D1393216

LORD OF WRATH

SOULLESS EMPIRE BOOK 2

JADE ROWE

SASHA LEONE

1

YELENA

I'm being watched.

Again.

I can't see who it is, but I can feel the unfriendly eyes. They whip my paranoia into a frenzy.

Paranoia. Shit. That's the last thing I can give in to now.

Today is too important.

My entire life depends on how these next seventy-two hours go. Yet every instinct is telling me to turn and run.

Instead, I plant my feet in the ground and glare ahead. Stubborn as always.

This line needs to move. Now.

So why won't it budge?

I tuck a strand of hair behind my ear as the noise in the Sweetwater Resort—a supposed oasis of serenity outside of Chicago—rises like a wave around me, threatening to overwhelm and crash me against the rocks of good sense.

Normally, I'm better at composing myself. But I've been in this line for way too long now, and I can't shake the cold tendrils creeping over my shoulder.

Someone is watching me.

It's stupid, I know. I'm here for a fashion conference. Of course, I'm probably being watched. Everyone is. That's the point.

But not everyone here has had the year I've had. If they did, maybe they'd be on edge too.

"I refuse," comes a snotty nasal voice, ripping through the fabric of noise, all the way from the front of the line, "to take that room. You're the concierge, so do something."

I can't hear the concierge's response, but the woman he's dealing with is holding everyone up, a faceless voice of privilege.

Behind me, someone mutters something about spikes and bringing back good old-fashioned public mauling. Usually, I'd find it funny. But the discomfort from being in the open like this, feeling exposed—defenseless and vulnerable—combined with all the licks of paranoia I've been experiencing for weeks now, leach any humor from the situation.

Yelena, you're not being followed. No one's stalking you. You've already dealt with this. Let it go.

As if in response, a shiver rattles through my bones. My gaze is ripped over my shoulder just in time to see a man in a wide-brimmed hat dip his head from across the other side of the lobby.

My breath hitches.

Was he watching me? It felt like he was watching me.

Screw this.

Flipping my portfolio in my hands, I hurriedly stuff it into one of my bags. The line still refuses to move. The nasal voice at the front grows with impatience, an increasing tone that screams *Don't You Know Who I Am?* I try to concentrate on that.

Instead, my gaze drifts back to the man.

He's still there. Chin dipped. Black hat hiding his eyes.

My heart beats fast. Hard. No matter how illogical it all is.

Then his head rises, just a little, and our eyes connect.

I don't know him.

There's no recognition, innate or obvious. Yet his gaze sears sickeningly through me, a hot, sharp knife.

I slam my eyes shut.

When I open them again, he's gone.

A figment of imagination.

Except he's not.

I know it. No matter how badly I try to convince myself otherwise.

A girl doesn't grow up in the shadow of the Bratva and not recognize certain things. Like when she's being watched.

Hell, a girl doesn't go through what I just experienced in Milan without learning what it's like to be picked out of a line as prey.

Stalked. Prey.

That's what it feels like.

It would be easy to give into it all, slap a label on it like paranoia, and call it a day. Hell, that's what I've been desperately trying to do.

It's just easier said than done.

Everything in me is on high alert.

I shiver again, whipping to my right, and this time a different kind of heat flares in my stomach, like someone else is looking at me too. I don't see them, just feel that slow beat of awareness, the kind of sensation that slides through skin and bone to nestle deep behind your senses.

Lifting a shaking hand, I push a strand of hair from my hot cheek.

Then, just like that, the mysterious gaze moves on. My senses settle, as if it was all just an extreme episode of paranoia, after all.

Shit.

Desperate and Paranoid. Maybe that's how I'll rebrand my new fashion line.

Get it together, I tell myself.

I shift on my feet, and a familiar fullness fills my bladder.

Double shit. I nearly forgot about that.

Here I am, talking to myself, fighting off invisible enemies and stalkers, trapped and exposed in an unmoving line.

And on top of all that, I'm getting desperately close to peeing myself.

Just another distraction I can't afford to have.

Right now, my career teeters on the brink, and after a snowball of setbacks, I need this conference to go well. It's make-or-break time.

I can't have the wrong people following me. I can't even think that the wrong people might be following me. Because then I'll start thinking about who exactly it could be. And there are too many culprits to consider. I could get lost in a deep, dark hole and never come out.

Unless...

I suck in a breath.

Valentin.

My best friend's gorgeous bodyguard. Her mafia boss husband's second-in-command.

A Russian masterpiece.

Sin incarnate.

I shake my head clear.

No. It's not him. I've ignored his texts. Let his calls go to voicemail. And for all the expletives I can think of that describe that dangerous, beautiful, frustrating man, the one thing he is *not* is a dog looking for scraps.

He wouldn't be caught dead following a woman. Any woman. A man like him is above that.

If I'm really being stalked, it isn't by him.

So why do I kind of hope it is?

Because part of you still wants to be that silly, naïve little girl you were before Milan, I catch myself thinking. *The girl you were back when he first stepped into your world.*

No. Stop thinking about Milan.

I'm not that silly girl anymore.

There was Yelena before Milan and Yelena now. I'm trying to rebuild without a sequined, couture lifestyle. I'm trying to pick up the pieces of my shattered dream. And I *need* to do it all on my own.

I don't have time for boys or men. No matter how tempting they are.

There is only my career.

Only. My. Career.

Suddenly, another shiver passes through me. It's followed by that same creepy awareness. I'm being watched again. But when I look back to my left, I don't spot anyone looking my way. That full-brimmed black hat is nowhere to be seen.

In my head. It's all in my head.

Goddamn. This is what I get for letting Valentin anywhere near me in the first place. He's a criminal. A made man of the Russian mafia. Being even the least bit associated with him *should* make me paranoid. No matter how ruggedly gorgeous he is. The last time anyone in my family got close to the Bratva, they ended up dead.

Great. Now I'm sad *and* paranoid.

Oh, and I still need to fucking pee.

"Goddamn it," I mutter, looking toward the front of the line. "That woman needs to shut up."

"That woman is Gia Ramone," says a soft female voice behind me. "The darling of Fabric."

Somehow, I swallow a gasp. Fabric magazine is what Vogue is to an older generation. It's the epitome of cutting-edge fashion, of the new houses and designers.

Gia Ramone is the *it* woman of the conference. The person to impress, a feat that's almost impossible.

"Darling of Fabric and fashion, maybe. But right now? She's being a beast." I keep my voice low as I turn.

The girl who greets me is so beautiful I have to resist the urge to breathe a sigh of relief. Because of course people were staring. Not at me. At her.

She laughs, flipping glossy black hair over one shoulder. "Bold words."

"You're the one who wanted to bring back... what was it? Public mauling?"

She shrugs. "It slipped out. I hate waiting."

"Me, too. Especially with a full bladder."

The woman tilts her head and smiles. She must be in her early twenties, around my age, but unlike me, she's next-level pretty. I bet I can guess why she's here.

"The line's not going anywhere, and with this conference, check-in will take a while."

I sigh. "I'm here for that conference. Check-in and registration and... ugh!" I hold out a hand. "Yelena Laskin."

"Kira Arendelle." She shakes my hand then snatches it back to point an accusatory finger at me. "I have one of your dresses from when you had that store. Hell-of-a seamstress and designer. You're with—"

"*Was*," I quickly correct her. Their name is the last I want to hear. I see it enough as it is. "I'm doing my own thing now. Kinda street meets couture." I eye her slender, elegant lines, already fitting her for clothes. With her face and body... "You must be a model."

"How flattering," she laughs. "But no. I'm a journalist with Chicago Daily. Here to cover the conference and hopefully write about the next big thing."

A thrill spikes my blood, and for a moment I'm back to when nothing could touch me and the world seemed to be at my fingertips.

"Listen, I can hold your spot so you can go to the washroom.

From what I've heard about Gia, she's going to be up there for a while. And even if she leaves now, there's bound to be a few more just like her in this line."

Biting my lip, I hesitate. It's a tempting offer, but my haze of paranoia isn't lifting. It's probably best to stay in a crowded area, just to be safe. I can go to the bathroom in my hotel room. After I've locked the door behind me.

"I don't know..."

"Your call, but the offer's there." She shrugs, her gaze shifting about the room. Then her eyes come back to rest on me. "Have you—" Kira breathes out, smoothing her hands down the front of her elegant trousers as she taps a foot. "Okay, I really love your designs."

I push out a laugh. I like her, she's got a sweetness that reminds me of my best friend Nat.

Oh, Natalya.

I get a sinking feeling in my gut.

I wonder if Kira here has also recently married the head of the Russian mafia?

No. Don't think about that. Don't think about your best friend Natalya or the Bratva or her ruthless husband Andrei or their gorgeous head of security. Don't get any more involved than you already accidentally are. Think of what's important. The conference. Your designs. Making connections.

"You haven't seen the new ones," I say, trying to stay on subject with Kira.

"That can be easily arranged." Kira swirls the end of an imaginary villain mustache, and I can't help but laugh.

"I mean, they might be terrible."

"Is that why you left—"

"Oh no, Miss Reporter, you're not gonna catch me talking shit about my past employer."

"Dang." She snaps her fingers. "So close." Her eyes twinkle and I'm struck again by how beautiful this girl is.

Being in the fashion industry puts me in contact with a lot of beautiful people. But there's something different about her. Something more natural.

"If you're looking for that kind of scoop, then you might get bored here," I say, hefting my bag onto my shoulder properly. "Fashion events are usually only interesting to the top tier. For me, though," I sigh. "It's more a fight in the dirt to try and get noticed."

"With your reputation?"

I flinch, I can't help it. And she's good enough to notice. I know she does. Those brown eyes narrow a little.

"Not here as anything from my past." My fingers tighten on the strap of the bag, "I'm hoping Dark One Eight—my new label—can stand on its own."

For a second, she doesn't say a word, and Gia's voice screeches in outrage, cutting through the noise. I can almost feel the shift of everyone in the room to her, and I'm sort of grateful. This way, if someone was watching, then...

They'd what? Stand out? Look the other way?

Either's fine by me.

Kira's cat-like eyes zero in on Gia and she leans toward me, dropping her voice. "That's good," she says. "But stay out of trouble. They say a lot of the houses, big and small, are funded by unsavory groups. Some of them even used to launder."

I bite back a quip about how laundering is normal to get clothes clean but don't because now I'm looking a little more closely at her.

What does Kira really know?

Probably not half as much as I do.

Still, I reply with a quiet, "I don't know anything about that kind of stuff."

"Hardly anyone does," Kira half smiles. "And that's why I took this job, actually. The rumors."

"Rumors?"

"Criminals." She almost shivers.

"You mean the general criminality that goes on everywhere?" I make myself ask. "Do the crime syndicates want new dresses for stylish B and E?"

She laughs, but it doesn't reach her eyes. "Just be careful," Kira whispers, leaning in. "I'm not kidding. Like I said, it's one of the reasons I'm here. There's something rotten bubbling under the surface. I'm going to dig it up. Word is it could be the mob. Russian mob. Maybe here looking for more avenues. It would be a huge story."

Valentin.

Fuck.

I flinch and paste on a smile. "I haven't heard a thing about that."

"You alright?"

"Yes!" I'm sure my voice jumps an octave. "I just really need to pee."

"Then go! I promise I won't steal your stuff—or do you not trust me?"

She's teasing, but I still feel bad. Maybe if I weren't so paranoid already...

As if on cue, the line finally shuffles forward an inch. I shake my head. "I can hold it."

"If you're sure."

I nod, trying to focus on anything but what Kira just said... or my bladder. But both tasks prove to be impossible. She mentioned the mob. Could that mean Valentin is here, after all?

No. That wasn't him in the black hat.

"You okay? You're all pale, Yelena."

Kira's soft voice pulls me back in and the noise of the lobby starts battering at my edges some more.

"Just thinking that devils wear lots of hats."

"But can they sew?"

I give her a sharp look. She's watching closely. Now that I know that she's a reporter, it couldn't be clearer.

"I mean," she adds, "you worked for a big name, and no giant company's clean."

"I'm not mafia."

She holds up her hands. "Not thinking that. Just... well, I'm trying to get my break out story and I figured if you know something, maybe we can talk? And I mean it about your designs. I really would love to see your new line."

"If it gets up and running like I want."

Without help.

Without interference in the form of an impossibly good-looking man who both scares me and makes my pulse pound faster than it should.

Valentin, I remind myself again, is dangerous. *Too* dangerous.

Reason numero uno why I haven't been responding to his texts or calls.

Just then, the phone in my hand buzzes.

I turn it so I see the screen and sure enough...

RED HOT DANGER

I instantly turn the screen back away. The sins of the father won't be repeated by this daughter. No matter how brutally gorgeous the danger zone might be.

Looking up, I see that Kira has also been distracted by her phone. She types something down and I take a moment to glance around.

Despite my best intentions, all I can search for is a familiar face.

Valentin texts and calls on occasion, but this week the calls and texts have gone from that to a few a day.

I don't necessarily blame him. His job is to protect, and in his eyes, I'm probably just a fragile little fawn wandering alone in a big, dark world; the best friend of his boss's new wife. To keep everyone happy, I need to be accounted for.

But it's more than that.

The way he looks at me. The way he acts.

The man won't leave messages on my voicemail, and his texts comprise of *Yelena*. And *Call Now*. Cary Grant charm isn't exactly in his wheelhouse it seems.

Not that I want that charm.

But he is charming, I admit. In his own way. Sledgehammer-style.

"Ooh, boy, what's his name and has he got a brother?" Kira grins, pointing at me and my phone.

"What?"

"You have a look."

"I don't have a look."

"You do."

Damn, she really is observant.

I shift, feet starting to ache. "I'm thinking about a pain in my ass."

She nods wisely, but before she can say anything else her phone rings. "Shit," she mumbles. "I have to take this. Can you hold my spot?"

"Of course."

Kira hurries off, and I try and placate myself with the thought of having made a new friend. One who could possibly help boost my career in the right way.

A small article won't have the same impact as the money and power someone like Valentin could throw behind me, but it's safer.

Besides, I don't want Valentin to know someone might still be following me. It's why I haven't brought it up to Natalya again.

He's smart. He'll work it out and know I'm desperate. He's

the kind of man who would take full advantage. I've been taken advantage of enough. I'm done with it.

Shoving my phone away as it starts to vibrate again, I look about for another familiar face. But I don't see that black hat or feel those shaded eyes. Just an all-too-common slight sense of unease that comes with standing so exposed.

But even that paranoia is quickly succumbing to another sensation.

Goddamn, do I have to pee.

Kira's made her way to the front door where it's quieter, and I silently curse not taking her up on her offer as my bladder starts to press—when she gets back, I'll do it. Or maybe I'll just ask her to join me. She looks like she can take care of herself.

I watch with increasing impatience as Kira nods, paces, nods again and then abruptly strides back over and grabs her things.

"Thanks," she says, frowning as she starts to look for something. She pulls out a card and thrusts it at me. The fun and sunny woman is gone. This one's darker, cloudier, and there's worry pulling at her mouth. I want to ask a million questions, but only one comes out as I take the card.

"Are you okay?"

"Fine." I know that tone. It's the one that says the person isn't fine at all. "I just..."

"Kira?"

"Hmm?" She shakes her head. "Did I give you—" Her gaze drops. "Do you have a card? Maybe we can connect later? Do an interview?"

Nodding, I give her one of mine. She shoves it into her bag.

"Great. I'm sorry, I have to go."

She doesn't wait for a response. Before I can process any of it, Kira turns and takes off.

I frown, trying to work out what happened. Maybe something personal. Work? I make a note to call her. Not just for the interview, but to check in and... Damn. I didn't ask about the bathroom.

Shit.

I suffer for what feels like an eternity. Then, I can't suffer anymore.

With one last hard glance around the lobby, I look for clear and present signs of danger. There are none, even if my body is still on edge—or maybe that's just my bladder.

Screw it. The line still isn't moving.

Biting back my unease, I load up my luggage and awkwardly head to the bathrooms, wheeling my cases behind me.

There's another long ass line at the closest one, and while that makes it safer, I'm beyond the ability to wait anymore.

Up ahead, I see another sign leading down to where the pool is. There are always bathrooms near pools. I take my chances.

But the further I wander from the lobby, the thicker the air gets. The chattery din disappears. It gets quiet.

Too quiet.

Despite my best intentions to push it down, my paranoia returns in full force. I can't shake it. Something is wrong. I'm being watched. Somehow, it's no longer a question. It's a certainty.

I need to get back to the lobby. I'll piss myself if I have to.

Sucking in a breath, I do a clumsy 180.

Then, I freeze.

Because there's only one way back to the lobby. And someone's blocking it.

The man with the black hat.

He wasn't in my imagination.

He's following me.

And he's gaining fast.

2

YELENA

My mind goes blank. There's no time to think, only react. Heart slamming, I drop my bags and stumble, narrowly stopping myself from falling.

Then, I'm running.

Past the bathrooms and down around a corner, and then another. I must be getting lost in the guts of the complex, because I have to dart around a few trolleys loaded with towels and sheets just to keep from crashing. Up ahead, there's a set of stairs going down and a big utilitarian elevator. The air fills with the overwhelming scent of detergent.

I look over my shoulder again, praying that this is all in my head.

But the man is still there. Still following me. Silently. His hat is pulled low, and he's got something gripped in one hand.

What the hell is going on? Who is this?

It's not like I can stop to get a good look. But I catch enough to see that he's pale, with a sweaty sheen to his face. He raises his face and squints my way, like he's sizing me up.

A crooked smile splits his mouth.

Fuck. It's the look of something going in for the kill.

Panic claws at me as I swallow a yelp and pick up my pace, darting down the halls. His heavy footfalls fill the heavy, humid air behind me.

I need a door, another stairwell, a person. Anything that can end this fevered nightmare. Instead, I'm only met by an endless maze of corridors and trolleys.

My breathing starts to hitch. I pass a men's bathroom and almost stop to hide in there before thinking better of it. I'd be trapped.

I keep running, Twisting and turning down the endless corridors until I turn my last corner.

What I see next stops me in my tracks.

A blank wall. No doors. No stairs. Nowhere to turn.

It's a dead end.

Just as the dread fills my gut, I hear a loud grunt fill up the hallway behind me. I fall to my knees and cover my head as a rattling crash reverberates down the corridor. I bite my lip and prepare for the worst.

Then, nothing.

I wait for so long that I don't even realize that all has gone quiet until the silence is so loud it's deafening.

"Hello?"

I look up. No black hat greets me. No greedy eyes or sweaty skin. It's so quiet I can hear my pounding heart.

That pounding gets heavier when I consider my options. Either I was just being chased or I imagined it all.

I'm not sure which is worse.

"Hello?" I call out, louder this time.

No one responds.

On shaking legs, I place my hand on the wall and cautiously lead myself back in the direction I came. When I poke my head around the nearest corner, my stomach drops.

Nothing.

No one.

With a deep, shaky breath, I look up at the ceiling.

"What the hell is going on?"

No one's around to answer.

Slowly, my racing heart starts to settle. I stare back down the corridor. My pulse jumps when I think of the bags I dropped. No matter where my head is at, I know one thing for sure. I need those bags back.

That stubborn determination drags me down the hallway as I retrace my steps. It doesn't feel like long before I reach the men's bathroom again. That's when I stop again.

The door is still swinging, like someone just went in... or came out.

And something dark and viscous is leaking out into the hallway, pooling at my feet. It looks like blood.

It smells like blood too.

I'm not sure if the scream that fills my head ever leaves my mouth, but it doesn't matter. The next thing I know, I'm running back to the lobby.

I almost don't stop when I come across my bags.

They're sitting neat, right where I dropped them. I sweep them up and start out into the busy lobby, not stopping to make sure I have them all. My mind is a jumbled, panicked mess. I need a cop, I need— Christ. A cop?

I remember what Kira told me. Are there even any cops here, or will I only find Bratva goons in fake uniforms?

I suck in a breath. I have to calm down. If I do something rash, my career—not to mention my life—is done.

But the blood...

That's not your problem, I tell myself. Someone will find that mess. You just check in and work out what to do next.

Like maybe go to the fucking bathroom.

I still need to pee, but not like before. And when I finally stumble back into the lobby, I see that the line has actually dwindled down to one person. Gia must have gotten her way.

"Shit," I mumble, hardly in control of myself.

Like a mindless vessel, I shuffle into place, eyes still wide with disbelief. In my mind, there's nothing else I can do. This is my defining moment. I can't let anyone take that away from me.

I close my eyes and picture the blood seeping out of the bathroom.

A thousand questions thrash through my mind. But when I open my eyes, it's my turn to step up to the concierge. So, that's what I do.

If he thinks that I look particularly disheveled, he doesn't let it show.

"Welcome., ma'am"

"I... I'm checking in." I pass my ID with shaking fingers.

He takes it and starts typing away on his computer.

Only then does he frown.

"I'm sorry, Ms Laskin, but our records show that you canceled your reservation."

My racing heart stops dead.

"What? When?"

"Three days ago, ma'am."

It's like a cold slap to my hot face.

"I... uh... Then I'll take another room."

He shakes his head. "We're all booked out because of the conference. But we have a list of alternative options just there." He points at a laminated sheet and turns from me.

Suddenly, my fear is incinerated. Anger takes its place. After all I've been through.

I'm ready to spit. I'm ready to kill.

My entire body starts to tremble. It's like the universe is conspiring against me. It's like...

I bite down on the hysteria. And then everything goes very still.

The concierge's eyes go wide as he looks over my shoulder. I stop trembling. A suffocating warmth spreads over my back.

"You."

I don't need to turn. I already know who's behind me.

I turn anyway.

I'm immediately greeted by a hard set of deep blue eyes. They glare back at me, unflinching.

"Lucky guess," Valentin smiles.

"I... you..."

He looks over at the concierge, then back at me. "Need a place to stay?"

I can't breathe. His voice is dark and heavy like rough spun silk. His gaze doesn't budge from me. His smile widens.

My chest flutters.

That smile.

It's filled with trouble... so much trouble. I've let it distract me before, but this time, I snap myself out of it and force myself to look at the truth behind his charm.

His dark hair is disheveled, like someone has grabbed at it with panicked hands. His big hands are splattered with crimson stains. His knuckles are clearly grazed.

My feet wobble.

Beyond his scent of spice and oud is the copper stench of violence. Instead of a pristine shirt, his bears the subtle touch of blood. Right at the cuffs.

Oh. God. Did he...

My vision blurs, then refocuses on the bag slung over his shoulder.

It's one of mine.

Of course, he fucking did.

I look up at those impossibly blue eyes again—it isn't the first time I notice the silver shards shattered within them.

"W-what are you doing here?"

"What do you think?" he says, that smile playing over his thick lips.

I try and breathe. Forcing my chin up, I smooth my hands on my thighs. "I think you're stalking me."

Valentin's smile loosens. He softly shakes his head.

"No, angel. I just got here. You weren't responding to my texts. I was worried." The mocking intimate and loving tone scrapes against me. "So, I had to come and make sure you were safe."

"You—" I stop myself before I can accuse him out loud. The blood on his hands may be obvious to me, but I'd bet the concierge is purposely looking the other way.

"That's right," he nods, understanding the implication. He places his big hand on my luggage and looks over the counter. "I'll take it from here."

I butt in. "No. You won't."

"I will," Valentin responds, unflinching. Those deep blue eyes study my frazzled cheeks. "And I won't take no for an answer. It's written all over your face, angel. You need a helping hand and a warm bed. Lucky for you, I've got both. And I'm willing to share."

3

VALENTIN

This fucking woman.

Her gaze narrows as she mutters, "In your dreams, big boy."

And then she turns.

Turns away and stalks off.

I take her in, and everything else here. No more suspicious people lurking. My men are on alert. And I'm here, near her, staking my claim.

Heading security for Andrei Zherdev, I know exactly how to blend in—even given my size—or make myself silently known. And with this little bird, you bet I'm doing the latter.

I flick a glance at the front desk, ignoring the silent stress. I'm not interested in anyone else. Only a contrary little angel who's probably more fucking trouble than she's worth.

"Yelena?"

She continues to ignore me, even though I know she heard.

"Yelena. Laskin"

She hesitates, then waves at the concierge again.

On a level, I'm fucking impressed. Not many deliberately ignore me. No one, in fact. Even if they don't know I'm Bratva, I'm hard to miss and don't put on a veneer.

No one who likes breathing tends to ignore me.

Except this girl.

The excitement of her reckless act shifts into higher gear.

But... places... times.

"Do not make me pick you up and haul you out of here," I warn.

"You wouldn't."

"I would. I'd do more, too. If I wanted. So, don't test me. Turn around."

Yelena looks up at me, those big eyes shimmering with a cold fire.

I take the opportunity presented and pull her away from the desk until we're in a corner where I can watch the damn lobby from a better angle. Despite its ritzy façade, this place is a shitshow. Yelena's lucky that the pissant private detective I found following her was so on the nose and incompetent even a fool could see him coming.

And I'm no fool.

That's the only reason I'm not losing my shit. I know what's going on here; what this event is and what it means to someone like Yelena.

Fuck.

Yelena Laskin.

Even her name is sweet to the tongue—and somehow oh-so bitter, too.

"No one's testing you," she says, voice dripping with contempt and Siberian winds. "Maybe you'd understand that if you could think, if your gorilla head could do that, just maybe you'd grasp that sometimes a woman ignoring you isn't playing hard to get, a plea for your idiot brawn or whatever you stupid thug-types do. Maybe she's just ignoring you because she doesn't like you."

I stare at her. Gor— wait, did she actually just call me a fucking gorilla? I start laughing.

"Oh angel, you're way off the fucking mark." And because I can and I more than fucking want to, I take her hand in mine and place it on my chest, then I move it slowly down, stopping right at my belt. "The mark's just below here. Can't miss it."

Her hand jerks, eyes widening at the meaning behind my words. But for a split second, she doesn't pull away.

Interesting.

Of course, decorum says I should let the pretty lady free. I'm twice her size and can take down armed men even bigger than me; one slender unarmed woman doesn't stand a chance. But we're past that now.

I'm fed up. She's been avoiding me for too long.

And now that I've had to save her life?

Shit. She'll be coming with me, whether she likes it or not.

Fuck decorum.

I spin Yelena around and walk her to the nearest wall. That's where I pin her. That tight little body stiffens against my weight, and I catch the sweet spice of orange blossom and cardamom she wears so effortlessly.

It drives me further down the rabbit hole.

Without thinking, I skim my lips along her throat, stopping to breathe on her carotid artery, and then to her ear.

The temperature between us flares to triple digits.

"This gorilla isn't here to get into your pantie... yet. I'm here because you're valuable property. Best friends with the boss's wife. My job is to make sure you're safe. And the only reason you are is because I showed up."

"I don't feel safe with you."

"Good. You shouldn't."

"Let go."

I ignore her. "No. You need somewhere to stay. So, you're coming with me."

"Kidnapping is illegal."

"You know full well I don't give a shit."

"Do you care that I fucking hate you right now?"

"I can smell the lie on your breath, angel. But don't worry, I lied too. I'm not just here to keep you safe."

I've missed our banter. It's time to take it to the next level. I grin slowly, taking her hand and sliding it down, over my cock. Her gasp is fucking music, fucking torture.

"What... what are you doing?"

"Exactly what we've both wanted to do since the day we met."

"I-I beg to differ."

"Now begging... you on your knees, that's something I'd like to see."

She lifts her chin and goes for contempt, which would work better if her breath didn't fall flat and her tits didn't rise and fall so hard and fast.

"In your dreams," Yelena spits.

Always, I almost say, but hold it back. She's in my blood, yes, down deep, drilling into bone, but she doesn't need to know that I'm so obsessed. Just like she doesn't need to know the added level of interest in her.

I've been promoted. And with that promotion comes unavoidable compromises.

Marriage is one.

Thing is, I like to corrupt compromise. Because if I'm going to toe a line, I'm fucking doing it on my terms, my way.

And Yelena...

A possibility.

I like the way she fights back.

"I need to be here. I paid for the room." Yelena huffs, looking away now.

"No," I say, "you didn't. Room got cancelled."

Her eyes cut back. "You did it."

"Me?" I lift a shoulder as I slide one thigh between hers.

Yelena makes a small sound. Hot blood rushes to my eager cock.

"Yes."

I laugh again, this time moving so my mouth's back at her ear, lips almost on her flesh. "Angel, I was standing right there when the concierge told you."

"Then you—"

"What?" I blow a strand of her hair, and she shivers. "Arranged it? If I wanted to make sure you weren't staying here, you'd never have stepped through the doors."

"I..."

"There's not going to be a vacant hotel in town. Shit like this always spills over."

I step back and Yelena looks around, her stressed gaze dropping to the blood on my cuffs.

"I'll call places outside of town," she mumbles. But I can feel her resistance melting. She knows there'll be no other options. "But, I guess, if I have to leave, you can bring my bags."

I can't help but smirk. "So, I'm coming with you then?"

"If I told you to leave me alone forever, would you?"

I remember the man who I caught following her. The man I murdered in the bathroom downstairs.

"That ship has sailed."

She grinds her jaw and flashes me a cold glare.

"Then I might as well make use of those big arms."

4

VALENTIN

By nature, I'm not a rule follower. Doesn't mean I don't do it when it suits me. When it gets me places. When it's the smart thing to do.

Smart being the operative word.

Yelena doesn't trust me. She fights the attraction.

I'm enough of an asshole to like that.

Usually, women throw themselves my way. And those who know who and what I am throw themselves harder.

Well, that shit's boring.

But this girl... she's the furthest thing from boring.

Glancing over my shoulder, I look through the glass front doors of the hotel. My car and my men are right there, waiting for a signal I've no intention of giving them.

With her back still pressed against the wall, Yelena starts calling all the places on the concierge's list. She won't find anything.

That's not just good news for me. It's what's best for her too. I may be a monster, but I'll protect her. And it looks like I'm not the only big bad wolf hunting in these parts.

The private investigator's blood still sticks to my skin, tightening my flesh as it dries.

What was the name that pig gave me before I ended his life? The man who hired him was called...

Alex Civati.

Yeah, that's it.

A burst of rage crashes through me.

I know all the players, and that name rings zero bells. But I'll find him soon enough. No one is allowed to go after Yelena. No one except me. I suppose I haven't made that clear enough yet.

Though, I guess our relationship isn't quite clear either. Maybe because there is no relationship.

I'll change that.

"Good luck with that," I taunt.

Yelena ignores me as she tries to wave down the concierge again. We both know it's hopeless. But she's stubborn.

Dipping my head, I take out my own phone and run Alex Civati's name through my personal database. It includes all the criminal outfits in and around the city. Italians, Irish, Japanese, you name it. I have thousands of names and rankings stored on this phone.

But no Alex Civati.

How odd.

Why the fuck was that name the PI's last breath?

I'll have to ask Yelena—once she's calmed down, of course.

"Goddamn it!"

Speaking of the devil. She throws the list on the ground, practically fuming.

"Problem?"

Putting her hands on her hips she looks upward, and then, heaving out a sigh even I catch, she picks up the list and shoves it in her pocket.

"Thank God it isn't Christmas or I'm pregnant because

apparently there aren't any rooms left within a thousand miles of this place, and I'm not sure the world's ready for a second coming."

"Trying to tell me something, there, Mary?"

"This," she bites her lip. "Why are you here?"

"Concern."

"Stalking."

I don't deny it. She's in my head, and it's been worse ever since my promotion. Because someone of my new status can't be a bachelor forever. I have responsibilities now, and that includes securing the future of my empire.

A woman. A wife. An heir.

But I can't stand to be ordinary. So, neither can my partner.

I need a challenge.

In that sense, Yelena's perfect. It also doesn't hurt that she's best friends with my boss' wife Natalya.

But unlike Natalya—whose own father was the leader of the last ruling Bratva—Yelena doesn't have any deep ties to the underworld, despite her Russian blood.

She's different. And that's exactly what makes her so fucking interesting.

"You've been ignoring me," I remind her. "This fashion conference is big, I know. But that's no excuse. Luckily, I showed up just in time." Looking down at my cracked knuckles, I offer my most charming smile. "So, how about you stop needlessly resisting and just stay at my penthouse already? It's big. It's safe. I have a bed you can sleep in."

"Nice try. I'm not having sex with you."

"Interesting, I never mentioned us fucking."

"Asshole."

"Now, angel, that's not nice." I mentally step back.

I may have been a bit testy earlier. But I was still coming down from the adrenaline of a fresh kill.

Taking a deep breath, I try to bottle the anger and concentrate on what matters.

Her.

"I'm not nice."

"Yes, you are," I say, pointing back toward the front desk. "And a nice, worldly, successful woman like you doesn't deserve the bullshit that goes on in there. The noise, the hassles. Stay with me, at my penthouse. It's brand new. Hell, they're still building it, but I'll stop the work for the weekend. You'll have a private car to take you back and forth, and you'll have a lot more room to move around in. Don't you want some peace and quiet?" *Don't you want me?*

"Well..."

The hesitation is all the answer I need.

Taking her wrist, I pull Yelena through the hotel's clear glass doors and signal for my car. A black, reinforced limousine quickly pulls up, and the driver, one of my men, steps out and scurries past us, back into the hotel. A moment later, he returns, Yelena's bags in hand. He loads them in the trunk as I open the back door and gesture her inside.

"Shall we?"

Yelena can't sit still.

The backseat is big, and while this isn't some cheap party limo, it's still got room to spare. Not my scene but I'll use whatever fucking props I need. I hand her a glass of white burgundy; expensive but not as pushy as champagne would be.

She almost jumps out of her damn skin.

"It's just a drink."

Her gaze slides over me. "You've bought into it all."

"I'm very rich, if that's what you're asking."

"I wasn't."

"Well, the more you know." I send a text making sure my penthouse will be free of workers, then I put my phone away. "The penthouse has a guestroom, but that's in shambles. So, you'll be sleeping in my bed."

"I'm not sleeping with you."

"Keep that up and I'm gonna think you definitely can't wait to wrap your thighs around my head."

"Valentin. Stop."

I sigh and lean back. "Take my fucking room. You need your rest. Your friend Natalya is making big changes across our properties with her new architectural firm. It'll be useful to help clean our money and create a legitimate presence everywhere, but all the construction can be fucking exhausting. The building crew has been at this place for weeks now."

She looks at me. "The building crew?"

"I own the building. I'm staying there until the renovations are done. After that, the penthouse will be rented." I watch her from under lowered lids. "The Bratva move with the times, darling."

She doesn't flinch like I expect her to at talk of the Bratva and crime and laundering, but there's something there.

The question of Alex Civati comes back to me, but I don't push it. Time enough when we're inside.

Her gaze is on the blood that stains my hands as we approach the penthouse. It's a lavish low-rise building on a hill close by, one that overlooks the resort. It's quite the sight, but Yelena hardly seems to notice. All she can focus on is the blood.

A sign of her innocence.

It almost makes me feel guilty.

Almost.

"Here."

The first thing Yelena does when I open the door is rush for the guest bathroom. The door slams shut behind her. Five minutes later, it swings back open.

She already looks less tense, but I don't say a word. Instead, I show her around. The tour ends in the master bedroom.

That's when she decides to stiffen up again.

"I... look, thank you, Valentin. But I can't let you sleep in that guestroom," she says, referring to the unfinished cement box we passed by earlier. "It's way too—"

"Yelena, don't insult me. I'm insanely busy. There's no time for me to sleep. Plus, I have a sofa."

The look on her face says it all. The picture of me trying to squeeze on the sofa is ludicrous.

"Valentin."

"Save it. I'm grabbing something to eat. You can join me... if you're hungry." With that, I turn and walk out.

Yelena is stubborn, but not even she is stubborn enough to resist the smell of food after a long, hard day.

I play that to my advantage. It hardly takes her thirty minutes to show up in the kitchen.

I know she's there before she says a word. Plating the leftovers, I pour a second glass of white burgundy.

"Finally."

"It smells good," I hear her quietly admit.

"Here." I turn to give her a plate and a glass. Our fingers brush.

An energetic warmth jumps through me.

She definitely feels it, too, and the troubled light in those pretty eyes tell me she's fighting it.

Then she steps back, as if remembering something horrible.

Her gaze falls back onto my hands. I remember the blood. The private investigator. The way I stole the life out of his pudgy little eyes.

"W-what happened to him?" she asks. The innocence is back. I can tell she's hoping that it's not what she thinks.

"Who?" I ask, giving her a chance to retreat. But she doesn't.

Brave girl.

"The guy who followed me."

I could spin tales. There are plenty of wives and girlfriends in the mob who don't want to know the gritty details. But I want someone who can take it. Who can handle me. So, I put Yelena through the ringer.

"I killed him. Slit his throat, let him bleed out. But not before I made him talk. Because make no fucking mistake, he was there for you."

"W-who was he?"

"Some low-life private investigator."

She swallows, brings up her glass, looks at it, and sets it down. "You just murdered him?"

"Yes."

"But—"

"But what?" I take a step toward her. "Is there a special rule against killing PIs? Men like that often do other jobs. Unsavory ones. And someone hired him to follow you. Report on you."

"Who?

"Do you know Alex Civati?"

"Fuck!"

I don't know what I was expecting, but it wasn't that. She's not scared, she's... Oh, shit.

"Yelena?"

She grabs the wine and downs it before settling into a glare. "That prick."

"Illuminate."

"He's my ex-boyfriend." She sweeps up the bottle and refills it herself.

Her hand's shaking a little.

"You want him dead?"

She snorts. "That isn't the answer to everything. He's a trust fund billionaire with deep ties to the fashion industry and..." She stops, takes a breath. "Alex wore me down to date him and... and it wasn't hard, he's handsome, but when we broke up, he got obsessed. Like really obsessed."

"I understand."

Of course, I fucking do. I understand the obsession with her, she gets in a man's head, in his veins. But there's something else there, beneath her words, lingering in her pause, the big outrage. She's not telling me something, and it links to the fear in her trembling hand.

What are you hiding, angel?

I'll figure it out. Eventually. But I know better than to push her right now.

She's had quite the day already. So, I let it lie.

But that doesn't mean this Alex fucker is getting off the hook.

Subtly flexing my fingers into a fist, I watch as Yelena gently nods and steps out of the open kitchen. Leaning against the wall, she looks through the window, to the half-built balcony. Right now, we could step out onto it. But it's not covered, and the railing isn't right. So instead of the soft light that will come in when this place is done, the lode-bearing beams spear the kitchen and living room with dark slashes.

"This place, it's kinda eerie," she whispers.

"It's not done yet."

Yelena turns. "It's almost like two worlds meeting, the polite one and the ugly bones beneath."

"A metaphor for life, right?" I shake my head, struck again by the different facets to her.

She's feeling vulnerable, I realize, and overwhelmed.

"Yelena." I cross the kitchen and take the wine from her hand. To my surprise, she doesn't put up a fight. "You're tired. Rest. You're safe here."

"I have an event tonight."

I motion her toward the bedroom.

"Fuck that. Go to bed and start tomorrow."

Her eyes glitter. "That's not how things work in the real world. It's a meet and greet, which is important. I have to get ready."

'Well, if that's how it works in the real world," I tease, before straightening up. "Alright. Fine. If that's what you want. Come on, then. We'll get you to your ball on time."

I lead her through the house to the master bedroom, where her luggage waits on the floor.

"Shit, I didn't realize what time it was."

Panic rises in her voice when she looks down at her phone.

"You better hurry then."

Standing in the doorway, I watch as she unpacks, pulling out a gunmetal and gold dress, shoes, panties, bra, and toiletries.

As she does so, a steady pink crawls up her throat to her cheeks, getting deeper with each item set out.

Without looking at me, she takes the clothes and scurries into the ensuite. A second later, the shower turns on.

I scrub a hand over my face and force myself to breathe.

Fuck me. I'm not a man who's used to holding back.

She wants me just like I want her. I'm sure of it. Reluctance and bullshit aside, it's there. Burning and spitting sparks between us. It would be so easy to set down the wine I'm still holding and follow her in there.

The door's not even fully shut. All I'd have to do is nudge it and all of Yelena's mouth-watering secrets would be mine. How could she stop me? Why would she want to?

Hell, she doesn't even have to know I'm there. I can enjoy the show from behind the slit in the door as she strips and showers. I can take in the way she lathers her body, slips a hand between her thighs, and maybe, just maybe, under my watchful gaze she'll start to work her sweet little pussy for me.

Fuck. I'm already hard as a rock.

The temptation is borderline irresistible—at least, it would be to a lesser man. But I won't stoop to a Peeping Tom.

Yelena didn't leave the door open like that as an invite. She didn't plan on providing prime-time front seat tickets, either.

Then again, she didn't fucking lock it.

A tease maybe, or a mistake. It doesn't matter.

It isn't an invite.

I'll get to her eventually. But tonight isn't the night.

Trying to draw the blood away from my cock, I bite down on my tongue and pull out my phone. It's about time I find out more about this dipshit ex of hers.

Alex Civati.

I immediately don't like what I see.

No wonder he wasn't in my criminal database. His sins are of a white-collar variety.

The exact opposite of me and my kind. Weak. Used to his own way for all the wrong reasons. Not one second spent on actually earning what he gets. And that, I'm guessing, is why he's so set on Yelena.

But was she really mercenary enough to date him for the advancement of her own career? Maybe innocent isn't the right word for her, after all. Not that I have a problem with that.

I know what it is to be hungry and willing to fight, to do what you have to in order to live well and get ahead. In a way, Yelena's no different than me.

We both found success.

But a man like Alexa Civati doesn't get that. He was born into his wealth.

I pull up a picture of him

He's soft and cowardly. It's all there in his face. Those eyes.

The difference between us is clear. He thinks money means he deserves it all. That he deserves her.

I think I deserve it all because I worked for it. Because I'll work for her.

I drink Yelena's wine.

"Thirsty?"

Her voice trickles over my shoulder.

"For wine?" I return, finishing off the glass. "Or for something else?"

"Attention."

I turn around and my jaw almost hits the floor. She's clearly annoyed that I'm standing so close to the door she just showered behind. But that's not what gets me.

It's the dress.

She looks gorgeous. Drop-dead. Not that I would ever say it to her face.

"Depends what you're offering?" I say instead.

For a moment heat flares, then her gaze dulls, like she's pulled down the shades.

"Nothing." She makes the fatal mistake of trying to push past me and we're suddenly both in that small doorway of her room, almost touching.

The dress is pretty, thin, and provocative. She smells sweet and fresh. The heat from the shower is still on her skin. My eyelids flutter with primal desire.

We're both breathing a little unevenly as I set the glass down on a side table.

Yelena doesn't run.

And her eyes—well, suddenly, they're not so dull and curtained anymore. No. Instead, they're like a glitter storm of light and emotion. And when our gazes meet, the heat burns up my spine and into the hair at my nape.

I take her hand.

She swallows. "What are you doing?"

I look down at her mouth and her lips part. I pull her close. "What I should have done when we first met."

"A little inappropriate."

"Fuck propriety, Yelena."

She doesn't pull free, instead her hand curls on my shirt and she sways into me, her tits brushing the material.

My cock swells. My heart pounds.

"Tell me you didn't want me then or now, angel."

"I barely noticed you."

Her punishment for lying is my reward. With a quick sneer, I lick a path up along the side of her throat. "Liar. A girl like you can't ignore a man like me. You didn't then, and you can't now."

She moans. "I..." The blush streaks over her. "Look, it's not that I don't like you, it's just..." She looks up and the misery in her blue eyes makes me loosen my hold just a little. "It's complicated."

I'm about to ask how this simple desire can be so complicated when my phone starts buzzing wildly. And I swear in Russian. Only a few people know this number. Whoever it is and whatever it is will be important, and in my line of work, that often means life or death.

"Saved by the bell." I grumble. Stepping back, I don't try to hide it as I adjust myself below the belt, because fuck it, she must have felt my hard on when I pulled her into my arms. "I need to take this, but don't leave until I say. I'm escorting you tonight."

"I don't need an escort."

My phone's still buzzing. "You do after what happened earlier. I'll put on a fresh suit. Do my hair. Whatever it takes to look like I belong. Call me your date, your security, fuck, ignore me, and I'll keep my distance. But I'm going. For your safety."

"It's not like I can just walk." She snatches up the glass and marches off to the kitchen. "I'll be in there. Drinking your wine."

She turns and she leaves.

I watch her go, gritting my teeth as I answer the phone.

"What?" I bark.

"Valentin."

I temper my annoyance.

This isn't a man to talk like that to.

It's my boss. Andrei Zherdev. King of the underworld. Pakhan of the Russian mafia. Leader of my Bratva. Husband to Yelena's best friend. And the man who I've sworn to protect with my life.

I know him well enough that it sends my stomach to my toes. That tone of voice. Something's seriously wrong.

"What is it?"

"We've got a fucking problem."

5

YELENA

His bathroom smelled like him.

Soaps, shampoo.

That strong, musky scent whispering over my skin as I bathed made it so tempting to pick up his soap and use it or his shampoo.

I didn't.

Of course I damn well didn't.

Something like that's too intimate, and I don't need to commit further acts of stupidity. Especially with a man like Valentin. He'd take it as a battle won.

Because there is a battle here, it hums in the air, like the precursor to a war that draws me in. He wants me, that's obvious, and the interest is apparent even if he didn't send me texts, if it didn't glitter in his eyes when he looked at me.

Pouring the wine into my glass, I take my time at the marble island, burying myself in the mundane task. But leaking booze into a vessel doesn't take long, and when it's over, all that's left in my spinning head is him.

Shit.

I sip the wine and try to get my thoughts in order. There's

no war or battle, just a bathroom a man uses as his own. That's all. I'm on edge because of the past few months. What happened at the hotel.

The blood on Valentin's clothes.

He dresses pretty, but there's no mistaking the violent, rough, and deadly man who hides behind the inexplicable charm.

Still, I told him the truth when I came out of the bathroom. It isn't that I'm not attracted to him. I am. I can't ever deny that. The effect he has is too strong, too electric to pretend otherwise. It's not that I don't want to. It's that I can't. I won't.

I would never survive him.

Valentin's the kind of man to devour whole. Suck everything down into the maelstrom that dominates his life. I let that happen with my ex, and I barely got out. With this man? Not a chance in hell.

I have to focus on trying to rebuild my career, make a life. And Valentin's world?

It drips with blood, violence, and death.

That's how clothes get stained. That's how *I* get stained. Forever.

Even if I'm protected, I don't want to be like Nat. Sure, she's building her own life as an architect extraordinaire, but it's in the cocoon of her husband's world. She has to fit. There's no meeting in the middle. Is there?

Shaking my head, I grab my bag and pull out my phone. I need another distraction. Sipping on Valentin's surprisingly exquisite wine, I run through the news feeds on my socials, ignoring the big, handsome Russian pacing behind me. He's still on the phone, speaking fast from the other room. I don't understand the low Russian growl he speaks in, and I don't want to hear. Best not to hear things I shouldn't. I'm much safer that way.

Shifting my focus to the feed, I find a thread on the conference and go through the star-studded guest list, picking out my targets for the night. Finally, I'm able to concentrate on something other than Valentin. I even set aside my glass. Just in time, too.

Because a split-second later, the bottom of my stomach hits the floor. My hands start to shake.

At the bottom of the conference's star-studded guest list is a picture of the last person in the world I want to see tonight.

His million-dollar smile greets me, along with his bespoke maroon suit that's sharp and runway ready, as is the ten-foot-tall, dark-haired model on his arm.

Alex.

My thumb twitches, accidentally clicking down on the image. I'm brought to his page.

It instantly becomes clear that my worst fears are true.

He's at Sweetwater.

He's coming to the conference.

No. Even worse. He's there right now.

Fucking hell.

I suck in a sharp breath and try to get my jumping, prickling nerves under control.

Why is he...? I grip the edge of the marble island and put my other hand to my stomach, the wine turning into vinegar in my guts. Nausea rocks me, sends bile, hot, bitter, burning, up into my mouth.

Swallowing, I walk carefully around the island and pull a glass from the cupboard near the sleek fridge. There's a sticker still on it. Some fancy name announcing in silver it's made of crystal, and I shove it under the water dispenser on the fridge, filling it.

I knock back the contents to try and soothe the burn, settle my stomach.

It doesn't work.

Why the fuck is Alex at this event?

Does he know I'm going to be there?

It's a stupid question. Of course he does. He sent a fucking private investigator after me.

Alex knows everything he wants to know, and I'm currently... shit. I don't want to think about what I am to him and what happened.

The bottom line is Alex is used to getting what Alex wants. And if he doesn't, he's not above throwing a dangerous tantrum.

Well, he didn't get what he wanted with me. So he'll ruin my life. He knows I'm going, so he's there too. Ready. Waiting.

Does he know about what happened in Milan?

God.

Wiping my hand down my face, I let out an agonizing groan.

I can't not go tonight.

Even as every instinct in me screams turn and run, I have to go. I need to be there. My future's hanging on by a thread right now, and if I don't go and make a good impression, that thread will be severed.

So, I need to ignore Alex. I need to be a star.

My damn livelihood depends on that. On me being successful tonight. If I am, I'll open all the doors that were shut on me in Milan. I'll make the contacts I desperately need.

I'll have a shot at my dream again.

I close my eyes and breathe slow and steady. Measured.

The only sound is the quiet of my breath.

Yet I know the moment Valentin comes into the kitchen area.

"You okay?"

Opening my eyes, I watch as the chiseled devil pours himself a glass of something amber from a bottle he's carrying.

"I'm fine," I lie.

Because he's clearly not.

His charming smirk has turned into a deep frown, and his blood-stained shirt has been swapped for something cleaner. A fresh suit. Three pieces, in the darkest of grays, the shirt snow white, the tie a soft sheen of silk in a coal black.

Fuck me.

He's stunning.

Even frowning, holding a bottle of booze like it's his new friend, he's dangerously gorgeous.

But suddenly, it's like I don't exist anymore. He takes a quick shot of his drink, then pulls his phone out and sends a lightning quick message.

I want to ask what's bothering him, but I know better than that.

Don't get attached.

Still, my heart flickers when his blue eyes finally flash back onto me.

"Yelena." The rough spun silk of his voice is something I want to wrap around me, because one word is all it'll take, and Valentin will protect me from everything. But the voice is a dangerous siren song, and its warm comfort comes at a cost. Valentin and all he is and will do for me comes at a cost I'm not prepared to pay.

"I'm fine."

A half smile turns up his mouth. "Don't lie, angel. It's too ugly for something so beautiful. What's bothering you?"

"Nothing."

The smile stays, but there's a hardness to it, a steel lining that tells me he won't let this go. "You know full well by now that I won't let this go."

I don't want to tell him about Alex, but I know there's no point in hiding it. Valentin will find out eventually. He always does.

"Remember my ex?"

"The fucker. Trust fund billionaire who hurt you. Yes."

The smile's gone.

I turn the empty glass in my hands, as he focuses on me.

"You want him dead? One word, Yelena."

"No!" At the narrowing of his eyes, I come forward, put the glass on the island, and I look up and across at him. "It's just... it didn't end well—as you can probably guess from the PI—but he's powerful, Valentin, and he's going to be there tonight. He could ruin everything for me."

I can see him holding back his rage as he takes another big sip of his bitter drink.

"Ruin. He threatened you? Did he hurt you, Yelena? Do something you didn't want?"

I swallow. "He has power, Valentin. And in this industry influence means a lot. He..." Shit how do I put this? "He told me he'd end my career if I didn't play ball."

"And did you?"

"No."

The anger is fast, violent. Valentin slams his hand on the marble and his mouth is made of granite, eyes so hard and brutal I can see all the blood he's spilled... and the need to spill more.

Specifically Alex's.

"I'm in one piece so he didn't..." I can't quite finish that.

"Hurt you? Maim you? Try and destroy you?"

"Valentin, leave it. I need to handle it. That's all. Play nice."

The raging beast forms tight fists as he brings them down on the counter. "Remember how I said I'd keep my fucking distance at this event? If you wanted me to?"

"Yes." I nod and relax a little. "Thank you. It—"

"Well, angel, I'm not giving you that fucking option anymore. You'll be at my side every second."

"You can't do that."

This time when he smiles it's dark and full of the wrong kind of promises. "Watch me."

"Valentin."

"No." The smile vanishes. "A real man doesn't frighten or threaten a woman like that. You'll be with me. Like we're one. And after? I'm going to have a few words with this Alex fucker."

Horror spreads through me like ice. The blood leaking from beneath the bathroom door at the resort. Valentin with his cuffs stained red and red blood on his knuckles and that knowing light in his gaze as he looks at me.

The one that says he will do anything and everything he pleases, that laws don't concern him. That to protect he'll kill.

He'll kill Alex.

I know that.

Look, I don't like Alex. In fact, I hate him. I want him punished for his crimes, his treatment of me, probably of other women. Of whoever gets in his way and he deems small enough to stomp on, to play with, destroy.

But Alex dead?

I don't want that. I can't have it.

I don't want blood staining my soul. The Bratva has ruined enough of my life. I can't let it have my future too.

"Please don't." I meekly whisper.

In response, Valentin rolls his shoulders and unfists his hands. "I do what I want and choose to protect who I please."

"Please, I'm begging you don't hurt him."

For a moment, the raging monster goes silent, dark head bent as he straightens and fusses with his immaculate shirt cuffs, and adjusts the subtle black and silver links. And he's utterly, completely, focused on me. "You still have feelings for him?"

"No! I just..." His gaze lifts and reaches mine, those blue eyes shockingly dark and hot. "I don't want that on me."

"It's not on you, sweet angel. It's on him. There's more to this than you've told me. I'm not stupid, and I've spent a life reading people. To me, you might as well be an open book. He hurt you. That's something I can't overlook. Worse, he'll fucking hurt you again, hold whatever he has over your head. Play games with you." He puts both palms on the counter. "That's not rough up territory, it's a death sentence."

"Valentin!"

"I didn't say I'd mete that out, Yelena, just stating I know the punishment that fits his crime." Then he slides his gaze slowly over me. "Maybe I'll rough him up when we speak. Just a little."

I hurry around and take his arm. He's warm and strong, those muscles steel under the fine material of his perfect suit. I sway a little. Being this close to him generates a special kind of buzz inside of me. That musky scent of his is stronger than ever. The hint of spice and oud is there too, and it wraps around my skin like it did in the shower, and—

I release him and shift back a little. "I asked you not to hurt him. At all."

"Yelena—"

"Please?" I need to be careful in what I say because I don't want him to know the depths of my desperation.

If I do, it's tantamount to asking for an IOU from the Bratva and that's debt. Dangerous and deadly debt. I don't ever want to owe him a thing. Owing him is owing the Bratva.

But...

If he threatens Alex then Alex will destroy me.

"Not even a threat, Valentin. Men like Alex are weak and not worth your time. And anyway, he's got too much influence in the industry. I need to play nice. Flatter if I can't keep out of his way."

"If I have words and point out the error of his fucking ways then he'll stay out of your way and maybe be nice to you."

Oh, God. Only Valentin could think his threats or violence could get me the results I want.

I try not to shake.

"He's not honorable. If he thinks you're threatening him—

and he will if you even speak to him alone—then his vendetta will get worse. It could push me back into working where he wants me to, under his thumb, and—"

Shit

It's true. The vendetta would be worse. More intense.

And that's not even the worst of it.

If Valentin killed Alex, the conference could be canceled. Either way, I'll lose chances for funding and clients. Those closed doors will remain closed. Forever.

"And what?" Valentin presses.

"And nothing. Kill him or hurt him and chances are the conference would end then and there. I'll lose these opportunities. Let me handle him. Please?"

"I could just buy this resort, now. Enough money and it's easy. Then this Alex fucker can't be there. I'd just ban him from stepping foot on the grounds."

"So instead of just behaving yourself, you'd rather buy the resort?"

"I have the money. More than enough. And the power."

"Valentin, be reasonable. You're rich, but Alex is rich too. And people like him get loud."

"I can shut him up. Or just outbid him if he tries to buy it from me."

I'm not sure how serious he is, but the way he warms to his own insane idea scares me. "No. The two of you in some ridiculous loud bidding war over a hotel because of a nobody like me? It would put a black mark on my name. No one would ever work with me again. They'd be too scared."

"Then I can be discreet."

"Valentin."

He laughs softly and grazes his knuckle soft against my cheek. "Fine. I won't buy the resort for you. I'll behave. I'll be good. I'll stay by your side. Okay?"

"No. You can't stick by my side. You'll scare everyone off." I shake my head and fold my arms. "You'll stand back on the other side of the room as we agreed. I know there'll be plenty of models to flirt with."

He strokes his thumb along my bottom lip and I almost moan. The rough pad of his thumb pulls my delicate skin just enough to make me want to feel his mouth there. His tongue. "I only want to flirt with you, angel."

"Stop it." *Please.*

"This is the deal." He drops his hand and leans in, all humor, lightness and flirting gone. "You're on my arm tonight. To anyone who asks, I'm your date. Whether you like it or not. Or, you don't go. Up to you."

My eyes widen. "You wouldn't!"

"Try me."

He would. It's there. On his face, in his voice. He would absolutely not let me go and then he'd probably go and kill Alex because he can.

I suck in a breath. "Fine. But if you're going to be my date, my *fake* date, then you better clean yourself up."

He glances down at his gorgeous suit, then back at me. My stomach twirls. The wicked light in his gaze licks at me. "You don't like this suit?"

"No. I'm sure you have better."

"There's no blood on this one. I checked."

I narrow my eyes, he wants a rise out of me, but I'm not giving him one. "You set your rules. I'm setting mine. Get changed."

"Fine." He kicks off his shoes and peels off his socks.

Oh my God, is he going to trip naked right in front of me?

"I was joking!"

"Never joke with the Bratva," he says, so deadpan my stomach flips. "I'll get changed, just like you said. Now, come."

I'm pulled by the wrist back to the bedroom, then placed at

the foot of the bed as he opens the closet and pulls out an identical suit.

My breath hitches as he strips down, those strong blue eyes glaring at me, daring me to turn away. I can only watch as he takes off the cufflinks. The tie. Unbuttons his vest, shrugs out of his jacket. Fuck.

With each discarded piece, he reveals more of his rock hard body. I swear my mouth starts to water. I'm waiting for him to stop, but as he gets down to his briefs, he shows no signs of slowing down.

"Wait!" I beg, but it's too late.

He pulls off his underwear.

Calling on some unknown willpower, I manage to whirl myself around before I get to see too much of his junk.

Still, I see enough that my toes curl and an irresistible heat clenches my thighs.

Valentin's laughter burns in my cheeks. "Shy?"

"I didn't think you'd actually strip in front of me. I was joking."

"I'm Russian. And Bratva. No sense of humor."

He laughs again.

"That's obvious because yours is terrible."

"Turn around and say that to my face, angel."

The taunt is obvious.

But I don't fall for it.

"Chicken."

"Smart."

"Debatable."

Two ties hit me in the back, draping over my shoulder.

"Pick one."

They're both charcoal, one is smooth and the other is beveled.

I pick the latter and turn. "This one," I say, holding my ground.

"You can turn around now."

Either I'm even more naïve than I thought, or I was just looking for an excuse, because when I turn myself around, Valentin isn't suddenly dressed.

No. He's still butt-naked, but at least his back is to me.

Not that the sight is any less drool-worthy. I can't help but stare, drinking in the muscles, the ink that covers his back and arms, and that tight ass that looks like it could thrust a mountain into pieces.

It's all too much. I'm essentially on fire as I throw the tie at him and turn away.

"Coward." Valentin laughs as I scurry from the room.

I don't disagree. I am a giant coward. But a smart coward.

Valentin can't see what he's done to me, even if he probably suspects it already.

My panties are soaked. My head dizzy. My throat dry.

The bastard. He's trying to drive me crazy.

And he just might succeed.

The conference lasts for three days. I need to be there for every single night. And I know Valentin's not going anywhere.

"Shit."

I stop in the living room and collapse against the barren wall. How the hell am I going to survive this conference?

How the hell am I going to survive *him*?

6

VALENTIN

These people are insane.

I already feel out of place as I walk by Yelena's side through the newly decorated lobby full of finely manicured, well-dressed beautiful people.

Don't they have more important things to do than lounge around like this?

Obviously not.

It's already pissing me off. But I keep my cool long enough to open the door for my fake date and ferry her into the main event.

Fuck. It's even worse in here.

If I had a scene this would be the farthest thing from it.

Though, it would be perfect pickings for a thief of my caliber... at least, back in the day. I'm above that now.

Grinding my teeth, I lead Yelena past a makeshift catwalk to the bar nestled among the lights and silvery curtains, and order champagne for her and whiskey for me. Drinks are free, and waiters circulate, but the bar is perfect to take it in, work out exit points, the safest places and any enemies.

"Oh, this is spectacular," Yelena breathes.

"It looks like a club crashed into a photoshoot that crashed into a high fashion show."

She takes a sip of her champagne and looks about as she bounces a little on her toes. "Just this world."

Lights, music, cameras, action and a whole lotta fake shit comes to my mind.

And Yelena wants to be part of this?

"Just," I mutter.

She turns to me. "There's plenty of talent for you." And she nods at the runway.

Fuck, there are even models in silver slinking along the black elevated stretch, striking poses to the music's beat.

"Not the talent I'm interested in, angel."

I give her a strong look and she blushes away.

But she isn't the only person here who's purposely looking away from me.

People know I don't belong here. It's a drip of acid down my spine. Like I'm picking pockets wrong.

The only time I like being noticed is when I want it. But here and now it doesn't seem an option. People stare and want to be stared at.

And they look. At me. Just out of the corner of their eyes.

They're scared. Or maybe they're staring at Yelena because she's a vision, something I have problems taking my eyes off, and yet, I do, to make sure all is safe for her.

It really doesn't matter if these idiots are looking at her or me or both; they shouldn't. Under normal circumstances looking at me, staring is for the very brave or very stupid and I'd fix it with a threat.

Permission should be granted and a woman like the angel on my arm is a privilege to look at. Something to be earned. Not a right.

Of course, Yelena wouldn't like that. She's fucking bossy when she chooses. It's why I had fun embarrassing her tonight, stripping down, changing. She's got an innocent air that flared bright when she turned away, but not before she ogled, not before that becoming blush painted her pale cheeks.

I'm getting hard just thinking about it.

But I'll control myself.

I did promise to behave, after all. So I will. I don't have to, but it pleases her and how upset she was at discovering her fuck of an ex would be here got under my skin, slid through ribs to nestle and urge me to put aside my natural inclination for her.

Still, I know she isn't telling me the full truth about this fucking Alex. Something very bad happened, I feel it. And I'll find out, but right now this is her night, and finally having her on my arm, to be seen as mine, is worth it.

I'll protect this moment with my life.

Not that it will keep my eyes chained to the floor. I can't help looking for my prey. Alex Civati.

I don't see him, though. Somehow I doubt she lucked out and he left. Men like him fit this place. Men like him love to be the center of attention. Ten to fucking one he's made a circuit, stepped out to the exclusive bar on the mezzanine level, or maybe to his suite, and will return to make a grand entrance.

"Oh, there's Sebastian Tyler." Yelena looks to her right and I follow to where a man with half white, half black spiked hair in sunglasses and what looks like a PVC suit stands, surrounded by pretty creatures of both sexes.

Shifting closer she stiffens like I'm holding a gun, and I ask, "Who's he?"

"Owner of Biopic."

"Let's go."

She looks at me in horror. "You don't walk up to a man like that, you wait for an invitation."

"Fuck invitations." I start to move off and she hurries after me, hand on my arm.

I hide my smile.

Yelena's fingers curl into the fabric of my jacket, pushing against my flesh. They're warm and a whisper away from a caress. "You promised."

"And what do I get in return?"

Her eyes flash as she looks up at me. "Satisfaction of a job well done."

"You could make it more interesting."

Yelena's lips part and she sighs, then drops her hand. "Valentin, I can't."

"But," I counter, "you want to."

Her gaze slips from mine and moves about the room as heat colors her cheeks pink.

If I wasn't in this fucking fashion hell, something that means a lot to her, I'd back her all the way into the wall and shove my tongue down her throat, slide my hand up to her pussy and make her purr.

But I don't. Not because she'd reject me, she'll try, against her base needs and wants, and then give in. I did promise to behave.

"Valentin." Yelena tugs my arm. "You just can't go up to him. Your ways won't work in here."

Naïve little dove, my ways work everywhere. But I keep that to myself.

Instead, I gesture to the idiotic-looking man as if I don't understand her request and her pretty mouth goes thin, so I let her lead me to the left wall, where there are standing tables, and she chooses one to hide behind and observe from.

I've seen her tactic in many before.

She's nervous, yes, but she's also trying to deny her attraction to me. Usually, when there's heat, a magnetic draw between me and a woman there's no battle, no war. A little resistance in the form of games—many women like to be chased and I indulge when it pleases me.

Yelena is different. She's not yearning for the chase, she fights herself as much as me. And every moment she makes me work, my obsession grows.

She's stubborn and wildly independent.

It would be easy for her to ask for help, even just hint at it. Monetary, influence, sheer brute strength.

But this stubborn angel doesn't ask. Doesn't hint. I get the feeling she'd reject that help. Just like she rejects her attraction.

She makes me work.

It's intoxicating.

"There are so many people."

Yelena's voice is soft, low, infused with nervousness.

"So we talk to the weird man in the terrible outfit, get him out of the way. If he's so important then start with him, others will come to you."

I know it's true, but I almost regret saying it. I don't want her to be the center of attention. No one's allowed to dote over her but me.

Suddenly, my hands curl into fists. I think of the man I killed earlier today. As far as I can tell, my men did a good enough job of cleaning up that mess. No one seems to be whispering about a murder.

But that doesn't put my mind to rest.

Yelena's ex hired that fucking pig to stalk her... maybe even to kidnap her.

But why?

There are too many loose threads laying about.

I prefer neat and tidy. I *will* get my neat and tidy.

"I told you. You don't do that," she says. "He's too powerful to approach head on. Like, you don't stare directly into the sun."

I grab her wrist and pull her so those pretty blue eyes are staring directly into mine.

"For you, I'm the only sun here. You look at everyone else, but you only stare at me. Understand?"

Yelena sneers and tries to pull away, but I hold her tight—at least, until I get a hold of myself.

"You can do whatever you want," I grunt. Then, I mutter some choice words in Russian under my breath.

Yelena quickly finishes her champagne, timing it so the passing waiter isn't there and she presses the glass into my hand. "Please get me another drink?"

"I'm not stupid."

She huffs out a breath. "I know. I just need to do this on my own. Schmooze without a hot, scary Russian at my side."

"You think I'm hot." I grin with delight and she rolls her eyes, even as her cheeks go rosy with her blush.

"You know you're hot. Every woman in here wants you."

"Including you?"

A beat throbs between us, sucking oxygen.

But she looks away. "Want has nothing to do with it."

I return to the bar. There are enough waiters I could have easily gotten her a drink that way, but I want to see who else may be here, who's looking for her with an agenda.

Even from here I can see her nervousness. It makes her look like a jumping bean. She's too smart and talented to be this hesitant. The Yelena I first met was in control, bold, confident.

Apart from her looks, her self-confidence is part of what drew me immediately to her.

Strong women don't change so much, so something is going on.

That fucker Alex Civati is my guess.

Whatever really happened between them, she hasn't told me the entire story. But I don't need the exact story. The change in her is enough.

Promises aside, I'm not sure I'll be able to control myself if he walks in.

More, I'm not sure I want to.

With a sigh I kick back against the bar, order another drink. The dark, biting anger in my veins isn't going to help Yelena. So I switch thoughts to Andrei's call.

Like some kind of psychic connection, my phone vibrates and I pull it from my pocket.

It's Ilya.

Third in command of the Zherdev Bratva. Right behind me, even though he's fresh off the boat from Russia. I don't hold it against him. The man is a bona fide computer genius. Invaluable to our operation.

I hit answer and speak in Russian.

It's easier with the noise in here. Ilya's English is perfect, but accented.

"Working hard, Valentin?" The sarcasm is gentle, and I smile.

"Given up English? Too hard for your small brain?"

"No, but I figured since you're partying I'd make it easy for you. Maybe your brain's pickled?"

I snort a laugh. "I'm drinking whiskey."

"They'll hang you for that."

"And here I thought I'd be first up against the wall."

Yelena is talking to a woman who snaps her fingers and two waiters appear, and soon a glass is pressed into my nervous angel's hand.

She's still jumpy, but not as much as before. I sweep for the fucker, but all I see are models and people in stupid outfits everywhere. No Alex.

"Did you speak to Andrei?" Ilya asks.

"He told me you think there's some vermin in our pipes."

"I don't think. I know. We have a rat problem, Valentin."

"Who?"

"That I don't know. They're careful, too clean," he says.

"Too clean?" I frown and sip my drink.

He sighs. Truth is I have a lot of time for Ilya. Some don't. Some see him as an imported upstart, but those won't last and I run through the names in my head, setting them aside to look at later.

Maybe one of those are this rat.

Ilya came to Chicago two years ago and is making strides in erasing his accent.

Some also see this as a bone of contention, think he's ashamed of where he's from.

He isn't.

He's whip smart, beyond computers. He sees big pictures. And part of that is knowing that he'll have an easier time if he sounds American.

"Whoever it is, they aren't leaving tracks."

"Which are almost like tracks?"

I can almost hear his grin. "Exactly. They clean up. I'm tracing it, or trying to, but the problem is if I push them further into the sewers, they could be even harder to find. And Andrei's empire is already vast."

"A lot of places to hide," I say.

"Exactly."

He breathes out and the quiet clack of computer keys comes at me suddenly.

"You think there's more going on?"

"There are the clean trails that lead nowhere, like the morning after a damp night and snail trails glisten, there's damage on the plants, but so many silver trails the fuckers could be anywhere in the cabbage patch."

I smile at the analogy, gaze on Yelena as she moves to someone else. Sure I promised I wouldn't leave her side, but sometimes the bigger picture is clearer from further away.

"What do you have so far?" I ask.

He pauses and there's more clacking. "I can't find the breach into the network, only the clean trails left in the wake of the missing documents."

"Do you know what was in the documents?"

"Information about our money laundering schemes."

"Shit."

Those are our big money makers, and the way we keep things looking clean when the government decides to take closer looks at our operation.

"Shit is right," Maksim grumbles. "My security team got the alert minutes before Andrei called you. I'm working on it now."

In my head something is ticking. This is bad and we both know it.

"Do you have any idea where the documents went?"

"Not yet, my friend. Only trails, a lot of clean trails."

"Treat them as fingerprints. We need to look for other incidents like this outside our operations."

"You want my job, Valentin? Pay's good, but not so many pretty girls."

Yelena turns and catches my eye and there's a flicker in her, back a little straighter, tits pushing out. Tiny, but I see it, and her glance curls inside me. I smile slowly and a blush eats a path up her throat.

"Less bloodshed," I say.

He laughs. "You might be surprised."

"If it's clean, it sounds to me like a robbery without the breaking and only the entering."

"Like with a key? Or a password? One of our terminals?"

I shrug and take another swallow of my drink. "I'm not the expert. But If I was looking at it as a criminal tracking a criminal that's what I'd think. Someone used a key, rifled the drawers because they knew the general vicinity—"

"Or wanted it to seem they weren't intimately familiar."

"—and took some things."

"So we're looking for someone savvy, unsuspecting and

with skills. Get in through the front door and then maybe the world's up for grabs."

"This is why I like you," Ilya says, very heavy on the sarcasm, "uplifting talks."

"If this is for blackmail..."

"I know. I've got my rat poison and I'm going to use it. Once I find the rat."

"I'll keep an ear to the ground, but we do work with the Italians." If I could, I'd spit.

He sighs, "And you think it's one of them or one of ours, or maybe an Italian in Russian clothing?"

I ignore the sarcasm.

"We did just form an alliance with a rival."

"The Italian alliance is heavily watched, on both sides, Valentin."

I snatch up my drink and down it, wishing it was quality Russian vodka. The stuff they have here is shit, hence the whiskey. Which I do like. I grit my teeth as Yelena is whisked off into a corner by another woman and a man. It's not hidden, and it's not near an exit, but I can't see her that well as people move around, blocking my view.

"Those fucking Italians," I grumble. Those mobsters think they're romantic and above the rest of us, and they're never satisfied. "It wouldn't surprise me if one of them secretly decided to step out of line."

"To try and weaken the Bratva?" Ilya clicks his tongue. "They wouldn't dare."

"They're arrogant." I straighten up from the bar and motion for another champagne for Yelena. "Think they're the ruling class. Wouldn't put it past those designer wearing fools to attempt some kind of takeover."

"And your love for them is so well known."

"I know what they're capable of."

"And if one comes in with Chekov's gun, I'll let you know."

"You called *me*, Ilya." I glare at the room. Too many people now. The glass of champagne lands next to me and I nod to the bartender and leave a hefty tip. "And that's not what the gun is—"

"I know what it is. I called to see if you've heard anything."

"Not a thing."

I end the call, making a note to keep my ear to the ground, but right now, I've got a lonely angel to keep company. And she's looking more alone than ever.

Anger streaks dangerously along my veins.

She's still in the corner, surrounded by a group of fresh fools. Misery radiates off her, melting through the mask of smiles she wears.

I take an instant to catalogue the people around her. One bored looking model-type, an older man who looks like he invented the word smarmy, a well-dressed mature woman and...

My hackles rise.

I recognize that face—even if I haven't met him in person yet.

Alex Civati.

He's dead.

7

VALENTIN

The need to see that fucker's blood soak the floor twitches in my muscles and my free hand curls back into a fist.

But then I feel Yelena's eyes fall on me and she calls, "Valentin!"

Beneath the fake happy note is real relief and warning. Relief I'm there, warning not to do what I intended to do; fuck him up.

Staying light on my feet, I approach the party and slide past my prey, lifting his wallet along the way. Petty move on my part, but fuck it. I'm just tucking it away when Yelena launches herself into my arms.

It's a complete surprise, and I almost spill the glass of champagne in my hand as I take her. Luckily, Alex is right there, and I manage to shove the glass into his chest before closing my arms around the trembling angel.

He has no choice but to take it.

I hold onto Yelena. Tight. Just like I've always wanted to.

She's warm, delicate and her face dips against my chest.

This is not acting. This is real. It takes everything I have not to cut eyes at Alex and mentally mark him for death.

"Vse v poryadke, angel. YA zdes." *It's alright, angel. I'm here.*

I speak to her, soft, in Russian, words of endearment mixed with how very much I want to kill the bastard for upsetting her, and I do it all with a crooning tone no one but Yelena can hear.

The moment she calms, and it doesn't take more than a handful, I tuck her to my side. Glancing around with the kind of dark smile I use before taking out human trash, I nod to the others by way of greeting, sliding a hand down over Yelena's soft, blonde hair.

The glittering hate, anger and want in Alex's eyes as he looks at her tells me what I want to know.

He's not happy, and he mistakes me for who and what I am. He's also clearly the source of her discomfort, something I see as reasonable cause for his demise.

But killing him right here and now won't do Yelena any good. So I hold back, but just barely.

"Yelena, you didn't tell me you got yourself a bodyguard." Alex sniffs, as if I smell.

I snarl back. "It's to keep the scum away."

"Are you calling me scum?" he laughs, nervously. I can see his hands shaking slightly as he puts the champagne glass onto a passing waiter's tray.

"Only if you plan on hanging around here the rest of the night."

Alex has to collect himself before responding.

"My bodyguards usually hold their tongue a little better."

"Well, then good thing you didn't hire me."

"He's not a bodyguard," Yelena meekly injects.

That raises Alex' greasy eyebrows.

I smile, scanning his eyes. "Of course not. Why would Yelena need a bodyguard... unless someone was trying to do her harm?"

He gulps. "I couldn't imagine anyone wishing harm on such a beautiful creature."

"I could." Stepping forward, I let the coward feel my size. But Yelena tugs back at me and I keep from getting too close.

"If you're not a bodyguard, then that must make you—"

"A friend," Yelena yips.

"Try again."

"Very close friends," Alex narrows his eyes.

"Closer than you think," I growl.

A tense silence follows before Alex lowers his chin and nods at Yelena. "Well, congratulations. I'm sure it's very convenient, dating your bodyguard."

"This is her trading up."

"Trading?" The word whore's implied but even he's not going to overstep. The fucker is scared. But not as scared as he should be.

Pulling on my shirt, Yelena glances up at me, begging for this to end. I kiss the tip of her nose as I slip one hand down to rest right at her ass.

Alex's gaze zeroes in.

"Trading," I say, "the trainer wheels are off and she's riding the real thing." I wait a beat. "By spreading her wings and branching out by herself. This woman doesn't need a bodyguard. She needs investors. Money to start her fashion empire. I'm just first in line. But I won't be the last."

I look over at the other people in our party and nod. They nod back, nervous but interested.

To my surprise, Yelena laughs, and if it's a little strained no one apart from perhaps the fucker notices.

"If she needs money—" Alex starts, but I cut him off, instead focusing on the others.

"You won't want to miss out. This girl is special. Have you seen her designs yet?"

They lean in, desperate to change the subject. I don't listen as they start to chat with Yelena. I just take some of the business cards poking out of her purse and slide them into my breast pocket.

I liked hyping her up. I plan on doing some more of it tonight.

But first...

"Shall we, dear?" I ask Yelena. Lifting her hand up to my lips, I kiss her fingers. Alex coughs, as if that will stop me rather than drive me forward.

Without a single ounce of fucks given for our company, I gently bite down on Yelena's ring finger, marking her in front of her overbearing ex. Then, I subtly lick the faint wound clean. It makes her shutter. The tiniest moan escapes her lips. The sound nearly makes me hard.

"We should keep mingling," Yelena whispers, her voice trembling. My gaze moves from her onto Alex. The rich snob is visibly fuming.

I give him my biggest smirk.

We glare at each other. Someone else in our little group asks Yelena a question. I loosen my hold, just enough so she can turn and talk.

Alex's eyes follow her, but I stay fixed on him. Leaning forward, I get nice and close.

"You should keep your tongue in your mouth," I say, so quietly only he can hear. "Or someone is liable to cut it off."

Ugly hate twists his refined features as he draws his gaze back onto me. "Is that a threat?"

"I never make threats. Only promises."

"Do you know who I am?"

"One of Yelena's groupies?"

The woman at Alex's side can't help but laugh. Suddenly, she starts looking at me with real interest, the kind I instantly understand. He does, too, because the laughter ends and he fists his hands, his face going a little puce.

"I'm Yelena's actual boyfriend," he rages.

The woman's face closes down into painted on smile mode and something tells me he's getting bare minimum from her tonight.

"Who's the one with her? You or me? Take your pissing contest somewhere else, I'm bored."

"She paid you, I know it."

I ignore him. From the corner of my eye, Yelena shakes hands with the woman she's talking to. The moment she's done I sweep her back into my arms.

"Done," I ask, seductively lowering my voice. "Because I think it's time we ditch this party."

"Valentin..." Yelena tips her face to mine and she nods. "I'm done right here and—"

"Good, let's go home. Tomorrow I'll cook you a big breakfast. Trust me, after tonight, you'll need it."

I give Alex one last sly look before sweeping Yelena away. I can practically feel his cheeks burning with anger and jealousy and shame. It's delicious. Though, not as delicious as seeing his blood will be, I'm sure.

But that will come later.

Shaking my head, I whisk Yelena out of the transformed conference room. We're already into the lobby when she pulls back so hard I have to stop or risk having her fall.

"What?"

"Valentin. Stop. I'm not done yet. I still have connections to make. I just meant I was done with that part of the room. I need to go back in there." She tugs again.

I refuse to let her go. "You're still shaking."

"Please." She glares at me. "I'm a grown woman. And now Alex knows to keep away."

"You're not going back in."

"I have to."

"Yelena," I say, pulling her up close to me so I can breathe in her sweet scent, "they'll be here tomorrow. And the night after that. Right?"

She hesitates, then slowly nods. "Yeah, but—"

I place my ring finger on her perfect lips.

"No buts. We'll do more socializing tomorrow. I'll help you win over a thousand new contracts."

"Why can't we stay for just a little bit longer.

"Because I don't want to."

"Sparing with Alex too much for you?"

"Fucking with him was fun," I admit. "Bashing his brains in will be even more fun. But that's not why I want to leave."

"Then why do you?"

I run my thumb up her palm, spreading her fingers. Then, I place them below my belt so she can feel just how hard my cock is.

"Oh my god. Valentin."

"Understand?"

"I... I..."

She doesn't try to pull away, and I take that as permission to wind my fingers through hers. "Let's go."

I pull her outside. The air's laden with the nectar of night flowers, and it hits me like a soft wave.

We stop for a moment, just outside the doors and take a breath of fresh air. It does little to curb my growing desires.

"I should really go back in," Yelena's whispers, but her heart's not in it.

"Not a chance, angel."

The sound of rushing water from a nearby fountain fills the space between us. I stare down at her, she stares back up at me.

"This isn't going to end well," she mumbles, almost more to herself than to me.

I gently pinch her chin.

"I can make sure we have a happy ending," I smirk.

"That's not what I'm talking about."

I can feel her desperate desire to sink into my fingers. But she just can't seem to let go of the tension in her neck. I drop my hand and caress her jaw. The warmth of her skin seeps through my fingers.

"What do you want, angel?"

"I... I don't know. I just know I can't have it."

"You can have whatever you want. I'll give it to you."

"No."

I slide my hand around the back of her skull and pull her into my chest. She comes without a fight, right up until her body sways against mine. Then she struggles, her gaze snapping into flight mode.

I don't release her.

This has gone on for long enough.

"Fuck it."

Pulling her head back, I give her one last look, just to make sure I'm reading her right. There's no doubt.

"Val—"

I shut her up with a kiss.

For a moment time stands still. Then, she starts kissing me back.

It feels even better than I hoped. And it sparks the ravenous side of me I was just barely holding back before.

Holding her close, I push us back against the outside wall of the hotel, pinning her between the hard bricks and my hard body. Yelena sighs and I groan, my hips thrusting into her.

"Was it worth the wait, angel?" I ask, running my tongue over her lips, teasing them open, and then plunging in to stroke against hers.

"Valentin," she sighs, grabbing onto my collar.

I don't stop. She tastes so sweet. Wet. Hot. Soft. All the things I crave. And this is just the start.

Pining my knee between her thighs, I spread her legs apart.

Her gasp is music to my ears. That tight little body melts into me. She starts kissing me back even harder now.

I lower my hand to yank up her dress. I'm so fucking hard it hurts. Aching. My need for her is feral.

"I can drag you back to heaven, angel," I rumble, my hot breath swirling into her open mouth. "But I think you'd prefer hell."

I can feel her wetness on my thigh. The hardness of her nipples through the dress I'm desperate to rip off.

"Hell," she whispers, as though struggling to decide if that's what she really wants or not.

It doesn't matter.

I'm not giving her a choice anymore.

"That's right," I say, ready to strip us both bare right here and now. "Are you ready for me?"

Yelena gasps for air, then says the sweetest word I've ever heard come from her pretty pink lips.

"Yes."

I can't help but smile.

"That's my girl."

8

YELENA

I'm drowning.

And it's not just because of the pressure swirling in my core, or the force of Valentin's body pressing against mine. It's his need. His desire. His *obsession.*

It all crashes against me like searing waves until I can barely breathe.

It's the most wonderful way to suffocate.

Every stroke of his tongue, bite of his teeth, slide of his fingers. Fuck. I'm going crazy.

What the hell is wrong with me?

Valentin moves back to kiss me again and I'm lost. He tastes of whiskey and sex. I want more.

I *need* more.

Almost as much as I need to run away.

"I'm not your girl," I gasp, trying hopelessly to fight back. "I don't belong to anyone."

"You do. To me." He sucks on my lip, making me moan even as I try to push him away. Between my thighs those big, rough fingers are working in steady strokes. I can't help but lift my hips to meet him.

"We have to stop." He isn't listening and one finger pushes at the side of my panties as a small spasm of heat clutches at me. "We can't..."

"Watch us."

I'm so turned on, and I don't want to be. This man scares me as much as he fascinates me. He's beautiful and dangerous. Soft and so hard I know he'd do horrible things in my name if I asked.

"Valentin." My voice is thick and I can't tell if I'm begging him to stop or to keep going.

"Tell me to stop and I'll stop, angel. Truly tell me to stop. No more lies. I can feel your desire. In your mouth, on your tongue, through your soaked panties. Your hips don't lie. Your tits speak the truth. You want this as much as I do. You want me as much as I want you. So let's cut through the cloaks already. Huh? Let's spread ourselves bare. We deserve it."

"It's not that."

"Then tell me what it is?"

My heart is ready to pound through my chest. But there's a fear mixed in with the arousal that can't be ignored.

I need to tell him. There's no other way to stop this.

"I... I'm a virgin."

Just like that, Valentin's ferocious advance halts.

Still, he doesn't pull away. Instead, his fingers stroke me a little softer, like he's trying to keep my motor revved and calm me, all at the same time.

"You're not lying."

It's like he's surprised to believe me.

"I'm not."

His lips glisten with my saliva. His jaw clenches.

"Virginity is antiquated, little angel. But I'm listening."

He lifts his head to meet my gaze and I can't help but marvel at the deep blue of his steely eyes. I try to breathe in fresh air but all there is around me is a haze of him. It permeates the air.

I know I shouldn't say what comes out of my mouth next, but there's no stopping it. Valentin wanted me to cut the bullshit, right?

"A-Alex was obsessed with it."

"The fucker is unworthy of you and small in every fucking way." The violence in his voice belies the soft stroke of his fingers. "He had the fucking gall to want it for himself?"

"I..." Valentin is more fascinating by the minute. I knew he was smart, but he's smarter than I thought and far more astute. Or perhaps I tried to paint him a certain way to protect myself when I helped him crash the barrier I built between us. "Yes."

"Men like him." He shakes his head.

I suck in more air, a warmth of sweetness spreading through me I want to chase and sink into. "He wanted my virginity as a gift, or as a reward. Something he deserved. I'm not sure. Whatever. I wouldn't let him have it."

"That's my girl."

This time, I don't fight back at the claim of ownership.

"Not because I'm holding out for marriage or anything," I awkwardly try to explain, "but, I wanted..."

Valentin watches me with those ocean blue eyes and I can't read the expression hiding beneath the glimmering surface.

"You want it to be with someone worthy of you." He gives a short, harsh laugh. "No wonder he turned so red back there. The idea that you may have been fucking me must have been driving him insane."

I ignore the crudeness of his words. "Yes. He was clearly livid." I clutch at him. "But he's not toothless."

"He buys sharp teeth with his money. Those are fake teeth. They don't dig deep. Not like mine."

"That doesn't mean I'm safe, Valentin."

God, he's being so dismissive. But Bratva or not, Alex can be vindictive. And I'm scared to tell Valentin the rest of the story. He's so territorial, and I don't want him to get himself into the kind of trouble Alex excels at. One with lawyers and bad press and word of mouth that can grind anyone into the mud.

Not that Alex will definitely go after Valentin. Instead, there's a good chance he'd turn his focus on a smaller target— like me. This time with the intention of burning me to the ground for good.

Fuck. How much worse could he get?

He's already hired someone to stalk me, maybe even kidnap me. What's the next level? Valentin can't protect me every second of the day.

Maybe, I amend, he can. But I don't want that kind of captivity.

"You're with me, of course you're safe. I'll protect you."

I stare at him. He just doesn't seem to get it.

"Alex is dangerous in ways you don't expect."

"Yelena." He's still stroking me between my thighs and I'm rocking into his touch, even as a million other emotions explode in me, I cling to that sweet touch. "Don't underestimate me."

"I'm not."

He snarls and leans in. close to my face. "You don't under-stand the power I hold, little angel. He's nothing to me. Nothing. But you know what the biggest difference between us really is?"

"What?"

He slides a finger under my panties, trailing the warm tip over my soaking clit. My body trembles.

"Alex has to play by the rules. I have no rules."

He kisses me, deep, carnal and then he lifts his head and pulls his hand away, slipping my dress back down and turning us so his back is to the wall and I'm plastered against him.

One arm comes about my waist and he licks his fingers. With a jolt I realize it's the one he touched me with.

"Delicious," he sighs. Looking up to the sky, he swallows me, his thick Adam's apple lifting. "I will protect you, angel. That's a promise."

I feel weak. My chin dips.

"Thank you," I whisper.

He can. For now. But the longer I stay in his world the more I'm in a different sort of danger.

Cranking his neck, Valentin looks around, as if only now having the sense to make sure there's no one watching. By some miracle, there isn't.

"Don't worry. I'm not going to defile you here," he grunts, pushing us off the wall. "I'll make sure your first time is worthy of you. Something you want to hold onto forever. It won't be the side of a hotel."

I'm not sure how to feel about that, and I don't get the chance to think about it much. Pursing his lips, he lets out a loud whistle. Then he takes my hand and whisks me across the resort's front drive.

We're hardly back outside the lobby doors when a black car pulls up.

Valentin opens the back door and hustles me inside. But before he can shut me in, I kick out my leg and stop him.

"Where are we going?"

A devilish grin fills his glistening lips.

"Back to my penthouse. So I can defile you the right way."

9

YELENA

The half-finished penthouse, a place of intense luxury and rough edges and stark places, stands around me like a suffocating dream. It's an embodiment of the man who owns it. Valentin.

I suck in a deep, jittery breath.

My heart's galloping and my stomach flutters as each breath draws in more anticipation and fear.

Valentin told me to wait, so I do, the stupid heels on my feet give me extra height but they make me sway. Maybe that's me. Maybe I'm beyond nervous and into another realm where everything's stretched to the limit. And it's suddenly hard to balance when my legs want to shake and my toes squeeze in the snug confines like they're seeking purchase.

Where did he go?

I clutch my bag and half go to pull out my phone, but what am I going to do? Call someone? No one's coming to rescue me here.

I'm not even sure I need rescuing, not when Valentin turns me on so much.

"Angel."

Whirling, I almost lose my balance and he stands in the hall leading to the bedroom, the light showing off his perfection.

Even in the suit, he's that. Pure perfection. My mouth goes dry.

Put him next to any other man and he's the only one I'd see. Like tonight.

How could I be aware of him when he'd been on the other side of the room?

I can't tell him one of the reasons I didn't lose my shit when Alex showed up was because I knew he was there. The moment Alex arrived, with his veiled and cruel put downs, the taunts and hidden threats, Valentin's presence soothed me down to where I could cope.

When he came to save me, he was all I saw, felt, smelled. Even over the cloying aftershave put on by heavy hands, the subtle clean scent of the spices and oud reached me like a lifeline.

"Valentin, I... thank you."

He comes toward me and removes his jacket, dropping it on the back of a chair as he passes it, then he undoes his tie, removes his cufflinks and places them with the jacket.

As he approaches I'm glued to the spot, everything in me throbbing with need.

"For what?"

"Not leaving me with Alex at the—"

"Enough about him. He's inconsequential, nothing. You're the only reason I didn't rip his head off." He stops in front of me and takes my bag, and crosses to the chair to place it down. When he returns he comes behind me, running his fingers down along my spine. "We don't talk about other men when we're alone. Understand?"

I try to breathe. He's going to... oh, God, this is the night.

"I understand."

The giddy wildness swirling through me is so at odds with who I am. I'm not sure what to do.

He toys with the zip of my dress and tugs it down, pushing it from my shoulders so it lands at my feet.

My stomach swoops down and heat rises through me.

Valentin turns me to face him. And my nipples bead as his gaze drops to them.

"Look at you." He traces a path from my collarbone up to my lips then down to rest at the base of my throat. "My perfect little virgin sacrifice. But, don't worry, we're not going there tonight. When we do it, I want you begging, I want you knowing how good it can feel. You don't know yet, do you?"

"No."

He leans in and tweaks a nipple. "Then I'll have to warm you up."

He lifts me in his arms and takes me into the kitchen where he puts me on the counter and he pushes my thighs apart.

Running his fingers down my leg, followed by his mouth and tongue, he undoes my shoe and tosses it aside. It lands with a thud. A wince. He repeats the same with the second shoe. When it hits the floor, I don't flinch as much.

"You're mine now."

Valentin comes in and kisses me deep and slow. My head spins as his warm lips mark every part of me. He kisses my eyelid, nose, cheeks, chin. He makes his way down the side of my throat, licking and tasting, his teeth grazing my skin and all I'm aware of is the sizzle of that touch as it spikes down to my clit, the bite of the marble and the heat of him between my thighs.

"You taste like heaven, angel. So fucking sweet." He lifts his head and peels my panties off.

I don't think I could stop him if I tried. And apart from a whimper of protest, I don't.

How can I?

My entire body is desperate for him. I've never felt anything this good before.

Sure, I've used a clit stimulator before. A vibrator, too. But nothing compares to this man touching me. Kissing me. Licking me.

Those roughened fingers slip down my stomach to my pussy and he slides through the wetness. My back arches at the touch.

"I've wanted you from the day we met," he growls, his breath hot and humid.

"That was a lifetime ago," I whisper.

"Nothing's changed."

He's wrong. "So much has changed."

I reach for the buttons of his vest, but he grabs my hands and nibble on my fingertips.

"No." He bites hard on the ring finger, then sucks it into his mouth. "I still feel the exact same way I did then."

Before I can say another word, Valentin kisses me again. His tongue presses against mine and I'm lost. Next thing I know, I'm clinging to him, kissing him back.

"I need to taste more of you."

Those wet lips leave my mouth to make their way down my body, sucking and kissing and biting at my nipples. Every single scrape of his teeth sends an electrified current pulsing under my skin.

I gasp his name. "Valentin."

"Yelena," he rumbles back.

I'm pulled forward until my chest meets Valentin's hand. His fingers spread between my breasts, my bare skin glistening from the marks left by his mouth. I'm angled like a sacrificial lamb, open and offered to him.

The dark and ravenous god takes my offering without hesitation, and it feels like I might explode under his desire.

"Valentin. Please."

I'm not sure what it is I'm asking. For more. For him to stop. Or maybe all of it. I don't know. My mind's spinning as he pushes a finger into my soaking pussy.

"Oh. My. God."

It's just one finger, but it stretches me out with unexpected pressure. My body clenches. My limbs quiver.

"Does that feel good, little angel?" Valentin asks, unbuttoning his vest.

He pulls it off and then picks me up, that thick finger pumping me further into delirium as he holds me around the waist with his other arm.

"Yes," I breathlessly admit, clinging to him as he curls inside of me.

"It will only get better."

He walks with me, feeding on my throat, sucking on my breasts, coming back to my mouth, teasing me, over and over.

Every time I get close to the edge, he slows, or shifts his focus, only to start all over again.

It's like he's trying to drive me insane. And it must be working, because I don't want him to stop.

"I'm going to make you erupt," Valentin says, his voice a low rumble in my ear. "Slowly. How does that sound?"

I hit a wall and he pins me there, suckling hard on my breasts until I start a high pitched, keening moan.

"I asked you a question, angel."

"Yes. Make me erupt. Please."

"Do you think you can handle it?"

What I can't handle is all this teasing.

"Just do it already!" I beg.

"No. Not yet."

Valentin drops down to his knees, holding me up so his hot breath crashes against my pussy.

"So fucking perfect."

When he finally licks me, I scream. His finger pulls out and

I'm pressed back against the wall. "Give in. I'll hold you up." His hot tongue flashes across my swollen clit.

"Please. Let me..."

I writhe and beg and plead, but Valentin doesn't give me anything more than exactly what he wants to give me. I grab onto his head and push him into me. He doesn't resist. Doesn't fight back. Doesn't give in—not until my nails dig deep into his skull.

Then he closes his lips around my clit and starts to suck.

There's no holding me back anymore. I lose it. "Oh my god, I'm going to—"

Just like that, the bastard stops.

There's a wicked glint to his eyes as he rises. I'm still shaking as he grabs my hand and whisks me to a nearby table. I'm carefully laid down on top. My thighs are spread for him. I look up at the ceiling, practically blind.

"This is what you deserve, Yelena. Don't you ever dare think differently, or else I'll have to keep reminding you. Over and over again..."

He leans over my body and starts to worship me with his mouth. That's the only word I have for it. Worship. The lick of his tongue, the scrape of his teeth. The suck of his mouth. The tiny kisses.

I'm no longer the sacrifice.

I'm the god.

My chest lifts. Grateful sobs jolt through my body.

A raspy cry breaks from my lips. "Valentin!"

"Tell me you deserve it," he roars.

"I... I..."

"Speak, angel!"

"I deserve it! I deserve it!"

"Damn fucking right you do."

His hot kisses land across my skin like searing drops of rain, overloading my senses until his lips find their way back to my pussy. This time, he doesn't just suck on my clit. He doesn't just slide his girthy finger into my begging hole.

He does both. At the same time.

And I'm gone.

But he's just getting started.

Another finger slides inside of me, stretching me further than I thought I could.

"It's too much," I gasp. "They won't fit."

"No. We're a perfect fucking match," Valentin assures me. "So fucking perfect."

He's right. Once the shock wears off, and I find it in me to relax around him, there's no other thought in my mind.

Two fingers are better than one.

I writhe as they lead me up and down, back and forth.

I pull at Valentin's hair, desperate for some sense of control. But he doesn't slow down. He doesn't stop.

Like a wild beast, he continues to feast on my body I can't take anymore. Then, as my body surges, he pumps his fingers in three hard and fast bursts, then pulls them free. I'm lifting up into his arms, gasping for air as he plants his soaking lips onto mine. I taste myself on his tongue, but I'm too weak to kiss him back. It hardly matters. His kiss is powerful enough for the both of us.

Valentin laughs at my weakness.

"You think we're finished, angel?"

I'm so satisfied it hurts, yet somehow more starving than I've ever been before.

I need him to keep going, even if I don't know that I can take it.

"Take off your clothes and—" I reach for his collar. But he stops me.

"No. This isn't about me, Yelena. This is about you. My clothes stay on... for now."

With surprising grace, Valentin takes my hand and pulls me

off the table. I'm whisked away. I hardly know where I am, yet alone where we're going. But it doesn't matter. Valentin hauls me up over his shoulder. Grabbing a handful of my ass, he turns and bites at my hip. A shot of electricity runs through me, sparking back to life.

This is a man who makes no excuses.

If he wanted to fuck me right now, he'd be naked already. He's be inside of me.

But he said it himself. He wants my first time to be worthy of me.

What a fucking thought. That I'm worth anything.

"I'm going to decorate this place with mementos to you," Valentin says, carrying me through the unfinished penthouse. "A marble bust of your perfect cunt, right where I first tasted your clit. A sculpture in the living room of your perfect tits."

He sets me down and pushes me face first into a wall to kiss my back. His lips leave a hot trail as they fall down to my ass.

"Right here, a painting of your perfect body." He spreads my cheeks and plants a surprisingly tender kiss on each side before lifting up again. "No. Two paintings. One of your front, the other of your beautiful backside."

I'm spun around so he can kiss me on the mouth again. We stumble backward until he decides to pick me back up.

I wrap around him, silently offering him my throat.

"Velvety wallpaper in this room." He turns and pushes me against another wall. It rattles as his fingers find their way between my legs again. This time, I mindlessly start to ride him. "So we can paint it with each other's cum. When I step in, I want to smell you."

Without thinking, I slip my hand between us and close it around the giant bulge in his pants. He's so big and hard I can hardly feel the edges. Still, I trace the girth and length, trying to get a mental image. It earns me a hard, long bite to the throat.

"Do you see how hard you make me?" Valentin rumbles.

My chest lifts. "I want to taste you."

My voice is thick and pleading. The desire comes from the most hidden parts of my soul.

But again, I'm denied.

"No. Not yet." Valentin moves his mouth close to my ear, his lips just barely brushing against my sensitive skin. "I'm not done planning out my shrine to you. Maybe I'll turn this section into our playroom. Add hanging ropes. Hooks. Would you like me to tie you up? Spank you? Tease you until you're begging for my cock?" His hand slides to my ass. "Claim every last one of your holes?"

He bites down on my earlobe and, in that moment, I want nothing more than for him to tie me up, to do what he wants with me, to make me his.

Something takes over me, and I press into Valentin's hard body, latching onto his throat with my mouth. I kiss the rough skin along his throat, licking my own path along his flesh. When I get to his enormous collarbone, I bite and suck until he grunts.

"I definitely need to restrain you," he laughs deeply.

His fingers wrap around my throat, lifting my head. It's a quiet reminder. This isn't about him. It's about me. I rest my chin on his shoulder, accepting my fate. My heavy eyes drifting. Then...

My heart skips a beat.

Something dark and ominous bleeds through the dim light. I blink, trying to shrug off the haze surrounding me.

Finally, I see it clearly.

It looks like a crest. Terrifying. Brutal.

And oh-so alluring.

The silver façade shimmers softly against the darkness. A black hole sits heavily beneath it. When I've blinked enough, I realize it's a vault.

The only decorations in this barren, unfinished room.

Valentin is kissing my neck, but he stops when he senses me tense up.

"What's wrong?" he asks.

I'm not sure what to say.

"I... what's that?"

I point, and he turns. The crest is absolutely mesmerizing... and utterly terrifying. I can't look away. A silver skull, screaming into the void. A black viper slithering through its sockets, fangs bared.

I swallow.

Below that, the thick vault is a deep black that sucks in all surrounding light. The only color to be found anywhere nearby comes from a small keypad below the handle that periodically casts a red dot in and out of existence.

"Ignore that," Valentin huffs. "It's just the crest of my Bratva." He starts to kiss my throat. "All you need to know is that it used to be gold. But when it was handed down to me, I turned it silver. Nothing else to worry about. What we're doing now is more important."

But I'm transfixed.

There's something so dark about the crest. Something so thrilling.

Shit. I must really be losing my mind.

"And the vault?" I can't help but ask.

To my surprise, Valentin stiffens slightly. "You don't want to see what's in there."

"But—"

"Enough." He stops what he's doing. "I said no. This is no time to share secrets. Right now, only one thing is important." He leans in close to my ear again. "Getting you off."

I'm going to argue more until he slips his fingers back into my tight pussy. It's enough to shup me up.

The crest and the vault fade from my emptying mind as I hold onto him for dear life.

"Now, isn't this better than asking all those questions?"

He bites down on my nipple and a hot white flash blinds me to everything else. My body throbs with a burst of release. For a moment, I'm in limbo, stuck between worlds. Then the release fades and I come hurtling back down to earth.

"Now, do you want to talk business or do you want me to keep making you fucking explode?"

A deep, shaky breath flares my nostrils. The is so obvious I don't need to say a word.

"That's what I thought," Valentin grunts.

Then, with a satisfied smile pulling at his glistening lips, he swings me up over his shoulder and marches us out of the room. My head spins as I'm carried into the bedroom.

Without sparing a second, I'm tossed onto the mattress. The sheets smell like him. Another aphrodisiac. So when he climbs over me, my hands instinctively reach for the buttons on his shirt.

This time, he lets me tug them open.

His shirt falls apart, reveling in the heat of his smooth, inked skin.

An involuntary gasp flies from my throat.

The tattoos are just as menacing as the skull and viper crest, but they stir me in a different way. There's a gothic passion to the art that covers his skin. I can't help but want to place my hands on each and every inch.

"It's like I'm touching living art," I mumble in awe.

Valentin looks down at me, the edges of his lips curling. "No, angel. That's you."

I try to touch more, but he rolls to his back and tugs me onto him so that his throbbing bulge is pressed directly up between my legs.

A warm shiver passes through me.

"Give me your mouth," he orders.

I do as he says, leaning into kiss him. When he's satisfied,

Valentin curls his hand in my hair and lifts my face back. "Now climb onto my face, angel. Suffocate me with your thighs."

Despite all that we just did, I'm almost to shocked to respond.

"Wha... what?"

"You heard me."

"I can't..."

"You'll do as I commanded," he says. "I want to feast on you. I want those soft thighs holding me down as you grind your cunt all over my tongue. I want you to come. Again. All over my fucking face. So do it!"

There's no fighting it.

I do as I'm told.

Valentin wraps his hand around my thighs and brings my pussy up to his mouth.

He licks me, suckles, from the bottom of my slit all the way up, and then down again. The rhythm of his tongue leads my hips. I start to sway, rocking against him, hands on the headboard.

It isn't enough. And like he can read my mind, Valentin shoves his tongue inside my slick hole.

I cry up to the ceiling, easing up.

Valentin pulls his tongue out.

"Tighter!" he commands.

I obey, gasping and groaning as he tongue fucks me. My eyes roll back into my head. I push down on him. Anything to keep him from stopping again. I need more.

He releases one thigh and pushes three fingers into me. He's not gentle. I feel his teeth hold my clit in place as he lashes at it with his tongue. When he sucks it in, I nearly collapse.

"I can't do it anymore."

I'm crying now, it's too much. My legs are going weak. I try to pull away, but that hand on my thigh clamps down and I can't escape.

"We. Aren't. Done."

The deep growl vibrates up through my soul.

"No, it's too much. Please." My words slip into moans as Valentin pushes and pushes until something splits.

It's unbearable.

It's unbelievable.

It's perfect.

I burst into a thousand little pieces.

One last cry rips from my throat, then I collapse down onto Valentin.

He reclaims his fingers and gently eases me off him.

He's a mess. His clothes are wet from where I've cum on him.

But a big smile fills his handsome face.

"Angel."

I try to speak. To reach for him. But I can't.

"Devil," I finally manage to rasp.

That was amazing.

It was also exhausting. I can't even call on the energy to move.

"I guess that makes two of us now." Valentin rolls off the bed and pulls the covers over me. "I'm taking a shower."

I want to follow him. I want to slide out of bed and let him fuck me under the water. I want to lose my virginity to him.

But I'm too far gone.

So, instead, I turn over in bed and watch his chiseled ass walk away. When the bathroom door shuts behind him, I sigh and sink into the sheets that smell just like him.

Like him and like sex.

A deep satisfaction fills my chest. My light head drifts off. My eyelids flutter shut. I hear the shower turn on.

The next thing I know, I'm waking up. Sunlight drifts in through the bedroom window.

I ache in strange places and when I stretch every part of me burns with a satisfying heat. I remember what happened last night.

Reaching out, I hit the cold spot where Valentin is supposed to be. Next to me.

But he's not there.

That satisfying heat is quickly replaced by a damp disappointment. A chilled sweat covers my skin. My heart sinks.

I fell for Valentin's tricks, hook, line and sinker. And now, I'm on my own.

Oh, God.

What have I done?

10

I'm still fucking hard.

My balls ache.

And her taste teases me, taunts. I want to fucking sink into her cunt and claim her. Make her mine. But I'm holding off. I need her to understand what it is to truly crave, to *want* to give me everything.

She will.

It's fucking inevitable.

When I left her last night, I took a shower and it would have been so easy to take hold of my cock and bring myself to orgasm to ease that ache.

Instead, I called on something I've always had trouble with. Self-control.

She's changing me.

Fuck.

I flip the pancakes, ones I've made from scratch, just like how I used to before the money. I remember those times with a strange nostalgia. Fending for myself, and others, in ways that seem so beneath me now—or at least, did, until Yelena.

I look after what's mine.

Protect it.

And in my way, nurture.

Like with food.

I place the syrup on the tray. Whipped cream. And a bowl of brown sugar, fresh cut lemon. Fruit. And a glass of orange juice squeezed fresh.

Yelena's going to want coffee, so I'll make that next.

These mundane duties help ease the ache in my balls. Stops me thinking about her naked softness in my arms as I held her while she slept.

Shit.

I adjust myself in the boxer briefs. Then, turning off the stove, I carry the tray down the hall, past all the spots I feasted on her, sampled, teased.

When I push inside the bedroom, Yelena sits up, a slight wince flashing over her features as she clutches the sheet to her.

It's like she's seeing a ghost.

Is that regret I see in her eyes... or something else?

"Hungry?"

I choose to ignore it.

"Who made that?" she asks, gaze lingering on the tray, sliding a little lower, then up to drink in the rest of me before returning to the breakfast.

"I did. You'll be sore after last night." I set the tray next to her and pull the sheet from her body so I can have my fill.

Reward or torture, I'm not sure.

I nudge her legs apart, ignoring the blush that paints her perfection, and I sit, picking up her left foot, kissing her ankle, running my fingers lightly up and down her inner leg, right up to the top of her thigh.

"Valentin." Her nipples are tight beads, her stomach flutters as her hand clenches the sheets.

"Yelena," I say, "you need your strength. So eat, I know you must be exhausted. Drink your juice and sample your food. Go on. You've got a big day ahead of you."

She makes a small sound. "You're so bossy."

"Assertive."

"The worst."

There's the Yelena I remember. I slide up the bed to stroke over her sweet rose of a cunt, all wet and red and ready. "In the best ways."

"Fuck." She grabs the juice and takes a deep swallow.

"Put it down on the bedside table. Try your pancakes."

She rips off a corner and dips it in the cream. That gives me an idea.

"That's not how you eat good pancakes, angel." I chuckle. "Pass me the cream. I want to taste your wetness and then make a meal of you."

Yelena gulps and moves her hips in a subconscious invitation. I lick her pussy, savoring her taste and wetness.

She's making tiny sounds that stroke against my cock. I could spend the day here between her thighs. But I raise my head. Tits up and nipples hard, her hand's on the tray.

"The cream, angel."

She looks down at me with a small frown. "Don't stop."

I laugh. "This is a pause." I ease a finger into her tight cunt, pumping it a few times before withdrawing. "The cream."

Yelena hands it to me and I dip in and paint her cunt with thick gobs of it, and then, I start to lick and eat it off her, licking into her, sucking on her clit, cleaning her and turning it all into a sublime and decadent feast. Her lips are so wet and soft,, and as I run my tongue along the inside, I push deep into her, nose against her swollen nub, breathing in that sweet, addictive scent of hers.

"Delicious," I rumble. "Truly fucking delicious."

Yelena moans, her hips rising. I feel her hands come down on me.

I need her restrained, tied down so I can have unfettered access to everything I desire. That will come. For now, this will do.

"You're still so tight," I tell her, slipping my tongue inside. "Too tight."

"Too tight for what?"

"You know what, angel."

As she's panting and moaning, I switch it up and come up to suckle and lick her clit, pushing three fingers into her.

She's even tighter than I remember and so fucking wet. My swollen cock twitches in my pants. I need to bury it inside her.

But if I do it now, she might shatter.

"Not that," she rasps. "Not yet."

"Soon."

Yelena pants, and moans my name over and over, with the word please and it makes me harder than it should, harder than when I've had a woman in ropes, unable to speak, taking whatever I choose to give.

All I'm doing is eating my angel the fuck out and it makes me harder than the kinkiest sex I've had.

Yelena is a wonder. A phenomenon all of her own.

"How soon?" she whispers, filled with cautious curiosity.

"Soon enough."

I hook my fingers right as her body starts to stiffen, as she begins to close on my fingers, and I bite her clit gently, sucking hard.

"Oh my god!"

She screams and explodes in violent movement, her body pulsating hard, the walls of her cunt squeezing my fingers and liquid gushes, liquid I want to drink, to bathe in.

But making her squirt is enough, because I want to make her ride this wave of orgasmic bliss, to writhe and come apart in my hands and mouth over and over, and then stroke her right back to that peak, only to shatter her again, this time her entire being.

And I do. She's crying out now, whimpering, fighting me.

"Too much, Valentin, please, I can't!"

I make her.

"You can. I believe in you, little angel."

Her cry when she cums is so loud that it fills the entire room. Her body convulses so hard that I can see the white of her eyes as they roll back in her head.

I can feel the wave of her orgasm. It's so strong it nearly snaps my fingers in two.

"Perfect," I whisper. "You are so fucking perfect."

When she comes down, I ease out, stroking her. Then, I crawl up her body to kiss and sip at her lips, to lick the tears of pleasure from her face.

"What is wrong with you?" she sobs. "Are you trying to kill me?"

I slide a finger into her mouth, and thrust gently. "See how good you taste? Do you understand now? I can't get enough."

She shoves me. Pulls my finger from her mouth only to bite hard on my fingertip.

The bolt of pain is sheer pleasure as it hits my cock.

"My turn."

"Angel—"

"My. Turn."

There's a red-hot rage to her voice that turns me on so hard my mind goes blank.

"Then take it," I sneer. "Take me."

I let her shove me on my back and she crawls, ass swaying, down to my cloth-covered cock.

She runs a cool hand over it and now it's my turn to thrust into her. "You're hard." Her whisper licks my skin. "Can... can I see it?"

I watch her through narrowed eyes. "Yesterday you were too shy to look."

"And now you've destroyed me. I want to see it."

"If you look, you have to taste."

Her pulse beats in her throat and she palms me again. "Is that a rule?"

"Yes. I want to fuck your face, Yelena. But I'll let you taste me, learn me, take it at your own pace."

She draws in a sharp breath. "And if I want more?"

"Ask."

I pull her up on me and take her face in my hands before kissing her deeply.

"Just ask," I say again.

She gives me a smile that's so purely hers that I groan. It reminds me of the girl I first met, back when she seemed to have the world by its cock. That deadliness is returning.

The thought is exhilarating, but also infuriating.

What the hell did Alex do to her to make her so closed off? I'm going to make that fucker pay dearly. But first...

"Get to work, angel."

"Don't tell me what to do."

Yelena shimmies down my body and sits on my thighs, pulling me free of my underwear. The cool air of the penthouse is a soft tease on my skin. "Holy shit," she gasps. "You... you're huge."

"Start slow," I advise. "Take a small taste, and we can go from there."

I wasn't planning on letting her go this far, but now that it's inevitable, I'm not stopping it.

"Slow, huh?"

Like a curious fawn, Yelena palms my balls and wraps her hand around my shaft as best she can, then she starts to pull.

"Just like that, angel," I moan. "Now, use your mouth."

To my surprise, she doesn't fight the order. Instead, she

lowers those glorious lips. I hold my breath. Her tongue touches the head and I buck, I can't help it. Teeth clenched, fists tight, I try and remain still for her.

"Does it feel good?" she asks, pulling back momentarily.

"Yes!" I bark. Grabbing the back of her skull, I lead her back down. "Don't you dare stop now."

Obediently, she licks a path up along my swollen shaft, to the sensitive spot under the head. My spine tingles with electricity. My balls get tight.

"Good girl."

Yelena bathes me with her tongue, slurping on the head, bringing it into her hot, wet mouth and I nearly lose my shit.

A groan breaks free.

"You like that?" she asks.

"What do you fucking think?"

"I think I want to make you beg."

I huff at her words. She has no idea the fantasies they set off, the ideas of punishment that leap into my head.

"No. Little one. I don't beg. Not even for you."

"I bet I can make you."

"How about you make me cum first?"

She takes that as a direct challenge.

Her lips stretch as she sucks me in, her hand working up and down my shaft.

"Fuck." She's already pushing me to the brink.

How?

"Easy." I growl.

It's a warning she doesn't heed.

Yelena keeps going, up and down, taking me as deep as she dares, coming up to swirl her tongue around the head. I can't help it. I take a fistful of hair and guide her, bringing her deep, deeper than she expects, and I set the pace, holding back the urge to hammer into her, to turn her into my toy.

"Just like that," I instruct. "Nice and smooth."

I let her have a modicum of control and when she wants to touch, I let her. And then... then she takes my balls as she comes up to suck hard on the head.

"Oh, fuck. I'm going to come." I don't know if this is English or Russian or a mix of the two and I don't care. From deep inside the orgasm rips through me, spreading sharp heated pleasure through my veins as I fill her mouth with cum.

When I'm done, when I have control, I take her hair and ease her up. There's cum on the corner of her mouth and I swipe it with my finger, pushing it past her lips. "Swallow."

"As you wish."

She does as instructed. Then she licks her lips. I pull her up and bury my tongue in her mouth.

"How was that?" she asks.

"Oh, we aren't done yet. I'm still hard, and—"

Suddenly, a shrill buzzing sound slices through the moment.

But it's not coming from my phone. Mine's in the kitchen still.

With a disappointed grunt, I release Yelena and reach for the bedside table. I manage to get to the phone before she does. I pick it up, but before I can get a good look at the screen, she snatches it from me.

"Something important?"

I get up and head for the shower.

Yelena rolls out of bed and mindlessly picks up my discarded shirt, draping it over her shoulders. I listen with pleasure as her tiny footsteps follow behind me.

"Valentin—"

The phone's in her hand as she hovers in the bathroom doorway.

"A reminder, I saw."

She rolls her eyes. "Not just a reminder, there's a scheduled event."

I nod and turn on the water. Then I turn around and take her phone, setting it down by the sink. "You'll need to shower before we head out."

"Are you saying I stink?"

"That's precisely what I'm saying." Tugging her by the shirt, I pull her in close and sniff her neck. "You reek of me."

"Better make the water hot then."

"That's just how I like it."

I pull my shirt off of her and toss it to the bathroom floor. Then I lead her into the shower.

"We have to hurry," she insists.

"Deep breaths, little one. Let me get my stink off you."

I pick up my soap and begin to bathe her.

"That's your soap," she points out. "I'm still going to smell like you. I can get my own stuff..."

She turns to leave the shower, but I take her wrist and stop her.

"I thought we were in a hurry?"

She rolls her eyes, but doesn't fight back.

"Fine. Be quick with it, though."

"I never am."

She turns and I keep going, this time soaping her tits, playing with her nipples, backing her into the shower's wall.

"Stop that." She slaps my hand as I go to push my fingers into her. Her hips move to me, belying her words. "I don't have time. And this..."

"Was inevitable."

"Fun."

I nod. "Inevitable fun and it's fun to discover the inevitable."

"Valentin." But my name ends in a moan, and I lick and suck on her throat.

"I mean it," she says. "I can't be late for this event. It's a chance for me to talk to some of the biggest players in the fashion industry."

"I'll set up appointments."

"No. I want to do this on my own."

I nod again. "With me by your side."

"You're not exactly made for the fashion industry. Although you do look good in a suit."

"But better without one, right?"

Horror crosses her face and I kiss her lips and slide those fingers into her. This is another favorite place of mine, inside her tight cunt.

"Valentin."

With a sigh, I stop and continue to bathe her, ignoring my erection. "Fine. Let's get moving."

"Thank you."

"I know how you can really thank me."

Her hand brushes my erection and she comes up to me. "Get out of the shower, I need to get ready and you're a distraction. We can play more later."

The minx.

"Look at you," I smile.

Without another word, I step out and dry myself off. Then I get dressed and head down to the kitchen to grab my phone.

When I return, Yelena's rushing like a mad thing, in bra and panties with clothes over one arm and her hair wet and wild.

"I'm not going to have time. I'm—"

"Easy there. I've already got a car waiting downstairs. Get dressed."

"I don't know what to wear."

"Go with your gut. It's always served you well."

She stops and looks at me like I'm proof to the contrary. Then she takes a deep breath and gets down to business.

I watch as she changed into a fresh outfit.

"How do I look?" she asks.

The skirt's long and tailored, reaching her narrow ankles. And she pulls on the sheer shirt with long sleeves and oversize cuffs. It's a take on a man's suit, and I'm no fashion expert, but I pull off my tie and put it, loose, around her neck, and then I remove my cufflinks and fit them to the shirt.

"Better naked." Her eyes go wide with annoyance and I take a step forward to ease her. "You look exquisite, darling. Now, put your hair back, it'll save you time drying it. We've got places to be."

Yelena bites her tongue and turns to look at herself in the nearest mirror. To my surprise, she nods, puts some shit on her eyes and lips and then pins her hair in a low, loose bun.

She slips her feet into black leather heels, and as she does so reveals the sexy and hidden split in the skirt. I'm admiring it, and all the things I could do to her while she's wearing it, when she smooths it down and grabs her bag.

"I'm ready," she says with more than a little sass, "let's get the hell out of here."

I smooth the silver and black tie I put on and the black and silver cufflinks catch the light as I do so.

"I thought you'd never ask."

I know she wants me to keep my distance but that's not happening.

This time the get-together is in the hotel restaurant and I check the place out, but it's secure and I'm packing. My driver is near, also armed and ready to spring into action should I need him to.

"Where's our table?" I don't wait and I go in, find it.

Yelena's at my heels. "Wait outside."

"You and me are glue."

"I don't think that's a saying."

"It isn't? It should be." I pick up the name card next to hers. "Who's he?"

"I don't know." This is a sit-down lunch and talk. After that, we move around and try to meet with those we want to.

I give her a look. "Who do you want meetings with?"

She rattles names at me, distracted as she looks around.

Since most of the people in here haven't sat, and none of the names at her table are ones she wants to sit with, I take them and switch them out, putting down some of the people she mentioned at her table.

I'm admiring my handiwork when my phone buzzes.

Ilya.

"Yelena, go ahead, mingle, but stay in my line of sight. I'll be over there." It's loud in here, louder than expected, so I point at the entrance.

She hardly nods.

"This better be good," I say in Russian, pressing the phone to my ear as I set up by the doors.

"Busy are you?"

"Very."

I don't explain myself or where I am. He probably already knows but it's not important. What's important to him is this fucking rat.

And what's important to me is being by Yelena's side.

"So let's get this fucking over with."

"Very well," Ilya responds. "Big news. We know where the missing documents came from. Our headquarters downtown. To use the snail analogy," he says, "I laid down cyber salt—"

"Do you have to sound so pleased with yourself?"

"Of course. I'm brilliant." He chuckles and then says, "I basically shut down all the paths that led nowhere, or came from the wrong direction, and focused on the ones that went to a specific place. Like downtown."

"You mean our empire's HQ and not one of the other ones?"

"That's what I'm fucking saying, Valentin."

I breathe out, leaning on the glass wall next to the entrance.

Ahead, I watch Yelena talk to someone, a man who's focused in on her. I read him, his stance, the touches he gives, the way he nods.

Not that he'd be a threat to me and my plans for her, but I like to know if I have competition. But it becomes clear pretty quickly that he's only interested in her on a professional level.

"Our new and improved base of operations isn't finished yet," Ilya reminds me. "We're still set up with the Italians."

"Our allies," he says.

I'm warming to the subject. "So you're thinking our rat could be Italian?"

Ilya doesn't answer and I bet he's throwing darts at the board in his office because I hear a small scream and a dull thud.

He still hasn't improved his game.

"Maybe," he says, finally.

"I told you. What did I fucking say? Those Italians aren't to be trusted, and certainly not with our database."

"We're not giving them all access clearance." He pauses. "Or any clearance to our protected files."

"So, an Italian with clearance."

"There are some. Low level. Like we have with them. And—"

"Who's fucked idea was that?"

"Andrei's?"

Andrei. What was he thinking? I'm about to launch into a modified tirade against my closest friend, the one I've protected and been with through thick and thin since the beginning, when I suddenly lose interest in the call.

Ilya isn't close to finding the culprit. He's uncovered some clues, but right now, that front is stalled.

And shit here just got real.

I watch with a twisted sneer as Alex walks in. Somehow, he immediately spots Yelena.

"Asshole," I growl.

"I'm not telling Andrei that."

"I wasn't referring to him."

Ilya starts talking but I'm not listening. I'm about to hang up when I change my mind. "Hey?"

He stops talking. "What?"

"Do me a favor. Get me everything you can on a fucker named Alex Civati."

"Sure, but, what does he have to do with the rat? Are you thinking outside influences? Remote access? Is—"

I hang up.

Alex makes a beeline to where Yelena just sat down and I'm hot on his trail, pushing through the crowd to get there first.

People are taking their seats and I know there's a spare chair next to hers, I did that on purpose. I just manage to bump Alex out of the way and sit, denying him a seat.

Yelena looks at me, unaware of what just happened. "What are you doing?"

"Sitting with you."

I turn, and smile a big, nasty grin at Alex who looks at me with hate and anger. I wish with all my fucking being that he'd try me. Any excuse to drag him out back and put him down.

"Get up." The words are snarled.

I can't help it. I stand up.

Not because he commanded me to.

Not because it's the best thing to do.

But because he pisses me off. I'm seething. The self-control I felt earlier is gone.

"You wanted something?" I sneer.

"Leave Yelena alone," he barks. "And don't you dare threaten me."

I step closer. "I don't threaten. I promise. And I promise you'll regret treating her the way you did." I let my gaze travel over him, thinking about how easy it would be to break every bone in his body.

"I treated her as she deserved to be treated."

I lose it. Flashing forward, I grab his collar in my fist. Someone nearby gasps. But I'm deaf to it all.

"Let me show you how we treat pigs."

My fist cocks back.

11

"Stop!"

I jump from my chair and grab onto Valentin's raised arm, holding on for dear life. To my surprise, he doesn't punch Alex.

Instead, he looks at me, face twisted in terrifying anger. My heart drops. The man from last night and this morning is gone. Only a monster remains.

"Yelena," he mutters, as if trying to find me through his furious haze.

"Valentin. Please."

His gaze softens in seconds. I know he's seething inside, I can feel it vibrating through him as I spread my hand on his chest. Valentin frowns. His fist lowers.

"He was trying to ruin your meeting."

"He's just trying to rile me up."

The fingers that were tensed and ready to kill soften as they reach for my face. He smooths his thumb over my lips and Alex mutters something, loudly.

"I don't want you riled, angel. Unless I do it, in the right way."

The smoke of his voice takes on a sex-filled twist and I almost swoon.

I shouldn't. I should run. He's taking over everything and yet, right now, I'm glad he's here, a buffer, as long as he remains that and nothing else. And doesn't injure my ex.

"I need you to behave. This isn't your world. You can't do whatever you want here." I'm telling him this isn't the Bratva.

And he knows. I see that.

But he likes to play, so I let him. Anything to take control of this situation. Panic claws at me, but I force myself to act calm.

Today is too important to lose.

"You need to leave," I quietly beg him. "You're causing a scene."

"He touched me first."

Valentin says this like it's reason enough to fight. And yes, Alex started it, but Valentin's way smarter than letting Alex and his little mind games manipulate him.

"Are you five?"

The words slip free and I steel myself for his wrath but an expression I can't immediately read comes over his face and then he grins slowly. "Angel."

It's half mollified, half rebuke, and all gentle humor.

"Can we get security in here to get rid of this ass?" Alex is looking around, voice loud. Then he throws me a look and slides it to Valentin. "I can destroy you."

"I wish he'd try," mutters Valentin so only I hear.

"Alex." I turn to my ex, gathering whatever strength I have, pushing the rush of nausea way down, meeting his gaze past Valentin as he shifts so he's blocking the very short path. "Valentin's with me and you started it."

He's about to say something when Valentin pulls out my chair for me, giving me no option but to sit. All eyes are on us.

"I apologize," the big man says, "but there are times when a woman's honor must be protected."

But he's not looking at Alex, he's looking at the men at the table and for the first time I take them in, too. Somehow, I've actually managed to land on a table with all the investors I want to see, and I can't help but cast Valentin a look.

"Can you move?" Alex isn't giving up, and the investors are talking among themselves and looking at me.

Valentin pats the seat next to him. "This is mine. You can sit there."

He pushes the chair out for Alex, who has no option but to sit there, which of course he does.

"I think we all know each other here," Alex says with a hearty laugh, one of those good old boys of money laughs that used to drive me insane. "All except you."

He doesn't even look at Valentin.

"I heard Yelena wanted to try her hand at this fashion business on her own and I knew she needed my guiding hand, so here I—"

"He's right," Valentin says, speaking over the top of him. "You don't know me, but you probably have visited one of my clubs, eaten in my restaurants, stayed at one of my boutique hotels. Valentin Constanov."

He hands out business cards.

Alex snorts.

"Here," Valentin says, "one for you, too."

"I don't need your crass new money."

"A pity. You know what happened to the dinosaurs? I like to look at old money like dinosaurs. All it takes is one event to wipe them out because they didn't adapt and stuck their heads in the sand." He looks at me. "I'd class the dodo as a dinosaur. They were birds after all."

I almost laugh, and it makes me realize how unafraid of Alex I am right now. That's a first. Sure, he stalked me to the luncheon, but he's not going to do shit. He can't. I'm with Valentin.

Speaking of the devil. His big, warm hand slips onto my thigh and rests there. Then he starts talking to a man I recognize as Peterson Grange, one of the richest, most influential guests at this whole event.

Of course, Alex immediately tries to butt in.

"As I was saying, Yelena is very—"

"Talented." Valentin offers a charming smile. "I'm just here to keep her company, she's beyond capable. Right Allan?"

"Alex."

"He agrees."

Valentin isn't falling for any of Alex's shit. If my asshole of an ex planned to come here and ruin my reputation with sly comments, then my current escort's presence might just make sure his plans fall short.

And what a presence Valentin seems to carry at this table. It's obvious already. The Constanov name must be known to some extent, or maybe it's just his businesses.

What was on those cards he handed out?

From what Natalya's told me before, the Bratva are involved in a lot of projects, apart from the illegal ones, and much power comes from that.

Valentin is rich.

No man who wears suits like his could be anything else.

But it's not just Bratva money. It's his.

With Valentin here, touching me, I don't feel intimidated by Alex anymore. And even as Valentin turned up and got ready to defend my honor, I managed to join in. Like the old Yelena would have.

Maybe I've finally turned some kind of corner again. Maybe I'm not as innocent and vulnerable as I thought I was.

After all, if I can survive the exquisite torture and deep appetites of Valentin, and even manage to please him back, too, then surely I can take on a rich pussy like Alex, right?

"But," Valentin says with a charming smile to Grange, "I'll let the star of the table field the questions."

And I do. Coffee is served by a passing waiter, but I hardly take a sip. Neither do they. Instead, we chat about my plans for Dark One Eight, and every time one of them slides a question to Valentin he slides it back, and I'm grateful.

There's one investor not here, Russian, and I'm thinking it's probably good. I knew she'd be out of town, but with Valentin …

It's bad enough he handed out cards, I don't need someone marking him for what he is.

The moment the thought comes to my head, Alex tucks his phone away, picks up his negroni and leans back in his chair. My stomach plummets.

"Sorry to interrupt, Grange, but I just found out something disturbing about our friend here." He turns his nasty grin to Valentin. "I'd be careful about who I invest with, considering Yelena's aligning herself with the mob. This man's connected."

Two of the investors murmur to each other and I don't know what to do. Fear grips me. Shit. Shit. Shit. This is one of the reasons I didn't want Valentin here. Why I didn't want help from the Bratva.

My mouth goes dry and my stomach churns. But Valentin just squeezes my thigh.

"I don't know about anyone else, but I don't want my money tainted." Alex finishes his drink and sets down the glass.

Valentin moves it. "Perhaps it's a little early for drinking?"

"You—"

"As you know, we Russians always drink vodka with every meal, eat cabbage and potatoes sprinkled with kasha and only read Dostoevsky and Tolstoy. And collect those little dolls."

The others stare at him and then start to laugh.

"Also we believe in Communism only, or is that the oligarchs, and we're all connected to the mob."

He pauses.

"Just like Italians only wear Armani and swear allegiance to the Mafia, and eat pasta all day long."

Valentin smiles.

"Would it be fair for me to accuse you of trying to bring concrete boots onto the catwalks for the savvy and well-dressed mobster?"

This time I laugh, I can't help it. Valentin's funny and charming and laser-like with his skewering.

"It's not the same," Alex says, a note of petulance creeping into his voice. "I've got no ties with the mafia."

"But you have Italian ancestry? And Italian money?" Valentin asks politely.

"I'm not mafia."

"Stereotypes are so boring, wouldn't you agree?" Valentin spreads his free hand in the air before landing it on Alex's shoulder. "We should embrace the diverse and new, just like you do in fashion."

"I like him," Grange says, "and he speaks the truth. Now where were we?"

Alex has turned a purple color, like he wants to explode with all the knowledge and dirt he has on Valentin.

After all, he must know, or at least suspect, that the man he hired to follow me is dead. And he must have his suspicions about Valentin being the one who did it. But he can't say shit. Because then he'd have to tell everyone he was crazy enough to hire that investigator in the first place.

I suck in a breath.

It's all going to be alright. It has to be.

Valentin takes his hand from me and gets his phone out. "Anyway, I'm not an investor in Yelena's business. Yet. But I've *felt* her designs, and she's shown me ideas for her menswear, how she could *accommodate* and *stretch* for a man as *big* as me."

My cheeks are on fire with his innuendo. Alex looks like he wants to knife someone and the others nod in ignorant bliss.

And Valentin?

He's not done.

"I offered to invest because I'm a businessman, one with varied interests. I like making money and I'm good at it. In honesty, my clubs are a passion, the restaurants a pet project, but they make me money. The big bucks come to me in construction." He pulls up some photos and passes his phone to me to show the others.

My finger shakes a little as I slide through the pictures and the worry I might find something horrible or damning isn't lost on Valentin. He trails his hand on my leg under the tablet.

And he continues. "I can smell a good investment, and Yelena is it. I want to *thrust* money at her, so I can *reap* all the rewards. Alas, she doesn't want investments from people she knows. She wants to do this the old-fashioned way. That's how confident she is."

The investor's eyes are on the phone's screen and it's clear they recognize a lot of the places, some of the restaurants are in there, and while the clubs aren't, he names them and other things he's sunk money into.

Valentin may have used dirty money to start his legitimate businesses, the empires that he's built under his name, things that stretch beyond his impressive portfolio of construction projects, but it's clear he's made his money make even more money with his business savvy.

And beneath all the layers of filth buried in his words for me, he's letting these people know what a great, low risk investment I'd be.

All while saying I won't take a dime from friends and family.

Their eyes glint with what looks like respect and Grange asks for my business plan and a glimpse at what I have so far.

The folio is tucked next to me so I pull it out and hand Valentin his phone back. With a brewing excitement, I place a slim leather binder onto the table, revealing my business plan, projections, and initial funding need.

While the table gawk over that, my phone buzzes. I pull it out.

It's a message from Valentin. His fingers are still drawing lazy patterns on my leg.

I want to eat your cunt right now.

My eyes grow big and I slam the phone onto my lap. His grip tightens around my thigh. A hot streak flashes through my body.

I bite down on my lower lip and turn my phone back around. From there I text him. *Stop that.*

Make me.

I gasp, my hold on the conversation slipping even though Valentin seems engaged, like he's not taunting me, not touching me.

He was being so good... but I should have expected him to taint his gift. He is the devil, after all.

"Pretty impressive, huh?" he says to the table, shifting in his chair.

They all nod, still distracted, as Valentin glances back down at his phone. When he sees that I haven't responded yet, he slides his hand further up my thigh.

My back straightens. I barely stifle a little yip.

"What is this number here for?" Grange asks, pointing at one of the documents.

Puffing out my chest, I try to explain everything to him, all while Valentin's thick fingers travel up my skirt to wrap around my panties.

My phone buzzes and I pull away from Grange to look down at the new message.

You said I couldn't claim you. Consider this your punishment.

Part those thighs or I'll stop with the innuendo and get straight to the good parts.

My breath catches, stutters as heat pools between my thighs.

He curls my underwear around his finger, then slips down between my thighs.

Just like that, I'm wet. I feel like what's going on is more than obvious. But the others don't seem to notice. Even Valentin doesn't seem bothered.

Except he shifts slightly in his chair like he's trying to get comfortable. I remember the taste of him, the size, the way he thrust into my mouth.

He's hard. I'm wet.

Fuck.

I place my phone on my lap and try to concentrate on the table. But when another text comes in, I nearly shake out of my chair. The vibrations run right through me. They might as well be playing with my clit.

Fuck.

I cough. Grange looks up and I give him an awkward smile, quietly begging him to look away. When he finally does, I sink into my chair, desperate to not give into Valentin's teasing, but also desperately wanting more of it.

As if in response, he eases my panties to the side. I'm practically panting. And then he stops.

I immediately drop my hand to my phone and swipe it open. Then I blindly text: *why the fuck did you stop?*

He doesn't respond for one beat. Two. Three.

The conversation happening around the table is mute to me. my ears buzz with need. The suspense tugs at every nerve in my body

My phone buzzes. *I want to make sure you really want it, angel.*

This is the punishment. Right now. Him revving me up and then stopping. How can he be so cruel?

I want the other punishment, the one where he keeps touching me.

I want him to claim me. Make me come in front of my shitty ex-boyfriend.

I want the real man to do it.

I want Valentin.

Punish me, I text him. *Keep going. Please.*

He shifts again in his chair and moves a little closer, his fingers pushing into me. Two of them, stretching me as he slips his thumb over my clit.

My anxiety bubbles... then, just like that, I stop caring.

Because Valentin starts to pump his fingers into me, curling his fingers for extra effect. It's a slow, agonizing thrust. One that forces me to feel every single inch of him.

My phone buzzes again and I look down, barely keeping myself together.

Keep your phone right there. Right over your clit. Hold it there. And don't answer when I call. Keep your eyes up. Look at your fucking ex while I make you cum.

He's insane.

But so am I.

Swallowing a gasp, I grip my phone, holding it in place just as it starts to ring. The vibrations pound through me. Over and over again.

Next to me, Valentin continues his conversation. The buzz of my phone and the little moans squeak from my lips are lost to the loud chatter of the room.

I want to roll my eyes back in my head. I want to cry out. Fall to the floor. I'm getting so close to losing it.

No.

Control yourself.

Biting down on my tongue, I try my best to look normal. A

tight smile holds my face as I scan the table, hoping to god that no notices what's happening.

Shit.

To my chagrin, Alex is staring directly at me, frowning as he talks to a man on the other side of the table.

The heat inside of my body climbs higher, but I keep my gaze fixed on that bastard. I do as Valentin ordered, no matter how hard it is to keep my shit together.

I need to scream. I need to cry out. I need something to hide the twists and turns of my mouth. But the only thing I can find is cutlery. Grabbing a spoon, I dip it in the nearest cup of coffee, then shove it between my lips, sucking hard as Valentin sends me spinning into a mind-blowing orgasm.

I start to shake and force a cough, to cover it.

"You alright, Yelena?" asks Valentin, withdrawing his fingers from me. Then he calmly takes the spoon from my mouth, places it in the cup of coffee, and stirs.

I wipe my lips as he takes a big gulp.

"You're fucking crazy," I mumble under my breath.

Out of the corner of my eye, I can see Alex throwing us a dark look. But he doesn't say anything. He's been put in his place.

And so have I.

I'm weak all over and when my phone buzzes again I jump, trying to ignore the soft laughter from the big, handsome Russian next to me. I snatch the phone away from my overly sensitive clit just in case he starts up again.

It buzzes again and I take a shaking breath and look down.

Valentin.

Good girl, he texts. *Such a good, filthy girl. My perfect angel. You're almost mine now. There's just one last part of you I have to claim.*

It buzzes again.

And I will. Soon.

12

VALENTIN

I lick my fingers, relishing the taste of Yelena's juices mixed with her coffee.

How delicious.

Cracking my neck, I settle back into the discussion around the table. But without Yelena to distract me, the meeting quickly drones on.

No one seems to suspect what we just did. Maybe Alex, but he's not willing to risk being made a fool of again. So even he stays quiet.

Smart man.

With him in his place, part of me wants to go up and keep my distance. Maybe even help Ilya find our rat from my phone while I keep an eye on Yelena.

But I can't move.

Because I'm rock hard.

Shit. I guess she got me as good as I gave it to her.

"Where were we?" I mumble, looking over at her.

To my surprise, Yelena is already getting up from her chair. She thanks the men, shaking their hands and telling them she's looking forward to setting up some further meetings.

"If you don't mind, though, Valentin and I have to run. We've got an appointment."

As quickly as possible, I lift the tablecloth so that it covers my waist and make a much needed adjustment, tucking my raging erection beneath my belt.

I just barely make it in time.

Yelena hurries ahead and I bid a curt farewell to the table before rushing off after her.

She doesn't stop moving until we're outside. She steps into a side path, one that's covered in potted trees and plants. The second I join her, she pushes up against me and lifts onto her toes.

"You fucking maniac."

The venom in her voice is softened by the kiss she plants on my lips.

But that softness doesn't last for long.

"You fucking vixen," I respond, prying her mouth open with my tongue. I close my arms around her as she kisses me, pressing those soft tits into me, and she breaks the kiss a moment.

"I want you."

I sneer with pleasure, my swollen cock pressing against my belt, threatening to snap it in two.

I know exactly what she means.

"Not here."

I take her hand. Then, as if on cue, my phone buzzes.

A message from Ilya.

Got the intel. Alex is part owner of the resort hotel, Sweetwater. But—and you'll love this—the other owners are in our pocket.

Despite the interruption, I smile slowly. This means Alex might have money, but he's essentially toothless.

Taking Yelena's wrist, I whistle through my teeth. A moment later, my car pulls up out front. We get in.

By the time we arrive at the penthouse, Yelena is jumping

with nervous energy. Touching her cheek, I smile, then lead her inside, taking her into the living room. Not the first one, with its half-finished state, but the second one, which serves as both my study and a place to relax.

It's still floor-to-ceiling windows, overlooking everything, but the view seems nicer from here because the room's finished.

"I didn't know this room was here," she says, stepping away from me and looking around.

"What do you think?"

Her pulse throbs in her throat as she looks at me. "I like the view."

"As do I."

A blush streaks over her face.

I pull my tie off and approach.

"I want you, angel."

I shrug off my jacket, then my holster. My vest follows.

"This is what those pretty eyes have been begging for ever since we met. And what you demanded at the resort."

She sucks in a breath, her head raising as her hands come up to my chest. "I didn't think I was ready."

Her gaze sweeps low.

"Are you ready for me now?"

"I hope so."

Lifting my hands, I start to unbutton her shirt. At first, I keep my kisses soft, warming her up. But when her shirt comes off, I can't help but take a harder taste of her throat.

Her bra falls to the floor next. It takes everything in me not to pounce.

Be patient, I tell myself. *Otherwise she could shatter on you.*

"You're ready," I assure her, kissing her clavicle.

Yelena's skin is on fire. Her limbs are trembling. Still, those elegant fingers smooth down my body, wandering below my belt to wrap around the bulge throbbing just beneath my tightening pants.

I take her hand and step back, admiring her perfect figure... and the wet mark on her little panties.

"You are definitely ready."

I can't help but smile.

Yelena puts her hands behind her back and looks down at the floor. Behind her, the world stretches out in a gorgeous vista.

It doesn't even remotely compare to her beauty.

"Eyes up," I order.

She does as I say. My cock twitches.

Surprisingly, something in my chest does too.

"Now, let's get started."

Stripping off my shirt, I wind it around her tender neck, drawing her in to me.

She doesn't need any more instruction. I feel her lips against my chest.

"Good girl."

Pushing into her, I lead her up against the window.

"Do you know how hungry I am for you, angel? Do you know how badly you've starved me?"

"You're insatiable," she whispers. "I could never satisfy you."

"Wrong. And I'll prove it."

Slipping my hand into her panties, I pull, ripping them from her waist.

The tattered cloth flutters to the floor.

I bite down on my lip. Hard. She's fully exposed to me now.

There is nothing between us. Nothing stopping me.

"Should we go to the bedroom?" Yelena asks, her long eyelashes fluttering.

"No," I snarl. "I'm tired of waiting. We're doing this here. Now."

The shirt I have looped around her neck slides down her back as I ease my grip. By the time it reaches her ankles, my hand has taken its place, fingers wrapping around her delicate throat.

"Take off my pants."

She swallows but obeys. I hold her tight, forcing her gaze to remain on me as she blindly fumbles with my belt and zipper.

Still, it doesn't take her long to do the job. Soon, my pants join her clothes on the floor.

"This has been a long time coming. Too long."

With a small growl, I grab her around the waist and pick her up.

"Valentin!" she gasps, instinctively folding her legs around me.

My name on her lips is music to my ears.

"I'll ask you one more time, angel. Are you ready for this? For me?"

I reach below my waist and guide my cock to her pussy. The wetness of her warm lips makes me tremble. She better say yes, because, at this point, I'm not sure I could stop myself.

I stare deep into Yelena's sparkling blue eyes. They sparkle with life.

I know her answer even before it leaves her lips.

"Yes. I'm ready," she whispers, innocence melting off of every quiet word.

With one stiff stroke, I push into her.

We both gasp. Loud.

"Fuck, you're tight," I grumble, almost surprise. She's even tighter than I thought she'd be. Or maybe I'm just that hard...

"You're so big," she yelps, her finger nails digging into the hard skin on my back.

"No. I'm perfect. You're perfect. We're perfect."

I can feel her hold her breath as I stay planted deep inside of her. She's clenches around me.

That won't do.

"Relax, angel," I tell her. "I promise it will feel better."

She digs her face into my shoulder. "It hurts..."

I splay my hand out over the small of her back. "Deep breaths, baby girl. Nice and slow. Let the pleasure come in waves. The pain will evaporate. You have my word."

Her chest rises and falls against mine. Little whimpers line every short breath. Then, she starts to listen. I feel her loosen down below, just a bit.

"Better?"

"Better," she nods.

"Thatta girl."

With that, I pull out, just an inch.

Then I push all the way back in.

"Oh my god."

Her nails dig into my hard skin, but the tension is gone.

I let her hold onto me for dear life as I let my tenderness crack and fall away. My strokes turn into thrusts. My thrusts into wild, frantic movements.

"We were fucking made for this," I growl. "You for me, and me for you. Do you understand that, little angel? Do you fucking understand?"

I plant a hand on the window behind me to steady myself, but I don't ease back.

"Yes," Yelena whines. "Yes!"

An unfamiliar feeling washes over me as her hot breath crashes into my tattoos. It takes a moment for my sex-clouded brain to make sense of it. Even then, I'm not sure it can be true.

I was born in hell. Raised in the flames. Damnation is all I've ever known.

But this...

Fuck. This must be what heaven feels like.

Salvation, in the form of innocent blue eyes and a pussy that has never felt another cock.

Yelena's hips start to sway around my waist, and the sensation grows. Suddenly, she's not just taking me, she's pushing back, trying to fuck me too.

Shit. This is no angel. And if she ever was, this has burned the last bits of her wings.

We may not be in hell anymore, but maybe this isn't heaven after all. Maybe it's something of our own.

How perfect.

"You are a fucking gift," I growl. "A naughty, perfect, mysterious little gift."

Yelena sobs into my shoulder, little laughs stuttering out in between each deep, burning breath.

Then...

"I'm going to cum," she gasps.

There's no hesitation in me.

"Then fucking do it."

This doesn't have to last forever. Not like I thought before.

She's not going anywhere. There will be time enough for this to happen again, and again, and again...

"Oh my god!" Yelena cries out.

"I am your god."

I pound into her harder. Faster.

Little ripples flutter against my cock as she starts to convulse around me. It's almost too much. I'm about to join her when I have a sudden change of heart.

No. This feels too good. I need to keep going. Just for a little bit longer.

It's a primal need. An animalistic desire.

Holding her against my body, I rip us away from the window. She trembles in my arms as I walk her to the leather sofa and sit down so that she's riding me. Her pretty little body sinks into my cock and I nearly bust again.

"Easy, little one," I grunt, wrapping my hands around her tiny waist. "If you make me cum too soon, there will be consequences."

"Like with the phone?" she squirms.

"Exactly."

A deep breath fills her chest. Then, the most devilish and subtle smirk lifts the corner sof her perfect lips

"Punish me then."

Her hips start to sway back and forth again. I grab her throat.

"Oh, you fucking minx."

I pull her face into mine and our lips crash together. She kisses me back, somehow maintaining the momentum in her hips.

My cock bends back and forth, side to side. I lean back and groan up to the ceiling.

"Bring me to heaven, angel," I urge her on.

Then, all of a sudden, her swaying stops. Her hands plant down on my shoulders and she starts to move up and down, riding me.

I let her take control, just for a moment, until she's panting and falling apart at the edges. Then, when her body starts to tighten around me, I dip by hand under her left thigh and spin her around.

Her ass pushes into my stomach. I rest my chin on her shoulder and palm her tits, looking at our steamy reflection in the window.

Our ghostly figures heave over the impressive view. I bite down on her earlobe and say, "See that, Angel? I own all that. Everything you see, I own."

She immediately understands.

"Even me?"

I stare at her reflection, dropping my hand to her swollen clit.

"Especially you."

Her entire body starts to shake under my grip as I lead her

to a final orgasm. Our reflection starts to blur into a single figure. My cock swells.

"I'm so fucking close."

I bring both hands to her hips and start to fucking jack-hammer her from behind.

"Oh my god!"

Her voice warbles as I spank her ass with my hips.

Then, it's all too much.

I pull her off just in time to burst all over her back.

13

YELENA

My skin is hot. Burning.

From my toes to my forehead. It's all on fire.

But nothing's as red-hot as my cheeks.

What have I done?

I can feel Valentin's sticky desire clinging to my back. It fills me with shame... and satisfaction.

There's a part of me that just wants to turn around, wrap around him and bury my head in the crook of his neck.

Another part of me wants to scramble out of his grip and run, naked, as far away as I can.

"Angel," he murmurs, mouth close to my ear. "You are a fucking gift."

Goosebumps cover my slick skin.

"No. I'm just a girl."

Flexing his hands, Valentin spins me around.

"My girl."

I swallow.

He thinks he owns me now.

And I'm not sure he's wrong.

How did that feel so fucking good?

"I should shower," I whisper, unsure of what else to say.

"I'll join you."

But neither of us move. Our bodies are exhausted. We still pant, our shimmering chests skin heaving up and down.

"Valentin."

I run my fingers lightly down the damp slick of sweat that covers his chest, tracing an intricate tattoo.

He spreads his hands out around the small of my back, spreading his seed. "Yelena."

His deep blue eyes flash with pride. It's hard to look away. But I do. Down to his chest. For a split second, the regret and shame vanish.

My first time could have been worse. Far worse.

This man is beautiful. Mouthwatering. A powerhouse of perfection.

If I don't move soon, I'll get lost in him forever.

"I need to wash myself off."

Valentin's gentle hands turn firm.

"Soak a little longer."

"Excuse me?"

"Let it seep through your skin..."

I'm not a meek person. I'm not weak. Yet he seems to have this hold over me that makes give in to his every command.

My throat starts to close up. I try and swallow.

"I-I'll go have that shower."

I climb off him shakily and Valentin offers no help. The moment my feet hit the hardwood floor I almost topple. Shit. I'm still wearing the heels. But I don't fall. Valentin is there, taking my arm to steady me.

"You're alright, angel."

"I'm not sure I am."

"No, I'll make sure you are."

The certainty in his voice runs ripples through me.

Stepping in front of me, he lowers into a crouch and

inspects my glistening privates. I can feel my own juices covering the inside of my thighs. I want to cross my legs and hide from him... as if he isn't already intimately familiar with my anatomy.

"What are you doing?"

Valentin extends his ring finger and brushes it across my inner thigh, taking a sample of my juices. Then he holds it up to the light.

"See, you're not even bleeding."

Suddenly, a fear takes hold of my chest. What if he thinks I lied about being a virgin? The thought is all-consuming. Then, just like that, it disappears.

He's not Alex. He doesn't actually care. Hell, he was obsessing over me long before he knew.

So why does my heart still beat harder?

"Disappointed?" I ask, using snark to avoid my own uncomfortable thoughts.

Valentin sucks his finger dry.

"How could I be disappointed after that?"

Valentin rises, more imposing than ever. But the boyish grin on his stupidly handsome face makes his blue eyes sparkle.

My stomach flutters.

"Can I shower now?"

"There's no point?'

My brows furrow.

"Why not?"

"Because I'm not done with you yet."

I gulp.

"We're not?"

"No." He removes his hand and walks me back to the window and his mouth skims my cheek to my ear. "We're not. Are we?"

My pack arches, My burning skin pebbles.

I'm still wet. Ready. Sore. But ready.

"Valentin—"

"Turn around, angel."

He gets his wish.

I tell myself it's because he's not going to give me a choice, but that's a lie. If I said no, he wouldn't force me. Somehow, I know that for certain. And it makes me want him even more.

I put my hands on the window as he kisses my neck, shoulders, and back. The head of his cock pushes into me. Then, he's in.

I can't help it. "Yes."

He thrusts into my tiny hole and nibbles on my earlobe.

"A perfect fit.

I close my eyes as he rests his hand on my hip and thrusts up, pounding me into the window until I'm flattened against the cool glass.

The heat of my body and the crispness of the glass add a new element to the pleasure rising inside of me. Valentin pushes deeper inside. Harder.

Mouth against my ear, he murmurs, "You made me work for this, angel. But it's worth it. You were so fucking worth the wait."

All I can say in response is the truth. "I'm going to cum."

"Then do it, right on my cock."

He picks up speed. I go weak. The cool glass covers my cheek, but everything else is on fire. Then I erupt.

The world outside the window spins. I collapse. Valentin catches me. I feel him pull out just in time to add to the masterpiece already staining my back.

I swear I must black out, because when I come too, we've taken a few steps back from the mirror, and Valentin is gently slapping me awake.

"You're alright, angel," he assures me.

I blink away the lightness in my head. I'm filled with a satisfaction so deep that I don't know what to do with myself.

"I... I'm alright."

"That's my girl."

Valentin lets go of my left hand and wraps his arm around my waist, holding me against him as his deep breaths brush the skin of my nape.

His thick, heavy forearm rests on my shoulder as he points to the glass.

"Look. We made a sex angel."

An involuntary laugh sputters from my lips. He's right.

There, on the floor-to-ceiling window, are the marks of what we just did. The breath clouds, the smudges of our bodies, the juices, the sweat.

My heart stutters in my chest.

That's the loss of my virginity, right there.

"And ode to you and me and this new beginning," Valentin says, holding me tight.

I'm shaking, glad he's got hold of me because I think I might collapse otherwise.

Leaning into him I stare at the glass, our blurry silhouettes tossed over the gorgeous skyline like a ghost of what was and what could be.

We could be that, a power couple, overlooking everything.

Or I've just temporarily lost my mind.

"It's stunning, isn't it?" I hear the grin in his voice. "I'm going to have someone cut it out and frame it. Artwork for the new place."

Even in ghost form he's ridiculously handsome. A man is made to be a king.

I shiver at that as I stare at our reflections.

Then something else catches my eye as he shifts us, taking a step back.

Light glinting.

But not from outside, it's from somewhere in here.

My heart hammers hard against my ribs as I recognize the reflection of something far less glorious than Valentin.

That terrifying crest on top of that vault. The door to the room is open. And I can see the screaming skull, split open by the snarling viper.

It's an instant reminder of who Valentin really is.

My stomach sinks like a stone.

My father was seduced by the seemingly easy glitter and siren song of the Bratva.

Now here I am.

Making the same mistakes.

Except mine are worse. I'm not seduced by easy money or even that offer Valentin is making me, because I can't pretend not to see it.

I'm seduced by a gorgeous face and a hard body, by hot sex and the fallacy of safety.

What I should be doing is playing everything smart, using Valentin to keep Alex away.

And yet I gave Valentin the one thing no one else can ever have. Something I easily kept from others for years.

But for this man, I stripped and begged him to take me, to have my virginity.

He turns me in his arms. "Are you alright?"

The blush in my cheeks must be turning pale. I look away from him and the crest.

"I need to shower."

"I'll join—"

"Alone."

14

YELENA

He's there when I step out of the shower.

"Miss me?"

I purse my lips, but let him wrap me in a big fluffy towel. He's warm and slightly damp, and I'm assuming he also took a shower in a different bathroom.

"Don't know if I had time to miss you."

"Well, I had plenty of time to miss you."

He sighs into my hair and leads me to the bedroom. I sit on the edge of the mattress, staring into space. He sits beside me, then lays me down.

I let him. Hell, knowing what I do now, how could I resist?

"Are you sure you're alright?" he asks, pulling at my towel.

"I'm very satisfied," I assure him.

"I already know that," he grins. "But that's not what I'm asking."

I stiffen slightly.

"How could you know that?"

He frowns, and for a moment a lick of fear hits me, but then I see the humor, the spark in his gaze. "I'm Russian. We are the best lovers."

"I think you'll find that's the French and Italians."

"And you're so worldly." His fingers down my body, lifting the towel up my knees. A warm shiver moves through me. "They stole their unfounded reputation. It's the Russians. I'll prove it. Again."

My hand snaps down to snatch his thick wrist just before he can lift the towel up any higher.

"I'm too sore."

"I understand. That's why I'm only going to give you a much-needed massage."

My weak little fingers are no match for his power. Valentin moves his hand under the towel, to my pussy. The back of his fingers brush over my lips and I sigh, desperate for him.

"Your grip is too weak," he notes. "Practice tightening it over something smaller than my forearm."

His free hand takes my wrist and leads it below his own waist. I know exactly where this is going.

"It's hardly smaller," I gulp.

"Hardly smaller is still smaller. Now, practice leading me where you want me to go."

I do what I'm told, stretching my fingers until they're wrapped around his cock. Even semi-soft, he's huge. And as I move up and down, he gets even bigger.

I bite my lower lip. My back arches.

"Thatta girl."

Valentin bares his teeth, as he slips his fingers through my folds.

"Oh."

I wince. And Valentin stops, bringing his fingers back together to thrust gently into me, his thumb playing over my clit as I work his cock.

"You are a bad little angel," he says, completely ignoring how he asked—ordered—me to take his cock, "one who should be punished."

"You've punished me enough," I rasp.

He starts to thrust into my hand. "I haven't even begun."

With his free hand, he rips the damp towel from my body and latches onto my hard nipples, one at a time.

I squeeze his cock. Hard. He only gets harder.

"This is your idea of punishment?" I rasp, already getting lost in another haze of lust.

Valentin laughs. Then suddenly stops, withdrawing his fingers and pulling my hand from his swollen cock. A cold emptiness replaces the suffocating warmth. "Is this kind of punishment more up your alley?"

I can see his jaw clench with barely restrained desire. Stopping like this is hurting him just as much as it is me.

"At least it feels like punishment," I whisper.

"For us both."

It's a strange flirt. One I can't get enough of. Like a proxy for the sweetest words that aren't being said and the snuggles part of me craves. The other part? It still wants to run.

Dipping his head, Valentin kisses me. "Good. We're on the same page, then. Punishment was fucking you hard. But I don't think you saw it that way. Did you?"

There's an odd twist of vulnerability to his words and it plucks at my heart. "No. I liked it."

The admission comes easier than expected.

"As did I."

I bury my face against him because words are suddenly hard. The raw note in his voice is almost too much. It calls on something inside of me. Something I'm not sure I want uncovered.

I'm not sure what to do or how to act. I want more of him. I need it. When he's kissing me, fucking me, I don't need to think beyond the drive and the pleasure. But here, now, when we're both wanting something else and neither of us knows how to express it or even what it is, then that's unnerving.

Some wall between us has been cracked. I'm not sure it can be put back together, even if I wanted it to be fixed.

Suddenly, the buzz of a phone makes me realize how silent everything has gotten.

"Hell," Valentin grunts, lifting the screen to his face. "It never stops. No matter how—

He stops. A frown fills his rugged face.

That's when I take a better look at the phone in his hands. The glittering case definitely isn't his.

It's mine.

"Who is this?" Valentin turns to face me. "Johnny K... You know you aren't allowed to talk to other men when we're alone."

My heart skips a beat. "Give me my phone."

I snatch it from him. Valentin's frown instantly turns into a playful, yet devilish smirk. He's fucking with me. But only a little.

There's no telling just how serious he is about locking me up for himself.

"It's another investor, Valentin."

"A man."

The tease in his voice becomes lighter. I try to ignore it with a straight face as I read the message.

Yelena, love to set up a meeting tonight to discuss your venture. I heard great things about the luncheon today. I'm free at 9pm, main room. Let me know.

I quickly text back, *I'd love to.*

"See? You're already setting up dates." He plucks my phone free and tosses it to the other end of the bed before rolling me under him to start kissing my throat.

"Valentin!"

Under all the teasing laughter is that possessive core I've seen burn in him.

And it's frightening, not just because of the need to own me, but because I like it. Well, a part of me likes it.

I like the warmth of safety he throws over me, when I'm with him it's like I could touch the sky, like I can do anything because Valentin is there, protecting me, watching my back, watching over me.

It's something I haven't felt since my father died.

But there's a reason I feel safe around Valentin. And it's the same reason I vowed never to get close to him.

He's Bratva.

Just as that thought settles deep in my bones, another ringtone cuts through the silent room.

This time, there's no mistaking it. That's Valentin's phone.

He sighs and rolls away to get it. A second later, the phone is tossed away and he's back on me. "Looks like neither of us have much time. But don't worry, I can work fast."

Without wasting a beat, Valentin parts my legs and shoves his face between my thighs.

"If we're going to pull this off, angel, then you're going to have to really believe it."

"What's that?" I ask, already distracted.

"That I'm your boyfriend. That we're a couple."

I cast him a look, but even he's not handsome enough to distract me from what's behind him. The glass doors that lead into the lobby of the Sweetwater resort.

The place is packed, but my focus is on the people inside. It's on our reflection.

Valentin is right—at least, partly. We need to make sure we look the part. But even more importantly, *I* need to make sure I look the part.

And for all of the distractions back at Valentin's penthouse, I truly tried my best.

But will it be good enough?

I'm in one of the black dresses I designed. It's sleek, with that modern street edge which makes it workable at a high-end classy event, a club, or pairing it with combat boots and a jacket for a low-rent day and evening out.

It's one of my visions, to have a line that can handle every type of situation. Of course, I want to have just evening wear and casual wear, but that's down the line. The name and the mood and vibe is what I want now.

"That's right," I mumble, as our car pulls away. "I believe it.

Valentin takes my hand and pulls me in for a kiss. "Good. If your stupid ex is watching, he's got to know. Maybe then, I won't have to bash his brains in tonight."

I snap back to reality. Valentin and I are on different wavelengths... but also on the same page, strangely enough.

"That I'm your fake girlfriend." I nod.

"That what we did wasn't fake."

He takes my arm and wraps it around his as we walk inside. It feels oddly real. Like I really am his. And I kind of like how it feels, no matter how dangerous it is to think that way.

The lobby is alive with people but not like when I checked in and I can't help but wonder about that reporter I met, Kira.

But all of that evaporates from my mind as we reach the main room where the big event is being held tonight. Valentin holds me closer.

"Did I tell you how stunning you look?" he whispers, leaning into my ear.

"Only a thousand times already."

He gives me a curious look and slips a finger beneath my chin and raises my head. "Just making sure you know it. Because you look nervous and you shouldn't be."

As if on cue, I feel his phone buzz through his pant pocket.

His eyes practically roll out of his head.

"Always something," I say for him. Then, I place a soft hand on his chiseled jaw and give him a kiss. "I'll be fine. You take care of your work, I'll take care of mine."

He nods, a solemn sense of duty taking over his features.

"Kill it, baby girl."

"I'd say the same to you, if I didn't think you'd take it so literally."

He laughs and kisses my forehead. Then, he's off, already swearing into his phone as I'm left to the wolves.

I stare at the crowd, feeling instantly overwhelmed. All of a sudden, I feel a big hand on my shoulder.

I nearly jump out of my shoes.

But it's only Valentin.

"Easy there, tiger." He's holding the phone to his chest, the classic and beautiful suit giving the brutal edge a layer of silk. It makes my heart squeeze. I already know what he's going to say, but I'm not ready to be left alone yet... not that I'm ready to admit that to him either.

"What is it?"

"I have to step out a second. Do you think you'll be alright?"

He eyes me like he's hoping that I'll say no. That I'll say that I'll come with him so he can keep a close eye on me.

But we both know I'm too stubborn to do something like that.

"I'll be fine. I'm just looking for my appointments."

He touches my cheek. "Take care of business, angel. And don't worry, I won't be far."

The phone's back to his ear and he moves away. But I don't doubt his words at all. His presence lingers.

There's something utterly empowering about it. I know it shouldn't feel that way, but it does. I guess that's the strength of a man like Valentin... and the danger.

He's always there. Always watching.

I take a deep breath.

I'll worry about him later. Right now, I need to focus on one thing: making the right next move.

So why do I feel like something is about to go horribly wrong?

15

VALENTIN

"And I'm telling you, Valentin, you need to get back to the city *now*." Ilya's laid back demeanor is taking a hit right now.

I'm not sure many people would even notice, but I do. I take an interest in the few people I happen to like, pay attention in case they need me to watch their back, even when they don't know it. Like with Yelena, which is why I'm here.

Why I'm not going anywhere.

At least not yet.

And Ilya's not happy about it. I stand in the corner of the bar. It's the same room they decked out with the catwalk, only now it's less party and more of a business-after-five vibe.

"Listen—" he continues, the concern and stress cracking his voice.

Scanning the crowd, I keep an eye on Yelena while the other searches for signs of Civati.

"No, you listen," I interrupt. "I'm basically in Chicago's city center."

We both know that's a lie and he mutters something not very nice about my mother.

I'd be insulted but I didn't know her.

"People keep calling you."

"They always do," I say.

"Yeah, but—"

"I answer the ones that are important." It's a small amendment, but I make it.

He pauses. He knows I always take calls. And he can guess why I'm being choosy.

"Valentin, pussy is pussy. Even sweet, tight pussy..."

"Do not," I mutter, "try to rile me into coming back into the city right now, not unless it's necessary. I like you, but not that much. If you say the wrong thing, I won't hesitate."

"In love, are you?"

"Not your fucking business."

He's been a little on the laconically nasty end, so he must be on his last nerve.

"Then let me remind you what my business is. This empire. Things have gotten worse, Valentin."

"Explain."

I tap my fingers on the bar. I can hold my booze, but right now I'm sipping water on the rocks in a low ball. The bartender didn't even raise a brow. Probably didn't fucking dare.

"We don't have any leads on the rat, which is a big concern. Usually, I can find that shit easily when I've tracked things, but this time, nothing."

"And what do you think I can do to help?" I frown, scanning for Yelena. I've temporarily lost her. She must be sitting down. I'd go in search but there's something in Ilya's voice I haven't heard before. Deeper than the little tells. He's beyond frustrated and feeling the pain from that. This is something else.

Ilya lets out a breath. "Anything."

"Anything?" Shit. He really is sounding desperate. "Why do you need me back?"

"The rat we can't track—" He stops. "That *I* can't track. Well, we just found out that the fucker tried to leak the documents to the FBI. And they're damning ones."

My chest thumps.

"All of our documents are damning."

"Yeah." He breathes out again. "We know some of what the FBI has, but the wrong thing at the wrong time..."

"Or the right." But neither of us needs to finish that.

It could bring our house crumbling down and leave our empire in tatters.

"Luckily," Ilya continues, as I signal the bartender for something stronger. I point to the whiskey, top shelf, because I think I'm going to need it, "the documents landed in the hands of the people on our payroll."

"But next time we might not be so lucky," I understand. "We could buy off all the FBI. What do you think that'll take? A few threats thrown in for good measure."

He snorts. "If we could do that, they'd be starting a bidding war."

"Become rich, form their own brand of crime syndicate."

"Isn't that already called the FBI?"

There's nothing funny about this, but a few exchanged wisecracks help lighten the mood slightly. I blow away the smog covering my head and I try to think.

"So we need to act quickly," I mutter, pulling out a fifty and laying it on the bar as my drink arrives.

I've got no idea if it's still an open bar, but greased wheels always buy standing time in places like this.

"That is what I'm fucking telling you, Valentin. We need you."

"I'm touched." I down half my drink. "But you know what to do, Ilya."

"Shit, we know we need to smoke the rat out, but without you here..."

"My leadership skills are that revered, huh?" I keep my voice light and jovial.

I don't give a fuck who might be listening on normal days, and the chances of anyone here speaking Russian are on the low side. But right now, considering the weight of the situation, I need to keep a hold on my emotions. If there are any enemies listening, I don't want them to read anything into my demeanor or tone.

"No. We need you because you're a fucking maniac who puts other maniacs to shame." Ilya's voice cuts through the speaker. "No one's going to get as violent as they need to without you here."

"We have an empire of grown men, they don't need to see me shedding blood to get into the mood." I take another sip of my drink. I'm more than aware of my reputation.

"Yes, they do. Your men need you to lead the way. You're stupidly brave, reckless and loyal. I've heard rumors you're also smart. The men respect you."

"Fear," I say, as I straighten up, "you left out fear."

"You're a maniac. Anyone in their right mind would fear you, but... they respect you, too." Ilya is pouring it on, though maybe I am a little reckless at times. "They follow you and your lead blindly and without you there, they hesitate. They're scared to make a mistake and incur your wrath."

"The one I threatened to blind did deserve it," I point out.

"I think it's more the things they've seen you do that they don't want inflicted on them."

I finish my drink. "So, you really want me to come back to Chicago, huh?"

"Yes! We need your fucking help."

I crack my neck.

"Find out what you can and as soon as I'm done here, I'll get back. I don't care if every password is changed and all computers are padlocked. Do whatever it takes. Diminish risk."

"You've heard the one about the horse bolting and then locking the gate?"

"Just in case there's another horse." I step away from the bar. "Do what you can."

I hang up the call.

"Fuck."

Ilya's right, I need to go back to Chicago asap.

But...

I look through the crowd until I finally spot Yelena again. She's talking animatedly with a smartly dressed man. He's older and she's smiling. He nods and listens to her.

I lean against the wall diagonal to her and just stare.

Is there anything hotter than a woman as pure looking as her just oozing confidence, strength and independence? This is the girl I first met while guarding my boss. She'd tried to get through security to see her friend. I stopped her.

Then, she stopped my breath.

I didn't know what it was then, not for sure. But there was something different about her. Something more than just her unmistakable beauty.

I became obsessed.

And now I'm here, and the light that made me obsessed with her is finally returning after being crushed.

I still don't know exactly what crushed it, but I know who's at least partly responsible.

My fingers curl into a tight, shaking fist.

Alex Civati.

It's a miracle I haven't killed him yet. But I guess Yelena is changing me just as much as I'm changing her.

My cock stirs at the memory of what we did earlier, of how dirty and depraved she became. Fuck. I'd love to drag her to the nearest bathroom right now. But I made a promise.

I'll control myself. For now.

I huff and fold my arms.

"What have you done to me, angel?" I mutter to myself, my mind drifting back to the conversation with Ilya.

There's a rat in our organization. That's bad fucking news. I shouldn't be this calm. Yet looking at her does something to me that eases my temper and makes me forget the nightmares I grew up with.

She is perfection. And I can't let her go.

I won't.

And as soon as this conference is over, and she's secured her investments, I'll take that fucker who crushed her light and make him suffer, nice and slow.

The thought pumps my veins full of red-hot blood.

I glance around. Where the fuck is he, anyway? Yelena's going to be busy a while longer, so maybe I should find him, just make him a little uncomfortable. Plant the seed in his head of what's coming his way. That should be enough to torture him until it's time to meet his maker.

Taking one last good look at Yelena, I start poking around. But he's not in this room, so I head out into the hallway. The resort is lined with conference rooms, each filled with people who all look the same.

The longer I look, the more the crowds start to blur.

Then, suddenly, someone stands out. Like a fucking beacon... or a warning sign.

But it's not Alex Civati.

I've just stepped into a fresh, bustling conference room when I spot a man who immediately catches my attention.

He's wearing an expensive suit, just like everyone else, but unlike everyone else, it's not fitted to his form.

The man's as out of place in a fashion conference as I am.

Our eyes briefly meet and he quickly looks away, as if he was just caught doing something he shouldn't.

That piques my interest.

"What do we have here," I mutter under my breath. "A spy?"

Acting as if he doesn't exist, I turn and head back out into the hallway. Then, slowly, I make my way to the outdoor area.

Sure enough, I can sense the man following me.

He knows he's been made. But the idiot isn't good at following people, at least, not people like me. Thing is, even with my size, I learned how to blend. How to hang back and stay where my mark is in my line of sight but I'm not theirs.

"That's it, stay nice and close."

Glancing at my phone, I act like I'm reading a message that sends me back into the room we just left. Sure enough, when I loop back, so does he. But the second I turn the first corner, and I know he can't see me, I pick up my pace and open the conference room door, hard.

I don't go inside, though. Instead, I make a beeline down the hall and wait.

The mystery man turns the corner just as I manage to step in the shadows, and I watch as he approaches the swinging conference room door and cautiously walks inside.

The fool.

Now, I'm the one following him.

Finding another entrance to the room, I slink inside. It's just as crowded as all the rest, and I make myself invisible amongst the talking heads as I catalog everything about my very own stalker.

"Who are you, big fella?"

Just shy of six foot, broad, probably well-muscled, the ill-fitting suit gives way to the tattoos spilling down his hands and up beyond his wrists.

Mafia. I recognize enough of one to know it when I see it.

Yelena is safe in her own crowded room. She won't leave without me, I'm sure of that. She's too scared of her vile ex to do that. And it won't take me long with this target.

The man looks confused, and I follow as he retraces his

steps, back into the hallway. After a beat, I join him, determined to get closer, maybe even have a few words and—

I falter to a stop.

Where the fuck did he go?

I glance down the hallway in both directions, but I don't see him. All of a sudden, he's vanished. I quickly check the shaded corner I hid in earlier. He's not there.

There aren't enough ways out here to have disappeared so quickly. The hall's too long for him to have made it back to the outdoor area already, unless he ran. But running draws too much attention, and there are other people here. Not many, but enough that they would have a look if a beefy, tattooed goon just sprinted past them.

But no one seems bothered at all.

I feel my face twist into a snarl.

I've lost a fucking mark.

That never happens.

What the hell did I miss? I check the bathrooms but they're empty. Shit. I underestimated this fucker. It's clear the guy is a pro. And he's here to tail me.

Why? I don't know.

Unless it's got something to do with the rat.

Maybe—

"Valentin!" Suddenly, Yelena grabs my arm.

Instinct nearly makes me throw her onto the ground, but when those warm fingers dig into my skin, I immediately calm.

Not that I should be calm. Not only did I just lose sight of a very dangerous man, Yelena just managed to sneak up on me.

I'm losing my fucking touch.

"Are you alright?" I ask, trying to shrug off my concern.

What the hell has me so fucking distracted.

"I'm fine," Yelena says, her bright blue eyes sparkling like fucking diamonds. That's when it all makes sense.

She's the one distracting me. My obsession with her is making me vulnerable; and by extension, her too.

Fuck.

"Are you sure?" I ask.

"Positive. I've been looking for you. My meeting ended and I couldn't find you. Is everything alright?"

I look over my shoulder, half-expecting to see my stalker staring from the shadows. But he's nowhere to be found. I'll worry about him later.

Right now, Yelena is all that matters.

"It is now," I say, sinking into her warmth. "I was just stretching my legs, but I'm glad to see you missed me."

"Maybe," she says, her voice so small and soft, "a little."

"Are you done here?"

She nods. "For now."

"Then let's go home."

I go to pull her along, but she stays in place.

"To sleep... just to sleep. I've got a big day tomorrow, and I can't—"

I pull her into my body and press her against my chest.

"I'll make sure you're nice and rested, angel" I whisper. "Or do you think I won't be able to keep my hands off you?"

She swallows.

"I'm equally as worried about myself."

I lift her wrist and kiss the back of her hand. "Let me worry about you. All you should worry about is getting a good night's sleep."

"I have far more to worry about than that," she sighs, a weariness weighing down her voice. "Tomorrow's the last day of the conference, so I need to be in my best form and try to make a big impression."

I let her twirl away from my chest, but I keep her hand closed in mine. "You already do."

A small pink blush fills in the tired paleness of her cheeks.

The weariness in her voice lifts a little as a small giggle escapes her perfect lips.

"You're just trying to get back into my panties."

I give her my most serious look. "I already know how to get into those. Right now, I'm just telling you like it is. The truth."

"The truth is that tomorrow's my last chance to secure financing."

This time, I don't have to pull her into my body. She comes voluntarily.

I hold the back of her head as she rubs her cheek against my chest.

"Then tonight you sleep." I grab a fistful of hair and gently pull her back so that she can see the look in my eyes. "Tomorrow we'll celebrate. And I know just what you need."

―――――――

After Yelena's in bed, I sit in the study and stare at the markings we left on the window earlier.

They float like fractured ghosts above the dark world below, beautiful and damning in equal measure.

Beautiful because of what transpired, the fierce pleasure that went beyond the physical. Damning because this budding relationship is dangerous.

It makes me weak.

She makes me weak.

Because my mind was half on Yelena, I let that fucker slide from my grasp. That's how you get yourself killed. That's how I get her killed.

Fucking hell.

I pick up a bottle of vodka and pour a slug into a chilled glass. The ice bucket for the vodka isn't ideal, but it'll do to keep it cold.

I'm not getting a minute's sleep tonight.

What I need is a plan. With the rat, with the man following me today, with Yelena. Because if I'm going to pursue this with her, think about making her my queen, she can't get so deep under my skin that I drop the ball with work.

Because then there will be no life to live with her. No future to spend together.

Someone snuck up on me today. Then, they got away.

It's sloppy.

And I can't let it happen again.

Even if it means pushing Yelena away.

16

This time, when I walk into the resort on Valentin's arm, there is no reservation, no fear or anger, just a strange sense of bliss.

I know it shouldn't feel this way. He's not my real boyfriend, even if he might want that, even if we've had sex, even if the idea feels almost right.

I squeeze onto his big bicep a little harder, remembering the dread I felt when he left me on my own yesterday. I was sure something was going to go wrong, and when nothing did, I realized that I only felt that way because he had left. Because without him, I momentarily felt like a meaningless speck, a nobody in a room full of somebodies.

Strangely enough, that understanding helped calm me. It helped me do better on my own. Because I knew he would be there waiting for me when it was all over.

And he was, even if I had to go find him myself.

Valentin took me home. He put me to bed. He let me sleep. And now he's going to help me shine.

I'm sure about it.

Taking a tiny breath, I look over at him.

There's no doubt he's the most gorgeous man I've ever met. But that's not why my stomach flutters. It's everything else.

"Right on time," he says, checking his watch.

It's a smart watch, one that cost an absolute bomb by the looks of the actual metal watchband. But it catches my eye because Valentin's not a man who wears such a thing usually, which says to me he's got something going down and doesn't want to be pulling his phone from his pocket.

I want to ask, but asking might actually get me answers I don't want. Answers that form a bond to him and his lifestyle. It's the last thing I want.

Even if there's little denying that I want him now.

"Ready?"

We walk into the main room and he gives my wrist one last stroke before letting me go.

"I hope so," I sigh, looking out into the crowd. Surrounding the butterflies in my stomach is a cage of tensed nerves and bubbling anxiety. This is my last chance. It's do or die.

"You're ready." Stepping up behind me, he gives my ass a soft spank. "Now, go get 'em, tiger."

I shift my shoulders, quietly hyping myself up. "What are you going to do?"

"I'm going to find that fucker."

Just like that, my nerves tighten.

"I thought we were passed that."

Grabbing my waist, Valentin plants a deep kiss on the back of my head. It might seem like an act of affection, but there's something else there too. He's staking his claim. Making it known to all who I belong to, once and for all.

It's part of the reason I have to do this alone.

"Please behave."

"Always."

One last gentle slap to the ass propels me forward. I stumble into the crowd, realizing that I haven't actually been thinking about Alex much lately. I guess that's the Valentin effect.

"You can do this, Yelena."

Patting down my dress, I make myself relax. Then, I help myself to a glass of white wine, and start the schmoozing.

There's a warmth on me as I move around the room, and I know he's watching. So when one of the potential investors from lunch grins over my shoulder, I don't need him to say, "Your watchdog is keeping you under his eye, I see."

"He's very protective." I offer a smile, an old hand at working situations similar to this.

"I see."

Dandridge might not be making moves on me, but these men don't like the idea of women being ready to drop out of deals to suddenly embrace family life.

It's old fashioned, misogynistic, but something that never quite goes away.

And to show me that his gaze drops to my ring finger.

Personally, he's my least favorite of the potential investors, but I can't afford to be picky. Besides, men like him can be handled.

One of the other investors I met earlier catches my eye, and he raises a glass in my direction. The bubble of laughter and conversation swells around us as I fix my gaze back on Dandridge.

"Protective, but content to let me run my own things, and I'm very determined to build my brand."

"Call my office and we'll set up a real one on one, I think we might have a bright future," he says, holding up his flashing phone. "But for now, please excuse me. Duty calls."

A thrill passes through me, but with a deep breath, I force myself to calm down. It's what people like Dandridge always say. That's no guarantee.

Everything here is bright, every deal is about to be signed on the dotted line, until it isn't.

But as Johnny K. waves me over, and I weave through the crowd, not even the man that bumps into my shoulder, and nearly makes me spill my drink, can dampen my mood. I just keep moving, ignoring his bad suit and ink-stained hands.

Because with one positive interaction here already, and with another on the way, it feels like I can't be stopped. The dread of yesterday is evaporating. Something good's going to come of this. I know it.

I *need* it.

"Yelena," Johnny says as I reach him. "I wanted you to meet—"

Before he can finish, he's interrupted by a room-shaking crash. That's followed by the sound of splintering wood. Then, a roar.

Someone in the crowd screams. There's a sickening crunch.

My skin pebbles. Everything in me goes cold and numb. The dread returns in full force.

Somehow, I don't even need to turn to see what's going on.

I know.

"No. No. No."

Johnny K and his associate step away from me, their faces pale with shock. I can feel more eyes on me. Judging eyes.

I'm already sick to my stomach as I make myself turn.

My heart drops.

Valentin, in his perfect suit, is beating the living shit out of the man who bumped into me. The guy's trying to fight back. But he's no match. Valentin slams his fists into the man's face, over and over and over.

Someone else has started screaming, and I slowly realize it's me. A group of employees start to race across the room, toward the commotion, but they're not security, and even if they were, they'd be no match for the feral Russian mobster.

I drop my glass and run. No one's doing anything, and if I

don't stop Valentin he'll kill the man in front of everyone.

"Valentin! Valentin! No!" I'm still screaming as I jump on his back, desperate to make him stop.

If he wanted to, he could easily fling me off. Instead, he turns and growls, his face dark red. But is that from effort or blood?

"Get the fuck off, Yelena."

"Please!" I sob. "Stop it."

He hits the guy again and I look up, two men in discreet security uniforms have arrived but they're not even real rent-a-cops, and the fear on their faces says it all.

"Get off him, now, Val," I yell in his ear. "You're ruining everything!"

Somehow, I finally manage to get through to him and tug him off the guy. But even I'm scared as he huffs and fumes with a ferocious glare.

"What are you doing?" he rumbles, getting up. There's blood on his suit and fists. Everyone's staring. I want to cry.

"You need to calm down. Please, Valentin. You're scaring me and—"

"Where did he go?"

The tattooed man is staggering to the exit and Valentin sees. Shrugging me off, he goes off after him. But I lunge forward and manage to grab onto his bloody cuffs just in time to get dragged out of the room.

"Stop! Please!"

To my horror, tears of anger burn at my eyes, spilling over my cheeks and onto his blood-soaked sleeves.

Somehow, that calms him immediately. He seems to momentarily blink out of enraged state.

"Yelena?"

"Please. Please," I beg.

He wipes his thumb across my cheek, soaking up the tears.

"Don't cry."

Behind us pure chaos has broken out. I glance over my shoulder. The crowded room is in shambles. Everyone is yelling and screaming and looking at us. People are on their phones. People are filming the blood-stained floor.

I can feel their fear and their judgment. It cuts through me like a thousand blades.

But it's only when I meet Johnny K's eyes that it really hits me. He doesn't just look horrified, he looks sick, like he'll never be able to look at me the same again.

That's when I know that it's over.

My dreams are dead.

Everyone knows Valentin and I are together. They all saw what happened. Every important name in the fashion industry knows what I'm associated with.

They're all scared.

And I am, too.

I let lust get in the way of common sense. I let it blind me to what I already knew.

The dread sits heavy in my gut as a new sensation over-powers it.

Pure, unadulterated hate. Frothing anger.

I grab Valentin's sleeve, not caring if I get soaked in blood, and I pull.

"Outside. Now."

"Yelena—"

"No." I say it quietly, but there's enough force behind it for him to go still. "I won't be quiet. Or stay and get arrested. I don't care. We're leaving. NOW!"

And with that, I turn and stalk out the door.

Valentin lets me reach the pavement before he grabs my wrist. But I shake him off with a boundless fury. "You're a monster, Valentin Constanov. Handsome, charming. But a monster. And the worst thing is, I knew it... and I slept with you anyway. Biggest mistake of my life."

Valentin straightens his back.

"Be reasonable, Yelena. He was a threat."

I nod and look him up and down, not caring anymore about those prying eyes watching from behind. "The only threat to me is you. I should have taken my chances with Alex..."

"Bullshit," Valentin barks. Stepping forward, he engulfs me in his giant shadow. But it's not warm anymore. No. It's fucking frigid. "I'm protecting you."

"And who's protecting me from you, huh?" I'm so angry I can barely talk straight. "You... you ruined me!"

In more ways than one, my words imply, and we both hear it.

"You're overreacting."

"How. Fucking. Dare. You." I step up to him and drop my voice. "This isn't some turf war or Bratva hit. This is my life and you stepped into it and turned it upside down and—"

"Enough."

The thunder of his voice cracks over me as he grips my arm and whistles loudly through his teeth.

A second later, his car comes screeching up front. I'm quickly bundled into the back seat.

My head spins as panic flares. Even through the buzzing in my ears, his presence is suddenly everywhere, and the click of the door is like the cocking of a gun. I scrabble for the handle, but he just sighs. Loudly.

"It's locked."

"Let me out, you psychopath," I seethe, pushing the words through clenched teeth.

"No."

I turn and glare. Next to me, as the car moves, Valentin calmly grabs a bottle of water from the counter built into the door. He pours some onto a white handkerchief and uses it to clean his hands. Behind him, the resort, with all of its staring, condemning faces, falls away. The night road takes over.

I hardly know what to do with myself.

"You bastard."

Growling, I reach past him, almost upending his water as I snatch the nearest bottle with shaking fingers.

I don't look at the label holding the clear liquid, just unscrew the top and take a deep swallow.

Gin. It's disgusting. I'm about to take another swallow when he grabs it from me.

"Easy, angel."

"Don't you dare call me that. You're insane. A brute. A thug."

He puts the bottle away and pulls another, pouring some of the contents into a glass. Whiskey by the smell.

"I am," he says, "exactly what I've always been."

"Bratva thug."

"Careful," he says, taking a sip of the liquid before turning the glass in his grazed-knuckled hand. "People have died for less."

I stare at him and my chest's so tight I can't breathe. "Did you threaten me?"

"No." One word. Emphatic. Reasonable, at least to him.

And I'm sitting trying to get air into lungs like a fish flopping on the dock.

"No? No?" The words hiss from me. "It sure sounded like a fucking threat."

"I'm just pointing out what kind of man I am... to everyone except you. A simple reminder, and an explanation for what happened back there."

"What happened back there? You mean how you went ballistic, beat up someone at a fancy hotel. Worse, the one where the conference to fucking save my career was happening. And now they know. At the very least, they know that I'm with someone unstable, or they realize what you are. Whatever they think, they're thinking I'm the last person they want to associate with now."

Those dark blue eyes barely flinch. And though he's calm I can't shake the feeling he's as angry as I am.

"Stop the car." I order.

"Then what, Yelena?" He sets down the bloodied handkerchief and picks up the drink. I snatch it from him, downing the contents. He just takes the glass and pours another. "Are you going to fucking walk? Hitchhike?"

"Anything would be better than being with you."

"That's your decision." He offers me the glass and I shake my head. I don't need to get drunk. I need to get out of here, away from him and the Bratva. "I'll take you where you want to go."

"I don't want to go anywhere with you."

"That man was—"

"I don't care if he was the devil. Since you turned up in my life again, you've killed someone, almost started a fight with my ex at a luncheon, and now you've ruined everything. You've ruined me!"

Valentin sets down the drink and slides closer to me. I'm immediately overwhelmed by him. The infernal heat of his body. The size. The scent. Fuck, I can't believe I ever found it arousing. Hell, even comforting.

Now, it's lined with the coppery scent of blood.

I go to shove him away, but he doesn't move, just wraps my hand in his and holds it to his chest. His breath teases my skin and my ear. "You gave yourself to me."

"I lost my head."

"No. You put it on straight. And I need to do the same thing. I need to give myself to—"

Panic scrabbles at my throat. "Stop. This is over. We're over. I'm... I'm finished. I'll never be able to work again."

"I'll be the only investor you need. I have more money than

most of those guys anyway. I—."

"No!" I'm drowning in panic and anger.

Panic that this was Valentin's plan from the beginning—to lure me into a false sense of security, then ruin all my other options so I had to rely on him for the rest of my life. Anger at how I lost my head and had sex with a man like him.

A monster.

"No," I repeat. "I won't be in debt to you. I won't disrespect my family like that again."

"What do you—"

"Don't." I push the word out as he shifts back, "don't you dare try to figure out who I am, where I come from. I don't want to know you. I don't want you to know me."

I stop and look out the window. We're pulling up to his place, the veritable construction site. I follow him out of the car and into the elevator. Not a word is spoken as we ride up to the penthouse, and I stand there when the elevator opens, not wanting to go in. Not wanting to cross the barren living room and go down the hall, past all the places where he fucked me.

I don't want to go into the bedroom.

But, suddenly, it all catches up to me, and I'm exhausted.

I'm so fucking tired.

My heels echo as I stomp through the penthouse.

Valentin doesn't follow as I throw my things into my bag. I wheel it out, the sounds preternaturally loud.

He still stands near the elevator, that unreadable expression on his face.

"I asked you to give me space. To let me do this on my own," I pant, fumbling for my phone to book an Uber. "And you couldn't. You couldn't help yourself. But that's not your fault. I see that now. You're Bratva. The worst kind. You use it to manipulate vulnerable women."

"You really believe that?"

He's in the same position, just inside the penthouse, face

giving nothing away.

"Yes. Why do you think I kept away from you, Valentin?"

"You didn't. Not over the past few days."

"I didn't have a choice. I was stupid and weak. I don't want your brand of help. And I don't want you."

"Angel."

"No, here's the thing, I don't want your filthy, tainted money. I don't want the kind of influence a Bratva thug can offer. The cost is too great, and it's a cost I'm not willing to pay. I don't want your life and I don't want you. I never want to see you again."

I turn and blink the burning blur from my eyes.

The last thing I'm going to do is cry. I'm not crying in front of him. Not again. Instead, I jab at the button for the elevator. I'll work out the Uber downstairs. And everything else? There's no working it out. He's ruined it. My career, my life.

And the worst of it is that I let it happen.

Never again. Ever.

When the elevator opens I step in, but he stops it from closing. The blood in my veins burn red-hot, all while a frigid gust blows over my skin.

If he wanted, he could trap me in here forever.

"Let go. I hate you. I don't want to see you ever again. I'll pay you back for your hospitality. God forbid I don't want to owe the Bratva a thing. Now, I need to go and get an Uber."

"My driver will be waiting."

"No—"

"This is not negotiable," he says, anger momentarily twisting his stoic façade before it settles back into form. "Goodbye, Yelena."

"There's nothing good about this."

Valentin releases the elevator door. It closes as he turns and walks away.

Good, I tell myself. *Leave me alone. Forever.*

I repeat that like a mantra, over and over again, all while my heart shatters into a million different pieces.

17

VALENTIN

1 month later...

It's been almost a month since I've been back in downtown Chicago and we're still no closer to finding that fucking rat.

"Get your head in the game."

I ignore Ilya as I stalk around the basement of our headquarters. Computers and servers line the wall, blinking in undecipherable Morse code.

This is Ilya's bread and butter. Not mine. I like to be able to see what's fucking me.

"How can you stand it down here?" I huff.

Ilya shrugs. "Because it's cool. Haven't you seen all the hacker shows and movies? They always are in rooms like this." He laughs like he's just told some hilarious joke.

"Funny."

I think about shooting him, but my guns have been through enough in the past few weeks, and I like Ilya.

"I don't need a view, Valentin. Just less distractions."

"I'm not distracted."

He isn't buying it. "You're still stuck on that girl. Don't be. There are plenty of fish out in the sea."

"Don't you fucking dare call her a—" I stop myself. As hard as I've tried, I haven't been able to stop thinking about Yelena, to stop defending her from even the slightest insults. Ilya doesn't understand. How could he?

"Where are we on the rat?" I grunt, cracking my neck.

Stay focused, Valentin.

Ilya sighs and turns in his chair, resting one foot on the opposite knee as he drums his fingers on his thighs. "I've shored up leaks, made it almost impossible for someone to steal files, but as to identity? I don't have anything."

I cross to him and lean against the desk, pushing my way through two of his giant computer screens. "Will you ever?"

"Never say never," he mutters, switching to Russian.

"You want to fit in, then speak English."

"My English is perfect and not on trial." He sends me a dagger-laced glare. "This is pissing me off too, Valentin. But short of torturing the people who used our computers around that time, we have nothing to go on."

"I'm not above torture."

"No one was in those files. That's the problem. And you're talking our people."

"Fuck." I pause. "Still not above torture."

I slap a hand against the table.

"Something on your mind, Valentin?"

"I'm thinking, what if we've made this too hard?"

"We're meant to make it hard."

I shake my head. "Making it hard pushes the rat deeper."

Ilya looks up at the ceiling, his eyes racing back and forth.

"What do you suggest? Planting fake files? It won't work."

I'm not too sure. Ilya is smart, way smarter than most, but he's thinking like a tech genius. What if we're dealing with someone who either got lucky or had a genius find them a path in? Or had something buried long ago to gain access when they needed it?

That muddies the waters. Italian or Russian, who's turned?

"What are you thinking, Valentin?"

"I'm thinking maybe we make it slightly easier."

"Like deliver something on a platter? Fake won't hold up."

"Fake or harmless information."

"They'll see through it."

"Not if the cheese we put out seems to be tasty in the right ways."

He's quiet for a beat. "Fake everything?"

"It's a thought." I shrug. "Flush the fucking Italians out."

"Italians."

"One attacked me."

"Oh, I'm aware. It took a lot to kill that story, brother."

"Your fucking job."

Ilya goes quiet as I rise and continue pacing. I can sense him judging my disheveled appearance. But I don't give a shit. I already know I need a change of clothes, a fresh shave, and an attitude adjustment. But that shit's not happening. Not until I figure this shit out.

With the rat and with Yelena.

No. Fuck that. The only thing that concerns me is work.

Everything else is meaningless.

"My job isn't running PR for you." Ilya puts his foot to the ground as he studies me. "You've been reckless, even for you. I told you to come back to do what had to be done, not turn into a fucking kamikaze with a death wish."

I pinch the bridge of my nose. "Isn't that pretty much what a kamikaze fucking is?"

"No—"

"Save it." I look at him and he sucks in an audible breath. "It's been a month since I was gone. I'm back. So fucking focus."

I straighten up and the wheels on Ilya's chair squeak as he shifts back.

He's got skills. And he's a killer in his own right. But he's no match for me and my wrath.

"You think you can give me fucking orders?" I bark, letting the rage take over.

I haven't seen her in a month. I haven't been with any woman. I haven't jerked off. Relieved myself. It's all pent-up and ready to explode.

"I just meant—"

"You think I'm you're fucking lapdog?" I squeeze my hand into a fist and stare at him.

He swallows audibly, his eyes going from my face to my hand and back again.

And then he gets up.

I know the fucking cost of that move.

Because he knows what I am.

What Yelena called me.

A monster.

Capable of anything.

"I'm no one's lapdog. And this thing, this rat? We'll locate them and then crush them."

"So are you ready to work together?"

I step up to him. "Yes, Ilya. I might be a fucking monster, but I'm not a fucking fool."

But I am.

I've lost my goddamn mind. And it's only getting worse.

Rubbing a hand down the thigh of my jeans, I sit in a corner of O'Leary's, an Irish bar in downtown Chicago famous for being a neutral hang-out spot for all sorts of scum.

It's also a good place for a drink when you don't want to be bothered with business. Fucking Irish and their sacred rules. No blood to be shed here. No deals. Neither one is easy to enforce but the first is met with dire consequences, the second... Well, in a place where anyone can walk in, no questions asked, deals are at the participant's peril.

But I'm not here for any of that.

I'm here to drink and keep my eye out for clues. To let my presence be known. I'm out of my suit. That makes me even more dangerous. It sends the message I'm not here to play by rules.

Word is out I'm looking for someone.

And my needs are very specific.

That Italian from the fucking conference. The one that ruined my chances with—

Fucking stop it.

This isn't about her. It's about why he was following you.

Thing is, lately, I can't keep my thoughts on track—not like I always have been able to do.

Yelena is too in the way.

It's not what she said to me that burns. Anger is anger, and she can be fierce.

It's her tone that's still branded into my brain.

She meant every word she said.

"Fuck," I grumble, shaking my head.

A woman sits next to me and for a moment my senses stir, gaze catching on her blonde hair, svelte form, perfect looking tits.

But that dies.

Because those perfect tits are a little too big, and she's a little too thin. Hair the wrong shade of blonde.

She isn't Yelena.

I'm not interested.

I give her a dead eyed look when she turns to me. Her flinch ricochets through me, but she stays and that gets my interest.

She's not here to try and pick me up. "Buy me a drink, Mr. Constanov."

"You know who I am?" Of course she does.

"Seems like it."

"I don't like strangers knowing my name. Maybe I'll kill you for it."

She sucks in a breath. "Maybe... but I hear that's frowned upon in here."

I signal to the bartender.

"Do I look like a man who gives a fuck about the rules?"

"You look like a man with a lot of power, and a hard-on for blondes."

Instantly, I know why she's here.

The bartender looks at me and I point at her, then lay money down for the tab.

She places her order, then puts her hand on my arm.

I remove it.

"Touch me again and you'll know exactly how little I fucking care. And tell Civati", I'm rewarded with the slightest widening of her eyes, "that I'm not easily distracted. If he's got something to say, he can say it to my face."

I get up and walk out the door.

Fuck this shit. That's not what I came down here for tonight.

I was hoping to overhear something, for someone to offer information in exchange for a deal. Rats don't exist in a vacuum, after all.

For the past month, I've been on a rampage. Busting into all sorts of places, guns blazing, blood-lust clouding my vision. I've shed more blood than the streets can handle. And it's gotten me nowhere.

So, Andrei, the great Pakhan, told me to try a new route. Now, I'm watching and listening. But that's not reaping shit either.

And now I have to deal with this.

The last thing I need is a reminder of Yelena. Especially one as despicable as Alex Civati. Really, I should just seek him out and put an end to him, once and for all. But something holds me back.

I'm not sure what.

Yes, you do. You made a promise.

Spitting onto the dirty street, I look up to the blank sky.

Maybe I should pay the fucker a visit anyway.

Part of me wonders what he wants. Hell, maybe his interests run beyond the girl who put my heart in a fucking headlock.

Ones that cross my path.

Sure, the blonde could have just been his attempt to rub my nose in the fact I'm not with Yelena anymore. Payback for what I rubbed in his face at the resort. But he isn't with her either.

I shouldn't know that for sure. But I do. Because of course I'm having her watched. How could I not?

And no one's come near her or threatened her since the conference. That's as far as I dare read in the reports. It's enough for me to know she's safe.

Or is it?

"I need to find a fucking fight."

Clenching my jaw, I stalk through the rougher Italian neighborhoods of Chicago. My thinking is justified. Make my presence known and maybe the rat will get skittish.

But really, I want to find the prick from the fucking conference. Not Alex. The other one. The one who helped me ruin everything. He's like a sturgeon that got off my line. The one whale I couldn't harpoon. Something's off about him, and it's driving me crazy.

From the ill-fitting suit to the giveaway ink on his hands.

No one in our allied Italians is claiming him. They say he could have come from one of the factions they don't control.

Maybe. Maybe not.

All I know is that I caught him trailing me at the conference. He managed to slip once, but when I caught sight of him again, I was ready.

We ran each other in circles until it all came to a boil. By the time we ran face first into each, I wasn't sure who was following who anymore.

That confusion led to the disaster that came next.

I didn't want trouble. Not there. I knew it would only hurt Yelena. But even apart from that, the place was too public. I should have tried to lead him somewhere more private, but he took the first swing.

After that, everything went to shit.

I blanked out. Next thing I knew, we were in that conference room and Yelena was pulling me off the guy, begging me to stop.

I deserved her wrath.

I handled everything so fucking poorly. But I was distracted. Never again.

My phone pings and I make a mistake of looking down; of reading the fucking report.

On Yelena.

She's still jobless. Everyone at the conference passed her over. And it's my fault.

Fuck.

I suck in a breath.

When I look up, I finally notice where my feet have taken me.

Shit. Not again.

Each and every night I find myself here, looking up.

Fuck it all.

Without thinking, I break into the building and climb the fire escape stairs. This isn't a great part of the city, and the elevator here is probably broken more often than it's working, but that's not why I'm not taking this route.

Once I reach the top floor, it's short work to open the door to the roof. People use it. There are some plants, chairs. A cheap grill. I don't like that others can easily get up here. Easily spy. Like I'm doing.

But no one's here tonight. In the sky above, dark rain clouds are forming. I'm all alone.

I go to the side where Yelena's building is and look at her window.

I shouldn't.

It's stalking, pure and simple. But I can't help myself.

Obsessive, I know, but what am I meant to fucking do? She's not exactly safe if I don't watch over her. I don't trust that fucker, Alex and...

I can't go bursting back into her life.

But I don't trust anyone else with her. Not completely.

And I *need* to make sure she's safe. At this point, it's not even a choice. Despite my best efforts, I'm hooked—even if I spend all day trying not to think about her.

Grinding my teeth, I stare off into the darkness.

A golden square of light fills up her curtained window. I see her silhouette behind it. Unmistakable. Impossibly beautiful. And then the light goes off, the window dark.

My heart plummets.

Maybe she's gone to bed. Maybe, but it's early.

"Go home," I mutter to myself.

Good fucking advice. I turn and take the dingy stairwell downstairs. I'm pushing my way out of the building's back door, when the front door to Yelena's building flings open.

I stop in my tracks.

The silhouette is just as unmistakable under the streetlights.

It's her.

The sight is a kick to the guts.

Seeing her in person is completely different than what I've

been limited to over the past month. Candid photos. Blurry security feeds.

But this is like my dreams. My nightmares.

Seeing her live, in person, within distance to touch if I crossed the street, it tears at me. Rips something open.

I'm ravenous.

It's a voracious hunger that knifes through my soul. I remember how she feels. How she tastes.

I fucking want her again. *Need* her.

"Where are you going, angel?" I whisper, stepping back into the shadows.

She's being tracked by my men. But I'm not about to let her out of my sight. Not now that I've seen her up close again.

I pull a small tracking device from my pocket. It's so small and thin that I have to keep it in a slender leather credit card fold.

"I should have done this back at the hotel." Stuck it to her phone, slipped it into her handbag. I didn't. I didn't think I'd lose the right to watch over her in person.

But I fucked up. And now I'm paying for it.

Am I evil enough to make her pay for it to?

"Yes."

There's a part of me that knows that this little tracker isn't to protect her. At least that's not its only purpose. It means I'm not ready to let her go.

That maybe I miss her. Maybe I need her.

That the memory of her aches inside me daily.

It doesn't matter how many people I kill or beat to a pulp in the name of justice or my job. None of it helps fill the hole her absence has left inside me.

Maybe it's time I stop pretending to be something I'm not.

I'm no knight in shining armor. I'm not chivalrous. I'm not above stalking.

I'm a monster.

Her monster.

And I'm going to do exactly what a monster does.

Dipping my head, I step out of the shadows and cross the road.

18

YELENA

Great. Just great. As if my life couldn't get any worse.

It's started to drizzle.

I wasn't prepared for this. My umbrella and coat are upstairs, and I definitely don't have time to go back up and get them. I'm already running late—and even if I wasn't, going back up means I might not come down.

I hate going out at night. For the past month, I haven't been able to shake the feeling that I'm being watched. The fact that it's not just possible, but likely, has me losing sleep.

I keep expecting to see Valentin or Alex, or someone they've hired to follow me. At any moment, I could relive that nightmare at the resort.

But no one has shown up. And I don't know if I'm more disappointed or relieved.

Actually, I know for sure that I'm not relieved. With all the stress I'm under, that's impossible.

Shaking my head, I take out my phone and look at the time, half expecting to see a missed call.

Valentin hasn't tried to call. I'm sure of it. But there have been other numbers trying to reach me. I have little doubt they're from Alex. I answered once, absent-mindedly, and no one answered on the other end. There was just silence and the implication that someone was breathing right into the receiver.

A chill skates up my spine.

It was just Alex, I tell myself. Harmless Alex, who sent a Private Investigator to stalk and possibly kidnap me. No big deal—at least, not compared to Valentin.

My heart squeezes at that thought.

Overbearing. Frustrating. Obsessive. Murderous. That's what comes to mind when I think of Valentin. That's all that should come to mind when I think of him. Yet, somehow, my twisted brain turned it into something to smile about, like I'm a fucked up girl who's dreaming of blood-drenched picket fences.

He's changed my brain chemistry. Fucking hell.

"Damn you and your handsome face and sneaky sense of humor," I mutter, putting my arms tight about myself as I duck my head and hurry along the streets.

There are people on the sidewalk, huddled under umbrellas or scurrying along. In the restaurants I pass, everyone looks so cozy and warm. I envy them. Not just because they look so comfortable, but because they have money to spend on restaurants.

I haven't been out to eat in weeks.

"Don't lose hope."

I cross the road and head down an empty side street, the best way to get to where I need to be. Ducking into a doorway, I take the opportunity to check for someone following me, but by now, everyone has managed to escape the rain.

I'm all alone.

And it's getting cold.

Reaching into my bag, I pull out the hoodie I brought just in case the weather turned. It's no raincoat, but it will have to do.

As I walk, the feeling of being watched grows. I pick up

speed. It always feels like this when I go out, but tonight it's more pronounced, and I can't stop my mind from trying to work out if it's Valentin or Alex... or which one I'd prefer.

Valentin, definitely Valentin, a part of my brain screams. My body warms in response.

But the problem is, Valentin comes with his own set of problems.

Really, I should finally swallow my pride and call up Natalya. But a strong, stubborn hand keeps me from doing just that.

"Maybe if things go poorly tonight."

I cross another street.

No. I can't crawl back to the Bratva. If I call her she'll get Andrei to put protection on me. And I know who'll volunteer.

"That's if he's not already following you."

It's driving me crazy and I've been staying in as much as I can, only going out for grocery runs and the occasional job interview. But those interviews don't extend into the fashion world. No phoenix is rising from those cold, burnt ashes.

I've tried. I've called and wheedled my way into even the lowest rung job interviews, but most of the time they've been cancelled. And my investors?

All of them disappeared into the woodwork.

I can't help but laugh, the bitterness acrid in my mouth. Valentin's little display made that happen. Chased them all off.

The warmth vanishes.

No one wants to be associated with a woman with a violent boyfriend. And a boyfriend that's connected? Never.

I could probably get past a violent man; people make mistakes, after all. And if I spread that the relationship is done, I'm betting things could cool down and my career would have a chance. But someone who's involved in organized crime? And yes, there have been whispers. No one wants to work with that. Mafia, Bratva, that stink doesn't go away.

So, here I am, on my way to Poppa's Burgers, a low-rent restaurant where I've got an interview for a server job.

Graveyard shift, which might mean money on weekends, but right now I'm not in a position to be picky and—

My breath catches.

Footsteps, coming fast along the street.

I hurry, not running, but moving fast. Whether these footsteps are after me or not, it doesn't matter. The sooner I get to where people are the better.

My lungs burn in fear. The last time I was followed, I—

Valentin. The PI.

What would that man have done if Valentin hadn't been there?

Because no one who's meant to keep an eye on me and report in follows their prey like that. And that's exactly what I felt like. Prey.

Still do.

I walk faster, and turn onto the next street.

The rain's coming down a little harder now, and there's no one on this street either. I risk a look over my shoulder but don't see anyone, just a growing shadow from the street I turned off of.

A scream builds, but I swallow it down.

If I'm in trouble, no one's going to help me. I just need to move. Fast. I wish I could afford a taxi or something, or to just stay home for the rest of my life, but that's a fairytale I'm not living in.

My life is a nightmare.

The footsteps grow.

Fuck it.

Fear griping my body, I dip my head and start to run. But when I turn the nearest corner, I run straight into a wall of solid muscle.

Warm, hard, familiar muscle.

Still, through the fear, I barely register the hands, the scent of him. I start to struggle, but he doesn't let go, just holds me tight.

"Yelena, calm down. It's me."

I gulp in air. "You were following me?"

"I saw you," he says, stroking a hand down my spine, "and wanted to make sure you were alright."

"Let go."

For a moment I don't think he's going to, and there's a part of me that doesn't want him to, either.

No matter how angry I am with him.

Valentin is a wall of protection.

Those footsteps were coming from behind me. They weren't his.

Then whose were they?

"I didn't mean to scare you." But he lets me go and I shift back from him, shivering.

There's something different about the way he looks, shabbier, but I'm too all over the place to concentrate on that.

Really, all I can see are those deep blue eyes. They practically radiate through the rain and the darkness.

Warmth thrums through me. I want to cry.

Not this again.

"Let's get you out of this rain," he says, sliding an arm around my shoulders.

He doesn't look behind me, but I can't let go of the troublesome thought that if he was the one coming after me, why did I run into him? And I think he's wondering that, too.

"I have places to be," I make myself say, "And I can get myself out of the rain."

"I'm just trying to help."

"You've helped enough." I take a breath. "Please, let me go."

He hesitates, then drops his arm. "Yelena, I'll take you—"

"No. You won't." I stop and turn. "I don't know why you're

really here, but you scared the shit out of me. I thought someone was chasing me."

"I didn't want you out here alone. It's dangerous"

I suck in a breath. The footsteps... they must have been from one of his men. That's why he's not concerned. "You couldn't have done that quietly?"

"You know full well I don't do things quietly."

I get a glimpse of his heart-throbbing smile before he purposely contains it. We both know that he's a wrecking ball. It's why we haven't seen each other in a month—at least, it's why I haven't seen him in a month.

"I'm well aware," I snap.

I see the muscles in his jaw clench and remember the way his tongue felt. A warmth flashes through me. That's followed by anger.

"You're trembling," he softly notes.

"Because you scared me. Keep out of my life, Valentin, you've done enough damage already."

The tension vibrates through him. "Those cowards at the convention don't know what they're missing out on."

"Those cowards" I say, shoving him, "are the ones who hold my livelihood in their hands. You're Bratva. Rich. You can do what you want. I can't. Those people don't know what I'm missing out on because of you."

"I can—"

"No." I lift my chin and glare at him, rainwater dripping down my cheeks. "I won't take your help anymore. That was the biggest mistake of my life."

"You're upset."

"Of course I'm upset! I thought Alex was after me. Or—"

"Has he been bothering you? Calling you?"

There it is. The subtle confirmation that Valentin has been tracking me. I wouldn't be surprised if my phone's already bugged.

"That's none of your business."

"I'm making it my business," he says, grabbing me and pushing me back against the rough brick of the wall. "And you aren't helping."

"I could say the same about you."

He laughs softly. "Sounds like we keep getting in each other's way. Could be fate."

"More like bad luck. Terrible, awful, luck."

"I won't let bad luck stop me."

"You should."

He shakes his head. "No. If I did, I would never be where I am today."

"You're where you are because of violence. Because you beat and torture and kill to get your way. I saw it at the conference. It opened my eyes. I know who you are now, Valentin. Truly. And I... I don't like it."

His heavy hands rest on my shoulders, feeling far too warm.

"Life isn't black and white, angel," he sighs. "There are many shades. I do what I do. And trust me, I might be a monster, but there are worse out there. And some of them hide it under layers of civility. I don't. What you see is what you get. And if you don't like that, if you truly hate it, well, then I'm sorry."

My heart drops.

His words are seductive in their ugly honesty. He's right. He doesn't ever hide who and what he is. He's just Valentin.

And that's why he's so dangerous.

"Who you are scares me," I mutter, almost feeling bad for being so harsh.

"Or maybe it turns you on."

That sets any guilt I feel on fire.

"Fuck you."

I want to pull him into my chest, stab him. Kiss him. Bite him. Claw. Ride. Fuck.

"That option will always be available to you."

He leans in and I can smell his hot breath on my wet cheek.

My heart thumps with wild blood. I clench my hands at my sides.

I don't want to be turned on by him. But how can I pretend I'm not when a touch from him makes me want to self-combust?

Problem is, the violence and the pleasure are so intertwined in him I can't separate them. He's just one big, hulking mass of sex and brutality.

"You're not sexy," I lie, clenching my hands so hard my nails dig into my palms.

"I'm not trying to be sexy, angel. I'm trying to protect you, keep you safe," he murmurs, pressing in against me, one thigh sliding between mine as his mouth skims a path to my ear. "And you fight. Even now. What are you thinking? Walking around rough neighborhoods at night?"

"I'm thinking I no longer have a way to make an income, because of you."

"You keep blaming me, but how about taking a shot at those who are too cowardly to see the genius in you? To risk it all for greatness. Are you willing to risk it all, angel?"

Frustrations swell, along with the bone-melting memories. The taste of him fills my mouth. I want to sob. I'm not over him. I want more. I want to press my mouth to his flesh. I want to breathe him in deep and long and hard.

I want to feel his arms around me, not in protection, but in passion.

And it would be so very easy to give in to those urges.

He is.

I can feel the throbbing heat of his erection pushing against me. I know he wants me. But there's never been any doubt about that. The true question is about what I want.

I want to feel wanted. To feel protected. Cared for. Supported.

I want to be treated with a sweet touch, and a rough hand.

But Valentin isn't a sweet man. He's dangerous on so many levels. And he gives in to his baser, violent sides.

What he did at the conference tells me that. Way too loud. Way too clear.

I can't rely on a man like this.

Even if he wasn't Bratva.

"Valentin," I whisper, tears burning in my eyes, tears I can't let fall, "please... just let me go. I'm going to be late..."

To my surprise, he steps back.

"I'll walk you."

He reaches out a hand, almost like a true gentleman would.

But I know that sugar-coated sweetness is only skin deep.

"No." I grab his shirt, only now processing that he's not in a suit. He's wearing black jeans and a long-sleeved black turtleneck. "I will walk myself."

For a moment, we just stand in the rain, steam rising from our bodies. For some reason, it reminds me of the marks we left on his window back at Sweetwater.

I let myself be weak. I won't make that mistake again. No matter how much it hurts to resist.

"I'll keep my distance," Valentin finally says. "But I won't stop protecting you."

"So I'm your prisoner now?"

"No. You are free to do as you please. As am I."

"And if I try to run?"

"I'll follow you."

I choke back my tears, unsure if I've already shed them or not. My face is wet, but that could just be the rain.

"Bye."

Without another word, Valentin steps aside. He just watches as I push myself off the wall and walk away.

I don't look back, but I can feel his warm blue eyes on me. That warmth fades. Then it's just me and the darkness and the rain.

I hurry away.

This time, no footsteps follow.

———

When I reach Poppa's Burgers it's raining a lot harder and I must look like an utter mess. I don't have much time left, but I take a few moments to calm myself. To wipe my eyes and smooth my hair.

I'm shaking. And I need to stop. But it's hard. How the hell can I, when I know I care more about Valentin than I want to? That his face haunts my dreams?

Worst of all, I hate him for making me feel this way, like I'm some kind of love-sick teenybopper who doesn't know which way is up or down.

It only took him three days to turn me upside down. Now, I've been suffering for months. That, in itself, should scare me to hell and back.

But I'm not falling into any more traps, and I'm not letting my wayward emotions win out.

What I WILL do is take back control of my own life.

When I'm calm enough, I take off the hoodie, smooth my hair as best I can and pull open the door to step inside the half-empty burger joint.

I need to make this work.

Because the last thing I'm going to do is ask anyone for help.

Least of all Valentin.

19

VALENTIN

It's been three days since I saw Yelena on that empty street, standing in the rain, looking miserable.

The image is burned into my mind, as is the pain of what happened.

I'm still suffering.

And it doesn't matter how many people I beat into unconsciousness, how many I kill, my murderous, violent rampage doesn't heal a single fucking wound.

It doesn't bring me any closer to the rat, either.

My life is falling apart.

Since the meeting with Yelena, I've been working nonstop, trying to find something—anything—on the rat. That includes going on another bloody rampage through the Chicago underworld.

It's not completely reckless. In a way, I'm being strategic. What I'm not doing is holding back. Not anymore. Those who need to suffer will. There's no tiptoeing around the subject matter anymore. Word is out that I'm looking for specific information.

In any other situation, fuckers would be crawling out of the woodwork with tips and leads. Anything to gain my favor.

But so far, nothing's turned up.

And Yelena...

Fuck.

I look down at my phone but don't open it.

I'm still getting reports on her. And when I'm at my weakest, I check the tracker I planted on her that night.

My fingers tighten around the black screen.

Then, it starts to ring.

I answer quickly. Anything to distract myself from that shit.

"Been thinking," Ilya immediately starts.

"How's that working for you?"

"About as well as your rampage."

I snarl.

"Why are you calling?"

Pressing the phone close to my ear, I try to ignore the chatter around me. I'm back in another dive bar, trying to snuff out anything from the lower end of the totem pole—at least, that's what I tell myself.

Maybe, I'm just here for a drink

"Remember how you suggested that our rat could be someone who got into the system years ago, even before I showed up?"

I frown. Ahead, a new batch of patrons filter into the bar. One in particular catches my interest. "Yes?"

"Maybe you're right. It doesn't bring us closer, but I might need to overhaul everything."

The man's got a greasy look. Small, thinning hair, skinny body, and too much jewelry. "I thought you already overhauled everything?"

"No. I changed everything. Passwords, server security, etc. But that might not be enough. I might need to recreate our systems from scratch."

"Sounds like a lot of work."

"Which is why I'm looking for a second opinion."

I chew on my tongue.

"Remember that cheese trap we talked about?"

"Yes."

"No bites yet?"

"Not that I can see."

"Then maybe we change up the plan a little. I'm thinking a more long-term thing. Replace everything with bogus documents—*everything*—all under the ruse of a system update."

"What kind of bogus documents are we talking?"

"You're the genius. Work it out."

"That's helpful."

This isn't my forte, but I can tell Ilya understands what I'm getting at.

"You can thank me later. So, what do you think?"

"Could work." He pauses. "Set a long-term trap?"

"And in the meantime, I'll continue this angle."

"You mean your murderous rampage angle?"

"That's right."

Static cracks as silence fills the call.

"Valentin," Ilya finally says. "If you find the rat, don't kill him."

"I know that."

"I know. It's just that you've been acting a little crazier than usual."

I hang up.

I don't need to explain myself to him, or anyone, for that matter.

Or course I won't kill the rat if I find them.

Not until I wring every last drop of information from them first.

"You'll do... for tonight," I mumble, staring at the slimeball with all the jewelry on. He's throwing money around like he's trying to show it off. Fool. "What was your name again?"

I close my eyes and filter through the memory banks.

"Ah, that's right. Big Len..."

From what I remember, he's got Yakuza links—a low-life pimp that helps keep their higher-ups happy. But he's useless enough to put the squeeze on without causing too much trouble. That is, unless I go overboard.

"Mr. Constanov!" Len's face lights up when he sees me. The fool. He probably thinks he can dump some overpriced girls. "It's been so long since I've seen that long face. Any chance you've changed your mind on my profession since our last meeting?" he asks, coming over to me. "Or are you here looking for freebies?"

"Neither."

He holds his glass in both hands and grins from ear to ear. "Then you must be looking for some information."

I sneer at him.

"I'm not here to play games."

"I wouldn't dare. I know you're a straight shooter, big guy."

"What do you know?"

"I know a lot." He turns so he's leaning back on the bar, facing out. But his voice is low.

"Someone stole some things. We'd like to know who."

"Word on the street is that your manhunt isn't going too well. Maybe ease back on the rivers of blood? Some good pussy could help calm you down. I just got a new batch in too. How about a free sample?"

"You keep talking about whores and I'll give you a free sample of my fucking fist."

His hand trembles slightly as he throws back his drink. I buy him another. For a coward, he sure is ballsy.

"Don't listen to me, I'm just talking out of my ass," he gulps.

"As per usual. Now, tell me who else is talking. What have

you heard?" I glance over his shoulder. "What have your hens heard?"

Len shakes his head. "My girls don't talk. What's said to them by a client stays between them."

Big Len isn't high class, but he gets girls who want to make bank. And his clients want his brand of low-level under-the-radar business.

"I don't know anything, but word is you might be in the market for someone with clout. Legit clout. Like the type that can have sway over the FBI, or knows how to do it. More than payroll personnel, if you catch my drift." His drink arrives and he downs it.

"I do." I pause as the chatting voices swell around us. No one here is interested in anyone else hearing what they're talking about. "You seem to have made it your business knowing mine."

"I make it my business to know everything about everyone." Then he pulls a scrap of paper from his pocket. "Figured you'd come asking eventually."

"How much?"

"What's it worth?"

"Your teeth staying in your head." I look at him, weighing up options.

Owing favors isn't my favorite thing, but sometimes the idea of one's worth everything.

"A favor."

"The Bratva will owe me?" His eyes light up.

"No. I will. And I'm fucking worse than them. So?"

He swallows and his hand shakes a little as he hands me the scrap.

"Deal."

I could go home and change, but I'm not in the fucking mood, even if a suit would definitely help me blend into this bougie downtown club a whole lot better.

Cracking my knuckles, I take in the room, with its tasteful dark wood walls, black leather seats, and stripped-back ceiling.

It's not the décor I'm interested in, though. It's the clientele.

In the back, I note a big man who looks like he's carrying. Must be the bouncer. And I'm betting the discreet door he's sitting next to is the clandestine part of the club. They'll call it members only and it'll be a mix of the Chicago rich, the Chicago low-level famous and the criminal type.

Exactly what I'm looking for.

Unfortunately, I don't have a ticket. Luckily, I don't mind making a scene.

"Name?"

The bouncer is quick to size me up when I approach.

"Valentin Constanov."

He checks his notepad. "I don't see your name on the list."

"Look again."

Lunging forward, I grab him by the collar and shove him against the wall. Before he can reach for his gun, I take it from him.

"Now, we can do this the hard way or the easy way. Your choice. Just know that the easy way means you live. The hard way..."

I click my tongue and shake my head.

His wide eyes tell me all I need to know. He won't be causing me any more trouble.

Without waiting for an answer, I release him and barge in through the door. From there, it's not hard to spot the VIP section. Two men stand outside a velvet rope at the bottom of a dark stairwell. I stride up to them, showing them their colleague's gun.

"Out of my way."

The one who's my height and build puffs up. "Who the fuck are you?"

"Your worst nightmare."

Without hesitation, I slam the butt of his buddy's gun into his temple. He collapses to the ground, a pool of blood already forming around his head.

His partner reaches for his own gun, but before he can get to it, I point mine at his head.

"Do what you want, but know this. If you fight back, I won't just kill you. I'll massacre your family. Your girl. Your friends. And his too..." I look down at the man bleeding out on the floor. "Same goes with your little friend out front. Tell him I'll even use his gun to do the deed. Understood?"

He's frozen still, but after staring at me for an uncomfortable amount of time, he finally swallows.

"Who are you."

"Valentin Constanov. I'm the fucking devil."

The door bursts open behind me and I take out my own gun. The bouncer stops in his tracks, staring down the barrel of his own weapon. My pistol is trained on his friend. My foot comes down on the back of their fallen comrade's neck.

"Who the fuck is Valentin Constanov?" The guy asks loudly, his shaky voice betraying his fear.

Out of the corner of my eye, I see someone stand up from his seat.

"Let him through, Con," the guy says.

"Why—"

"He's Bratva. And crazy, clearly." The other guy's eyes flicker to me. "No disrespect. They should have let you in without a fight."

"Apology accepted." I turn to Con. "Easy or hard?"

Con studies me and I know the word Bratva has him unnerved but he sees something in my face that turns him ashen and he steps away.

I give them all a curt nod, then I step over the bleeding head at my feet and take the stairs up into the darkness.

The door at the top is heavy. I have to use my shoulder to push it open.

I'm not shocked by what I see.

One guy. Four girls. One's riding him as two others make out. The fourth lies on a table, legs spread as he fucks her with a dildo.

He stops the second he sees me.

"Fuck."

I aim my gun at him and the girls scream.

"No need to move, General. You look so comfortable there."

The old fuck must have eaten a vat of Viagra before this.

"If you're going to kill him," one of the girls suddenly says in Russian, "wait until we leave. Please. I'm not in the mood for a blood bath."

She must know who I am.

"No one's going to die here," I tell her, keeping my gun pressed forward. "Isn't that right, General?"

"What the hell is this?" he booms.

"Hush now, or you'll scare the girls." Nodding my head, I gesture for everyone with a pair of fake tits to scram. They don't need to be convinced.

They gather their clothes and scurry past me.

I wait until the heavy door clicks shut behind them before I continue.

"Now, let's begin."

General Briggs sputters. "Don't you know who I am?"

He's a big, beast of a man. Iron gray buzz cut, muscled. When he stands up, he's almost as tall as me. The proud man may be butt naked, but he juts his chin and meets my gaze.

"I know exactly who you are, General. It's why I'm here."

His grey eyes dart back and forth as he tries to figure out what's happening.

"I'll have you thrown in prison for this, you pissant Russian pig!"

I click my tongue at him and shake my finger. "No. You won't. But you will answer my questions."

Stepping forward, I kick his trousers toward him. "Put those on. I'm already sick of your wrinkled dick."

"You better not shoot me or they'll throw you in fucking Guantanamo..."

"Don't worry about me. Worry about yourself. This isn't going to look good."

"What the fuck is that supposed to mean?"

I wave my gun up to the corner of the room, to where a little red dot is just barely discernable through the shadows.

"See that?"

His red face goes pale.

"A camera?"

I nod. "Don't worry, the owner didn't know about it. It was the pimp who betrayed you."

"Fucking Len."

"I'm sure your wife will find this very enlightening. She works for the government, too, right? Up for reelection? Wouldn't want this to get out.

"I'll wipe the floor with your thug ass," he says buckling his pants and pulling on his shirt.

"You can try." I point to the chair he rose from but he refuses to sit. Fucking military man who thinks I care about his clout.

I do, but only in regard to what it can do for me.

"We can do this," I say, "the easy way or the hard way. Up to you."

"I'll ruin you."

I laugh. "You'll ruin me? To use your words, do you know who I am?"

"No."

"Good. All you need to know is the Bratva has taken an interest in you."

His eyes narrow. He's very still, tense, waiting to make his move. Then, all at once, it seems to hit him.

"I'm listening," he relents.

"Good. Good. It's pretty simple, really. I just need you to use your government access, Mrs. General's too." He bristles at that. "There were documents leaked to the FBI. Documents that weren't their business. We caught the documents, but we need the rat. I need you to trace where those documents came from."

"You want me to betray my country to a Russian criminal?"

"No, I want you—a man who cheats on his wife with two-dollar hookers—to help the Bratva find it's rat."

The general stares at me for a moment before shaking his head. "I don't help criminals, and I don't betray my country."

"You betrayed your wedding vows, cheated on your wife. You can cheat on your country. Just a little."

General Briggs comes up to me and shoves his face into mine. I let him. I want to see what he's made of. So far I'm not impressed.

"I'm more powerful than you can dream of," he snarls. "Do you not understand the kind of trouble I can bring down on you? I've killed dozens in battle."

"And I've killed hundreds for fun." With that, I move, elbowing him in the throat and grabbing his hand as he falls.

Bending his middle finger back, I wait until I hear a crack before I stop. He howls and I let him go.

He falls to his knees. But a proud man like him can't stay there for long. The second he's back on his feet, though, I turn and kick him hard in the kneecap, sending him to the floor again.

He curls up in pain.

"I could cut off your left nut, slice your Achilles tendon. I could break all your ribs and shatter your jaw." I kneel next to him, right on those nuts of his. "How's that for power?"

His scream is high and thin.

"Please."

I press harder on his nuts. "See, real power isn't having a bunch of shiny badges, or a wife with a stuffed ballot. It's having complete freedom to be as sick, twisted, and depraved as you want to be. It's not having to follow any rules. And I don't. With a snap of my finger, I can buy this club and everyone in it. I can set up your wife in a sex scandal so vile she'll never get a job again. And if you try to retaliate? Then I'll hit you back, a thousand times harder. And I'll do it all with a smile on my face... or you can do what I've asked."

I stand, releasing him from the pain, but not from the humiliation. Pulling out a stack of cash, I toss it down on the general, bill by bill, like he's a stripper.

"There's your money, now do your job. I'm sure your veteran benefits will cover your medical bills. Let's not add your wife to those bills, too, eh?" I head to the exit and stop. "And don't worry, I'll be in touch."

With a mock salute, I leave.

———

Once I'm on the street I give in to the urge that I've been ignoring.

Yelena.

The tracker app on my phone shows her location.

She's home.

Leaning against the wall, I allow myself to breathe. Honestly, I expected to feel a little calmer after all that. At any other point in my life, beating the shit out of a General would have been therapeutic. I should be brimming.

But I'm not.

In fact, I'm angrier than ever.

I don't like cheats, I never have. Not in cards, in honor, and not with relationships.

Honor counts. I'd die for the few people in this world I'm loyal to. I'd tear the world for their well-being.

I watch the dot that represents Yelena flick on my phone screen. It fills me with emptiness.

This isn't going to work for much longer.

Sucking in the cool damp air, I straighten up. The emptiness inside of me is slowly filling with fire. I know I only have two choices.

Go to her and try to smother the flames once and for all... or feed them.

I think of the flashing dot. I think of her.

She doesn't need to burn in my hell. She deserves better than that, than me.

She's an angel. I'm a blood-soaked animal. The devil.

I can't go to her. Not ever again.

But I'm too restless for sleep. So, I decide to do something I've been holding back on for far too long now.

If I'm cutting the cord between us, then that means my promises are void.

I look back down at my phone and text some of my men.

Tonight, we're going to set this town on fire.

And I know exactly who I want to tie to the first stake.

20

YELENA

If I was a big drinker, I'd be wasted right about now.

I flick the channels on my TV and chuckle weakly to myself, eating some microwave popcorn, aka dinner.

"If only I could afford to actually get drunk anymore."

Swallowing my pitiful laugh, I flick the TV off and pull my legs up under my chin on the sofa.

It's been four days since the interview at Poppa's Burgers. And three days since I got rejected. I didn't have high hopes. Waiting tables isn't exactly in my wheelhouse, but I thought they might at least give me a chance.

I was wrong.

They wanted someone with experience in the industry. And I only have experience in one industry. The industry I've been shut out of, seemingly forever.

Shit.

Since that rejection, I've only managed to secure one other interview. And— Shit. My phone beeps. The alarm.

I need to get ready for that interview—even if I don't really want the job. It's as a nightshift concierge at a fancy apartment building, one of those full service ones where half the people are put up by their employers.

Like I'm going to get that.

If I know nothing about waiting tables, I know less about this.

Still, I get dressed and do my makeup the best I can, all the while thinking about how it's all so useless now.

I'm not getting this job. This isn't despondency talking, it's my understanding of the world. I've spent my time outside of school, and inside of it, doing my dues in fashion. Cleaning studios, sewing, tailoring, fetching coffee and the glossy magazines for the so-called talent.

Thing is, I could be a receptionist or personal assistant. My life leading up to my fall from grace in the fashion world gave me the experience for that. I don't even care that I've already paid my dues. That's now dust. I'm not above picking up a magazine or a triple almond nonfat latte made with ethically sourced beans.

But these people won't even hire me for that.

I've been blacklisted.

Valentin finally did by accident what Alex had been trying to do on purpose for years.

Shatter my dreams.

So why do I still feel bad about how I treated him that night in the rain?

Maybe because he got so close I couldn't help but remember the good times we shared. The passion. The tenderness. The warmth.

That's gone now, too.

But, unlike the fashion industry, it still wants me back.

Or did I ruin that, too?

"What am I doing."

Smoothing down the black high-waisted trousers, I step

back, ready to head out. I intend on being early to this stupid interview, no matter my views on it.

A girl needs money to survive, and I'm getting sick of having popcorn for dinner.

My phone starts to buzz as I pack my handbag. Probably one of my friends. Worse, it's probably my bestie, Natalya. She'll know something is up. The others will think I'm just busy, but not Nat.

She knows me. And, she's got a sixth sense when I avoid people. I've just been hoping she's caught up in all her business ventures with her husband, Valentin's big boss, Andrei.

Reason number one I'm in avoiding mode.

But it keeps buzzing.

"Leave me alone," I mutter as it starts to buzz yet again.

I'm too ashamed to speak, and too exhausted to put up any kind of façade to hide my depression from Nat.

Knowing her, she'll ream out Valentin and then he'll turn up and—

And I don't want to deal with any of it.

When it starts to buzz again, I cross my small living room to snatch up my phone so I can turn it off. That's when my eye catches the name on the caller ID.

Kira Arendelle.

My heart skips a beat.

Oh my God. It's the beautiful reporter I met in the lobby at the conference. I almost slide the phone into my bag when something makes me hesitate.

She knew my name.

Chances are she's calling for dirt about the incident with Valentin... but what if she just wants to interview me? Not about Valentin, but about my work? Didn't she say she liked it?

From somewhere deep within a small kernel of hope flares into life.

Could this be the break I'm looking for?

Trying not to let that thought grow wings, I answer the phone.

"Yelena!" Kira's voice chirps over the receiver, maybe a little too perky. Or maybe I'm just hearing things out of my desperation. "So glad to have caught you. I know you're probably swamped. Not sure if you remember me from the fashion conference."

I bite back a sharp retort, and paste on a smile Kira can't see. "Hey Kira, how are you? Of course I remember you, what's up?"

"I was just thinking about how much I enjoyed our short time chatting in that line, and well, I'm wondering if I can interview you for a story I'm doing on young fashion entrepreneurs in the city."

My heart leaps up with a wild yes, but I temper it. "Oh, I'm not sure—"

"The paper will pay you for your time, of course."

Money. God, I need some money.

"When were you thinking?"

"I can do right now, if you can?"

Her eagerness takes me aback.

"I.. I have an appointment, but I'll see what I can do."

That wild, leaping hope is threatening to overtake everything, even as I keep my voice calm and hesitant.

"I understand. Listen, if your schedule frees up tonight, I'm going to be at Diner. It's a really small hole in the wall on the edge of Near North Side and Old Town—"

"I know it."

I don't, but I can find it.

"Great, I'll be there at seven, just having a drink by myself. Stop by if you can?"

"If I can."

There's an awkward silence, then Kira says goodbye. So do I.

When I hang up, I clutch my phone to my chest. There's no holding back. I can't help but give in to the hope that floods my veins. This could be something good. Finally. The beginnings of a new turn in my life.

It's like someone's lifting the heavy shades and instead of a perpetual storm outside, there's light streaming in.

This could be better than good.

It could be huge.

A write up is almost as good as a clean slate, and I can push the agenda of a young, single independent designer who's focused solely on her career. One who's doing it on her own, without the help of the big name investors. The grassroots reinvention of me. And that whole idea fits my line and label.

There are smaller people out there who are into helping newcomers. Suddenly, my world is alight with possibilities and all I need is this article.

I could even paint myself as a brave young woman who escaped an abusive relationship to take the fashion world by storm.

No. Even if it's true, I couldn't drag Alex into this. He would take any opportunity to fuck me over, even if it shed him in a negative light. He's too rich to care about bad press.

And Valentin was never abusive. Not to me, at least.

I'll leave that story on the cutting room floor.

Still, my mind races with other ideas as I check the time and begin to pack up all my best designs, including my business plans and financials.

Screw my job interview. I wasn't going to get it anyway.

But this...

This could finally be the big break I've been dying for.

Diner is quiet, low lit, and full of old world charm with a modern twist.

It's the kind of place that wouldn't even give me an interview, let alone a serving job. But for the first time in a month, I'm not at a restaurant to find work.

I'm here to rebuild my dream.

"Yelena!"

Kira spots me before I see her. She waves me over to her two-person booth, and I try to hold back my big smile.

This is it. I'm finally doing it. And on my own.

"Sorry I'm late," I say, scooting in.

"You're not. Want a drink?"

I opt for water, and we settle down to it. I have to keep my mouth from running wildly as Kira starts out with casual small talk, then eases into more formal questions. She asks why I chose fashion, what I thought of school, and why I quit a big label to go out on my own.

I try to avoid any details on that last one.

I'm still not ready to discuss what happened in Milan. Not publicly, at least.

These things are full of minefields, but I've gotten good at negotiating the waters and slipping around all things explosive. I tell the truth as best I can, and I've got all the generic answers regarding Alex and what he did. That's something I can't open. It's full of grievances that always make the up and comer female look bad.

My word against his.

And, as far as I know, no one else knows what actually happened.

The further under the waters that sinks, the better.

Still, I start getting more comfortable as the night goes on, sinking deeper into my set as I tell Kira about how I really want to take what I've learned and make something new. Something of my own.

"I'm far from street, but I can't be the only one that doesn't want to have to change my whole outfit every time I'm going to a different event. We need something that can easily switch off from streetwear, to club attire, to classy event garments."

Kira nods and makes a note in her pad, even though her phone's sitting on the table as she sips her tea. "I love that idea, to have something that's cool and I can wear anywhere. Even if it's just by a change of shoes."

"It all depends on what it is. You don't need to wear sequins and six-inch heels anymore to dress up, but I love the idea of building it in. Something for everything, as well as things for special occasions. Levels, you know, both in items and styles."

Kira is charming and sweet and so easy to talk to, and I find myself really letting loose with some of my bigger dreams, like one day working with a shoe designer, and to have a look book for customers, one where they can mix and match on the page before they start shopping.

"I mean, haven't you loved a brand before, but wished they did something that wasn't exactly on trend? Something that felt like it was made for you?"

"Made to order?" she asks.

I shake my head. "It's a possibility with 3D printers in the fashion world now, but I was thinking below that, by seeing what people want, we could spot specialized trends before anyone else, or even just for our customer base."

"Like special but also for everyone."

"Exactly."

I show her my designs and she oohs and aahs over them, even flipping through the proposals as well.

Then she sits still for a moment. "This is all great and I think you have a real future. Like I told you before, I've always admired your work, and I swear I want to write about it. But I have to ask—the fight at the conference..."

I freeze.

"I don't know if you heard, but apparently, there was also a body found in one of the bathrooms at the start of the conference. Listen, I'm not throwing accusations around, but I couldn't help but notice your involvement with that very handsome thug. Who is he?"

Panic wraps tight about my throat.

I can't speak. Fuck. How the hell do I get out of this without incriminating myself, without ratting out the Bratva? Valentin?

She looks around and leans in. "Yelena, I think it was mob related. I think the man you were with is in the mob. Someone said he was heard on the phone speaking another language?"

I swallow, already feeling faint.

"Is... is that a crime?"

"Russian. And the Bratva are known in this part of the world."

My mouth's so dry I can barely speak, but I make myself. "How is that a story?"

"A dead body? A man trying to beat another man to death? Russians? Talk of organized crime and threats? How is it not?"

I'm going to hyperventilate. "Why would I know about it? About any of that?"

"You were with him. The hot guy. The thug. You're Russian, aren't you? Is that man your bodyguard? Friend? More? Are you related to the Bratva?"

Everything implodes at her words. I stare at her, face burning, tears blurring my vision.

Kira is too lost in her tale to notice.

"You don't strike me as the type to date the run of the mill thug. And considering he was dressed in exquisite suits that I'm positive were made for him, he had to be connected. The Bratva are making moves and I figured after something that brazen, I'd speak to you."

On legs that don't belong to me, I push back my chair and get to my feet.

"This is not what I came here for," I rasp.

Kira stands up, too. "Yelena, I'm not saying you're involved. Please, believe me. This isn't an interrogation. I'm worried about you."

"No."

I clench my jaw.

This is a nightmare.

Kira isn't interested in me and my work. She's interested in Valentin and the world of trouble that comes with him.

Even if I wanted to, I couldn't tell her anything.

They'd kill me.

The Bratva is ruining my life all over again and I'm nothing more than a fucking idiot who thought someone might actually be interested in what I brought to the table.

I look down at my designs, feeling like an utter fool. I blink rapidly as a few tears escape and a small sob slides free.

"Yelena?"

Christ, I'm an idiot. With shaking, jerking motions I grab my things and shove them into my bag, not caring if something rips. Who cares? All of this shit is useless.

"Yelena. Are you alright?

Kira reaches for me, but I shake her hand off. "I-I have to go."

"No, wait—"

"I can't." I stumble back as Kira frowns, biting her lip, looking for all the world like she really cares. But she doesn't. If she did, if she was concerned, she'd never have gone where she did. "I have to go."

I can't stop saying that and the words tumble out a few more times before I manage to turn my heavy feet around.

Kira hurries around the table and I recoil, nearly knocking the table off its legs. Kira catches it.

"Please," she says, "don't go. I didn't mean to upset you. I thought... it doesn't matter what I thought. Are you okay? Did they threaten you? Do you need help?"

I swallow and hurry to the door, Kira hot on my tail. She catches me as I step out and drags me away from the entrance. "Listen, I can get you help. Protection. I have sources on the police force. Yelena, if you do, please let me know. If I can do anything, I will."

"I thought you wanted to know about my work."

"I do. I want to write about both. Your story is the tie in. The girl who rose from the ashes of that disastrous conference. The fashionista who survived the mob. It's the story of the century. I just need to—"

Another sob breaks free and she tightens her hold for a moment. "Listen, I'll always help someone over getting the story. Screw that thug and screw what I said earlier. Let's go back inside. I'll buy you dinner. I'll get you a cab home. Hell, I'll walk you there myself."

But I shake my head.

Somehow the fact that I believe her makes this all so much worse.

"That guy you're asking about, I don't know him." It's a lie and we both know it. But she doesn't push.

"The reason I'm writing this article—"

"I don't want to know. If you're smart, you'll drop it," I warn her. "Messing with organized crime, with the Bratva, doesn't do anyone any good."

"So you—"

"No, I don't. I've just read stuff, that's all. I wouldn't ever get involved with a criminal and neither should you."

Valentin and his people would kill her if they knew she was poking into their business. I don't even want to know why. And if she's seen talking to me, it's over.

Fuck. In all likelihood, it's already too late. Valentin's probably watching. Or someone from his gang is.

Kira doesn't know the danger she's in.

Then again, maybe she does.

She knows about the dead PI.

This girl's trouble. And the last thing I need is more trouble.

"Goodbye, Kira," I say, holding what's left of me together just long enough to storm into the night.

"Yelena, wait!"

I can feel the papers falling from my bag. I don't care.

My dream is dead.

And soon, everyone involved might be too.

21

"Your computer is a mess, Valentin."

The thump of dance music fills my office at Club Silo247. These walls are supposed to be soundproof, but that's only when the door's shut. And right now, it's wide fucking open. We're waiting on one of my men to show up, and he's taking his sweet time getting here.

"My computer is fine," I say, putting my feet on my desk from the other side. "And don't get too comfortable in my chair. You're far too small for it. You look ridiculous."

Ilya doesn't respond, apart from an eye roll.

He might have a point, my office is a little on the hit-by-a-storm side, but that's only because I'm busy... and no one's allowed to touch a thing in here without my direct permission.

That means no cleaning staff.

Some things in here are too valuable to risk falling into the wrong hands.

Ilya taps away on my computer as I look over his head.

My crest floats above him like a gothic halo.

The skull and viper. Its silver paint gleams, giving it a life of its own. The fresh coat makes it look new.

It isn't.

If you look closely, you can see that it's covered in marks and scars. The marks and scars of history. Of war.

It's been through a lot.

So have I.

With a sigh, I get up and walk behind the desk, tracing the smooth black and silver detail with my fingers. Sometimes, the memory of what it took to get this crest calms me. Other times, it infuriates me.

Right now, I'm somewhere in the middle.

"Ever going to tell me what's in there?" Ilya asks.

Looking over my shoulder, I can see his sharp eyes glancing at my reflection on the computer screen.

"Maybe someday, if you're a good boy."

"You know, I might not do it as much as you, but I can fight, too."

"Is that a challenge?"

"I win and you show me what's in the vault behind that crest."

I consider it for a second, but, "No. We can fight after we figure out this rat problem. Until then, let's keep our eyes on the prize."

"That's no fun."

"No. But it will be rewarding. For you, at least."

The memory of when Andrei handed me the keys to this place and showed me the vault behind the crest is still bright in my head.

I take a deep breath.

I've kept some of the original contents buried deep inside. I split the rest of the contents into different vaults on different properties, including the one at the penthouse near the resort.

The one that Yelena saw.

Fucking hell.

Yelena.

I remember how she felt in that moment. The dark curiosity that came over her. I wanted to share everything, spill my insides out.

Then it all fell apart.

I think about that night in the rain. How badly I screwed up. Her fury. Her desperation. Her sadness.

It's all my fault.

But I'll make up for it. Somehow.

"It's been too long," I mumble, opening the vault. I don't care if Ilya sees what's inside. Someday, this will all be his, I'm sure of it.

But until then...

"What's that?" Ilya asks after I've shut the vault door again.

"I'm not sure," I admit, twirling a black box in my hand.

I still don't know how to open it. All I know is when you hit the side, the front opens and two silver bowls appear, each with a small hole in the center of each, like drains.

Apparently, Andrei knows how to get inside. But he won't tell me. Not until I'm ready, he said.

I guess I'm not ready yet. Because no matter how hard I've tried, it's still impossible to crack.

"Want me to give it a look?" Ilya offers.

"No. This is for me to figure out."

I think the reason I like holding it, like trying to open it, is there's something about it that's almost alive, like it's full of possibilities, some kind of future path that's mine if I can find the right way to reach it.

Recently, since the fucking fashion fiasco, I've been holding it more.

Strangely enough, it feels connected to Yelena in a way I can't explain. Like she'll somehow be the one to help me become ready enough to open it.

Fuck. I must be losing my mind.

"Where is that fucker?"

Putting the box away, I grab my phone and flick through the security footage around Yelena's place. Those are new. I might have gone on a bit of a bender after our little encounter in the rain.

It's for her safety, I tell myself.

And my sanity.

I need to protect her. At this point, it's a compulsion.

Three days ago, one of my men told me about how Yelena met up with a reporter. Left basically in tears.

That's troubling. The fact that she spoke to a reporter is bad enough, but that she left crying too? It took everything I had not to pay that reporter a visit.

That will come.

After I deal with Alex, of course.

But that fucker's been out of the country for the past few weeks. That means I have to show some restraint. As long as he's not sending any more PIs after my girl, I can wait until he gets back before I make him pay for his transgression.

Until then, I have to concentrate on work. Because, without Yelena, that's really all I have.

"Valentin. You there?"

Ilya's voice breaks through my thoughts. I shoot him a look.

"Yeah, I'm right fucking here. What is it?"

He smirks.

"Your recently retired general did his job."

I put my phone down. "Finally, some good fucking news."

"Good news, indeed. I've got access now. And that means results."

"Don't keep me waiting."

Ilya nods and turns back to the computer.

"Our little rat didn't use some super advanced hacking methods, after all." Ilya rubs a hand over the back of his neck. "They did it the old-fashioned way. With a camera."

"A camera?"

"It's deceptively simple, really. Snap pics of the screen, and then wipe a whole series of paths clean. All without downloading anything. And it's nearly impossible to find."

"They sent selfies to the FBI?"

"Well, no. Selfies are when you take a picture of yourself. Not when—"

"You understood what I fucking meant."

"I did. I did. But did you understand me when I said what they did made them nearly impossible to find?"

"Nothing is impossible for the great Ilya Rykov."

"Correct. I tracked it. Took some doing, as they jumped through some servers to get the info into FBI hands. Seems our rat didn't want to talk to the FBI."

"Who does." I tap my hand on the table and look at the computer's screen. Ilya has brought up a map. A location is already marked. "Where is that?"

He pauses for dramatic effect.

"A computer store in Little Italy."

We look at each other and I whistle low. "I fucking knew it."

"You really think the Italians would be this stupid?"

"I think they'd be this arrogant. But there's only one way to find out."

"What are you going to do?"

Stupid question. I take out my gun and make sure it's loaded. "Seriously?"

"Thought I'd ask."

I look at him. "Interested in a road trip?"

Ilya grins.

"Thought you'd never ask."

I pull on my suit jacket and grab a second weapon, check the clip situation and holster it. But before I move to the door, I take a second to check my phone—because no matter what else is happening, she's always on my mind.

"Be good, angel," I murmur, taking a quick look at the security feed around her apartment. It looks like she's still at home. And with the perimeter, I've set up around the area, she should be safe.

"What's the hold-up?" Ilya asks from the doorway.

"Don't worry about it," I say, putting my phone away. "Call Andrei and tell him shit just got real. We're having Italian for dinner tonight."

Ilya's smile is almost too big for his face.

"Aye aye, captain."

22

My life is over.

I turn in the bed and pull the covers over my head. It's about all I can manage.

I can't believe I thought I could make it as a designer. Just like I can't believe I thought Kira was interested in me and my designs, instead of Valentin and the Bratva.

It's been three days, maybe four, since I saw Kira. Since the bottom fell from my world. Again.

No one tells you how depression seeps into your pores and invades your bones, making them heavy. No one tells you how everything goes numb.

How you can't help but focus on the one thing that ever made you feel good, no matter how bad it was for you.

Valentin.

He's everywhere. In my dreams, my thoughts, my blood.

And I hate myself for wanting him.

It's almost physical. The one thing that penetrates the numbness.

The monster under my bed. Bane of my existence.

The only touch I need.

I'm so weak to want him. So pathetic. It only makes me feel worse.

Maybe I just need to purge him from my mind.

At least, that's what I tell myself as I slide my hand down over my stomach until I reach my panties.

Tears stroll down my cheeks as I start to stroke myself, thinking of him. But my touch isn't enough to mimic his strong, steady hands.

With a deep breath and a tightness in my throat, I roll on my side and open the bedside drawer. The vibrator is stuffed beneath used tissues and old phone cords. It feels heavy in my hands.

"I should have thrown you out ages ago."

But I've never been able to manage. It's one of those rabbit vibrators, a joke gift from Natalya. I've barely used it in the past. But over these past few days, it's sat in my bedside drawer like a tempting drug.

I finally give in.

Pushing down my panties, I set the vibrator into place and think of how Valentin fingered me. How he dragged me all over that penthouse, playing with my body.

He was in complete control, and it was amazing.

I try to let the vibrator recreate that experience.

It hums against my clit, filling me with a warmth that I can't help compare to the real thing.

It doesn't compare, but any bit of heat will do. My world's cold. I need a fire.

Closing my eyes, I slide the tip into my hole. It's tiny compared to Valentin's thick cock, but the sensation is enough to let me pretend.

I picture his deep blue eyes. His hard muscles. His dark tattoos. I find comfort in the image, in the memory of how he held me so powerfully, yet so tenderly.

Then, I think about our last encounter.

Out in the empty streets, alone under the rain. A different kind of heat rises from my core. Hot flames flicker up from between my legs. My back arches. I sigh.

The darkness seems so inviting. But not any darkness. His darkness. A darkness we can only fill together.

I should have let him take me, right then and there. Then, maybe, I could have kicked this habit...

"Valentin." His name is on my lips as my hips start to sway. I remember how his hot cum felt on my back. Our ghostly silhouettes strewn across the glass of his penthouse window. The rhythm of his thrusts. The strength in his hands.

"Valentin!"

I explode.

The warmth spreads, then recedes. This was no substitute.

If I'm going to quit Valentin, I might need to get one last taste of the real thing.

No! a lazy voice croaks from somewhere inside me. *Be strong.*

But I'm sick of being strong. It's gotten me nothing but misery.

I toss the vibrator from my hand, and it buzzes on the floor, rattling the cheap, rickety wood until I can't take it anymore.

But when I turn over, I realize the vibrator's off.

It's my phone that's causing the commotion.

I don't even want to check. But something drags me across the bed. An alert for an email pops up on my screen. **High Importance,** it says, still buzzing.

"What could possibly be more important than this?" I sarcastically mumble.

But when I open the email, my breath catches in my throat.

It's from Pierre Olivier. A well-known investor in the fashion industry. And a rival of Alex's.

No. Don't even dare to hope.

My mind searches for excuses. Instead, I can only

remember the last time I saw Pierre. It was when I was still with Alex. He had crowed about how I was going places and how he had me and my career in his hands. Later that night, we had a blow-out fight because I told him didn't appreciate how he made me sound like his whore and personal pet project. We eventually sorted it but that, for me, was the beginning of the end of us.

I wipe away the tears drying on my cheek and read the email.

Yelena,

I'm sorry I missed the conference and meeting you properly, and I'm also sorry it took a turn for the worse before I could.

But I love your designs. I got a peek at the look book you brought to the event and I'd love to meet up with you to discuss a deal. Call me at your convenience. Any time works.

Pierre.

I read it again and again, hands shaking. This can't be real, right? It's got to be a dream from my fevered mind. A trick.

Yeah, that's it.

I'm being fooled.

I'm seconds away from deleting the email and throwing my phone next to the vibrator. But something stops me.

Desperation.

I'm hooked on Valentin. And right now, I need him, in more ways than one.

The only way to wean myself off of his memory, is to make memories of my own. Memories that he's not in. Good memories.

Could tonight be one of those good memories in the making?

Careful, I tell myself. *Remember what happened last time you dared to have hope.*

I remember all too well.

But what's the worst that can happen? If I take this chance, and it's another dud, then I'm just back here, right where I already am.

What else do I have to lose?

With a deep sigh, I click "Respond to email".

Hi Pierre—would love to chat about working together. Let me know when and where. Yelena.

I hit send and collapse back on the bed, already exhausted from my inner conflict.

But Pierre's response is lightning quick, and it comes in as a text.

Tonight, 8pm. Petit Agneau. It's Pierre btw.

Holy hell. He's just named one of the fanciest restaurants in the greater Chicago area. It's also just outside of the city limits, beyond where public transport can take you. And I can't afford to take a cab.

No. You can't afford not to take a cab. You need to get there, Yelena. Scrounge up your designs and get there!

If I say no or suggest somewhere close to me, then he'll think I can't afford it, and while that's more than true, no one of his caliber wants to work with the desperate or the broke. I need to look and act successful.

He must not know the gory details of what happened at Sweetwater, or maybe he does, and it was just worse in person.

I need to take advantage of that.

Whatever I have to do, I'll do. I go and grab my computer and pull up Google maps. I'll find a way.

Fingers shaking, I text him back.

See you there.

I leave so early I barely have time to shower, do my hair and makeup up and choose the right outfit. One of my own, obviously, and though I've designed a lot of my line to go from street to nightlife, this is one occasion where I need to put on heels. But those I drop in my bag.

Three buses and some good old-fashioned pavement pounding later, I'm at the restaurant. A lush suburban house with faux Colonial vibes that has been turned into a sprawling destination restaurant with beautiful grounds. I thank the Google gods and my phone's ability to lead me here without any wrong turns as I rest against a nearby window and change shoes.

I finish my walk in the three inch heels. Just in time too. It's started to rain.

If the front of house is shocked I'm not pulling up in a car or being dropped off by a service, they don't say a word, just lead me inside.

And it takes all I have to keep my Queen B façade in place. I'm all about faking it until you make it, and in here—unlike at the conference when I thought I had a chance—I'm pulling out the stops to hide the beaten-up ego inside and the uncertainty that hounds each step.

I'm not a quitter, no matter how much wallowing I've done.

In the past things haven't worked out.

But at some point, things have to change for me. And this could be it.

Finally.

No. It has to be.

I give my name, and as I'm led to the table in the classy, romantic and dimly lit restaurant, I feel better with each step.

"Hello there, darling."

Pierre Olivier is even more handsome than I remember. Older than Valentin—and if I stood them side by side this man would fade into the wallpaper—but I'm not here to compare. I'm here for work.

He stands and pulls out a seat for me.

"Thank you, Mr. Olivier," I say, sitting down.

"My pleasure," he smiles, joining me.

I'm not sure why I'm sitting next to him, but I try not to think about it too much. Maybe there will be others joining us later. I shift in my seat, trying to get comfortable enough to keep my bright, friendly, professional smile in place.

"Glad you could join me on such short notice."

"How could I resist the great Pierre Olivier?" I smother on the charm. "I've got—"

"Wine good for you?" he interrupts. "I took the liberty of ordering an eighty-six pinot noir. It's light enough to go with most things." He winks, touching my arm. "I don't believe in the red and white thing for meat or fish; it's about the lightness of the wine, and there are light reds and heavy whites."

I swallow down misgivings. "Oh, that's fine, anything really. I thought—"

"We can wait to talk shop. It seems a shame to waste such a special atmosphere. I've ordered the tasting menus for us. Everything here is exquisite ,and it's a lovely way to get a feel of what Petit Agneau has to offer."

"Okay, but I've got an early appointment tomorrow."

He laughs, waves his hand and the low light catches on his wedding ring. The sight of it eases my misgivings. Besides, in this industry, most meetings involve booze and fancy dinners. I'm just not used to one-on-ones yet.

Maybe everything is like this.

Our first dish arrives quickly enough, and we make small talk until Pierre straightens his back.

"Did you ever think of becoming a model, Yelena?" His gaze lingers on my mouth then drops lower before coming back up as he refills his glass.

"I'm too short, and that side of fashion never appealed to me. I'd rather design the clothes than display them."

He comes in close, holding a forkful of lamb on jus-drenched potatoes up to my mouth. I'm given no option but to take a bite. "Pity, you're very pretty, you should be on display..."

My stomach flips in the wrong way. A greasy, hard slap of unease. The delicious food I'm chewing on loses all taste.

"I... uh... thank you."

The night continues on like that, with Pierre sitting a little too close, refilling my glass, complimenting me and my work. And yet each time I try and turn things to business, he changes the subject.

Dessert can't come soon enough. By then, I feel like I've been here five hours instead of two and we haven't discussed my work. At all.

The desperation has its hooks in deep, and I pull the look book out, along with the five year business plan I have. I place them in front of Pierre, ready to put my foot down.

"Yelena, we're having so much fun."

Fun is the last word I'd use, but I just smile and nod. "Yes, but I did come all this way to discuss an investment, and I wanted to show you my business plan."

Without touching the look book, he picks up the business plan and folds it into his jacket's inside pocket.

That horrible fear grips me again. I can't let this go, I can't. "I do have other offers." The lie comes easy and he just smiles.

"I'm sure you do. Hmm..." He finally flicks open the first page of the look book. "You're very talented, but I never realized quite how young and inexperienced you are."

"Which means I've got a long career in front of me."

"I guess I can discuss it with my partners."

It's slipping away, all of it, and... God, I can't let it.

"Please, Pierre," I say. "I know I can convince you to take a chance with me. I promise you won't regret it."

"It's not me, Yelena, darling. It's my partners who need convincing." He checks the expensive watch on his wrist, a

Piguet. "It's still early. I can take you to them, and you can work your magic."

I glance at my phone. It's 10pm, not exactly an ideal time for any sort of business meeting, but then again, this isn't official.

Shit.

A cold, heavy weight slides down my spine.

I know this is suspicious. I know this is wrong. But I'm desperate and he's not exactly a stranger. He's a well-known businessman who reached out to me.

Remember what happened in Milan, a voice comes from the back of my mind.

I shove it away.

I'm here *because* of what happened in Milan. Even if it wasn't my fault, I need to rectify it.

Pierre's not exactly asking me to strip naked. He's offering to let me plead my case.

I take a breath. "I'm more than happy to set something up tomorrow."

He sighs. "Wish that I could, Yelena, but two of them leave tomorrow for a month in Europe, and earlier they told me about a couple of other young designers. Right before you showed up."

"It's late," I say, hesitating. "Maybe we could do a zoom call?"

"Sure we could, and we could leave it until they return but," He shrugs. "It's risky. And I'm sure if they meet you, you'll get your deal."

I know better than to get in a car with a man I don't know, even one as well-known as Pierre Olivier. But I'm also pretty sure that Valentin is still having me followed. He's too controlling not to do that. And he'd never let anything bad happen to me, right? After all, the man followed me to a job interview, no way would he didn't have me followed here, too.

The coldness at the base of my spine spreads.

Still, I open my mouth and I can only say one thing.

"Alright. Let's do it."

At the very least, I'll get a ride back to Chicago.

Pierre instantly calls for the bill, and the next thing I know, we're out front, hiding from the heavy rain under an awning, as the valet pulls up.

The staff hold umbrellas over our heads as we walk out. It's gotten cold enough that I can see my breath.

"My dear," Pierre smiles, opening the back door for me.

I swallow my anxiety and dip inside.

Pierre's car is more lush than Valentin's. The inside is like a small limousine, with two long seats that face each other. He slips in next to me, telling his driver to take us the long way to Old Town.

Then he presses a button and the partition goes up.

I try to breathe calmly.

"Thank you for the opportunity," I say. "You don't know what it means."

He slides his arm along the back of the seat. "I'm about to find out exactly how thankful you are. And how much it means to you."

Pierre rests his hand on my thigh.

I shift, crossing my legs. "I have a lot of ideas and—"

"Sweet thing…" He pushes my leg down and slides his hand up, brushing against my panties as he hooks one of his legs over mine. The hand on the back of the seat comes down to my shoulder, diving into the loose top. "I don't give a fuck about your ideas."

"Pierre!"

I try to pull away and he grabs my wrist.

"Come on, Yelena. You know the deal. You did it with Civati, I'm actually offering to invest in exchange for what's under that dress. Fuck me, keep fucking me, and you've got a deal. It's a no-brainer."

For a moment, I'm completely paralyzed. Then, a flash of red-hot rage bursts out from somewhere deep inside of me.

"Fuck off!" I shout, shoving Pierre off.

He grits his teeth and shifts back to me. "Don't do something stupid, girl. I know—"

I slap his mouth shut.

"I'm not having sex with you," I heave.

Pierre just stares off into space, his hand rubbing against his red cheek.

"Then we're done," he finally says, straightening his tie. With my hand print seared into his face, Pierre pushes a button and the partition lowers. "Pull over."

The car does just that. Pierre looks at me, opening the door. "Last chance for you to spread your legs or wrap those lips tight about my cock. If I'm honest, after all that, you'd probably have to do both. We're talking a lot of money, and you're a risk now. So I expect you to whore your heart out to me and some of my friends. Or you can get out and walk home. And lose this deal."

My body burns with shame and anger. "I'll walk."

"Have it your way."

He stares as I struggle my way out of the car. The second my feet hit the ground, Pierre slams the door shut and the car screeches off.

Cold rain pounds down from the black sky. All I can do is watch as the tail lights disappear into the distance.

On the horizon, I can just barely make out the Chicago skyline through the haze. My breath turns to smoke in front of my face, obscuring it even further.

I shiver, already soaked.

"Things could be worse," I try to tell myself, just as a monstrous roar of thunder rips through the night sky. "Fuck."

I try to ignore the tears pushing at me as I kick off my heels and do the only thing I can do.

Start walking.

I can only hope I make it somewhere warm before the hypothermia sets in.

23

VALENTIN

Heads are going to fucking roll.

I speed through the rain, racing toward Yelena's last known location. Fuck, of all the times for me to back off with physical surveillance.

I tear around a truck in front of me, not caring if I'm breaking the speed limit. Let a cop try to pull me over.

Fucking hell.

When I checked my phone earlier, I thought there must have been a mistake. What the hell would Yelena be doing on a lonely stretch of road just outside of the city?

At first, I thought it was a glitch. So, I got Ilya to take a look. He's the one who pointed out the obvious.

There was no mistake. Yelena was stranded out in the rain, slowly making her way back to Chicago.

Walking. At this hour. In this weather.

Something had to be wrong.

I grip the wheel, flip the indicator, and overtake another car.

It's been a hell of a few days, and I needed to take care of shit tonight, so I didn't see her location until it was too late.

But my men should have fucking warned me.

Though, I guess they did. Sort of.

I knew that Yelena was going outside of the city. I heard that she was tracked to a pretentious French restaurant in the sticks. I figured it had to do with business.

Then, someone told me the name of the place.

Petit Agneau.

I'd heard of it before.

It's not a place you take a client.

It's where you take a date.

That had been enough for me to slam off my phone and fill my eyes with fire.

She wasn't just trying to move on. She was trying to move on without me.

Then, when my killing spree was over, I couldn't help but check up on her again. Part of me was hoping she was at a nice apartment. Somewhere I could break in to. But she wasn't.

Instead, she was on the side of the road. Slowly trudging through the darkness and the rain and the cold.

She was in trouble.

The thought stabs through my chest like an icepick as I switch lanes and turn at the next exit, heading to where she is.

If anything's happened to her. If she's hurt…

Blood's going to spill.

I look down at my phone. I'm close. It shouldn't be much longer until…

"Yelena!"

I see her, finally, a huddled thing plodding along the side of the road, head down, soaked to the bone. Even as I pull up beside her, I can feel the misery radiating off her tiny figure. It fucking kills me.

"It's just me," I say as I open the door to get out. I don't want her spooked. I don't want her here, but a sixth sense tells me to go easy on the fallen angel.

She doesn't respond or turn, but her shoulders start to shake and she might as well reach into me and rip out my heart right there and then.

"Hey." I ease her wet body into my arms and she clings to me, going boneless. "You're all right. I'm here."

I don't really know if she wants me here, but I'm sure as fuck not going to leave her. I hold her in the rain, running my fingers down her spine, rocking her gently, and speaking soothing words to her in Russian.

I tell her she's safe, she's mine, she's a good girl, the best. I tell her I'll take care of her forever and keep the other demons at bay. A demon to ward off all the others. I tell her she's beautiful, smart, talented. Special. And when she stops her silent tears and her shoulders calm, I kiss the top of her head.

"Teper' ty v bezopasnosti, malyshka." *You're safe now, little one.*

When I manage to get her in the passenger seat, I don't immediately drive off. Instead, we just sit in the car, in silence, the heater running to help her dry out, to warm her frozen bones, and I don't say another word.

I grip the wheel so tightly it's a miracle it doesn't snap, and I wait for her to speak.

"Thank you," she whispers. "I... I was so stupid."

I swallow, count to five slowly. "You're far from stupid, angel. What happened?"

"An investor asked me to talk over dinner and..." She stops, takes a deep audible breath as her hands ball up into fists. "But he just wanted to sleep with me."

Extreme violence, that's what I want to inflict on this man. Anger surges. "Name?"

"Valentin. No."

"I just want to know who it is."

"You'll hurt him."

I cut her a look. "Is that a problem?"

"Yes. Valentin, violence isn't always the only answer."

I disagree. But I can save it for later. Once she's settled and safe.

"Okay," I say as gently as I can. "No bloodshed." For now.

Yelena closes her eyes and settles in her seat. I want to ask her more questions, to get to the bottom of this, to get her revenge. But I know an interrogation is the last thing she needs.

She needs to know she can relax with me.

So, I wait.

Putting the car into gear, I start driving. We'll head to my main residence in Lincoln Park. She'll be comfortable there.

"I should have known, Valentin. I should have been smarter."

"It's alright, angel."

"It wasn't a date, I swear."

"Whatever happened, it's not your fault."

"It is." Her hands clench and unclench and clench again. "Because I ignored all the warning bells, like I always do. I guess me being drawn to assholes, the only men I've ever dated, makes me an idiot."

I want to say something. Anything. All sorts of words press at my lips but none of them seem right. So I stay silent.

Ten minutes later, we're in the city.

"I'm taking you to my place, Yelena. Not to do anything. Just so I know you're safe. We can talk, or not, and there are plenty of rooms. You don't have to sleep in the same one as me. Best of all, I have a big fireplace to help warm you up."

She laughs but it's a sad sound. "I could use a nice fire."

"No jumping in," I say, trying to pick up her mood a little.

"No promises."

Her sigh is like a knife to my heart.

I failed her.

It won't happen again.

"How are you feeling?"

"I'll live." Her voice breaks and she swipes at her eyes. "I guess I've felt unsafe for so long that it's almost a part of me."

"Because of men?"

She sighs. "This isn't the first time something like this has happened, the reason I got fired in Milan was because one of the company's higher ups tried to sleep with me and I said no. He killed my career."

A small growl escapes my throat.

"I wasn't dating him, but he was another asshole who invaded my life. That's how the industry is. That's how life is. I should have known it was bound to happen. I should have played it safe with the money I'd made. Losing that job took me from riches to rags in an instant. But if I hadn't put myself in that position, I..." She shakes her head. "I probably wouldn't have been desperate enough to have a meeting like this one."

"People do it all the time."

"People in the Bratva, maybe. People like you."

"I hate to break it to you, angel. But everyone in this world is like me to some extent. I'm just the best at it."

We near my street and Yelena unclenches her hand, taking in the opulence of the neighborhood, with its garden filled lawns and sprawling mansions.

"I should run from you, too, Valentin. You're everything I hate. The Bratva offers shiny things, sweet deals, but they come at a cost. The Bratva... they... they stabbed my father in the back. We lost everything. He was just a businessman who wanted to expand, and the Bratva, they... they might as well have killed him themselves. They ruined him. He was so ashamed. A shell of the man I idolize. He tried so hard, but the debts were too much. And my mom was so sick. The Bratva didn't have to get their hands dirty. He took his own life. My mother died a few years later."

Just like that, it all makes sense. Her resistance, her shame, her conflict.

My heart grows heavy.

"How old were you?"

"Ten."

I almost want to sigh with relief, but that would be distasteful. "That was the old guard, angel. The old empire. Corrupt and riddled with loyalty problems. You know Andrei. And Natalya." And me. "They wouldn't—"

"Bratva is Bratva. The mob. Organized crime."

"We're not the same as they were," I assure her. "We're the new guard. The Zherdev Bratva prides itself on loyalty and building strong relationships in the community. We don't cheat civilians. We empower them. It's the criminals we threaten. Only the criminals."

And once in a while, a stubborn old general.

Yelena shakes her head. "It's not safe. *You're* not safe. And yet..." She swallows and glances down at her hands as I type in the gate's code on my phone. The ornate iron barrier opens. "I feel safe with you."

My heavy heart suddenly feels as light as a feather.

"Because you know the truth."

Yelena looks at me as I pull into the garage. "What truth?"

"That I'll keep you safe. I don't care for most people, Yelena. But the people I care for are the people I'd kill for. Die for. You're one of those people, angel, whether you like it or not." I lean over and touch her cheek. "So, I'll be your shadow, your cloak, your armor. Protector. You'll always be safe with me. I promise."

My staff have left the fireplace burning and retired to their quarters. I don't have more than a housekeeper and a few guards here full-time, and I wouldn't even have that if Andrei hadn't put his foot down when I bought the house.

Stop being so stubborn, he'd said. Let a few warm bodies into your life. *It won't kill you.*

How wrong he was. Because I've got the warmest body in the world in my living room, and I feel just about ready to die.

"Easy now, angel," I say, helping her to the bathroom.

She's shaking so bad I have to help her strip down, but there's nothing sexual about it. I don't even stare. I just take her hand and lead her into the shower. Then, I turn the shower on and look away.

Part of me still wants to climb in with her, scrub down her skin and wash away every part of her that bastard touched. But I know that's not what she needs. Yelena needs a modicum of autonomy, to feel she can stand on her own two feet. Some privacy to get herself together.

So I give it to her.

I take her clothes and dump them in the laundry, then I go upstairs to my room and raid my closet. A long sleeved T-shirt and boxers are all I have that will fit her. I take them down and leave them on the bed, forcing myself to retreat.

The pattering of the shower filters through to the wide hall as I go into the kitchen where I heat up some soup left for me by the housekeeper. Simple and hearty chicken barley loaded with vegetables. I know she ate, but at least this is wholesome and maybe it'll help calm her.

I don't know. I'm at a loss for what to do. This isn't my wheelhouse. Nurture is foreign to me.

But she needs it, so that's what I'll do.

When the soup's heated, I cover it with a protective lid and carry it out to the living room to set it on the coffee table. Then I kneel on the big rug and tend to the fire, feeding it another log of wood.

I know she's behind me before she says a word.

"Valentin?"

Turning, I rise slowly, trying to breathe. She looks so vulnerable and bruised.

Not physically but her aura. I want to mend her.

But I stay where I am.

For Yelena's sake, I need to be gentle. I need to be patient.

But that doesn't mean I'll hesitate for a second longer. Hesitating is what put her in danger. I let her flutter in the wind.

Easy pickings for the sharks and bottom feeders out there.

So no more fucking hesitating about our relationship.

I want her. I need her. And I will protect her at all costs.

"There's soup." I gesture to the coffee table.

She nods and walks slowly over, perching on the edge of my whiskey-colored suede sofa. "This place is beautiful."

I shrug. "It's home."

She takes a sip of the soup and a calmness comes over her. "It's delicious."

"Eat it up, angel. I can get more when you're done."

I keep my distance as she finishes the soup. Then, I let her digest it all in silence.

That silence lingers until I can't control myself anymore.

"Yelena. You need to tell me his name."

She shakes her head, gaze desperate, despondent. "No. I shouldn't…"

"I can find out on my own," I say softly. "Call the restaurant, go through the names, describe you. But I'd rather hear it from you."

Her shoulders shudder. Her head dips. "Pierre Olivier."

The flames in the fireplace are nothing compared to the red-hot anger I feel inside. But I keep it contained in front of her.

"I know him." I nod to the bowl. "Eat your soup. There are throws and pillows in a basket between the sofa and armchair. There's also a wet bar in the back of the room, in case you want water or soda… or something stronger. Be here when I return."

Her eyes grow big. "You're leaving?"

"That's right."

"Why?"

"Why do you think?" I spread my hands. My gun's loaded but I'm thinking of using a knife. "I'm going to kill that motherfucker."

24

YELENA

"You're still awake."

Valentin's words are soft as I sit up from my spot on the sofa. I haven't been able to shut my eyes since he left. Instead, I've been watching the flames twist and dance, their pops and hissing crackles somehow soothing.

"I couldn't sleep."

I turn and he's in the doorway, taking up so much room. The coat and vest he left in are gone. His holster hangs from his shoulder.

He's covered in blood.

I try to find it in me to be disgusted, to be afraid.

But I can't. It's not there.

All I feel is the warmth this fire couldn't provide. His warmth.

"What did you do?"

He half smiles, his gaze intense. "Don't worry about it, angel. Just know, Pierre Olivier won't be bothering you ever again... or anyone."

"You killed him?"

His eyes flash as he drops the holster and kicks off his

shoes. "By the end, he was begging me for death. I gave it to him. But only because he asked. With his last breath, I made him understand consent."

Unbuckling his belt, Valentin reveals a bundle of clothes that he had hanging from his backside. I instantly recognize the outfit. Pierre's. The same one he wore to dinner.

It's soaked in even more blood than Valentin's clothes.

"Why... why did you bring those here?" I ask.

"To feed the fire. To warm you up."

He walks by me and tosses the items in the fireplace. The flames spark, licking up the chimney. A new wave of flickering heat fills the living room.

I watch in awe as Valentin strips down to his briefs. His massive silhouette practically steaming against the orange fire.

"You still look cold, angel. Come, join me by the fire."

It's like I'm in a dream. There's no resistance. I float over to him. The next thing I know, I'm lying on the floor next to the man who just killed for me. Again.

This time is different, though.

I hold onto him like a life preserver, sinking into the hellfire he stokes for me. His body is hard and damp from sweat, but the longer we lie there, the smoother his comforting skin becomes.

It all evaporates in the heat. Everything.

Including my need to keep him at arm's length.

"Easy there, angel. You've had a rough night." Valentin stays stiff as I hug him from behind, burrowing my face in his broad, tattoo-filled back.

"You... you've made it better," I sigh. There's a sadness in me that won't quit. It comes from the knowledge that I can't do it all on my own. The world is too dark and mean. But something else rises above the sad black mud. A new knowledge. One that shines a soft white light over all the sadness.

I'm not alone.

Valentin is here. And if I give him the chance, he always will be.

"Thank you," I whisper, gently kissing his back.

He turns around, those giant hands caressing my jaw.

"No. Thank you, angel."

"For what?"

"For giving me something real to fight for."

He kisses me so tenderly that I swear my lips melt. Hot tears of relief streak down my cheeks. He soaks them up in his rugged shadow.

"I'm so alone," I quietly sob.

"No. Not anymore. You won't ever be alone again, angel. I promise."

My weak hands lift to take his face. I kiss him back, tasting the salt of my tears on his lips.

"I'm so tired."

"Then, let's go to bed."

Valentin starts to rise, but I place my hands on his wrists and use what little strength I have to keep him here. "No. Please. Let's stay here. By the fire. Together."

"As you wish, princess."

For a while, we just drift off in each other's arms. Then, for some reason, I start kissing him again. It's an unconscious desire. A dreamlike passion. It starts slow, then picks up speed.

I push myself into him so hard it feels like I could slip under his skin, and I can feel that he wants to do the same with me.

Instead, he forces himself to be gentle. He caresses me with caring hands as we entangle into a sighing, moaning web of flesh and need.

"Not tonight, angel," Valentin whispers. "You've been through enough."

"Make it all worth it," I silently plead. "Please."

Slowly, his resistance melts away too.

The fire rages behind us as we start to sweat. But the slickness of our skin just makes us hold onto each other tighter. The warmth in my core billows up. Valentin's briefs come off.

Then, he's inside of me, and everything that felt wrong feels so right. So perfect.

My soreness evaporates in the heat. My sorrow too.

We sway against each other, moans growing as the pleasure builds. Then, I'm over the hill. Dipped beneath the searing waves. The warmth spreads out, filling me with relief.

Valentin pulls out just in time to spray his relief on the warm carpet.

This time, I don't feel any emptiness after the act, only satisfaction.

Whatever I was before, whatever he was, it all burns up in the fire. Something new rises from the ashes. Something that doesn't belong to either one of us.

This special feeling isn't his or mine.

It's ours.

I wake up to the familiar buzzing of a phone.

It doesn't ring for long, though. The moment Valentin's eyes open, he turns over, switches it off, and throws it across the room.

I must drift off again, because the next thing I know, I'm startled awake by what sounds like a doorbell.

Booming knocks echo through the house as Valentin grunts and finally sits up.

"Fucking hell. He rolls away from me and goes to a small unit on the wall near the door. "Andrei is here."

The peace surrounding us shatters.

"Does that mean Natalya might be—"

"No. It's just Andrei and some of our men."

A small sigh of relief escapes me. I couldn't face Natalya right now. Not after all I've kept from her.

I look over to the smoldering fire. Little wisps of smoke billow up from the ashes. Without Valentin next to me, I'm starting to feel cold again.

"Do you think it's serious?" I ask, hoping that they might go away if we ignore them.

"If Andrei's showing up in person, it's probably very serious. It takes a lot to drag him away from his family these days."

To my dismay, Valentin starts picking his clothes up from the floor. I can't help but feel a little hurt as he gets dressed.

I know he's Bratva, and I know that's something I have to come to terms with if anything is to come of this.

But now?

When we've found each other? When we're exploring our private bliss?

His job is more important?

Even in my head I sound like a petulant child.

Yet I can't help it.

He doesn't come to me and kiss me before he leaves. In fact, it almost feels like he's forgotten I exist as he pulls on his shoes and presses a button on the wall.

He starts speaking through the intercom in rapid Russian.

"Wait here, angel. I'll be right back."

He doesn't wait for a response. A second later, he's gone.

A chill fills the room. I shiver and reach for my discarded clothes. My skin is sticky. I'm cold. Valentin is gone.

I decide to find a shower.

Slipping on my dress, I pull myself onto my feet and start looking. It doesn't take long before I find a set of stairs. I take them up and then start walking down a winding hall.

But this place is like a maze, and I quickly find myself back at the top of a different set of stairs.

That's when I hear the voices.

They rise up from below. One of them clearly belongs to Valentin. I crouch down, peering through the railings to get a better look.

At the bottom of the steps is a large sweeping foyer. Massive mirrors fill up the walls on either side. Looking at the left one, I can just make out the reflection of what must be the front door.

Valentin is standing inside, while a group of men stand just outside. I instantly recognized one of those men as Andrei Zherdev. Natalya's husband. Leader of the Bratva. And, apparently, Valentin's best friend.

Their deep voices echo through the sprawling foyer, and I already know where this is going. They have work to do. Valentin is going to leave me here all alone.

"Of course," I whisper.

I know I should walk away, but something keeps me frozen in place. I strain to listen.

"Okay," I just barely make out Valentin say. "Thanks for the heads up. Now, get out. I've got things to do."

"Things or women?" asks an accented voice.

"Don't make me ruin your pretty face, Ilya. It's all you have going for you."

"Don't forget my brains."

"I'll smash those in too."

Without waiting for another response, Valentin slams the door shut.

My heart starts to race as I watch his reflection turn and start to come my way. I start to scramble back, like I'm afraid to be caught doing something I shouldn't, but before I can even straighten back out, Valentin has spotted me.

"Yelena," he smiles. "Glad to see you up."

I take a breath and pat down my crinkled dress. "Are you busy?"

"I'm always busy, angel."

My heart beats fast and I don't know if I can bear being cast aside right now. "I can leave, if you need me to."

He frowns. "No. That won't do." Stepping up the stairs, he offers me his hand. "Come with me."

I'm led through the maze of his mansion like a feather on a string until we turn into a sprawling office.

"Wow," I gasp, looking up at the bookshelves that reach to the ceiling. I would have never pegged Valentin for a reader.

"It's not much," he chuckles. "Now, sit here."

We walk around a giant mahogany desk and Valentin sits down in a big leather chair. Then, he softly yanks at my arm, pulling me onto his lap.

"What are you doing?"

"Work."

He opens up the desktop and starts typing in passwords.

"I won't be a distraction?"

"No, angel. You'll make it all worthwhile."

I let myself sink into his chest as he clicks away at the keyboard. I try my best to stay silent, but the rapid-fire images and documents popping up on his screen are impossible to ignore. My interest piques.

"What are you doing?" I ask.

"Checking documents and evidence."

"Evidence for what?"

"Anything. We have a problem we're working on, but right now... here I'll show you how we track strangers—persons of interest to us—using information from police servers."

"You have access to police servers?"

Of course he does.

"All thanks to a newly retired general," Valentin smiles. "He was so kind as to help us in this important matter."

My breath catches at that. I can read between lines. Forced to help. And perhaps something shows on my face because Valentin says, "Don't worry, angel. He isn't a good man. Cheats on his wife. He got us access to these servers in exchange for our discretion. With his help, I might just be able to crack the code. Spot a pattern... something like this."

I watch as Valentin clicks through countless files and documents. It's all a whirlwind to me, but the importance behind it isn't lost on me.

Valentin's letting me into his world the only way he knows how, through his work. This is his opening up. Exposing himself.

Valentin-style.

It makes my heart swell.

Resting his hands for a moment, Valentin nuzzles my neck. "If you had the strength last night to stop from doing what I did to Pierre, would you have?"

"I'm not ready for that question.

"I don't know."

"Yes, you do, angel."

It's like he's trying to figure out if I can really hack it in his world.

"I... I mean, there are so many men like him in the world. We can't just go around killing them all."

"Watch me."

I can't help but laugh.

"Revenge. Wrath. Those are nice thoughts, but really, it's success that makes the best story."

"You'll get there."

I sigh.

"Will I, though?"

Valentin turns me so I'm facing him, thighs spread now over his lap as he holds me by the hips. "Sure, your dreams are a little dented—"

"Dashed."

"Dented," he corrected. "You're too talented to put yourself at the mercy of animals and those who don't respect you." He runs a hand over my wrinkled dress. "Who else could have invented an outfit like this? One day, it's going to take the world by storm. *You* are going to take the world by storm. Just like you took my world by storm."

"Maybe in my dreams."

He kisses me softly. "Time passes, angel, and don't worry about money. I'm here. I'll always support you." This time, his kiss is harder. "Even if you're too stubborn to accept that at times. I am your mountain that can't be moved."

His words are sweet, but they still leave a faint bitter taste in my mouth. Because I wanted to do this without support. I wanted to go out there and build a dream on my own, not have the cushion of a rich man to cradle me—no matter how much warmth I find in his embrace.

"What if that mountain crushes me?" I whisper. "What if it's too big and powerful for me?"

"And what if it's not?"

We kiss again and a subtle relief washes away all my fears.

He reminds me of my childhood, the comfort and warmth and safety that could be found there.

Before the Bratva tore our lives apart.

But Valentin is more than just the comfort and safety, he's thrilling, fascinating, completely unexpected—even while being exactly what he says he is. A violent, charming man. But one with depth, with the capacity for caring.

He's familiar and unfamiliar.

Comfort and danger.

He... he feels like family, I realize, astonished. A new kind family.

I stare at his handsome face.

Am... Am I falling for him?

"Now, back to work."

Valentin kisses the top of my head before turning me around again.

He gets back to work and I watch in a daze, oddly at ease with everything. I must zone out, because it doesn't seem like that much time has passed before he leans back and lets out a yawn.

"You know what? I haven't had a lazy day in forever. Indulge with me, angel?"

Lazy day. Those are words I never thought I'd hear come from Valentin's mouth. But that doesn't mean they don't sound good.

I nod, suddenly grinning and he scoots me off his lap and takes me into the kitchen to make sandwiches with ham and cheese on black rye bread, thick with cultured butter.

He squeezes oranges on his juicer and then he pops a mountain of popcorn with melted butter and a touch of cayenne.

I raise my brows at him as he loads me up with the drinks. He adds pickled cucumber to the plates and then he carries those, along with the popcorn bowl, into the living room where the fire still burns, making the room toasty. There are two sofas and two armchairs and he sets up on the coffee table and moves the pillows and cushions and throws from the sofa opposite the fire to the one that runs lengthways.

"You can be very domestic when you want to be," I point out, hardly hiding my surprise.

"I can take care of myself." He picks up a remote and a screen comes down. It quickly lights up with a streaming service. "And I can take care of you, too."

The thought of this domesticated side of Valentin makes me want to giggle. It also makes my insides melt. Who would have thought?

We eat the sandwiches and drink the juice, watching some sitcom I barely take in. I'm so full after eating that I keep drifting off. At some point, Valentin hands me a remote control and picks out an iPad from under the coffee table.

"I thought you weren't going to do any work," I quietly note.

"Lazy day, angel, not work-free day." He kisses my temple and feeds me some popcorn as I settle in to watch the next episode.

"It's always something with you," I joke.

"It's always you with me," he chuckles back, pulling the throw over me. Instead of turning on the iPad, though, he rests his hand on my waist.

It feels like something's changed. Like the walls between us have crumbled. Like there's nothing standing in our way.

"You fit right in here, angel," Valentin says, sinking into the cushions.

"It's alright... I guess," I say, stifling a yawn. "I suppose I could get used to it."

I'm not lying. For all its sprawl and opulence, Valentin's place is surprisingly cozy. Right now, I don't ever want to leave. And I don't want him to go anywhere either.

My pulse hammers at the craziness of that thought. Because it is crazy. Completely and utterly unhinged.

And yet, Valentin's opened himself to me.

I yawn again.

After all that's happened in the past two months, from losing investors, to Pierre Olivier, to Kira... all these things that sit so heavily on my chest seem so much lighter as I lie in Valentin's arms on the couch, without a care in the world.

It feels safe. It feels right.

It feels like being home.

25

VALENTIN

The morning sun has just barely started to spill through the curtains when my phone rings. I'm already awake, working in bed.

It's something I never do. But then again, I never have Yelena and her blonde tresses sprawled on me, sleeping, either.

Still, I know I'll have to take the call eventually. So I slide out of bed, then send a text stating I'll call back in a few. After a quick shower, I dress and head for my office. That's where I call Andrei back. He's with Ilya.

"You got something?" I ask, turning on my computer. My phone connects to the screen and a clear video feed pops up.

When he sees me, Ilya raises a brow. "Pulled yourself away from that—"

"Be very careful with your next fucking words, Ilya."

"New friend of yours," he finishes. "I've been up all night."

"I joined him a little while ago," says Andrei with a nod. "We got something."

"On the Little Italy computer store."

I let Ilya's words settle. When we paid that little Podunk store a visit, it quickly became clear that it was a front.

What we didn't know until later, was that it was a front for more than one enterprise.

"So, how many schemes are they really involved in?" I ask.

Andrei nods. "Three."

"Different ones." Ilya frowns.

Thing is, lots of places are fucking fronts that cover a whole host of things. A lot of places are dedicated fronts. But they're rarely dedicated fronts to more than one thing, and three?

I lean back in my chair and stare at the computer screen, flicking through the files Ilya is sending me. "Money laundering, we knew. And the guns. But the third... information selling?"

Alarm bells start to ring.

"On the surface, it's your usual black market and dark web shit; dirt on people and organizations," Andrei says. "But Ilya found an order for very particular dirt on an untouchable West Coast mafia outfit; very similar to what we had stolen."

"Crush them. I'll get a team ready." I'm already standing up when Ilya speaks.

"That's the problem. On one hand, it's almost too obvious they did it to us, and if they're the middle man, which they seem to be, all their clients for information are almost impossible to track."

"From the request to payment and delivery, they have so many loops and ping backs set up it's made so things are anonymous. As in their clients. I can't track it and—"

"If we rake one of the operators over the coals to get them to talk, we might shoot ourselves in the foot. Have we got anything else from the general?" I ask.

Andrei laughs. "So much shit we're going to have to buy a bulldozer. There might be something but it's taking ages to sift through everything new we're getting and it's not filtered. What did you do to him, Valentin? This smacks of a man fucking petrified of you. He's slinging everything he can at us."

"We had... words. Came to an understanding."

"Valentin, never let me get on the wrong side of you, or at least give me time to find a nice, roomy panic room to camp out in for the rest of time." Ilya looks pleased with himself for that.

"We got what we needed from the general," says Andrei, taking a sip of coffee, "the pile of crap that keeps coming, we'll go through. Who knows what we'll find useful down the road."

"Maybe we do risk taking someone else," I rub my temple to ease the tension suddenly building.

Andrei shakes his head. "There's a difference between taking a worker and one of the goons. Goons go missing all the time. But the workers are all surface respectable, and they just might be. So, I think your first instinct is right, Valentin."

I fucking hate being so close and so far from answers. When we visited the store in Little Italy, we busted some heads at a connected tavern. We took a goon who looked like he knew something.

He's been locked in one of our personal torture chambers ever since. My men have been interrogating him and roughing him up. Turns out, he works a number of places for that mafia offshoot, but mostly at the store. So, it stands to reason he might know something useful.

Someone knocks on the door and Andrei rises, heading out of view. When he comes back, he gives me a look.

"Ask the fucking universe and it gives." He holds up a piece of paper. "Seems our guest broke a few minutes ago. Gave us a name. Sandro Barella."

Ilya types furiously and the information pings on my computer as he starts talking.

"Barella's notoriously tough, not on our radar on the whole. He's a relatively small time criminal who broke off from one of the Italian mob families a few years ago to make a name for himself," he says.

"Interesting," I mutter, brain working furiously.

"His crew's beyond violent and they're still very much fringe as they're not that well connected."

"What about money?"

Ilya shakes his head. "Their pockets aren't deep enough to explain the leaked documents. He uses the computer store, but the price our stuff would have cost? Astronomical. Especially as he doesn't have access to us."

"Unless," I say, "he was working with one of the Italian families who do."

"That's a big risk," Andrei says.

I give him a dark look. "They're fucking Italians."

Hate isn't a strong enough word for how I feel about them. I used to be the middle man between Andrei and the Italian fucks. I know they're slimy, sneaky and would sell out their own grandmother for a bigger slice of power. I'd love to destroy every last one of them.

"Do you have more on this Barella?"

"I'll send the rest." Ilya does just that.

I open that file and freeze.

This one comes with a convenient photo.

The face is more than fucking familiar. It's the same one who followed me at the fashion conference.

What the fuck was he doing there? I hadn't been looking for him. We were focused inside our ranks, not looking outside.

If he's the key to finding the one who did the original leak or who knows who sanctioned it, had he gone there to kill me before I found him out?

And how did he know I was there, anyway?

Something tells me this is perhaps even more important than finding out this man is linked to the rat and the leaks.

I don't know how or why it is, but it is. And I learned a long time ago to trust my instincts. After all, they've kept me alive this long.

We need to get out on the street. I need to shift through the shit myself and find Barella.

But...

"I've got a situation," I say.

Ilya rolls his eyes. "The girl, huh?"

Andrei smacks him on the side of the head.

"Fair enough," Ilya says. "Sorry."

"It's Yelena." Don't need to say more. Andrei knows who she is. "She's been through some shit. And right now, she needs me."

"Someone giving her trouble?" Andrei asks.

"Someone did."

"And you took care of them?"

"Instantly."

He nods. "Good."

My heart stays heavy, though.

"But she's vulnerable, skittish of our world, her father..."

"I know the story." Andrei says this quietly as he studies me. "Natalya told me."

"She's scared, and I don't want her to run. I..." I search for the words.

"I understand, brother." Andrei sits, leaning forward. "I know the feeling well. I felt the same way with Natalya. One wrong move and everything implodes, right?"

"I just want to protect her, treat her how she deserves to be treated." Fucking talking about feelings is not my favorite thing. So, I leave it at that.

But Andrei isn't done. "You still have the box I gave you?"

"With the silver bowls?" I nod. "In the vault at Club Silo247."

"Roll up your sleeve and check that scar."

I do. And I remember vividly how Yelena stroked over it with her fingers when we were naked in front of the fire. It's been covered by tattoos for so long now that sometimes even I forget it's there, but she felt it.

Andrei rolls his sleeve up, too, showing me his matching one.

"From when we became blood brothers, over a decade ago," I remember, "but what has this got to do with Yelena? I should slice into her arm?"

"This," he says, "was a ritual. And the message still stands strong. The bond of blood is powerful."

I wait, because I know he's not finished.

"The box, Valentin, takes a similar offering. Blood. From two people who want to be connected for life. That's how you open it up and see what's inside, with blood. A small offering in each bowl."

So, he finally tells me how to open that damn thing.

But I don't want to cut Yelena. I never want her hurt. Ever.

Andrei grins and I know he's guessing the directions of my thoughts. He knows me better than anyone else.

In the way I hope Yelena will know me.

"Of course, it's not magic, Constanov. You could just put your own blood in both bowls, but where's the fun in that?"

"And how the hell do you know that?"

"There was another box. I figured out how to open it and found an engagement ring inside. The one that Natalya wears. I gave it to her when I proposed."

"Woah, I don't know about..." I drift off.

I want to know Yelena better than anyone, just like I want her to know me, but this is a different level.

Do I really want to take it to that next step?

The answer comes so quickly I'm a little shocked.

Yes.

I've never in my life even entertained the thought of marriage, not until I first met her. But even then, it was more of a duty, a responsibility to find the queen to my king, someone to make an heir with. Nothing more.

Now, though, there's something else involved.

Something I never thought I'd feel for another human being.

I want to marry Yelena. Call her my wife. Own her completely. And have her own me.

She'll be my wife.

My queen.

The one to rule by my side.

But first I need to be able to offer her a stable empire. I'm happy being Andrei's second, ruling over my own piece of our kingdom. But if there's a rat and other factions threatening to tear it all asunder then I need to fix that first.

And right now, we all know that starts with finding Sandro Barella.

"If Barella's the rat, then I can't leave Yelena here alone. He was at the fashion conference. He'll know we're connected. If he thinks we're hot on his tail, he might come after her."

Ilya looks up from his computer. "You need to be out on the street hunting this motherfucker down. No one else in our organization can do it quite like you."

"He's right," Andrei nods.

I shake my head. "I need to make sure she's safe."

Ilya rolls his eyes. "I mean, I guess I could stop by and do my part from your place while you're out. She's not loud, is she? Because I need complete silence to—"

Andrei slaps him on the back of the head again.

"Stop playing around... but that's actually a good idea. We need you out in the field, Valentin. And as long as Ilya has a computer, he can work from anywhere. So, what do you say?"

The idea of relying on another man to keep my girl safe immediately rubs me the wrong way. But it is Ilya we're talking about. For as annoying as he can be sometimes, he's still one of my best and most loyal friends.

"Shit," I grumble.

I look up right as Andrei catches my eye.

I'm not worried she won't be safe with Ilya—he pretends to be more casual than he actually is; he'll keep a close eye on her —I'm fucking worried that with her vulnerable state, the emotional beatings she's taken, that she'll get cold feet. And run.

I blow out a breath.

"It's up to you," Andrei assures me. "Look, I get it. This feels like a terrible risk. What if she runs? Am I right? But the thing is, if it's truly meant to be, she'll be there when you get back. Yelena will understand. Love always understands."

Love.

The word fills me with a heavy dread chased by uncertainty.

Is this love, or is it just an obsession? I know I want to marry her but will I feel that way in a week? A month?

A calm seeps in. This is more than obsession. Much more. I don't see me losing interest. Ever. I've obsessed over women before, even thought myself to be in love once. And yet I never shared my real life with them, showed them my work, became tender with them. I never even considered marrying any of them.

Maybe Andrei is right. Yelena will be here when I get back. But if I lock myself away with her in here, our empire might not survive. Then what will I have to give her but a shoulder to cry on?

"Okay," I grunt, curling my hands into fists. "I'll go hunt this fucker down."

Andrei smiles.

I look from him to Ilya.

"Ilya?"

"Yes, boss?"

"I need you to bring me the box from my office vault. Andrei has the password." I look at Andrei. "And I want our best security detail here, backing Ilya up."

"Got it."

"Ilya," I say, rising, "I'm relying on you to keep her safe while I go hunting."

"Obviously." Ilya starts packing up his computer. "I bet I'm a better bodyguard than you."

I grab my phone. "You better be, because if anything happens to her, it's your head."

"If anything happens to her, I'll do the chopping myself."

Andrei pats him on the shoulder and looks at me.

"Gentlemen, let's settle this, once and for all."

26

YELENA

Things I didn't know existed hurt. But it's that good hurt that comes from a great workout. And I stretch in Valentin's bed, strangely satisfied.

There's a smile on my face I can't seem to get rid of.

Maybe it's where I am, maybe it's because I know why I'm sore.

Or maybe it's the delicious aromas that waft up the stairs and into the bedroom Valentin must have carried me into after I fell asleep last night.

He must be cooking again.

Sniffing the air, I force myself out of bed and grab the first shirt I can find. Then, I head downstairs.

Valentin's in the kitchen. He's wearing black trousers and a black-t, and his muscles bunch and work as he leans over the stove.

I bite my lip. No matter how sore I am, no matter how satisfied, just the sight of him is enough to make me want more.

No wonder I kept away from him.

He can devour me whole, just by being in the same room.

Except now I know what it's like to be devoured by him and I'm thinking it's possibly better than the pancakes he's cooking.

My stomach squeezes as my heart spins.

Is there anything hotter than a ridiculously gorgeous, burly, tattooed giant of a man cooking breakfast for you?

There's even a white tea towel casually tossed over one shoulder. The bastard must know how sexy that is.

For a second, I just stand there, staring.

"You might not be wearing shoes, angel, but I know you're here. Come in and keep me company while I make you breakfast."

My smile grows as I cross the tiled floor to him, my gaze catching on the sweater and coat on the chair at the kitchen island, and the holster, gun and lethal looking switchblade sitting near them.

Does my smile falter a little as I pass them? Yes, but mostly because I'm guessing he's going somewhere.

But I do as asked, wrapping my arms around his waist and resting my cheek against his back. I breathe in the scent of him, deep.

"I thought you might be hungry this morning."

"You have no idea."

"I guess that makes two of us." Turning around, he slaps my ass and lifts the hem of the t-shirt. "Hmm. No panties."

"You stole my panties."

"They are in the wash. And you don't need them with me. I'm a full access kind of man." He turns back around and flips a pancake, then presses a glass of orange juice into my hands.

I take a sip of the fresh, sweet juice. "Easy access."

"It's the same thing." He puts the pancake on top of an impressive stack and measures more batter into the skillet.

I grin. "Impressive."

"Angel." He shoots me a disapproving look. "Besides killing, making pancakes is what I'm best at."

My skin heats as I run my finger down his shirt. "Well, I don't think that's true. I can think of something else you're good at. Excellent, actually."

He turns off the stove and looks at me. "And what is that?"

"Don't play dumb with me."

He grins wide and takes the juice, setting it down. And then he pulls me in close, placing my hand against his hard cock. "Why don't you remind me of how good I am at that? My memory isn't so good sometimes."

"You need a reminder?" I give him a squeeze.

He draws in a sharp breath. "Fuck yes."

Valentin's gone down on me so many times I'm practically salivating to return the favor. There's something so delicious about the idea that I'm on my knees quicker than I came downstairs for breakfast.

"You sure you can handle that?" he asks, cheeks lifting.

"There's only one way to find out."

I look up at him and he leans back against the bench, forking a small pile of pancakes onto a plate and drizzling them with syrup.

"How about we have breakfast together?" he asks. "You can have two courses."

I don't need him to say anything more.

"Then bring on the first course."

Before he can do it himself, I pull his trousers down, then his briefs. His cock springs directly into my face. Instinct opens my mouth, desire closes it around his giant shaft.

"That's a good girl," he groans as I try to take him as deep as possible.

I barely get a third of the way before he hits the back of my throat. That's when his hand comes down on the back of my head. He starts leading me back and forth. I flatten my tongue, doing all I can do to take him.

"Delicious."

My eyes are starting to water, and when I look up I can hardly believe what I see.

Valentin has the plate of pancakes in his hand. He cuts out a piece and starts to eat, casually chewing even as his whole lower body tenses from pleasure.

I take it as a direct challenge.

Obviously, if he can concentrate on anything else while I'm blowing him, I'm not doing a good job.

You beautiful bastard.

Keeping my lips stretched, I use my own coat of saliva like lube and take the base of his cock in my hand.

I want to break him like he breaks me, I want him to lose control, and come apart in my hands and mouth. I want to taste the salt of his cum on my tongue.

I start to stroke and suck and choke and gargle until I can feel him twitching.

The plate lands on the stone bench with a clatter and Valentin's whole body jerks, like he's physically holding himself back.

"Oh, fuck, angel."

He twists one of his hands in my hair as he trembles, coming apart at the edges. I've already won a small victory. The pancakes are gone. But I'm not satisfied. Not until he is.

His hand stretches back around my head and he holds me in place as he starts to thrust, face fucking me with increasing force.

His movements are jerky, without the forceful finesse he usually has, and soon he's speaking to me in Russian. I don't understand a word, but his voice is so deep and rough that I'm worried I might stain the floor with my wetness.

"Don't stop," he orders, his thrusts picking up speed.

I feel his cock swell just as he erupts.

With a roar, he cums hard, spurting hot, thick liquid into my mouth. With one last thrust, he reaches the back of my throat and holds me there forcing me to swallow every last drop.

When he's empty, Valentin eases himself out of my mouth and he holds it open so he can look inside at his deposit.

The smile is so filthy, so satisfied, so weirdly sweet that I almost cum then and there., too

"Swallow," he says, voice a whisper as he pulls me up into his arms.

"I already did."

"No. There's still some left on your tongue. There's no need to save it, angel. I can always give you more."

Closing my mouth, I take a big gulp.

"Good girl."

With that, he lifts me off my knees.

"Now it's your turn to eat."

Stepping behind me, he lifts the back of my t-shirt up.

But before he can go down on me, we both hear approaching footsteps.

He quickly steps back, zipping himself up just in time.

"Excuse me, Sir, but your guests have arrived."

It's a slim older woman. I'm guessing a maid.

"Already?" Valentin groans and nods and my heart sinks as he tightens an arm around me.

"Guests?"

Valentin nods, shifting away from me as he takes me in. "You need to go put some clothes on. Come on."

He leads me up the stairs as voices start to filter up from the living room. They speak Russian, but I recognize Andrei's voice. The other one is new to me.

"I'm sorry," he says, pushing open the door to the master bedroom, the sheets are fresh, I note, the bed made and my heart sinks.

It's like I'm being erased.

"For what?"

He disappears into the closet briefly and when he comes back out, he's holding a pair of ripped jeans, some boxer briefs, and a sweater.

"Your outfit for the day," he says. "You'll be nice and cozy in these."

I ignore his fashion advice.

"What are you sorry for?"

"I have to leave for work. Remember what I showed you yesterday? I'm hot on the trail of a lead, possibly the person who's causing all our problems. I need to find him and I'm the only one who can do it. Otherwise, I'd stay. I put it off as long as I could, but Andrei and Ilya are her..."

My heart twists and pain skitters along my nerves.

I get it. He has to work, but surely as a boss he can work from here and send others out for him, right?

Right now, I need him. It feels like I'm made of glass and he's the only one with gloves on.

I stop. Okay, I'm feeling vulnerable after Pierre. I know that. However, I also know Valentin is not the kind of man to sit back on a throne while others go out and do the dirty work for him. He's a warrior. He needs the battle. And I know he's not about to let others do what he won't.

If he's going to support me, I'll need to support him, too.

"It's okay," I say. "I understand."

He kisses me softly. "Thank you, angel. Now, get dressed."

Forming a soft fist, he gives my jaw a playful tap. I can't help but giggle.

"Don't be long."

"I wouldn't dream of it."

We share one last long kiss before he leaves the room.

When I'm dressed, I head downstairs just as Andrei is leaving to take a call. Still, we exchange knowing glances and he smiles at me.

I do my best to smile back, no matter how guilty I feel for shutting him and Natalya out of my life lately.

"Yelena, come here. there's someone I'd like you to meet."

I turn into the living room and Valentin slides his arm around me and nods toward a man with dark brown hair and a small streak of what I can only assume is very premature gray.

Is there a damn handsome man farm somewhere in Russia? Because he's super attractive too. Not Valentin-level, but definitely on par with Andrei.

Valentin puts his mouth to my ear. "That's Ilya. I like him so don't fall in love with him and make me kill him. Besides, he's useful."

"Whatever he's saying, it's a lie," Ilya butts in. "But only if it's bad. If it's good, then it's the truth."

Valentin rolls his eyes. "Ilya, this is Yelena. Filthy hands off or you'll have to learn how to type and communicate with your forehead." Valentin points to the doorway. "Sergei is in charge of the security team. There are twelve, a few inside, the rest outside."

I want to ask if this is overkill, but it's Valentin and I don't think he sees anything as overkill as long as I'm safe.

As they fall into conversation I head off and explore, finding the library next to his office.

I select a book, some dime store detective novel, complete with a Sam Spade type on the front. Valentin said he wouldn't be long, but I know better. He can't control what happens out on the streets.

I might as well get comfortable. So, I curl up on the nearest couch to read.

The book's pretty good and yet my attention keeps wandering off as too many things crowd my head. Admitting defeat, I set it down and go in search of Ilya.

He's in the living room, fire blazing, stretched on the sofa with a laptop on his chest, and another on the table. A glass of something dark amber sits next to what looks like rum on the floor.

He's wearing black rimmed glasses he's pushed to the top of his head.

"Bastards!" He glares at the computer and types furiously before laughing like a maniac. "Take that, fools. No one ever bests Mad Ilya."

He lifts his gaze to me.

"What do you think about the nickname? Mad Ilya, yes or no? I'm still workshopping it."

He's got a cavalier air about him that's light to the hot headed yet deliberate seriousness of Valentin's darkness.

"It's cute, I guess."

I edge closer. I don't want to be alone and he's sort of fascinating.

"Cute? Shit. I'm not going for cute, honey. I guess it's back to the drawing board."

He clacks away at his keyboard and I look at him with genuine curiosity.

"Are you playing computer games?"

"Me? Do I look like I play such things?"

"Yes?" I shrug. "Isn't that what you're doing?"

"Please, little one." He snatches up his drink and downs it then refills it all without looking. "I have no time for such frivolities. But back to the matter at hand. What if we switch around the words? Does Ilya the mad sound better to you?"

"Do you need a nickname?"

"Ouch," he fakes hurt. "But no, it's not necessary. I'm just trying to keep up with your man."

I blink. "Valentine has a nickname?"

"You've never heard of Val the Heartless?"

"There's no way," I can't help but laugh, perching myself on the end of the sofa. "Does Valentin know you call him that?"

"God no. And no one does. I just thought if I'm getting

myself a moniker to strike fear into computer nerds every-where, I'd give him one, too. Valentin hates being left out." Ilya shakes his head as I laugh. "Sometimes this job is boring. I'm sifting data right now, so..."

"Well, if you're going to put me on the spot. Then I prefer Mad Ilya."

"Then Mad Ilya it shall be." He sets the computer down and taps a few keys. Data runs across the screen.

"What's my nickname going to be?" I wonder out loud.

"Oh, don't you dare. Valentin will kill me if I steal the honor from him. You two figure that out. I'm getting a drink. You want one?"

He stands up.

"I... It's not even lunch time."

"I'm Russian." He pauses and picks up his glass and takes a sip. "Vanilla, cinnamon, honey and orange, that's what I'm getting. And for me it's... actually, I don't know what the fucking time is. I haven't slept since yesterday. Too much to do."

I swallow, unsure if I should leave. I don't want to.

"Should I go?"

"God, no. Save me from boredom." He winks. "Besides I'm tasked with keeping you safe and happy. So I should probably keep you in sight."

"You and the five million guards."

"It's six million," he says with a small laugh. "And they're just keeping us both safe. They don't care for happiness. It's a rare feature in most Russians."

I plop down on the sofa, feeling surprisingly comfortable. My head shakes as I try to hold back my laughter.

"I get it now," Ilya says.

"Get what?"

"Why Valentin's so hung up on you." He shifts a little and takes another sip of the rum. "Everybody's falling in love these days."

Color spreads through my cheeks.

"Love?"

I freeze. I don't even want to ask if he heard Valentin say that. I don't know if my heart can take it.

But I can't stop thinking of that word.

Love.

Does he love me?

Do I love him?

The blush grows deeper, wider.

"I'm sorry for what happened to you at that fancy restaurant," Ilya continues, hardly seeming to notice that I've turned bright red.

"Valentin told you?"

"He told Andrei. I was just there in the room. Men should act like men, not beasts. And you are too sweet to have a man try and... you know... hurt." He pauses, looks at the ceiling, then at me. "It is not your fault."

I sort of love how his accent grows thicker when he gets all tied up in his own words and I can see why Valentin has time for him. Behind all the muscle and tattoos, he's a good guy, too.

"I... thank you, Ilya—I mean, Mad Ilya."

He grins.

"Me? I'd have chopped the fucker's dick off, turned it into little canapes and fed it to him. But that's just me. Also, I'd have stolen all his money by hacking his accounts. He was a bad man, Yelena, he deserved it." Then he nods.

He's as lethal as Valentin with his charm, and that awkward bent to it is going to melt someone's heart sooner or later.

"I'm glad you have your Heartless Valentin to keep you safe." He leans back in his chair, apparently exhausted from trying to comfort me, because I'm pretty sure that's what he was doing.

"He may try a little too hard to keep me safe sometimes."

"He's very protective, but that's a good thing. You know,

Valentin would never have let you see a man alone like that—not because he wants to control or doesn't trust you, but your safety is that important to him. If he wasn't so busy with work, I'm sure he'd never leave your side. And that... is a little dangerous. It's been distracting him. And without Valentin at his best, our empire is vulnerable. At least, that's what goes on in his head, I think."

I breathe out. "So, Valentin's going to beat himself up for me being stupid and getting in that car, but if he spends more time with me then things could go wrong? What's the answer?"

Do I leave town? Do I tell Valentin to back off?

Thing is, I don't want to.

But I also don't want to be his downfall.

Ilya runs a hand through his hair. "The answer is that girls are trouble," he laughs. "at least, that's how they teach it in the motherland."

A small smile teases my mouth. "Well, what do they say about women?"

"Also trouble."

"You know," I say, relaxing into the chair, "if you asked politely I could help you adjust that attitude, and maybe you could meet a woman of your own."

He snorts a laugh. "I'm fine with women. That's the problem. And unlike Valentin, I sometimes pay more attention to them than I should. Then I have to shove them off with a pole. It gets messy."

"I don't doubt that, you're very handsome. Though, not Valentin-level, of course."

He rolls his eyes. "You're biased."

"And thank you for your less than subtle way of telling me Valentin isn't a man-whore."

"Neither am I."

"It's the pole that gets in your way, women don't like being shoved away with one."

"I'll review my methods."

I doubt that he needs to. I don't doubt that he does just fine with the ladies.

"So... what brings you to the Bratva?" I ask, genuinely interested.

"Money, fame, glory. All of the typical stuff. What about you?" The counter is soft and genial.

"Well," I wonder where to start. "As you probably already know, my best friend married Andrei, but, I mean, honestly, I wanted to keep far away from your organization. And not just for the obvious reasons. I have a bad history with the Bratva. My father got messed up with you guys decades ago. It ruined him and my family. I know it doesn't seem like it now, but I grew up with money, then the Bratva snatched it all away."

Somehow, he sees through the flippancy. "I'm sorry."

"You didn't do it."

"Andrei and Valentin aren't that type either." He shrugs. "I know a little. Greedy bastards in the last Bratva empire. Why it fell. But no Nero to fiddle while it burned." He goes quiet as he checks something on his main computer and then takes another sip. "My family was rich, too. And we lost it all. Not me personally, but when Capitalism came to the motherland, with the Oligarchs and the corruption and the rise and fall of the great experiment, everything was torn apart, taken. I was nine. I remember it vividly, going from riches to nothing overnight, it seemed."

I sigh. "I was about ten."

"In mother Russia, it is a hard life being poor. But I credit the years of riches for helping start me on computers and tech. I'm grateful I had those opportunities. Many didn't. Then..."

"You joined the many?"

"It's very boring when I think back. But I worked hard, hand to mouth, when my parents died. Surviving on my skill set as I flew through school. I'll admit, I worked for people who make Valentin and Andrei look like saints. Which, I guess, they are—

at least, in how they run things. Loyalty means something to them. But outside of their organization, that is rare. I'm glad I ended up with them."

Suddenly he snaps his fingers. "Oh, shit, I just remembered."

Ilya puts his glass down and fetches a leather satchel by the door. He pulls something out and brings it over, handing it to me.

I'm immediately drawn to it but I don't know why. I do, however take it from him.

It's a heavy, smooth black and silver box. "What is it?" I ask, turning it in my hands.

"A mystery. Andrei says you push on the side and hey presto, two silver bowls appear, put a drop of blood in each and all will be revealed."

"And what's inside?"

He holds up his hands. "It's Valentin's, so I'm not opening it."

"You don't know?"

"Nope. That's why it's a mystery."

His phone starts to ring and he picks it up and sighs dramatically. "I have to take this." Ilya also grabs the main computer. "And this."

The moment he's gone, I'm studying the box.

I need to know what's in it. Pressing on the side, the top opens and two beautiful silver bowls appear.

Setting it down, I start searching for something, anything to prick myself with. I eventually manage to find a silver letter opener on the wet bar.

Either I'm really bored or I've just lost my mind, because I hardly think as I take it over to the sofa and jab my finger with the tip. "Ow!"

Squeezing the wound, I let a drop of blood drip it into one bowl, then the other.

They click and creak and, slowly, the box opens like a strange flower.

I stare down at the contents.

My jaw drops open.

Holy shit.

27

I stand in the dive bar, surrounded by people. Well, technically, they're not people anymore.

Bodies. Corpses that we just created.

In the next room, the manager's office, Andrei's interrogating one of the few survivors of our massacre.

The world won't shed a tear for anyone here. Scum bags, lowlifes. The kind of criminals not worth our time, the type who push drugs to kids, rape whoever they please, and kill whoever they dislike.

But that's not why we came here—though, it is a bonus. I like to do my bit in making the world a nicer place.

Someone groans. Not all dead. Yet.

I step over some bodies and put an extra bullet in the fucker. The groans stop.

Then I help myself to a quality vodka, shaken, not stirred. I leave the bottle on bar, a calling card for whoever the clean up crew is. They'll report the vodka to certain Italians and they'll know not to fuck with us.

I was careful. The bar's supposedly neutral but it's owned

by a mafia family not affiliated with us. In future, perhaps they'll be more careful with who they align with.

And who they don't.

But this lot in here tonight? All Sandro-adjacent. All living it up because Sandro likes to splash money for his associates.

Maybe the mafia family who owns the place is associated, maybe not, but I'll bet a cool million they won't be after tonight.

They want in with us, not trouble.

This lot thought they were better than the Zherdev Bratva. Thought they didn't have to talk. They kept refusing to squeal. So, I took matters into my own hands.

The three survivors will spread word.

Do not mess with the Bratva.

I pour another drink.

Normally, I revel in this kind of thing, but after searching for Sandro now for days and meeting dead end after dead end, I followed my instincts. Those landed us here.

It's not a dead end, but...

It's not what I wanted, either.

"It doesn't feel right," I mumble to myself, heading to the office. Two of the people are tied up and bloody. The one in Andrei's hands isn't faring better.

"You're going soft. Bougie," he says to me in Russian. "Tsar-like qualities are appearing."

I ignore that. "Anything?"

"No. This one says the same as the other two. He's claiming Sandro hasn't been seen in weeks."

"How many weeks?"

Andrei kicks the man. "When did you last see him?"

"A month ago, please! We drink here on the cheap. It's where we get word from him when he wants to reach us, so we come regularly. But we're not—"

"Who's we?" I ask.

I don't even have to offer a threatening move to make him

cower back against the desk. "Whoever. It depends. If people want work, they come here. And we've been getting a lot of work from Sandro's crew lately."

But I've stopped listening to him. I know operations like this. Sloppy, lacking in loyalty. They also come with a certain level of anonymity. But that's not why I've stopped listening to him whine.

A month?

That would have been around the time of the fashion conference.

"Wait." I crouch down, stopping Andrei just before he can kick the man unconscious. "Were you meant to see him?"

The man's good eye darts between us. "Not me personally, but the man's pretty consistent with work."

I stand. "Maybe we take him with us? See what else he knows."

"I collect. That's it. Just collect money for him."

Collect, beat people up, break bones.

"You check his wallet for his address?" I ask in Russian.

"Of course."

I switch to English as Andrei downs a drink. "Easy to find if we need him."

"Or discover he's lying."

But I want answers now. It's been over a month now since that fucker Sandro ambushed me at the conference. I need to know why.

I now also need to know why he disappeared afterward.

"You done?" I ask Andrei.

He gives a cold smile. "For now."

"Good. I'll send in the clean up crew."

We both walk back out to the bar with the man pleading behind us. Andrei takes a swig of the bottle I left on the bar and we head for the exit.

There's no real clean up crew. Not for this job. Just a couple of my men who'll help the survivors home. Maybe check in on them over the next week or so. Just in case they remember anything.

Outside, the car's waiting and I get in after Andrei. He's looking at me. Normally I'd already have a plan of attack, a place to hit next, people to mess with. But tonight...

I'm not in the mood and he fucking knows it.

"Heading home?"

"You know the answer to that."

"Yeah," he says with a sigh, "I do."

I scowl as I check my phone. All's well at the mansion, according to Ilya. "I can do my job."

"Did I say you couldn't? Listen, I like Yelena. She's good for you...."

"There's an if there."

He shrugs. "There's always an if at the beginning and you know her history. She's not a fan of the Bratva."

Of us and what we do. But I also have never lied or hidden it from her. Or my intentions. Not from the moment I laid eyes on the blonde angel. "If she can't accept who I am then..."

I don't finish the sentiment.

I don't need to.

"Love finds a way, Valentin."

"Did I mention love?"

He laughs softly.

"I will get to the bottom of this. Sandro hasn't been seen since my run in with him at the fashion conference. Which is strange." I look out the window, noting where we are. There's a bar I want to check out, an informant I want to see.

The woman knows everyone and everything. She might not be there, but if she is, a quick exchange might do us a world of good right now.

"Stop here."

Andrei glances out at the bar. "Did I not just say you deserve a break? The only one pushing you to work insane hours is you."

"I just want to drop in. Do me a favor and pick up Ilya and order Yelena to stay put."

"I'll suggest it. Not order."

But the car pulls over and I head into the bar. It's a swanky place, low lit and shadowy, full of velvet and leather and secrets. But my informant isn't there tonight. So I send her a message and call my car.

Usually, I'd head off to search and poke another angle and wait to see if she calls. Or visit another friend of the Bratva. I can work all night and day and often do.

Part of me still wants to do that. To avoid confronting the four letter word Andrei just dropped on me like a sledge hammer.

Love.

I'm not ready for love.

But I am ready for Yelena.

And she's at home. Waiting for me. My own, personal angel. One who's expression haunted me through the killing spree. Fuck, Yelena looked at me like she didn't want me to leave, like she needed me.

I don't think I've ever been needed. Not like that and it feels... good. Special.

So what did I do? Neglected her in her time of need.

It couldn't be helped. Now it can be.

I want to show her what she means, how she should be treated.

And I know what I'm going to do.

Take her to dinner.

I know just the place.

But she's going to need to dress up. And I don't have the proper attire at my place.

So, I get the car to take me to her shitty little apartment. I'll have to break in, but... that's in my skill set, too.

And a little B and E is good for the soul.

Picking the lock to the building is a little time consuming. It's sturdy but old and soon I'm taking the stairs to her apartment. I'm betting she has two or three locks and all of them crap.

I'm right.

But something else is wrong.

They're already picked. Broken apart.

Fuck. I inhale sharply, trying to get a handle on the sudden rush of anger.

Someone has beaten me to the fucking punch. My hackles rise.

Who the fuck is after my angel?

Immediately, one man comes to mind. Someone who's had her followed before.

Alex Civati.

I send a text. From this moment on, Civati is under my eye at all, he won't be able to piss without me knowing. I don't care if he's out of the country. We're tapping his phone. Following his people. Reading his emails.

Everything.

Pushing the door open, I make sure to keep a hand on my gun as I step inside. But when I switch on the light, no one's there.

Whoever broke in left hours ago.

I download the surveillance footage to my phone. I'll watch it on the way home.

Might as well do what I came here for.

The place is small and the furniture cheap, but Yelena's made it work, and it looks and feels more comfortable than it should. Still, things are slightly out of place.

Whoever went through here, did it carefully.

This wasn't a random robbery. This was personal.

It's enough for me to make a decision. One I'd already unofficially made.

Yelena is not coming back here. Not alone.

No. She's moving in with me.

It's something I should have made happen right after the fashion show. I protect what's mine and it's fast becoming clear Yelena needs protection of the very personal, hands-on kind.

I go to the bedroom and pack up some clothes. Pretty dresses, prettier underwear. Nice shoes. There's a bag of make up in the bathroom and a brush. Some face creams. Her toothbrush. Shower crap. I pack it all.

I'm about to leave when I spy something on the desk set up near the window.

Sketches. I stroke my fingers over the one on top, the sharp lines and fall of the design, something with edge and heat. Something I could see on Yelena. There are a whole bunch of them. So, I flick through them until I reach her look book.

I pick it up and go through it slowly.

These are real. There's a rack right in the corner with the outfits pictured in the Look Book hanging from it, but I flip back to the start and go through it again.

Even in my limited experience, I can tell these outfits are gorgeous. I've seen my fair share of high end clothing in my time, but nothing like this. At the back of the look book there are even some men's clothes, too.

God, she's so fucking talented.

Why these idiots haven't been shoving money in her pretty face is beyond me.

Fucking hell.

I helped kill her dreams.

It's time I helped revive them.

I stack the designs and the look book and slide them into the portfolio she carried at the conference. It comes with me.

I've got an idea.

And it might just help make up for all the shit I've put her through.

28

I keep fidgeting with the strap as I sit on Valentin's bed, waiting for him to come back. I don't think I've been so nervous before in my life and that includes the first time I pitched to an investor.

A couple of hours ago, Andrei arrived to collect Ilya. He told me Valentin would be back soon, and in the meantime, a whole army of guards would remain.

I was asked to stay put until then. Well, more like ordered. But I didn't mind.

I wanted some alone time to gather my thoughts. Now, though, all I want is to see Valentin again. To feel him.

To show him what I've found.

Somewhere outside the bedroom, a door slams and every atom of me bursts into life.

Second thoughts race through my mind.

But it's too late to back out now.

I touch my neck, feeling what I found in the box Ilya gave me, and hope that I'm not in over my head.

Valentin's speaking to me from the stairs but my ears buzz with nerves and I can't make them out. Slowly I rise and kneel on the ground, hands behind my back, eyes down. A calm washes over me.

I'm not sure what makes me do this, only that it feels right. Like I'm being led by an invisible hand. His invisible hand.

"So I thought—"

Valentin bursts into the room and immediately stops talking. He takes an audible breath as two bags thump on the ground next to his feet.

He swears in Russian and I know what I must look like.

A naked little submissive. Hair up, eyes down and wearing a diamond studded choke collar around my neck. It pricks my skin from the small pointed studs that line it.

It's gorgeous, a black viper—like the one on his crest—wrapped around my neck, sparkling in the bedroom light. A long leash-like strap hangs down from the side.

I stare at the floor as Valentin's hand silently slips over my head.

"What are you wearing, little one."

He pulls me up to my feet.

I meet his gaze and take a breath, the little studs catching at my skin. "It was in the box Ilya brought, the one with the silver bowls. I wanted to see, so I pricked my finger, and... are you mad?"

"No. I'm hard as fuck." And Valentin puts my hand over the bulge stretching his pants. He's not lying. "What a wonderful welcoming gift."

He touches the collar, eases a finger beneath the edge, and frowns.

"There's a velvet layer that covers the studs. I could put it on. But I thought you might like it like this."

Valentin takes the strap and winds it around his hand, pulling me in and kissing me in a slow, long breath that unravels the softness in my center.

"This is perfect, angel. You. Are. Perfect."

He kisses me again, dipping his head down to smother the line of the collar and my throat with his lips.

When he returns to claim my mouth, I kiss him back with everything I have. I'm hungry for him. Starving. And he knows it.

I gasp as he starts playing with my nipple, then drops his other hand to slide it between my thighs, teasing my pussy and pushing the heel of his hand into my clit as my entire being builds out from the searing pressure between my legs.

"You are a fucking queen." He eases back but keeps hold of the leash. "My queen."

"So you like it?"

"I fucking love it. But it's going to have to wait. I have other plans for you tonight. Now, get dressed before I fuck you senseless. I'm taking you to dinner."

My gaze falls to the bags he dropped in the doorway. Silky, silver-threaded material spills out from the openings. Those are my clothes. "You brought my outfits."

I don't even bother asking how he got into my apartment. I know he broke in. He's Valentin. Nothing stops him from doing what he wants. And a streak of heat whispers in my veins at the thought.

"I thought we needed your clothes here," he says, like I'm moving in and we've already discussed it. Another very Valentin thing. "As much as I like you in my clothes, I've seen the contents of your lingerie drawer. And think your clothes might be better."

He tugs on the leash and I tumble up against him.

"For you?"

"Well, I don't want you parading in your sexy little panties without a bra in front of Ilya."

"I don't wear a bra now?"

"Not when we're alone." Suddenly, he grins and bites my ear, whispering, "I will buy you enough handmade lingerie to fill a thousand closets. You'll need plenty of backups. Because I don't slip off bras and panties, angel. I fucking tear them apart."

"Valentin."

He looks down at my naked body and his jaw clenches.

"Let's go fucking shopping."

I gulp. "Now?"

"It isn't that late. Put on something simple from the bag. You have shoes, too. Leave the leash on."

I do as he says, and half an hour later, I'm wearing a simple velvet-lined dress in the back of Valentin's car, staring through tinted windows at the tall buildings downtown.

He strokes my cheek, that big hand impossibly gentle as he smiles.

"Hungry?"

"I could eat."

"Good. Hold onto that appetite. I want to see you stuffing your face in your new outfit."

"My new outfit? I thought we were just getting lingerie?"

"We'll get some of that, too. But first…"

Valentin points out the window as the car pulls to a stop in front of an exclusive, cutting-edge boutique. I instantly recognized the place. It's not the most luxurious in terms of labels, but it's the most expensive. They have an acclaimed collection of labels. Old, up and coming, new. The style's eclectic, but anyone who's ever had their clothes for sale in the boutique has eventually made a huge impact in the industry.

It's been a secret dream to have my label in their stores, but they don't attend conferences. They're too rogue for things like that. Instead, they go by instincts and pure chance.

My gaze darts to Valentin as he comes around to open my door and help me out. He's taking me there. Has to be. It's the only store open on the street right now.

I can't move.

"Angel, what's the matter?"

"I'm not dressed for this place. They..." They've never responded to the few times I've reached out to them. "I don't belong here. Look at me."

"And? You're fucking gorgeous. The most beautiful woman I've seen." He reaches in, but ignores my hand and picks up the leash instead, tugging it so I have to get out. "And I'm Valentin Constanov. I don't let any door or opinion stop me."

"That's true," I mutter. "You are Valentin Constanov. But I'm not."

"That's right. You're Yelena Laskin. And you need to have the confidence to match such a prestigious name," he says, leading me into the store.

"Valentin," I hiss his name. "How the hell do you even know this place?"

He shrugs, looking entirely at home in his charcoal suit. "I do my research. And I have deemed this place worthy of you."

Oh, Lord. Only Valentin.

We step in through the doorway and I take a nervous look around, a sigh filling my throat. But before that sigh can leave my lips, it gets caught in the back of my mouth.

I freeze.

"What is going on?"

Right at the front of the store, in a prime location, is a rack of very familiar-looking clothes. Above that rack is a sign.

Dark One Eight

The exclusive and exciting new line.

Coming soon.

"Valentin. What did you do?" But I already know. When he left me earlier, he wasn't just out taking care of business and breaking into my apartment to bring me my clothes. He was doing far more than that...

I step forward and notice that the walls surrounding the rack are lined with my sketches. They've been framed and placed next to sketches from some of the most brilliant designers I know of.

"No. You can't do this." I mutter.

"Why not?" Valentin touches one of the dresses they have for a sneak sample sale. "I'm shocked they got this up so fast." Then he takes my hands. "Yelena, when I saw these at your place, I was blown away by your talent. I've overheard Natalya talking about this place. So, naturally, I stopped on my way home to check it out. It was underwhelming, to say the least. They had nothing that compared to your line."

"But..."

"I asked for the manager, and then asked to speak to the owner, who just so happens to be Chicago-based. When she saw the designs and these samples, she jumped at the opportunity to put an order in."

"I... Valentine, you didn't have to..." I'm not sure what to say. So, I just glance around, astonished that my clothes are in the same room as some of these other designer outfits.

Then I realize something.

"There are no customers."

Valentin chuckles. "That's because we're in after official store hours. I made sure they kept the store open, though, just for us. I promised you a new outfit, after all."

"Valentin, I don't think you appreciate how expensive some of these designs are."

"Oh, I'm not paying."

Reaching into his pocket, he pulls out a thick cream envelope and hands it to me.

"What is this?"

"Why don't you open it up and find out."

With shaking fingers, I do just that. Inside is a check. Addressed to me.

I count the zeroes and almost faint, my knees wobbling. "A million dollars? What? Why? Valentin..."

"It's not from me. They want exclusive rights to your designs for the first two years. This covers that only. They will pay you royalties on the clothes, too. They seem to think it's a good deal for them."

I can't breathe. I can't. My head spins as I try and wrap my brain around it all. He negotiated me one hell of a deal.

"I don't know what to say."

"You don't have to say a thing, angel."

He wanders off and rifles through the racks, picking out a few dresses. He comes back, holding them up against me as he considers which one looks best.

"Now you don't have to be with me for my money. You can follow your dreams, with or without my help."

"I'd never be with someone for money."

He kisses me softly. "I know. But it's better that it's not in the way, don't you think? You're rich now. So, that begs the question: do you still want to have dinner with me?"

I laugh, my stomach fluttering. I can hardly believe this is real.

"Of course I do."

"Good," he grins. "Now, what will you wear? I like these, but you can pick out anything you wish." His smile turns wicked. "Actually, I fucking insist."

"You want a private fashion show?"

"I wouldn't object."

I eye one of the price tags and suck in a sharp breath. Even with that check sitting in my hand, I can't quite believe the prices. "Valentin, they're so expensive."

The old me would have spent this money without batting an eye. But now I know better.

"No," he says. "They're not. The stores were expensive. The dresses are free."

I open my mouth and close it again. No words come.

Finally, I force them. "Did… did you buy the store just so they'd take my clothes?"

It stings, and—

"It went the other way around."

"But this check is from you, technically?"

"Yelena." His smile fades. "My success is your success, it's true, but I'm not a fool with money. I negotiated the deal for your line because they wanted it. And then I realized the worth of this place and the chain, so I bought it. And when you're ready, I will invest in your own brand-name store."

I want to fight him on it, but I can't. It's like he handed me a way to reach my dreams. And if they wanted the clothes first…

"I still don't know what to say."

"It's a good business deal. That's it."

"For who?"

He laughs. "Angel, you need to pick your battles. This isn't one. I'm just trying to make more money. That it happens to be good for you is just a bonus."

That's clearly not entirely true. But I don't fight it.

Instead, I appreciate what he's really saying.

Valentin believes in me.

No one, apart from Natalya, has ever done that. Not since my parents' death.

"Well, if it's good for both of us…"

For once, I force myself to relax and take it all at face value.

Pushing any doubt from my mind, I pull out a few dresses, including the ones Valentin has picked, and I take them into the most lavish dressing room I've ever seen. It's huge, with velvet seats and a small table with bottles of booze and an array of snacks on it.

That's insane. Even the dressing rooms here are catered.

Valentin is quick to join me. Without a word, he takes a seat and pours amber liquid into a glass.

After a long sip, he looks up at me and smirks. "Strip."

I do, and I'm a little self-conscious at first, just standing there in my panties, but Valentin offers me plenty of direction. "Panties, too. Then come here."

I lower them, shifting down my thighs and off my feet as he watches intently. The focus in his deep blue eyes makes my toes curl.

When I'm completely naked, he leans forward and wraps a hand around the leash. Then he pulls me to him. "Now, climb on up and feed me that beautiful pussy."

"Valentin!"

"My store now. My rules."

Another tug sends me sprawling into him.

Digging his hand under my ass, he helps me climb onto the seat. Then I'm guided into position.

The second he kisses my clit, I nearly fall to the floor. But his strong hand tenses around my ass, keeping me in place as he eats me out.

Ecstasy lashes up from every flick of his tongue, forming an intense pressure that builds out from somewhere deep inside of me.

I dig my hands into his hair for good measure and let my body succumb to his will.

"Fucking delicious," he growls, lapping up my wetness.

My hips start to sway into his face. I pull and push at his head until we sync in a perfect rhythm. It feels so good that I nearly pass out.

Somehow, I manage to keep my wits about me. But even if I couldn't, I know I wouldn't fall. Valentin's got me.

It's like some depraved version of a trust fall.

I trust him. To hold me. To catch me.

To make me fucking erupt.

And that's exactly what he does.

"Cum for me, angel," he demands. "Fucking drown me."

The words alone are enough to send me over the edge.

The pressure in my core cracks, spilling out over the rest of my body as I explode over Valentin's face.

"Oh my god," I pant, every inch of me trembling. "That felt amazing."

Tugging down at my leash, Valentin brings me face-to-face with him.

"Just wait until I get you home tonight," he warns, before kissing me hard and deep.

I can taste myself on him.

"Yes," I sigh, filled with satisfaction.

'I wasn't lying, was I?"

"About what?"

"About how fucking delicious you are."

My cheeks flush as he releases me.

"I guess you weren't lying..."

I stand on shaky legs as Valentin runs his gaze over the dresses in the changeroom. After a moment of consideration, he nods at the blue one.

"That one."

I carefully pluck it from the hanger, trying not to note the two thousand dollar price tag. But before I can put it on, he leans over and grabs it from me.

Like it's nothing, he uses the expensive dress to wipe his glistening lips. Then, as if that wasn't enough, he yanks me forward by the leash and uses it to clean up between my legs before dropping it to the floor.

"Valentin do you—"

"I own it." He reminds me, checking his watch. "Look at that, we're running late. We'll save the rest of your fashion show for another time. Tonight, you're wearing the silver dress."

I don't bother negotiating. I grab the outfit and pull it on.

"It... it's amazing."

That's no exaggeration. It clings to me like a dream, dipping low in the back, almost to my ass.

Looking around, I spot a small pile of panties in the corner of the changeroom. Valentin must have brought them in. But when I make a move toward them, he shakes his head.

"I've changed my mind. I don't want you wearing anything else tonight. You're going to be nice and bare under that dress, just in case I'm in need of dessert before we get home."

He stands and holds out his arm. I take it.

"It's quite the dress," I acknowledge.

"Nothing compared to your designs."

Winding the leash around his hand, he pulls me nice and close.

"Now, let's go to dinner. I can't wait to show you off, my queen"

"If I'm your queen, does that make you my king?"

He smiles, and those deep blue eyes glisten.

"It does."

I can't help but like the sound of that.

29

VALENTIN

We walk into the hottest restaurant in Chicago, hand in hand, and Yelena looks right at home.

No. Better than that. She looks like she owns the place.

And in a way, she does.

Because *I* own it.

Leaf. This place makes that French restaurant Yelena got dumped out of look like... well, a dump.

But it's not just the décor and food that make this place special. This is where the rich and famous love to be seen. And I want her to be seen. I want her treated like the queen she is.

What better place than my establishment?

The exclusiveness of the place isn't lost on Yelena at all. I saw that when we arrived. It shone bright in her eyes.

But that's not why her grip around my hand is loosened. Why those perfect blue eyes are wide and shimmering and half-lost in a daydream.

No. It's not my restaurant that has her speechless. It's what happened back at the store. The realization that one of her dreams finally came true.

And they did come true.

I didn't lie to her. It unfolded exactly as I told her. Almost.

I left out the part where I made them sell to me, made an offer they couldn't refuse because I wanted to make sure no one could ever exploit my angel again, not even when I get too busy to keep my eye on every single detail of her life.

And it seems like it's all going to work out.

Everyone's happy.

Yelena, I hope, most of all.

On my end, it's also a great investment that'll get me excellent returns. Because I might be a controlling brute, but I like making money. Especially clean money to balance out the dirty.

"Impressed?" I ask her, as we're seated in the private mezzanine level.

Here we can overlook the rest of the restaurant and the glittering people filling the space below.

And they can see us—more specifically, her.

I want the world to see the beautiful creature I'm with.

"It... it's very impressive," Yelena agrees, trying to gather her bearings. "But... listen, I need to know. Did you buy the store just to give me money?"

"A complicated question." I wait for our personal waiter to pour us the wine. An organic orange wine I've been informed is perfect for a pre-dinner drink. "The easiest answer is: I only solved your problem because it will make me lots of money. And it will only make me lots of money because you're so talented."

"Is that why you're taking me to the most exclusive restaurant in town? To celebrate our business deal?"

"No. This doesn't have anything to do with business. This is about us."

"And what are we?" She almost looks nervous to ask.

I just smile and touch my glass to hers before I take a sip.

"King and queen."

She relaxes a bit as bewilderment fills her light laughter.

"I've got to admit, I never thought I'd get into a place like this, even if my designs took off someday. Do you know how long the wait list is?"

"I'm aware."

"Then—"

"I wanted you to eat like the queen you are. This place has the second best food in Chicago. And you're overdressed for a taco truck."

Her eyes widen. "Tacos? What?"

I slip my fingers into the leash's handle and tug her close. "I own more than this place, angel. And while this spot wins out in décor, nothing beats the food at my taco truck."

"What an eclectic businessman you are," she teases.

I nod. "I love food. And money. And both restaurants have proved insanely profitable. I don't spend money if I don't believe in the product."

"And you believe in my designs."

"I believe in you and your designs, yes."

The shock starts to dissipate from her face as Yelena's chest finally puffs out a little with pride.

"Alright," she says. "I believe you."

"Good. Now, take a look at the menu." I lean in a little closer and sip a kiss from her soft lips. "I think the other patrons have seen enough of my queen for one night."

I lift my free hand and snap my fingers. Just like that, heavy curtains are drawn along the balcony, blocking off the rest of the restaurant and its ambient noise.

"You are now for my eyes only."

"You're too much," she giggles, shifting in her seat before getting up. "But... mind if I use the lady's room?"

I nod, and she starts to walk past me, but pauses to put her hand on my shoulder. "It goes both ways, you know. I don't need them vying for your attention. You look..." she leans in and kisses me on the cheek and then whispers against my lips, "like the most handsome man in the world. You take my breath away, Valentin."

Heat flares in my chest. My heart squeezes tight.

I stare at her perfect ass as she struts away. Knowing she's going commando underneath that pretty dress is enough to make my cock hard. I'll have to check if she's as aroused as I am when she gets back.

Until then...

When she disappears from view, I pull my phone out. It hasn't stopped buzzing since we entered the front doors. But I've been ignoring it.

I'm about to put it on silent when I see Ilya's message.

You're right. Definitely him.

A muscle ticks in my jaw.

I reviewed the footage from our security cameras, but now I've got the official confirmation. I don't feel vindicated, just fucking furious. That motherfucker wore a disguise, but some things, like fucking tattoos, are dead giveaways.

Sandro broke into Yelena's place.

I'm going to make sure he pays dearly for it.

Ilya's been coordinating security footage from all around the city, trying to find out where he went.

I'll get him. Find out why he broke into my angel's place, and kill him.

Okay, maybe I'll torture him first, get the information we need, and then kill him.

Because I need to know why he's doing this.

Is he just a power-hungry savage? Is he working with Civati?

Apart from being Italian, I haven't found a connection between the two of them... yet. But that doesn't mean there isn't one.

I order a whiskey and down it, my fingers curling into fists.

I don't know what the fuck Sandro did in Yelena's apartment. I don't have cameras in her apartment.

All I know is he left with seemingly nothing. So, he didn't take anything, and if he did, it was small enough to hide on his person.

Or he put something in her place.

Like a bug.

But why?

My phone buzzes again. This time it's Vlad, head of my security team. He rarely texts, so I'm instantly curious.

But all he tells me is the perimeter is secure around the restaurant and at home.

This is why I handpick my people. Vlad's smart and intuitive and, while I don't need this personal reassurance, I do appreciate it.

I'm still trying to figure out Sandro's angle when Yelena returns.

I instantly put my phone away and pull her into my arms.

"There you are."

When she's around, everything else can wait.

"I was just in the little girl's room," she giggles. "It's amazing in there."

"Well, I'm glad you're back. I was getting hungry."

"You could have ordered without me."

I pull at her leash until her lips are on mine. While we kiss, I make sure she feels my hard-on.

"I didn't mean I was hungry for the food."

Her stomach growls and we both laugh.

"I guess I am, though."

"Then let's get to it."

Standing up, I pull out her chair and wait until she's seated. "Thank you," she blushes.

There's a dreamy little smile on her face that goes straight to my chest. Then she sighs. "Natalya called so I had to take it; otherwise, she'd be interrupting all night."

"I had the same problem," I grin. "But we can fix that by drowning our phones in vodka."

She laughs. "You wouldn't. Would you?"

"I'm a man of my word."

"That's why I like you." Yelena flips open her menu, but then she flicks me a glance. "What is it?"

"Nothing."

"There's something."

Is it that obvious that Sandro's still bugging me?

"Work shit," I say, not daring to tell her the truth. She's involved in this work shit now. And that's dangerous.

Yelena nods. I can tell she wants to ask more, but by now she knows me well enough. Tonight is about her. About us. I'll do my best to keep the outside world at bay.

"Okay, so what should we eat?"

She starts reading through the menu and I watch as she picks and chooses.

I've had most of the dishes here, even though the menu changes frequently. I'm interested in what she'll choose, so I don't push or guide. I like hearing her opinions, her hesitations, the questions she peppers the waiter with when he comes to refill our glasses.

But beneath it all, I'm fucking furious.

How dare Sandro involve her?

I want heads off and smashed. And I know Yelena picks up on it, but she remains coy. It's not that I don't want to share. I do. I want to open up my world to her, invite her into every corner. But she's had enough worry in her life the past few months.

I want to treat her, not concern her.

I'll figure out what's going on, then I'll handle it. Hopefully, she won't have to know a thing. Because she doesn't deserve the darkness of my world, only the light and the riches.

Only the fancy restaurants and million-dollar checks.

Not the competitive freaks breaking into her apartment because she's connected to me.

Fucking Sandro Barella.

His fate is sealed. He's a dead man walking.

And my girl? She'll be protected. By me.

Yelena smiles, touching my hand. "I can't decide. What do you think?"

"Your choice, angel." I pick up her hand and kiss it. "What does your heart desire?"

"Everything looks so good."

"Then everything is what you shall receive."

A blush stains her cheeks and I'm left breathless by her beauty all over again. "No, Valentin," she laughs, knowing I'm serious. "That's a waste of food."

"How about we do chef's choice, then? And after, we can decide if we want more?"

"That sounds better."

I grin and kiss her ring finger. "Perfect."

I soak in her excitement as we order, knowing that she won't particularly enjoy what must come next.

This will be our last night out for a while. That's why it has to be so special.

One night. Before I have to lock her away for her own safety.

30

YELENA

Dinner was amazing.

Honestly, I don't even think it was the food—though it might have been the best meal I've ever had.

It was the company. The impossibly handsome man at my table.

Valentin.

He walks in front of me as we make our way through the back halls of our third destination of the night. His club. Silo247.

"I'm sorry, angel," he says, opening the door to his private office. "I've got to take care of a little work."

I want to ask if it can wait, but I don't. The words feel mean, ungrateful to a man who clearly wants to spend time with me. A man who Natalya took great pains in her call to tell me would work 48 hours in a single day if that was possible.

Basically, up until me, she says, he was the biggest workaholic she'd ever seen, and that includes her husband.

And now, Valentin's making time.

For me.

He punches in a code, the throb of the music filtering into

the hall and I glance up at the security feeds. The screens show everyone down below as they drink, dance, and wait in line.

A small shiver works its way up my spine. I briefly remember how it felt before our most recent reunion, where I could almost sense someone watching me at all times.

Was it Valentin?

Almost certainly.

Like he can read my thoughts, Valentin turns his head and smiles. "The cameras are just a safety precaution, angel. I'm not sitting here and staring at them all night long."

His gaze slides over me and heat surges.

"Now, maybe if there was something better on TV..."

"You know, I've been to this club before, right? It seems like a different lifetime ago now."

"I'll have to bring up the footage. I'm sure you looked incredible."

His hand splays out on the door and he pauses for a moment.

I can feel his deep blue eyes on me, but suddenly, I can't look at anything but the door.

The heavy panels are painted in a dark black coat. But not even that pitch-black paint can completely cover the subtle scars, bullet holes, and blood stains that crisscross the frame.

I hold my breath at the heavy reminder.

This is what I'm getting myself into.

Is Valentin worth it?

After tonight, only one answer comes to mind.

Yes.

"Let's get you inside, angel," he says, his deep voice nestling deep in my bones.

He pushes the door open and we tumble into the office, and when it clicks shut behind us, the fear from the scars outside disappears. In its place comes a strange kind of comfort.

That door. It keeps all the bad stuff out. It protects us.

Just like Valentin protects me.

"Take a seat," Valentin gestures to a chair on the front side of an impressive mahogany desk.

I look around the office, sinking into the warmth of that strange comfort, when I spot something that threatens to shatter my sense of safety.

"The crest…"

The words slip out of my mouth.

Sure enough, Valentin's silver crest floats in the darkness just behind his desk. It's the same as at the penthouse. The same viper that coils around my neck.

"That's right," I hear Valentin say. He walks behind the desk and opens up the panel behind the crest. Another vault is revealed. "Do you want to see what's inside?"

Nerves nip beneath my skin and I find myself nodding and moving closer to him, like my feet have a will of their own.

"Or through there," he says pointing to a door I almost missed, "is a safer, more comfortable suite than this. There's a bed, booze, food, a bathroom."

"Are you preparing for Armageddon?"

"Not tonight. Tonight, I'm offering you a choice. You can nap while I do more work, or we can look in the vault."

I don't miss the wicked gleam in his eyes. "No one's sleeping when you have a series of mysterious vaults lying around."

"That's my girl," he grins. "The vault it is."

He punches in another code and it opens. But it's too dark to make out what's inside from this side of the desk. All I can see is what Valentin takes out.

And that's enough to make my mouth go dry…

And curl my toes.

Restraints.

Candles.

I meet Valentin's eye, but he just raises a brow and sets the items on his chair before clearing his desk.

Suddenly, it doesn't look like a desk anymore.

It looks like a sacrificial altar.

A familiar pressure returns to my core. As does an exhilarating little jolt of fear.

"Strip, angel. But leave the collar and the shoes on, then get on your back so I can admire the view."

"W-what if someone comes in?"

He laughs. "No one would dare. Besides, the door's locked."

With a deep breath, I slide the dress from my shoulders until it pools at my feet. Valentin holds out his hand and helps me on the desk.

His gaze moves slowly over my body.

"You truly are perfection." He skims his finger along my flesh, over my hard nipples and down to my pubic bone, touching me everywhere but where I ache to be touched most. "One day, I'll show you what's in the penthouse's vault. And my other ones, too. But for now, we start with this. Let's see if you can handle it."

He moves out of sight and the lights dim to a soft glow. I stare up at the ceiling, swallowing hard, trying to get a grip on what's about to happen.

My mind's racing with ideas of what he can do with the restraints and candles.

I find out soon enough.

First, Valentin lights the candles, then he sets them at the four points of the desk. If I move, I could knock them to the floor.

So, I stay as still as possible, even as a thrilling, erotic fear slides over my skin.

"Do you trust me, Yelena?"

Valentin's voice is deep and assured.

"I do."

"Good."

Leaning over me, he hooks the leather restraints into something out of sight. I try to keep my breath steady as he takes one arm and positions it right at the candle, wrapping a soft black cloth around my wrist before locking on the restraint.

The same ritual is repeated on my other arm, then my ankles, until I'm stretched out, open, a sacrifice for him and his desires.

"How's that, angel?" He tests to see if the restraints are too tight, totally consumed by the task. His level of intensity makes my breath flutter.

"It's alright."

"If this gets to be too much, I want you to say viper. That's our safe word. Not no, not stop, but viper."

"V-viper."

"That's right. Say it and I'll stop. Promise." His hand comes up around my throat, above the choke collar. "But I think you're strong enough to take it all."

This time actual fear beats in my blood. "Take what?"

"This."

Valentin picks up a candle and holds it above my ribs, then tips it, letting the hot wax drip and bite at my exposed skin. I hiss at the pain—or maybe it's the shock that gets me first, because it only hurts for a split second before morphing into something sharply pleasing. Something exciting.

He does it again, and again, holding the candle closer so I feel the heat of the flame. All four candles are used as my body is covered in a coat of wax. The searing drops paint my nipples, nip at the tender skin of my inner thighs.

I close my eyes

"These candles are handmade in Russia," I hear Valentin say. "They were brought here when Andrei and I first overthrew the previous Bratva boss."

Each drop makes my back arch sharper. Away, toward, I'm not sure. It feels so good, but only after the initial tinge of pain.

It heightens my senses. Turns me on. Makes me whimper.

"That man was unworthy of the title. We were not."

Leaning slightly, Valentin covers my soaking pussy with the palm of his hand, protecting it as he playfully drips hot wax onto the surrounding area.

At first, I jump and shake, but the calming presence of his hand somehow eases the pain and elevates the pleasure.

"These candles were burning when Andrei was crowned. When my life changed forever."

Valentin's protective hand softly lifts, and I tense up, waiting for the wax to drip onto my most sensitive area. Instead, I only feel the wet heat of Valentin's lips as he kisses me gently. Despite the tenderness, the act threatens to overwhelm my senses.

"They also burned when I was named second in command. And they burned as we retook our blood oath, the one that made us brothers. Family. The scars on my arm? On his? We reopened them and sealed that bond."

Drip. Drip. Drip. I try so hard to focus on the wax and where it hits. But Valentin's tongue circles around my clit. I want to erupt. To scream. But I clamp my lips shut and whimper in silence.

I don't want to interrupt this.

It's too special.

"You are part of my family too, now, angel. But I never want to make you bleed again." He pauses, his hot breath washing over my wet lips. "I took your virginity. You pricked your finger when it should have been my blood. So, we do this ritual instead."

He rises up my body and licks a path down my throat to the collar.

"The wax symbolizes the shield I am to you. The one that will always cover your soul, flesh, and heart. I'm your protector, Yelena. And you will never suffer again in your life. This is the last of your pain."

"I-I'm not suffering," I whisper. "Not too badly. It feels good."

"Perfect. Then let's continue."

The wax starts to drip near my nipples again, and my hands turn into fists, clenching in excited and dreaded anticipation.

"You are so strong, angel," Valentin says, his free hand finding my soaking pussy. "So brave. So. Fucking. Beautiful."

His thick finger finds my clit and I nearly jump off the table. But the restraints hold me down, and he leads me in circles as I rattle and shake with pleasure.

"I'm going to cum," I pant, every part of me trembling.

"Do it. Cum for me, angel. Now."

My body obeys.

I explode. The pleasure erupting in relief across my body.

"Yes!" I cry. "Thank you! Thank you!"

"My fucking pleasure."

I never want this feeling to end.

I need Valentin inside me. I want to worship him, too. Let him do more to me. Anything. Everything. I just want whatever he has to give. I want to give him all I have.

"Such a good girl," Valentin rumbles, but I barely hear him.

I'm moaning. Loud. My breathing deepens as he blows out the candles and unties me, tearing off a piece of the black cloth as he does so.

Then, without a word, he pulls a switchblade from his pocket and cuts into his ring finger.

The blood drips onto the cloth.

He wraps his hand on the leash and tugs me to him. "I don't want to make you bleed again—"

I immediately understand what he's doing.

"But you need my blood."

Even through the satisfied haze filling my head, I manage to take the knife and stab the top of my ring finger. Valentin doesn't stop me. Instead, he just stares into my eyes, a look of pride and hunger filling his ocean blue gaze. Without losing eye contact, he wraps the cloth around my finger, letting my blood mix with his.

"Now it is done right. We belong to each other in a way no ring can ever hope to match. You are mine. I am yours." He folds the cloth and slides it into his pocket. "I'll never go anywhere without this cloth. It is my pledge to you."

Then he takes my finger and sucks the blood. Without thinking, I do the same to him.

He groans. "You are incredible."

With surprisingly soft hands, he picks me up off the table. I let him, going completely limp in his arms as he carries me through his private suite, then into a bathroom.

I'm placed back down on my feet as he turns on the shower.

"Let's get you cleaned up," he says, stripping down.

For a second, I can't do anything but stare at his big, tightly muscled, tattooed body.

He's so fucking gorgeous I can't breathe.

I remain hypnotized by him as he pulls me under the hot water and helps wash the dried wax off my body.

Every touch feels like a miracle. His big, violent hands caress my sensitive skin like butterfly wings. He's so gentle, I almost don't notice how hard he is.

Almost.

But he's too big to miss. Too mouth-watering to ignore.

"I see that look in your eye," he says, placing me against the slick wall. "Do you think you can handle more?"

I swallow and nod. There isn't an ounce of doubt in me.

"Then that's what I'll give you."

My thighs wrap around him as he pushes into me. When his cock breaks my threshold, I lose my breath and my nails cling to his back.

He welcomes the pain, grunting as he thrusts up.

My mind goes blank. He fucks me hard and fast, the intensity building as the shower fills with steam.

Then, we both erupt together.

The hot water dances over our heads, trickling down our faces as we pant in place, faces buried in each other's bodies.

I lap up his wet skin. He runs his hand through my soaked hair and pulls my face back.

"Let's go home."

All I can do is nod.

Home.

That's exactly what this feels like.

31

VALENTIN

The frantic knocking and ringing of the doorbell rips me awake.

I'm immediately on high alert. I drag on underwear, and grab my gun, leaving Yelena sleeping in bed.

My poor angel's exhausted from the club, the shower, and the fun we had when we got back here.

The knocking doesn't stop and I check the intercom.

"Ilya." I press the button. "Hold on."

Even though I knew it would be one of my people, I still don't ever take that for granted. Taking the stairs, gun in hand, I race downstairs and rip open the door.

"What the hell took you so long?"

Ilya pushes past me and I slam the door behind him, following as he heads to my study.

"What are you doing here?" I demand to know, checking the time on my phone.

He takes over my computer, types something and spins it. A map.

"I tried calling but you didn't answer."

"It's three a.m."

"The wicked never sleep." He jabs a finger at the computer. "Look."

I set my gun down and lean over the computer. "Sandro?"

"Bingo. I managed to track his location. He's been holed up there for days—with security, of course. But right now, it looks like he's alone." Ilya glares up at me, a wild look in his eyes. "It's now or fucking never, man. I don't know why, but Sandro is essentially alone. We finally have him in our sights."

"He's got some fucking questions to answer."

"Damn right."

We share a knowing nod and Ilya takes my computer as I turn and head for the stairs. Opening my phone, I text Vlad.

Need you here and at least four of your best.

Home protection? he asks.

Yes. I pause. *Yelena.*

Got it, boss. On our way.

When I get back to the bedroom, Yelena is sitting up in bed, hair a delicious mess and one pink nipple showing. There's a bite mark above it that reminds me of last night.

The warmth. The wonder.

That's all on pause as I pull on clothes. Trousers, a long sweater, boots. The clothes I can fight in. The clothes that'll hide blood.

I want Sandro to see me and fucking quake. In the bathroom, I catch my reflection. It's savage rage and ruthless ice. If he's smart, he'll be pissing his pants.

"What's wrong?" Yelena asks.

"Duty calls. I need to head out?"

"Can I come? It won't take me long to get ready."

A whip of pride spreads through my chest.

She's not afraid anymore.

"It's not safe, angel."

"So?"

"So, you're going to stay here and live to be brave another day."

I cross to her and touch her cheek, too aware of the ticking clock in my head, and of Ilya waiting down in my study. So, I stay standing.

"Well, I can just go home and—"

"No. You're not leaving."

It's sharper than I mean it.

Yelena narrows her eyes, pulling the sheet up to cover that pretty tit. "And what if I insist?"

"I'm sorry. I'm not giving you a choice. This is for your own—."

"Am I your prisoner?"

I know how it must seem to her. And she's not wrong. But by now, my motivations should be clear.

"You are my queen. And queens stay behind palace gates. They listen to their guard. I have a whole army coming to protect you in my stead." I blow out a breath, hating the sudden stillness to her. "Then, when I get back, we can go anywhere you want."

She's quiet a beat too long. "I understand."

It's clear she doesn't. At least, not entirely.

It kills me to see her like this. She wants to join, but she can't. She wants to ride the high of getting her own clothing line, but she can't. For her own good, she needs to sit tight just as the world seems to be turning her way.

"No. I understand," I assure her, leaning down for a kiss. But her lips are surprisingly cold. I force myself to chalk it up to her being tired. It's the only way I can pull away.

Ilya shouts at me to hurry.

"I have to go. You have everything you need here, and when I get back things will be better. I promise."

"Be safe," she murmurs, even through her disappointment.

I can't stop myself from taking her cheeks in my hand. Planting one last tender kiss on her lips, I catalog her scent.

She's so sweet smelling, so soft and warm that it twists inside me, and I whisper, "I love you, angel."

Those words have been there, waiting, and it occurs to me I didn't want them to have freedom until the time was right. They disagreed.

And now they're out. I'm lighter than before.

"I love you," I say again. "It's the truth."

She sucks in a breath, her hands clutching at me, but she doesn't say anything back.

It hurts.

But I don't know if it's because she's too stunned, too mad at me for keeping her here, or just still half asleep.

Or maybe she simply doesn't love me back.

Not yet.

I don't have time to find out, and I also know how hard they are to say until you say it.

Ilya shouts from downstairs.

I straighten up.

"Bye, angel."

The walk from the bed to the bedroom door is the longest of my life. I stop just outside, wanting to look back. But I stop myself.

I wasn't expecting any of that.

What a fucking disaster.

With my heart sitting heavy in my chest, I stomp down to the foyer. Ilya waiting, holding my holster for me.

I slip it on, taking my other gun from him and then my jacket.

"Have a nice little nap up there?" he teases, checking his own gun.

But I'm in no mood.

"Let's go."

He seems to get the point.

"We're picking Andrei up along the way," he says, glancing down at his phone as we get into the car. "Looks like Vlad is joining us, too."

I scowl.

That motherfucker is supposed to be coming here. I've got a precious package for him to look after.

Checking the rearview mirror, I stare back at the mansion and consider abandoning this whole hunt.

Ilya seems to read my mind.

"Don't worry. Vlad is still sending his best men over. And you have a good security system, right?"

"The best," I grumble.

But none of that matters. If Sandro was the one threatening Yelena, then she should be safe while I'm out cornering him.

"Let's go get this fucker, Valentin. That's what we've been working for. Then you can come back here and take a nice long vacation. How does that sound?"

I sneer. He's right. I have a job to do... plus, it seems like Yelena needs some space. She'll be safest here, all while I make the world out there a safer place for her.

"That sounds like a fucking plan," I growl, cracking my neck. "Let's go kill this fucking rat."

32

Valentin's words ricochet through my head.

Not just the words of love, but how he essentially told me I'm trapped here until further notice.

He can paint the scene however he likes, pretty it up or whatever, but it's still obvious I'm like a pet to lock indoors.

And that's making me feel uneasy. Like he chose me deliberately because I ticked criteria off for him.

I know how these things go.

The traditions.

It's what happened to Natalya. Sure, she seems happy now. But at what cost?

I shudder.

To be completely respected, Valentin needs a wife. It's the way the Bratva works. Like a do-it-yourself future dynasty. Find the right woman to pop out the right babies and—

It hurts to breathe.

The harsh reality of his words hit hard.

It's one thing to fall for a man and have him fall for you. Another to be a deliberate choice, manipulated into this position.

Maybe I'm just sleepy. Maybe he's just left me in the lurch one too many times, maybe I'm unreasonable, but there's a dark bile in the back of my throat I just can't shake.

I've gotten so lost in the feeling of home that he inspires, that I haven't seen the prison bars that line the windows.

I've been distracted. Vulnerable. Foolish.

The man is too good looking, too charming, and real in a way that calls to me, and I thought we fell for each other naturally. He made it seem that way.

He said he loves you.

But he bought his way into my career, used money to purchase my dreams, my future. He showers me with nice things. With sex and adoration.

It's hot. There's no denying that. And there's no denying I'm falling for him, too. Maybe I've already fallen.

But what recently felt like a dream now drips with unshakable dread.

That million dollar check, the business, my career; Valentin didn't just buy me a fast track path to success. He's bought me.

He owns me.

My clothes. My designs. My business.

I'll report to him, work for him, answer to him, bend to whatever he might want. Until that contract is up—and I'm sure he signed on my behalf. He's Bratva, he doesn't follow rules—I'm at his mercy.

Even now, I'm under lock and key. His prisoner.

Not that I wanted to go anywhere. I just didn't' want him to leave. Again. Then something slipped between us, and it felt like, momentarily, I saw the true side of him.

It made his unthinkable words feel shallow.

He said he loves you.

I almost said it back. But the dread wouldn't let me.

With heavy eyes, I throw back the covers and get dressed. Why did he have to tell me I couldn't leave? My heart beats fast.

If he hadn't, I'd never have thought of maybe going out, or... I don't know.

But as I head down to the kitchen, I realize how wrong that is.

It's clear I'm not meant to go anywhere.

The place crawls with guards. At least four roam the area between the front door and the kitchen, though it's hard to tell the exact number because they all look down and scurry away as I approach.

My heart twists. Valentin must have given orders that no one's to look at me.

It's a funny kind of loneliness that builds as I float into the kitchen. It makes me feel like a leper, stuck in some twisted, gothic fairytale.

It's suffocating.

At least if Ilya was here, I'd have someone to talk to. Instead, I make a bowl of granola and yogurt and pile on the berries. I'm not overly hungry, but I need something to do and I have to eat. I don't want to come down again for a while and this... well, it'll hold me over.

I set it down with a bottle of water by the bed and climb back on, even though there's a perfectly good sofa and chairs to sit on nearby.

With nothing better to do, I start reading through emails on my phone. When those turn out to be mostly junk, I scroll through Instagram and all the fashion blogs. Sure enough, the sale of the exclusive store is there, but no word on the mysterious buyer, just that things won't change much, apart from hosting an exciting new line.

I start to smile, but it freezes as I remember who the buyer is and that maybe this new line—mine—isn't that exciting at all.

"Stop it," I mutter, flipping to a celebrity gossip feed. "Just keep calm."

Easy advice, hard to follow. But for my own sake, I try my best to. Maybe I should call Natalya, but then again, what would that do? She's so involved in the Bratva life that she sees Valentin as a good thing for me.

And I bet she'd tell me he's just protective. Like Andrei is with her. Like I'm a fucking child.

If there weren't guards, I'd try to leave, just go home and breathe in my own space.

Instead, I pull up some fashion TikToks, not because they'll unleash something brilliant in my head, but because I desperately need some harmless, mindless fun—

My phone suddenly flashes with a text.

Kira.

I frown. Of everyone I thought I'd hear from, she's low down on the list. After how the interview went, how I left, she's got some fucking nerve contacting me.

A small growl escapes.

She better not want to try to get an interview again. Shaking, I read her message.

Yelena, I'm so sorry again for what happened. I never meant to upset you. I'd never publish anything about you without express permission. It's always off record until you say otherwise. So, if you want to talk, I'm here. But I have to warn you

The message suddenly ends, like she got interrupted and I stare, heart leaping.

Warn me about what?

I grip my phone tight, fingers hovering over the keys, when another message comes through.

about the danger. I think I cracked the code of what happened at the conference. You're in danger. Pls call/text. I'm here and can help.

I'm practically sparking with fear and confusion. Does she know something I don't already?

With all I've been through, it feels hard to believe that she does.

Still, part of me wonders if I should call or text her back. Or maybe it's some kind of trap. I don't know.

For a while, I just stare at my phone. Then, I try to distract myself from making a decision by going back to my socials. But Kira's text pokes at me.

With a deep breath, I read her message one more time.

Then, I decide to call her. Maybe I'm just bored. Maybe it's the dread of being trapped here. Bought and paid for. My best friend is part of this life. If I needed help escaping, who else could I rely on?

Kira.

If I don't like what she has to say, I'll—

Shouts and yells break into the silence of the room. I look up from my phone... then nearly jump off the mattress as a rapid succession of booms rattles the air.

My stomach drops.

I know that sound.

Gunfire.

I scream off the bed, as if that will protect me.

The gunshots get louder. Quicker. Then people start yelling. I hear screaming.

I look frantically around for a weapon as my adrenaline spikes and my blood turns cold.

What the hell's going on?

The bedroom door shakes and I freeze. Someone's trying to get in. I glance at the bathroom. Instinct pulls me onto my feet. I try to run and hide in there.

But it's too late.

The bedroom door slams open and smoke curls in.

So does the scent of blood and death. I fall to the floor. When I look up, I can see a pair of boots. Black liquid pools around their ragged soles.

I'm instantly flooded with flashbacks of the bathroom at

Sweetwater. The dead PI.

Blood. It's blood.

Oh God.

The smoke clears as someone steps inside the doorway.

My stomach falls through the fucking floor.

"No..."

It's Alex.

"Well, hello, *whore*. Fancy running into you here," strengthening his immaculate suit, he takes another threatening step forward. "Tell me, is this the bed he fucks you in? What a pity. Such squalor. You deserved better. But I guess you like being treated like a common bitch. I can do that, too. In fact, I insist. Or maybe, I won't touch used goods."

Suddenly, four burly men in black tactical gear appear out of the smoke behind him. They hold massive guns. The smell of death follows them in.

I'm so scared I can't move.

"What the hell are you doing here?"

Alex clicks his tongue and shakes his head. "The mouth on you. I'll have to clean it out with soap... or maybe something worse."

I swallow, a cold chill pebbling my skin.

"Valentin. He... He'll kill you."

The words slip out. I have no idea what's going on.

But one thing's clear.

Valentin isn't doing any killing here.

Because he's not here.

No one's coming to save me.

I'm totally fucked.

33

The construction site is abandoned. It feels like a graveyard.

Or a trap.

It's not one of our projects or even an Italian one—at least, as far as Ilya could work out. Just some project financed by an absentee billionaire who barely ever visits Chicago.

Still, because it's not one of ours, we approach everything with caution, especially as we head up the concrete stairs in a hollowed-out, half-finished office space.

I make eye contact with Andrei and he nods, holds up two fingers and points. We have men scouring downstairs and Vlad's at the gate, making sure troops keep the area around the building secured.

This is do or die.

Breathing lightly, I keep my adrenalin contained. I can't lose focus. Every sound is filtered and cataloged. The steps and light clangs of our people as we move—and then, something else.

Above.

I live for shit like this, it makes me come alive like nothing else. Or, it did. Now something else does that. Yelena.

Fuck. Yelena. The look on her face as I pulled away.

I told her I loved her, and she...

No. Not now. I push her from my mind. It's too dangerous to think of her here. I need to be on my game.

Andrei and Ilya step out, making their way across the open concrete room.

I wait, looking for a way up. The barren stairwell is the obvious way, but it's also the most dangerous. When I peer up, the darkness above is dense.

Anything could be up there.

Again, I hear that suspicious sound. The scrape and soft clang that comes from above.

Noises in empty spaces have a way of ricocheting, of being disorientating, but this... no. It's above.

Fuck.

Making my way to an empty doorway, I scan the dusty ceiling. Andrei and Ilya are at my back, guns out, ready to attack.

They heard the sound, too. Andrei tells Ilya he thinks it's from this floor, and it sounds like it when you stand where we are now. The hesitant and light crunches and clangs, like someone's shifting, moving, trying to hide. But it isn't from this floor.

I look up.

There, a few feet in front of us, a giant section of the ceiling is missing. I stare through the darkness, searching for shapes in the shadows.

Then, something flashes, light on metal, the shift of an arm.

I swing out and point my gun. "Above!"

Andrei and Ilya jump into action, stepping up and pointing their gun in the same direction as mine.

For a tense second, nothing happens. No one shoots. No one shouts.

Then, I take matters into my own hands.

"Get down here now, Sandro. We'd like a little talk. Words, bullets, your choice," I say.

"The place is crawling with our people," adds Andrei. "You'll never make it out, even if you manage to shoot us first."

"And believe me, you're not quick enough to get all of us before we get you. So, put your gun away and get the fuck down here."

A deep, hoarse laughter echoes down from the darkness.

"Liars. You don't have anyone else, or they'd be here."

"Maybe we don't need backup," Andrei bluffs, giving me time to press the call button on my phone. It's a signal for Vlad.

"I'm disappointed in the big, bad Russians not being able to fucking find me without my help. The city deserves better. The underworld deserves better." The sound of a cocking gun descends from the darkness. "The underworld deserves me."

"Feeling a little unappreciated, there, huh? You fuck," I growl. "I get it. Overlooked, not accepted to a position you want in any of the many mafia families you've tried to join. A grunt man. Grunt men don't lead. They follow. They die."

I shouldn't be trying to piss him off, but I can't help it. No matter how much I try to push Yelena from my mind, all I can think about is how he was in her apartment. How he ruined her chances at the conference.

I'm going to rip him to fucking shreds.

"I'm going to destroy everything you ever worked for," Sandro hisses. "Shatter the natural order. You lot are pathetic. Weak. I'll overthrow you just like you overthrew the last guy. And it's going to be easy. After all, you served yourself up to me. And after I take out you three, the rest will come tumbling down. I'll own the Bratva and the mafia."

"Our men won't follow you." I want to shoot him so bad, but I still can't see shit up there. He keeps shifting around, and the barren architecture carries and stretches the sounds so far that I can't manage to pinpoint him.

"How did you get the documents to leak to the FBI?" Ilya asks.

"Did the Italians help?" Andrei adds.

"No," Sandro spits "Those pussies are going down, too. Pathetic bunch of losers. They were too afraid of their overlords to help me. Everyone in the underworld was too afraid. Turns out, I didn't need the underworld. I found a stooge who was stupid enough to be my patsy. And he should be finishing up his end of the bargain right about now…"

I want to ask why he bothered breaking into Yelena's apartment, but I hold it back.

"Who the fuck would help scum like you?" Andre asks instead.

"All in good time," Sandro chuckles, switching between maniacally amused and furiously angry. "You Bratva, you surround yourselves with guns and muscle and money, so bringing you down head-on could never work, for anyone. I had to be smart. Think outside the box. I needed to sabotage and distract. And what better way to do that than put you up against your greatest and most powerful enemy? The government."

"And the documents?"

"Easy to pay someone to take photos. To get access through an old computer that was linked." He laughs again. "Some expert you are, Ilya."

"I'll fucking tear you apart, rat," Ilya growls.

Sandro doesn't seem to hear. "But once I had the documents, leaking them without getting caught was hard. Hell, I'll admit, it looked nearly impossible. No one wanted to feel the wrath of the Bratva. Cowards. So, I found another way to weaken you all. And I found that way through the most primal, beastly member of your organization."

I can feel his words latch onto me.

For a moment, my blood runs cold. What am I missing? Did I fuck something up to let Sandro get an upper hand?

"You didn't do shit," I bark, my eyes darting back and forth from the hole in the ceiling. I need to find a way up there. I'm with Ilya. We need to tear this rat to shreds.

Sandro laughs again. "Imagine when Valentin turned up at a fashion conference, sniffing about a blonde babe. I got to see his interesting interaction with a certain billionaire. I first thought of kidnapping your blonde bitch, rough her up, use her as bait, or even keep her as hostage and have fun. Valentin's clearly smitten like an idiot, and if she got sullied or hurt he'd have lost his shit. Am I right?"

I nearly go blind with rage.

"You fucking animal—"

"But you're not all brawn," Sandro loudly declares, interrupting me. "There's a brain behind that swollen face, and you locked her the fuck down, didn't you? So, I found my patsy. The one, the only..."

My heart drops.

"Alex Civati," I suddenly realize.

Sandro howls with laughter. "See, I knew you were smart. Well, just smart enough to get fooled."

I aim my gun at the darkness above and fire out my entire clip.

Sandro hoots like a deranged clown as my bullets ricochet harmlessly off cement and steel.

"Easy there, cowboy. I'm not done rubbing it in yet."

"Get down here and fight me like a fucking man!"

"I'll kill you like a king!" he roars. Coughing, he contains his manic fury to continue his bleating. "You see, I made a deal. A deal with a man outside our world. A deal you could never make. The blonde cunt is to stay alive at all costs... and the giant Russian pig is to die. You, Valentin, are to die."

A bullet hits the ground near my feet and I jump to the side, reloading my clip for a firefight. Andrei and Ilya fire up into the darkness. The thunderous applause of gunfire echoes through the cement coliseum.

But no more bullets come out of the darkness.

Sandro is fucking with us.

I don't care. I'm sick of waiting. Of listening. He can't talk about Yelena like that. Threaten her.

"I'm going to make you suffer," I snarl. "I'm going to—"

"Valentin." I ignore the low almost inaudible warning from Andrei.

"Let me finish!" Sandro booms. "All this work requires an acceptance speech. I've earned that much, haven't I?"

"You've earned a bullet in the head," Ilya bites back.

"No. I've earned your crown, Andrei Zherdev. I've earned your power, Valentin Constanov. And I've earned your knowledge, Ilya Rykov. I've earned it all. And I'll get it... just for the price of a pathetic life and a used cunt. It's a good deal, don't you think? For me, anyway."

His words about Yelena... I'm going to fucking wipe the floor with him, make him beg for death.

But he's clearly baiting me on purpose. Sandro wants me to lose my mind again. Give in to my base urges. Make a mistake.

I can't let him win. Not just for my sake or for the sake of our empire.

Something even more important is at stake.

Yelena.

Even if she hates my guts. Even if she doesn't love me back. I will protect her. Always.

And right now, I only see one way to regain control of this situation. I have to pretend like I don't give a shit about Yelena.

Easier said than done.

"Take her," I say, shaking as I try to control my rage, keep the disgust from my voice. "Just tell me how you think you'll take the Bratva's power? It's more than us. We have a whole web twisted around our fingers. And I don't see your pathetic government here backing you up right now."

Beside me, Andrei and Ilya trade glances, then look at me. I instantly understand.

"Do it," I silently mouth.

They nod. And as silently as possible, they start to branch away, looking for a way upstairs.

My job is to keep Sandro talking. For some reason, he only seems to be interested in me.

Well, me and Yelena.

Bastard.

I tighten my grip around my gun.

"The government," Sandro guffaws. "They want you dead, too. The billionaire has his own government connections. Now, they're mine. Soon, your corrupted webs will be mine as well. It's only a matter of time."

Out of the corner of my eye, I see Ilya gesture at Andrei. It looks like they might be close to finding a path to Sandro. I just need to hold his attention a little while longer.

"I see how it is," I sneer, biting my tongue. "This wasn't your plan at all. Civati's the brains. You're the real patsy. The hired help. He has the connections. You're just here to do the dirty work."

It physically hurts to give that fucker Alex any kind of compliment. Intensely. But I need this to end. If we can get it done without a battle—if I can goad him into showing himself for a clear shot, I'll fucking take it. Put a bullet in him and take down Civati.

"Bullshit." The disgust in Sandro's tone is almost as deep as my own. "I'm the brains, he's a fucking stepping stone. I manipulated him. He didn't want to get the government involved. He was too scared. But I convinced him. And he went out and got me a fucking general. Did you know that? Well, know you do. I, Sandro fucking Barella, had a general do my dirty work. He leaked the documents to the FBI. Said they landed on his desk. But he put them in the wrong hands. Corrupt hands."

"Our hands," I say. "Not very smart."

"You're right. Not smart. Genius. But my pawns are stupid. They've given me too much leverage. When this is all over…"

I tune Sandro out when I see Ilya's head pop out from around the corner up ahead. He points his gun up at the ceiling. They've found a way up.

"Are you listening to me?" Sandro bellows. "I asked you a fucking question?"

"I'm done listening. You ramble like a fool. It's time you answer one of my questions."

"Hit me with it," Sandro quickly returns.

"If you're so fucking smart. Why are you here all alone?"

His laugh starts small, then grows, expanding to fill the entire building. It's like we're surrounded by hyenas.

"Poor fool. You truly are blind. By anger. By ambition… by love. I'm not alone, Valentin Constanov. But you are."

Before I can respond, a horn blasts from somewhere nearby. The shuffle of countless footsteps follows, like roaches in the walls… or rats.

"It's a trap!" Andrei shouts in Russian.

I can't see him, but I jump to the side, using a concrete wall as cover while I prepare myself for bloodshed.

"Now, I don't understand Russian, but I can guess what he just said," Sandro continues to laugh hysterically. "But let me tell you this, whatever you think is coming, you're wrong. I'm not like you anymore. I don't have an army of thugs. I have an army of mercenaries. All thanks to yours truly. Mr. Moneybags himself. Alex Civati. My. Patsy."

The first gunshot rips through the darkness. Then, the world erupts.

"Goodbye, you fucking dinosaur." Sandro's shrill voice disappears behind the hall of bullets.

"Fucking hell," I rumble, cocking my gun.

"Over here!" Andrei yells.

I crouch low to the ground and race toward his voice. If we're going to survive this ambush, we need to do it together.

"Behind you!" Ilya yells, pointing his gun at me as I turn the corner.

I hit the deck and his bullet whizzes over my head. Something hits the ground. I look over my shoulder and see a twitching body, dressed in all-black tactical gear.

Fresh bodies are already storming up behind him.

"You fuckers!" I shout, twisting around to fire at them.

They disappear in a cloud of smoke and I scramble back onto my feet, joining Ilya just in time to spot trouble for Andrei.

He's stuck reloading his gun. And I can see the tops of approaching heads down a newly discovered stairwell.

"Brother!"

Andrei looks up just as I leap in front of him, knocking him to the ground as the first bullets dig into the wall behind us.

Ilya stays put, and he manages to catch the first few by surprise, putting them down before they can get through the doorway. But there are more coming.

"This way," Ilya shouts, gesturing toward a wall behind us.

I drag Andrei to safety as bullets rip through the concrete above our heads.

"You didn't have to do that," Andrei pants, leaning back against the wall as it cracks from gunfire. It's mostly tubing and I don't know how long it will last.

But, for a moment, at least, we have a chance to breathe.

"What? Save your ass?" I huff, reloading my guns.

"I can save myself."

"Well, I'd leave you— " I glance through a hole in the wall and empty my clip on a few more fuckers, then duck down and reload. "But Natalya would kill me."

Ilya takes the other side and Andrei covers our left.

"Shit," we all seem to grumble at the same time.

"We're fucking surrounded."

"Oh well," Ilya says, nearly laughing. "I guess I'm going to have to use all my bullets. Shame."

Andrei has a similarly light tone to him. This isn't the first time we've been in a spot like this.

"Admit it," he says, shooting another man in black tactical gear as runs at us. "You just want to get back to Yelena."

"To the right, Ilya!" I bark and shoot over his head to the left.

We may be surrounded, but we're not done yet.

We didn't come alone. All we have to do is survive long enough for Vlad and our men to fight their way up here. Andrei has undoubtedly sent him the signal by now. And even if he didn't, the gunshots would be enough to get his ass moving.

"Let's both live long enough to get back to our girls," I say, peeking around the corner as a sharp pain fills my chest.

Is Yelena really my girl anymore?

I thought she felt the same way about me, but when I left...

Sadness fills my chest, before quickly being replaced by rage.

"We need to end this," I grunt.

Every second I'm here is another second Yelena could be in danger. I don't care if she doesn't feel the same way about me. I wasn't lying. I love her. And my home's a fortress, but I didn't set it up to withstand this level of moneyed assault. We're facing a fucking hired mercenary group. Can't say I've ever done that before.

It would be fun, if so much wasn't at stake.

"Next time," says Ilya, "we should just go for ice cream."

"Honestly, I'd rather this," Andrei chuckles. He looks over at me, but when he doesn't see a smile on my face, he understands. "Hey, if you're not having fun, we can hold down the fort."

I shake my head. "I've already had to save your ass once."

Andrei purses his lips. "You know damn well I can take care of myself."

"What about Natalya?"

"She's safe. I promise you that. She understands the safety precautions. I've had her under lock and key for days now. Sandro must know that. But Yelena?"

"She's not used to it..."

"If Sandro has more mercenaries, then there's a chance they could be on their way to your place."

Panic grips my body. "I can't leave you—"

I need to stay. I need to go. Never in my life have I been so torn. Family and family, because that's what Andrei is. That's what Yelena is.

Family.

Mine.

Andrei grabs me. "Go. Make sure she's safe. We can handle a few out-of-towners."

"Don't believe in us," Ilya taunts, right before turning to empty another clip. More bodies hit the floor.

They're right.

These fuckers can handle themselves.

Andrei hooks his fingers in my top. "Remember our blood oath? We're blood brothers. Stronger than any shared parentage can fucking mean. We die and kill for each other. Go. It's an order."

"I'll protect him." Ilya crawls up, his humor gone, mouth thinned. "Now get out of here. And after all this is over, we can meet up for ice cream."

"We'll cover you," Andrei nods.

I nod back.

Without another word, I turn and make my exit, shooting like mad man. Bodies fall in front of me, but I don't hit them all, and by the time I'm back on the main floor, I can feel a whole fleet coming up my rear.

I need to hurry. I need—

Suddenly, a bullet nicks my sleeve.

"Fuck." I spin, taking down the shooter just before he can fire a second round. But he's slowed me down, and hot blood spills from my arm as the others gain on me.

I'm ready for a dogfight.

Then, all of a sudden, the fuckers following me start to fall. One by one, they become corpses. I don't see who's shooting them to know who it is.

Vlad. Our men. Ilya and Andrei. They've got my back. They know what I need to do.

And so do I.

Yelena Laskin.

I don't care if she doesn't love me back.

No one else is allowed to touch her. Threaten her. Desire her.

I'll rid the world of everyone who does.

I just hope I can make it to her before they do.

34

I wake in a fit, jolted awake from a bad dream I've already forgotten.

That's bad enough. And then I start to remember what happened.

It comes in pieces. My mind's still foggy.

I was drugged. Taken. By...

I blink, trying to orient myself.

Panic is there. The heart-pounding, wet-your-pants kind, but it's weirdly distant, like I'm separated from it, from feelings, from everything apart from the strange softness infusing my brain.

I go to put my hand to my head and it snaps me sharply into the world of feeling.

I swallow.

Alex.

He drugged me. Oh, God. Alex. He-he ripped through Valentin's house and jumped on me, smacked something stinkingly sweet and piercing over my face and then something sharp stabbed my arm.

That's when everything went black.

And now I can't move.

But it's not just because I was drugged. I've been tied to a chair.

I breathe slow. But the panic is pushing now, slamming hard against my ribs and veins.

Glancing around, I try to gather my bearings.

I'm in a large fancy living room. Giant arched windows fill the walls. In the distance, I can just make out the Chicago skyline.

Where am I?

The room's beautiful, except for the wooden kitchen chair I'm trussed to. And the weird post-modern black and white wallpaper, it's asymmetrical, no real pattern, and...

Wait.

It's not wallpaper.

Photos.

A big picture of me. Candid, like it was taken with a zoom feature from a great distance.

Fear joins my panic.

The walls are covered in pictures of me. Hundreds and hundreds of black and white photos of varying sizes.

My stomach lurches and I want to throw up.

Me. Going into my apartment, leaving. At my window.

Walking down the street.

Talking to Kira at that diner. Kira grabbing my arm. There's a close up of my face. I look miserable.

Then there's me and Valentin outside the fancy designer store. His collar winking in the light as I look up at him with shining eyes.

His entire face has been scratched out.

My eyes dart around.

Any picture with Valentin—or any other man, for that matter—has the man's face blacked out. The Valentin ones, though, are gouged with particularly violent strokes.

My heart contracts. My fingers turn numb. Tears burn my eyes.

I've been watched. Followed. Stalked.

And not by the man I fell for.

Someone else is obsessed. Someone vindictive. Someone who despises Valentin for getting close to me. Someone who's taken me from his bed and tied me up.

Alex.

"Nice of you to finally wake up. I hope you had pleasant dreams... because you aren't going to like what comes next."

The voice comes from behind me, and I jerk in my restraints, trying to get a better look.

"You bastard."

Sure enough, Alex stands near a door, leaning on the wall, arms crossed, staring.

"Maybe I am," he nods. "Maybe I am."

"No. I take that back. You're not a bastard. You're a dead man. Valentin's going to—"

Alex interrupts me with a loud, fake laugh. "Valentin's not doing anything anymore. I hate to be the bearer of bad news—oh, wait, in this case, I fucking love it—but that beast is dead."

"No!" I hear myself cry, not believing it. "You're lying. You could never kill a man like that."

"I didn't have to. My partner on the other hand..."

He looks so confident that I can't help but start to believe him. No. Don't. He can't be telling the truth. Valentin is invincible.

"Who would ever work with you?" I croak, trying to hold back the tears. "You're a liar."

"Am I? Why isn't he here?" Alex shrugs and rolls his eyes. "I mean, it could be worse. He could just be sick of sticking his dick in your worn-out cunt. Stupid little bitch, aren't you? I did everything for you and you fucked me over by giving yourself up to someone else. To that BEAST."

"You're the beast." I blink hard and pull back the tears as best I can. Crying won't help. Never has, and never will. And this man, he's a monster. A real one. And he hides his nature. Valentin never has. He's always told me what he is.

And my heart pulls apart at the thought of him.

"I wasn't a beast when we were together. But I am now. You turned me into this."

"Fucking lies..." I mutter.

"Tell me the lie. Fucking do it!"

"You were trying to..." I stop. Swallow. "You found my contraceptives. I only ever took them for my skin. I told you that. But you just said if I was already getting fucked by every man in town, you might as well get some of it, too. I told you I was a virgin. You didn't believe it. You said you had to see for yourself. I told you no..."

Alex huffs.

"Don't act like l took anything from you. If I were the man I am now, I would have. But I thought I had to be chivalrous. I thought I had to earn your approval. I was naïve. An idiot. Now, I know better. I don't need your approval at all. I'll take what I want—even if it's already been taken from you. No, he couldn't have taken it all. Tell me, Yelena, has that beast tried your other holes?"

A sudden burst of anger cuts through my fear and panic.

"You picked the wrong girl to fuck with!" I shout. "Valentin's going to cut you into pieces."

"Valentin is dead," Alex heartlessly reminds me.

"Then his Bratva will come for you. Andrei. Natalya. Ilya. They're my friends. They'll fucking hunt you down like the pig you are."

The realization hits me like a ton of bricks. I've spent all my life running from the Bratva. Now, they're all I have. My only friends.

And I'm proud of it.

But Alex just shakes his head. "I don't care about that underworld shit. But my new friend Sandro does. And he also has beef with your man, along with the precious criminals he plays around with. He came to me with a plan to make you and that fucking ugly beast of a Russian pay for your insolence. Well, how could I resist?"

"Sandro?"

Who the hell is that?

"Your boyfriend knows him. Thing is, being close with the new king of the underworld is just icing on the cake." Alex comes over and looms above me. His expensive perfume invades my senses. "It's actually exciting. I enjoyed ordering those men to storm Valentin's mansion. Ordering them to kill his security was quite the thrill. It made me feel like what I am. Big. Strong. A real man. Something you tried to take from me."

He pushes up his sleeves.

"You know what else makes me feel like a big strong man?"

He lifts his hand and brings it down hard on my face.

Pain lances through me as my head whips back, and for a second I can't breathe. Everything is bright white and hurting.

"Beating you into submission. Teaching you who's in charge and who you love. And if that doesn't work, it doesn't matter. I think I'll like hurting you."

He hits me again and pain blooms outward.

I taste the metallic salty heat of blood as my lip throbs.

"You little fucking cunt. You had no right to give away what belonged to me. I—"

He's going to hit me again when someone taps on the door. At first, I can't see anything through my blurring eyes. But when I spit out some blood, everything becomes clearer.

I recognize that man.

But from where?

Suddenly, I realize. It's the asshole who fought Valentin at the fashion conference.

Is that the Sandro Alex was talking about?

"What?" Alex snarls. "I'm a little busy here."

The man's eyes are flat and lifeless. They briefly fall on me before turning back to Alex. "It's done."

"Fuck yes!" Alex punches the air and turns, grabbing my hair and wrenching my head painfully back. "Valentin is dead. You hear that? Dead."

"No, no, no!" I struggle not to cry, but the tears spill hard. Everything inside is ripping apart and the pain is like nothing I've felt. I'm not sure I can bear it.

Valentin can't be dead, he can't. I didn't... oh, God, I didn't tell him.

Why didn't I tell him I loved him?

It's there, in this moment. The love. And I can see it without all the bullshit, the sheer sweet sharpness of it. I love him. I fought it because... because a man like him demands everything, even though he'd never ask. It's just him. Valentin demands it because that's what he gives: everything.

A lifetime of getting to know him lay ahead and now...

Valentin's dead.

There's no place for the love I didn't tell him I shared.

No place for a lifetime or a future.

The truth came way too late.

Valentin is my family.

Was.

And I blew it.

Now, it's too late.

I'll never be able to tell him what he meant to me.

Alex is talking, but I can't listen. Everything in me feels numb. I look up, lip hanging.

Sandro is still there, and he's frowning suddenly at his phone. There's something in the frown and the stillness that grabs my attention.

He gives a heaving sigh of annoyance.

And then he pulls out his gun and turns to Alex, shooting him point black.

Alex's words stop, mid-sentence, and he falls, dead, to the floor.

I start screaming.

Sandro hits me and I almost black out.

This time blood pours from my nose. Through the pain, I stop the tears, the screaming. I stare at him.

"Shut the fuck up, you annoying little bitch? I need to think." He glances at Alex's corpse and shrugs. "What? He's not useful anymore. It looks like they fucking survived. Now, I need a hostage, or at least more bait, and he wouldn't have let me take you."

"What—"

"I said shut the fuck up!"

He pulls out his gun and shoots it at the giant arched windows. They shatter. We're high enough that a violent wind rushes in.

The panic and fear sink deeper. But something else rises from the depths of my despair.

Hope.

Did... did he say Valentin survived?

Sandro sneers. Then a maniacal little chuckle escapes his dry lips, and I forget about the hope.

All I can feel is fear.

"Now," he says, cracking his knuckles, "let's get you hooked the fuck up."

35

"Give me something fucking good."

Desperation has me in its grip as I frantically drive like a demon, armed to the fucking teeth, away from my mansion.

I'm furious, scared out of my mind.

"We're free."

I ignore the teasing note in Ilya's voice. Under it is stress and yeah, I'm fucking beyond happy they got out alive. To lose them and Yelena? I'd fucking destroy the planet. I'd go on the kind of spree that would make the nutters spread their arms and prepare for the second fucking coming.

"What have you fucking got?"

The anger in me is wild.

These fuckers stormed my castle, killed my men. Took my girl.

Civati.

He's going to suffer. So is Sandro.

But first, I have to find them.

"Talk to me."

"We're here, Valentin," Andrei says, sounding close to losing it himself, "keep it together."

"Sandro must have fucking planned for Civati to take Yelena while we were busy chasing him. We fucking fell—" No. This isn't anyone's fault but mine. "I fell for it."

I smash a hand onto the wheel.

"Where the fuck are they?"

"I'm in the car," Ilya says, "I'm fucking trying to coordinate the security footage to track him down. When I get it done, we'll meet you—"

"Don't bother." I grip the wheel hard as I head downtown, "find me an address for Civati. A second place. In the city limits. Nearby. Get me that and I'll get to her. I'm sure of it."

"Got it," Ilya says a few seconds later. "Penthouse, top floor, downtown. Pinging your GPS with the address. We'll meet you there."

It's a race against the clock.

I swerve in and out of traffic, blaring through red lights and traffic jams until I'm there.

Andrei and Ilya aren't far behind.

"Valentin, look—" Andrei is the first to spot it.

I'm already halfway to the building when I look up.

And stop.

Horrified.

My gaze zeroes in on the most terrifying thing I've ever seen.

Yelena.

She's bound to a chair.

And the chair's dangling down the side of the building, just barely holding on by a thin thread. It must be tied to something just behind the shattered penthouse window.

Bait on a hook.

Fucking hell.

"Andrei. Ilya." I speak in rapid Russian. "Create a distraction. Call every fucking man we own or can get a favor from to come and fill the streets. Make it so this fuck can't take his eyes off them. I'm going up there. I'll kill Civati and Sandro. I'll get Yelena."

"He'll have people."

"Bring it the fuck on. I'm ready."

In the distance, I hear sirens wailing.

If Sandro and Civati aren't dust on the sidewalk by the time they get here, I'll have failed.

And I am not failing.

Not with Yelena's life on the line.

"Hold on tight, angel. I'm coming for you."

I make short work of getting in, there are two men in the foyer. One shoots at me but I'm quicker. I shoot him dead and run at the front desk. The other man barely has time to load before I shoot him.

He's still processing his death when I grab the keys attached to his belt.

Then, alarm bells start ringing.

I empty my clip and reload as I race to the elevators. The nearest one dings open just as I reach it.

It's filled with armed men.

They don't even have time to understand what's happening. It's like shooting fish in a barrel.

They all go down, filling up the elevator with their bloody bodies. I decide to try the one next door. It closes just as some more men reach the main floor. They can't do anything but watch as I'm lifted away.

I reload again and prepare myself as I'm brought to the top floor.

It's not her floor. Alex's penthouse is above this, but I'm quick to find the emergency escape stairs. I use the biggest key on the ring to open up the door to the stairwell.

Funnily enough, it also opens the door to Alex's floor.

Just like that, I'm pushing into the penthouse hallway, not giving a fuck who's there.

Someone takes a shot and the bullet hits my shoulder. But I ignore the burn and shoot him back. He falls to the ground, another dead body.

Suddenly, another man jumps at me. Knocking me to the ground, he wraps his arm around my neck. I reach back, ignoring the sear of pain from the gunshot, and slam my thumbs into his eyes.

He screams.

I flip and use my weight to pound him back into the floor. Then, I jerk free, straddle him, and pound his face into pudding.

This is taking too long. I need to move faster.

Shoving my guns back into their holsters, I spring to the door at the end of the hallway. It has to be my way in. But I don't bother looking for the right key. Instead, I keep my pace and lower my shoulder, blasting through the thick wood like it's nothing.

I don't have time to recover from the brutal sting that explodes through my body.

Because the door falls at the feet of fucking Sandro Barella.

His gun is pointed directly at my face.

"Weapons on the floor," he smirks.

I grit my teeth, resisting the urge to take my chances. I can't. But it's not just because Sandro might kill me before I can rescue Yelena.

It's because the only thing stopping her from falling to her death is Sandro's foot. He's stepping on the rope her chair is precariously tied to.

One wrong move and she's done for.

The fucking maniac.

"You're making a mistake," I growl, carefully laying down my weapons.

"That's what they all say," he shrugs. "Now slide them over."

I do as he says, hating him more than I've ever hated anyone

in my life. Emptying my pockets. Guns. Knives. Everything—
except the piece of cloth I ripped from her that night at my
office. The one stained with both of our blood.

That stays with me. Until the fucking end.

"Let her go, Sandro. This is between you and me."

He ignores me.

"Not so big and brave now, are you? Stupid fuck. You're
going to be the first of your little Bratva to fall. I'll bury you
right next to the billionaire. How does that—"

Suddenly, an explosion booms from below, shaking the
floor. Sandro turns his head.

That's enough for me.

I lunge forward, pulling the piece of cloth out, hoping that
it's long enough.

Sandro turns back around just in time for me to stomp my
foot down on his, clamping it into place. He aims the gun at my
gut, but I knock it away and wrap the black cloth around his
throat.

"You fucking—"

He struggles and we both slip.

Our feet come off the rope.

I hear Yelena scream.

My stomach drops.

"No!"

With a roar, I lunge forward...

Just barely grabbing the strand before it plummets over the
edge. Even through the bloody cloth, the rope burns my palms,
but there's no time to grimace. I turn over quickly, pulling
Yelena back up.

But Sandro isn't having it.

"Enough of this," he yells.

I loop the rope around my ankle as he charges me, fire
burning in his eyes. I have to take his first punch, just to finish
the knot. It cracks my lip. I stumble. The rope slips a little more.

Yelena screams.

"I won't fucking lose her...' I rumble, planting my feet in the ground.

Sandro starts swinging at me again, desperately trying to knock my foot out of the loop but I take his punches and angle to the side.

All it takes is for him to miss me once, and I'm able to wrap the cloth right back around his throat. He grunts in surprise as I yank him up against my body.

Every inch of me hurts, but I don't give a shit.

This has to end.

His eyes start to bulge, his face turning red as he struggles to breathe.

Then, I catch the glint of silver right before he plunges a knife into my stomach.

The pain explodes, but I can't push him away, can't let go. I need to choke him out, right here and now. Otherwise, he'll be able to grab one of the weapons I dropped.

So, I hold on, choking him as his knife plunges into me over and over again.

Blood soaks my clothes and my head swims. But through that blood loss, through the pain, I focus on keeping hold of my angel.

I'm going to die, it's in the grayness and the way the pain turns cold inside of me. But I can save her.

I need to save her.

My hand slips a little, but I reassert my hold and strangle him harder.

She's all that matters.

The thought of her is what makes me hold on.

"No... stop..." Sandro chokes. Then, suddenly, he stops stabbing. The knife drops from his hand. He starts to twist and jerk.

And then he goes still. I make sure the last bits of life leave him before I drop him to the floor.

I collapse right beside him.

My foot slips and the loop unravels.

My vision's dim. Blurry. All I need is to sleep...

... But Yelena.

My reason. My heart. My everything.

The rope is slipping. I look over my shoulder and see it pulling on a piece of window frame. The shard juts out from the floor, bending it at the base.

Yelena's screaming.

From somewhere deep inside, I find the strength to throw myself on the rope. But it slides through my bloodied hands and I'm dragged up to the broken window.

I stick out my foot. It somehow finds a beam just before I can plummet over the ledge. Searing pain rips through my body.

I must black out, because a second later, I'm opening my eyes.

Miraculously, the rope is still in my hands.

"Yelena."

Biting through the pain, I pull... and pull...

And then, the tension in the rope goes loose...

And the chair spills into the penthouse.

"There you are," I smile.

"Valentin!"

Her cries become more and more distant.

I try to touch her, untie her, but I can't make my hands move.

She's there. Next to me. Sobbing. Gorgeous. "Don't cry, angel. You're safe."

"Valentin, Valentin." Her breath is warm and sweet on my face. "You're alive."

Darkness starts to close in.

"Hmm." A warm wave is overtaking the cold inside of me.

"Valentin, open your eyes, I love you. Please! Do you hear me? I love you. Stay with me."

I cough. The taste of blood coats my lips. I drag myself from the darkness and laugh weakly. "You love me?"

"I do! I fucking love you. Please."

I stare lazily down at my bloody chest. "That's all it took? I should have done that earlier..."

The words fade in and out with the world.

"You're going to be alright, you hear me? We're going to be alright. It's over now."

I lift my heavy eyes back up to Yelena's face. That's the last thing I want to see before I die. But...

"Your face."

She's hurt.

"I'm fine. You saved me. I... I love you, Valentin. My beautiful man. I love you."

"Then I can die happy."

I get lost in those beautiful blue eyes one last time before the world goes black.

36

Everything has changed.

Even with the mansion almost back to normal, it doesn't feel like it did when I first got here.

And Valentin...

"Just focus on what's in front of you," I tell myself.

It's all I can do.

I'm up to my ears in designing a series of bespoke suits for when he gets better. In gorgeous fabrics and colors, with all kinds of additions for his weaponry. So he can reach it easily, and it won't ruin the lines.

My man's got pride.

And he loves his suits. He likes beautiful things. Quality. Food, guns, clothes.

Of course, he loves me and—

A small sob escapes my lips as I look down at the latest outfit.

He *will* get better.

"Yelena?"

The voice comes from behind me. Natalya.

I straighten my back.

"Sorry," I quietly offer. "I didn't hear the door."

I take a few deep breaths in the living room where I've been sleeping and working and try to get myself under control before I turn and put on a smile for my best friend.

But when I do, Nat sees right through my happy façade.

"Honey." She rushes up and hugs me tight.

I hold her, trying not to cry.

Lately, I've been saving my tears for after hours, when everyone's gone.

But I keep that to myself.

My heart's in a million pieces, held together with string that could fray at the wrong word. Two words really.

I don't dare think them, though.

"That's because my husband's a total monster and has no manners," Natalya says, looking around at the ordered chaos. Her gaze slips to the pillow and throws on the sofa. "He's got keys to the place and figured we'd let ourselves in. But we did see some suits at the front." She sits in a nearby chair. "I'm guessing they're for Valentin. Is he...?"

"No different."

My words are dull and she just nods. "Andrei is beside himself, too. Those boys are like brothers, you know. And... He'll be alright, Yelena."

I purse my lips and nod as a pair of new voices filter into the mansion. Ilya and Andrei.

I want to hide my face.

They're all so strong, and here I am constantly on the verge of tears. I can't even bring myself to tell Natalya that I'm scared. I swallow and twist my fingers in the sumptuous fabric swatches I have in front of me. I can't lose him.

"More suits?"

"I can't think of anything else, and designing clothes for him distracts me from the terrifying thoughts that..."

"He'll wake up," Natalya assures me. "Valentin's strong and stubborn. I know. He won you."

I sigh.

"He's been in that medically induced coma for the past week."

"And you're a mess." Her gaze wanders back to the sofa, to the insanity of all the designs.

I point to the room next door. It's where they've set up a private hospital room. It's filled with doctors and nurses who take care of him around the clock. "I have to be close to him."

"You really love him, huh?"

"Yes."

The word's so simple I can't believe it took so long to leave my lips. And now, I just want more time.

"I understand," Yelena says, a tight smile painting her lips. "Anything you need, just ask. We're sending over some food later. We've heard you haven't been eating what the house-keeper makes."

"I'm not hungry."

"You need to eat. I'm gonna turn up and inspect the plates."

I find a hollow laugh.

There's a knock on the door and I whip around, heart in mouth. But it's just Ilya and Andrei. Ilya crosses to me and gives me a hug. "He'll be all right, Yelena. He owes me ice cream and he's sticking around for that. Also, I think he likes you."

He waves to Natalya and salutes Andrei.

"There, did my good deed for the day. Now I've gotta get back to work. Someone needs to pick up the slack since pretty boy's slacking off in there."

He leaves and I know he's worried, too. I've found he makes a ton of jokes when he's upset.

Andrei sits on the arm of the chair, an arm around his wife. "I hung the suits up for you." He plucks a design up from the side table. "You know, Yelena, I had a peek at one. Did you build in a hidden holster?"

"Yes, I needed something to do."

"Well, here's something for you to do. I want some suits, too."

Natalya hits him.

He grabs her hand and bites her fingers. "What? I'm not allowed to benefit from her love for Valentin? I'll pay. He'll make me."

I chew on my tongue as tears spring to my eyes. I don't know how much—

"Excuse me."

The bottom of my world drops out as the doctor appears from next door.

Andrei immediately rises.

The doctor never turns up like this.

"I'm sorry to interrupt, but I thought you might like to know... Mr. Constanov is awake. I took him out of the coma last night, and he's just coming off of it now."

My knees buckle. "You didn't say!"

"I wanted to see if he needed to go back under before I made any official announcement. But everything is fine. He's out of the woods, stable and awake.

Andrei makes for the door at the same time I do. Natalya stops him. "Andrei."

"I want to see him first," he says.

She shakes her head. "Yelena first."

I'm only vaguely listening as I push past him and the doctor. I honestly don't care that Andrei is the big scary Bratva boss. All I care about is my Valentin, and I run into the room, full speed.

He turns and my heart swells.

Sure, he's pale and needs a shave, and there are bruises and cuts and dark circles under his eyes, but he's the most beautiful man I've seen.

I grin just as he does.

"Angel."

He holds out his hand and I take it. "Valentin." I want to throw myself on him, but there are so many tubes and bandages that I settle for a kiss. "You're alive. Thank God. I thought..."

He laughs. But that laughter quickly turns into a coughing fit. "Sure, I thought about dying," he smiles, wiping his lips. "But then I decided I wanted to spend a little more time with you. So here I am."

"I love you. I love you so much. I'm so sorry. About everything. I got caught up in other bullshit, but when you told me you loved me..."

"I do. I love you and it's okay. It was a bumpy path but here we are."

"Promise me something?"

"What's that?"

"Don't ever die."

He laughs again, his hand falling to his ribs as he grits through the pain.

"Not sure I can promise that. But I'll try my best. For you."

"You better." I kiss him again, peppering his bruised face. "At least live for the rest of my life."

"But staying alive is such a drag," he kids.

"Do it for me."

"For you?"

I nod.

Valentin's deep blue eyes glimmer. The pain melts from his face.

"Anything for you, angel."

My heart skips a beat when Valentin walks into the room.

There's still a limp in his step, and it's clear his body aches, but I can tell he's doing better than yesterday. And that's all we can ask for.

That every day be better than our last.

So far, so good.

Those deep blue eyes shimmer as he flashes me a smile. We don't even share a word. Our bond runs deeper than that now. He just grabs his laptop and sits on the sofa next to me, pulling me in so we warm each other as he works.

For the past few months, we've found a sweet niche. He works mostly from home. I keep him company as I prepare for my big launch.

I just got off a big video meeting with my new fashion company. It's all a little overwhelming, but with Valentin's support, I know I can do anything—at least, eventually.

After all, he originally wanted me to run the whole company. But I need to build up to that, and I'm content learning the ropes and creating my designs until then.

"What are you thinking, angel?" he asks, stretching as he looks up from his laptop.

"Just daydreaming?"

"Sweet or dirty?"

We laugh.

"With you, there's no difference."

He smiles at me and my stomach still flutters as hard as the first time.

"Guess what I'm thinking."

"Is it how lucky you are to have such a wonderful girlfriend?"

"Girlfriend? No," he clicks his tongue. "I prefer to think of you as my future wife. Mother of our future children. And—"

"So, you're daydreaming about weddings and babies?" I tease. "How manly."

"You dare question my manhood?" he grins, sliding a hand down under my waistband.

My sigh is mixed with a wicked giggle.

"No babies until after marriage," I say, biting down on my lip.

"Then I guess I'll just have to marry you." He plants a gentle kiss on my neck and I grab onto his thigh.

"You better hurry. Natalya is due any day now, and I want our kids to be roughly the same age so they can grow up friends."

"We're only nine months behind."

"We can always wait for their next one."

"You know I don't like to wait. Plus, we've got to show them how it's done."

"Always the competitor."

"Or maybe I just want to put a baby in you. Watch your pretty belly swell. How many babies should we start with?"

He nips my lobe and I melt and giggle and moan.

"You can't control how many—" I gasp when he bites down harder. "Fine. One baby."

"To start," he counters. "And we start now."

"Where's my ring?"

His laugh is deep and warm.

"Alright, I'll throw you the wedding of the century first. Then lots of babies."

"Valentin."

I wiggle, but it only allows him to slide his hand in further under my waistband. His fingers gently play along my pantie-covered slit.

I'm already soaked.

"It's a deal. I'll marry you. And to show you I mean it, we don't have to have those babies."

"But... I want a baby with you."

His mouth comes to my ear and I feel him smile. "Good,

angel. Because I'm waiting to propose. It needs to be perfect, just like you." His finger slides aside my panties and I melt into the warmth of his touch. "But make no mistake. You're already mine. You belong to me. Forever."

I part my thighs and move to unbutton my trousers to give him better access. "And you make no mistake," I say, moving my hand from his thigh to his hard cock. "You belong to me."

"Forever."

Our lips meet and I know he means it.

This is the kind of love that lasts a lifetime.

And we're going to spend that lifetime together.

EPILOGUE
VALENTIN

3 months later...

"The penthouse?"

Yelena's gaze swings to me as I turn the car up to the familiar building. There's a touch of amused annoyance in her expression. "That must mean..."

Glancing over her shoulder, she tries to find traces of the Sweetwater resort.

"Don't bother," I taunt. "We're only here for one thing."

"And what's that?"

"You'll see."

So much has changed since we first stayed here, all those months ago—least of all the building. It's finally finished.

"Keeping secrets, huh?" she teases.

"I prefer the term surprises."

I park out front and lead her through the doors.

"Wow, I never thought I'd see the day," Yelena gasps, ogling up at the gleaming lobby.

"Pretty wild to think how far we've come."

"Are we going upstairs?"

"Not yet." I take her wrist and pull her into my body. "This way."

"Valentin!" Yelena yelps with surprise as I lift her onto my back. Her arms and legs wrap around me as she holds on for dear life. "Slow down!"

"No way. I'm tired of waiting."

"For what?"

"Patience, angel."

"Look who's talking."

On the far side of the lobby is a giant set of double doors, A private conference room. We burst inside and I put her down.

"That was quite the ride," she laughs, trying to catch her breath as she pats down her outfit. I watch as her gorgeous blue eyes wander around the giant room. "Now, what do you—"

She stops when she sees it.

Up ahead is a giant banner. It hangs from the fifty-foot-high ceiling covering up nearly the entire back wall.

"Your very own fashion show," I say, stepping up behind her.

"... Featuring Dark One Eight. My brand..."

I didn't think I could shock her anymore. How wrong I was.

"I thought this would be a perfect place for a new beginning."

"It's perfect," she whispers. "There's so much room in here. We'll be able to fit—"

"Oh, the conference isn't happening here. That sign is just for you. You need a bigger space than this. I think the resort down the road might do..."

"Sweetwater?"

I can hear the apprehension in her voice. For all the good memories we share here, there are an equal amount of bad ones.

But I want to drown the bad memories out. Replace them with new memories. Better ones.

"Sweetwater," I nod. "Though, I'm thinking of renaming it?"

Yelena turns around. "What does that mean?"

"It means I bought the resort. We're going to bulldoze it to the ground. Natalya is already working on designs for its replacement. She's going to make sure it's a perfect space for hosting this event. This is where the fashion industry will get its first real taste of its next queen. You."

Her eyes wander back to the giant banner.

"I... I don't know what to say, Valentin. Are you sure it's not too much? How could I ever repay you?"

"With your heart."

"You already have that."

"Then how about your hand?"

Reaching into my pocket, I pull out a tiny black box and get to one knee.

"My hand?" Yelena asks.

Slowly, she turns back around.

When I can see the blue in her eyes, I open the box.

"Yelena Laskin, would you do me the honor of becoming my one, my only, my partner, my queen. My wife."

She gasps, her hand snapping to her mouth.

"Valentin."

Those bright blue eyes are already filling with tears. Her cheeks turn pink.

"You are my heart, my love, my life. Angel, will you marry me?"

Her hand falls and the vast room fills with a scream of pure joy. I barely get a chance to stand up before she's on me, arms wrapped around my back.

"Yes! A thousand times yes!"

We kiss and I almost fall back to my knees. She kisses like a queen. With all the power, strength, and love that comes with the title.

But she's not just any queen.

She's mine.

Pulling back, I use my thumb to wipe away the happy tears streaming down her face.

"Let's see if it fits," I smile.

I take her hand and slide the ring on.

"Like a dream," she whispers, staring at the diamond in awe. "It's gorgeous."

"Look familiar?"

Her brow scrunches as she takes a closer look.

"Actually, now that you mention it. Where have I seen it before?"

"It's from the choke collar you found in my box."

Her eyes go wide with surprise. My heart swells.

"You devil," she laughs, sniffing away the tears.

"An angel and her devil. Sounds about right.

"I love it," she smiles, wrapping her arms around my neck. "I love you."

"And I love you, angel. So much that one ring wasn't enough."

She pulls back, confused again.

"There were seven diamonds on that collar. So, I had seven rings made. All different, gorgeous cuts."

Her jaw drops.

"You have six more of these for me?"

"Backups?"

She huffs playfully.

"I don't plan on ever losing this ring."

"When you live as wild and recklessly as we're going to, it's always smart to have backups."

"You spoil me."

"Oh, this is just the start. Wait until you see what's next."

"Next?"

I spin her in my arms and pull out a remote, then point it up to the banner. "For example..."

I click and the banner falls, revealing the hidden artwork behind it.

Yelena gasps.

"No. Valentin. Is that?"

"The window I took your virginity against," I grin. "Smudges and all."

I had the floor-to-ceiling glass from the penthouse taken out and brought here. Now, it's immortalized. A grand piece of art representing our love.

"Valentin, you're..."

"Let me guess," I say, leaning into her ear. "The devil."

She spins around and grabs my collar.

"No. Not the devil," she shakes her head. "My devil."

"And I always will be, angel. Forever."

We kiss and Yelena's diamond flashes through the darkness behind my closed eyelids.

I hold her tight.

My queen.

My wife.

My angel.

Forever.

EPILOGUE
YELENA

2 months later...

I stare at the vault in Valentin's office as he works at Club Silo247.

My fiancé's idea of work is me on his lap as he takes breaks to kiss and bite and nuzzle my neck, turning me into a pool of melting desire. Sometimes we end up fucking, half-clothed, or me naked... But not tonight.

So, I stare at the damned thing as he talks about the security details for my upcoming fashion show to someone on the phone. Probably Vlad.

I should probably be paying attention, but the vault utterly fascinates me.

I can't help but wonder if I finally have the guts to ask what else is inside. Our sex life leans into kink, but how far can we really take it?

A warm shiver runs over my skin.

I can only imagine.

"Alright send them over, I'll talk to you later."

Valentin's call ends and I swallow, working up the courage to ask.

"Hey," I practically whisper, as he swivels in his chair and wraps his arms around my waist. He plants a soft kiss on my ass, and his hands slip up the underside of my dress.

"What's on your mind, angel?" he asks.

"I... I think I want to see—"

Suddenly, the office door bursts open. We both rip around to see Ilya charging in. He stops in his tracks when he sees the position we're in.

"Oh, shit. Sorry," he says, not sounding completely sorry at all.

Valentin glowers and I bite my lip to stop from laughing.

I've never had family like this. Ilya's sort of appointed himself my older brother—whose goal is to annoy Valentin and me. In good fun, of course.

"What is it?" Valentin growls.

"I didn't mean to interrupt," Ilya says, "but I need to talk shop with you, Valentin. It's urgent."

Valentin huffs, but before he can object, I turn and kiss him on the forehead.

"You boys get to work. I'll be outside."

"You'll pay for this," I hear Valentin threaten as I walk into the hall, winking at Ilya as I brush past him.

"Do you take checks?"

The door clicks shut behind me and I head to the mezzanine that overlooks the dancefloor.

Two of Valentin's men stand nearby. I wish Nat was here, but she's home with baby Konstantin, who is beyond gorgeous, and Andrei is—

Like he heard me, the big bad Bratva boss breezes up, stopping to kiss my cheek. "Valentin?"

"He's in the office." I wipe a spot of baby spit from his jacket, my heart twisting. "How's Konnie?"

"He's perfect. I'd still be at home with him if I didn't need to talk some things over with the boys. Natalya sends her love."

We share a nod and he heads off. I can't help but watch him go. For such a big, bad scary mob boss, he's also a doting, hands-on father and loving husband. It makes me think of what Valentin will be like as a dad. Protective, I'm sure. But also supportive and caring, I have no doubt.

I sigh and lean on the railing, taking in the people dancing below.

It's weird to think I used to be one of them, so naïve to the dark and wonderful world that lay just out of sight.

That world is mine now. And I wouldn't leave it for anything. But if you had told me that just a year ago, I would have called you crazy.

Hell, the Yelena who once dragged Natalya to this very club would have instantly run out the back door if she knew it was run by the Bratva.

Now, I'm staring down at the dancefloor, thankful that—

Suddenly, I spot a familiar figure amongst the crowd.

My heart stops. The faint smile on my face vanishes.

Kira.

I grip the railing.

She's standing in the middle of the dancefloor, surrounded by dancers and she's staring up. Right at me.

Our eyes meet.

I suck in a breath as Kira starts waving madly at me, like she's desperate to talk

I don't know what to do.

Glancing around, I take note of Valentin's guards. They already seem to be on high alert. I don't know how they do it, but they always seem to know.

Or maybe they read my body language. I look back down and Kira isn't just frantically trying to get my attention, there's a real vibration of stress running through her. I can read it from here.

But I can't go down. Can I? She's a reporter. One who's interested in bringing the Bratva down.

It would be a stupid, foolish thing to do.

But Kira was so nice, even when I didn't give her anything about Valentin and the Bratva. She truly sounded like she was just trying to keep me safe.

And right now, it looks like she's the one in trouble.

Maybe I can repay the favor.

"I'm going to get a drink," I say, breezing past the guards. They know better than to question their boss' fiancée, but I also know that they'll be keeping a close eye on me.

By now, I'm used to it.

"Let's hope that this isn't a dumb idea," I mumble to myself.

The music seems louder and the club more crowded when I reach the bottom of the stairs. I can't see Kira anymore. But I figure if I head to the bar, she'll find me.

Sure enough...

"Yelena!"

She appears next to me, pushing her way between the throngs of people.

"Five minutes, Kira," I say, trying not to look around to see who's watching. "I can give you five minutes."

Kira's gaze falls to my ring, and she leans in. "I know what's going on. I know who your new fiancé is, and I know what this place really is. But I didn't know where else to go or what to do. I need information. Desperately."

"Information on what?" I ask.

She frowns. "I know you know something, and I know you're too afraid to talk."

"No, I—"

"It's okay," Kira says. "Look, I'll try and protect you, but I need you to help, too."

My head's spinning because I'm suddenly not sure what she's talking about.

"Kira—"

"I have to get the Bratva, bring them down. Make them pay."

My eyes go wide. "Make them pay? What are you—"

"It's personal. They stole my big brother from me. Got him killed. Destroyed my family. So—"

"Kira." I put my hand on her arm and I tighten my grip in an effort to make her really understand what I'm saying. "I'm so sorry for what happened, but I can't help you. I don't know a thing. I don't know anything. And I have protection. From my fiancé. If you need money, I can help."

"I don't need blood money."

I take her in. She's not just frantic, she looks rumpled, disheveled, like she hasn't slept in days. "I'll be all right, and so will you... if you let whatever this is go. Please, take care of yourself. And if—"

"No." Kira's voice goes flat as her shoulders slump. "It's fine. I shouldn't have come. I'm sorry." She turns and pushes through the crowd, head down. Defeated.

I feel bad, but I know I can't go after her.

If helping her means hurting the Bratva, then I can't do it.

Breathing out, I order a drink. When it comes, I take a sip and turn around to head back upstairs.

But when I look up at the mezzanine, my blood runs cold.

Ilya stands there, watching.

What did he see?

"Fuck," I quietly curse.

Trying not to act suspicious, I make my way through the crowd and join him by the railing.

"How'd the meeting go?" I ask, trying to change the subject before he even brings it up.

But Ilya is no fool

"Who was that?" he asks, nodding toward the dance floor. An intense expression dominates his handsome face.

"Why?" I try to play it cool. "Want me to set you up on a date?"

My attempt at humor falls flat.

He continues to look out, strangely interested, at where Kira had been. "That girl... I didn't get a good look, but she seemed oddly familiar. I don't know why. Who is she?"

Fuck, I don't want to get Kira in trouble. "Oh, just a girl I know from the fashion industry."

"Is the front as pretty as the back?"

My stomach drops.

The last thing anyone needs is for Ilya to become interested in a reporter.

"She's beautiful, but she's not for you.'

"Worried about her?" he grins, the intensity draining from his face.

"Worried about you," I counter. "She's trouble."

To my dismay, Ilya's grin widens. "Trouble is just the way I like them."

Shit, shit.

"So now you like trouble, huh? Well, if you really need my help getting women..." I look down and pick out a pretty blonde. "She looks fun and uncomplicated."

"Boring!" He snorts. "No, I've been thinking about our conversation about troublesome women and maybe, maybe I need some of that to spice up my life. Like your fashion friend."

"She's a fashion reporter. You get the last part of that, right? Reporter?" I take his arm with my free hand. "So leave her alone. She's going through enough without your brand of help."

"I never said I'd help. I said I want to meet her."

"No, Ilya." Now I don't know who I'm protecting. Maybe both of them. "Reporters and the Bratva don't mix. She doesn't need your kind of trouble and... she could also be dangerous to our empire if she's let too far into it."

Ilya narrows his eyes and steals my drink.

"Interesting," he says. "Maybe I'll have to personally neutralize that threat. Right up close. Tell me all about her, starting with her name. And, if you don't, you know I'll be able to find out for myself..."

Printed in Great Britain
by Amazon